FELICE

Random House
New York

FELICE

Angela
Davis-Gardner

*Grateful acknowledgment is made to the following for permission
to reprint previously published material:*

Macmillan Publishing Co. and A. P. Watt Ltd.: Five lines from "A Dialogue of
Self and Soul" from *Collected Poems* by William Butler Yeats. Copyright 1933 by
Macmillan Publishing Co., Inc. Copyright renewed 1961 by Bertha Georgie Yeats.
Reprinted by permission of Macmillan Publishing Co., Inc., M. B. Yeats,
Anne Yeats and Macmillan London Limited.

Library of Congress Cataloging in Publication Data

Davis-Gardner, Angela.
Felice.

I. Title.
PS3554.A9384F4   813'.54   81-40234
ISBN 0-394-52009-2   AACR2

Manufactured in the United States of America

24689753

FIRST EDITION

For Charles

What but a soul could have the wit
To build me up for sin so fit?
So architects do square and hew
Green trees that in the forest grew.

—ANDREW MARVELL,
A Dialogue Between the Soul and Body

When such as I cast out remorse
So great a sweetness flows into the breast
We must laugh and we must sing,
We are blest by everything,
Everything we look upon is blest.

—W. B. YEATS,
A Dialogue of Self and Soul

FELICE

1

WHEN BLANCHE MELANSON UPSET A DISH OF CRAB-APPLE JELLY
on Mother Superior's pristine white tablecloth, Sister Agatha proclaimed it a sign. A sign of what, she did not care to say. But she was
not pressed on this point, for of all those present in the convent dining
room that December noon—and this included not only the nuns and
their students but a guest, the Abbé Sosonier, who looked, seated
amongst the black-frocked females, like a fly serenely caught in molasses—of all these observers, only Felice Belliveau paid attention to the
content as well as the form of Sister Agatha's outburst.

All the others seated at the three circular tables looked outraged or
amused, according to their general dispositions, when, after the jelly
upset, and after Sister Theodota's reprimand of Blanche (which
stained that girl's normally pasty cheeks as red as the pickled beets
upon her plate), Sister Agatha stood and, with her finger trembling
like the gelatinous mass she pointed toward, cried, "A sign, Sisters,
a sign."

"Ridiculous," Sister Theodota countered, with a volume that carried to the head table at the far end of the room. At that table Mother
Superior rose halfway from her chair and looked sternly toward the
offender, while beside her the Abbé, who was famous for his
equanimity in trying circumstances, attended to his fish and potatoes
as though nothing were amiss. The Doucette twins, seated at Mother
Superior's table by virtue of the pink good-conduct ribbons they wore
pinned to their collars, smirked. At Sister Agatha's table Sister Claire
looked worried, Sister Theodota's brow lowered as threateningly as
the Nova Scotia sky before a winter storm, Felice's best friend, the

irrepressible Celeste Rouget, giggled, and the novice Evangeline crossed herself. But no less than an hour later, when the young ladies worked at their needlepoint in the parlor and the nuns, preparing their souls for confession, knelt in the chapel, most members of L'Académie du Sacré Sang had doubtless forgotten the particulars in the sequence of events that climaxed with Sister Agatha's being unceremoniously hustled from the dining hall up to her room.

But not Felice. Permanently stored in her memory was the image of the aged nun rising from her place just across the table, pointing at the offending glob of jelly (had she raised her finger just six inches she would have pointed straight at Felice's heart), and moistening her lips with the old-woman's tongue that seemed too large for her mouth. Recalling the moment later, it seemed to Felice that she had sensed, an instant before Sister Agatha spoke, what the words would be. "A sign, Sisters, a sign": Felice, months afterward, would imagine her lips moving in silent unison as Sister Agatha uttered the prophecy to which only she had attended. And all her life Felice would remember the moment just after, when Sister Agatha's eyes, wobbling and magnified behind her thick spectacles, found her own face, focused and fixed there, the nun and the girl held together for one long, breath-holding instant before Sister Agatha was rudely jerked down.

Felice had always been attentive, even before her Uncle Adolphe had deposited her at the convent school on the western coast of Nova Scotia about a year ago. But in this harsh and unfamiliar climate—the dank halls, the classrooms so cavernous as to swallow up her timid, reciting voice, the dormitory, where she lay looking up into the dark, willing back tears—here Felice's powers of observation were greatly heightened. Conversation, glances, the inclination of a head or hand, the juxtaposition of objects in a room, the shapes of clouds gathering above the bay, the language of the waves that spanked the cove just below the cliff—everything she saw and heard, and even that which she tasted, smelled, and sensed—everything Felice collected as evidence. As evidence of what, she had no clear notion; the collection was itself random but thorough, impressions stored up in much the same way Mother Superior saved bits of string, scraps of cloth, candle-ends, material that might be useful later.

Yet it was not only this general penchant for close observation (the ferocity of which would have surprised anyone looking upon the girl's smooth young face) that caused Felice to notice and to mull over all particulars of Sister Agatha's behavior. Much of the attraction lay in Sister Agatha herself, whom Felice had watched from across the table three times a day (except on fast days, when she watched her in the chapel, or on the days of Sister Agatha's illness, when the girl tiptoed up to her cell and asked if she could be of service); it was Sister Agatha, her sad and powerful and mysterious presence, who was particularly compelling to Felice.

When eating, Sister Agatha sat poised like a bird of prey, her attention fixed on the dark pottery plate, bowl, and cup below her with such an intensity as to seem vengeful. Once upon a time, the kitchen-maid Soukie told Felice, Sister Agatha had eaten from Mother Superior's prized Haviland china like everyone else; when she began to mistake the roses patterned on the plates for morsels of food, Mother Superior had ordered the black dishes for her. Stark against the white cloth, these dishes were now the only objects on the table her eyes could distinguish in the gray flicker of her visual world. All the more wonder, Felice thought, that Sister Agatha had pointed exactly at the jelly; but then, as the nun had often warned her students before her forced retirement, her ears had eyes, and, as she had once confided to Felice, her bridegroom Jesus sometimes caused her to see everything suddenly illuminated in one great glorious burst of light.

Sister Agatha had been at the convent forty years, long enough for a body of legend to accumulate about her. Felice spent a good deal of time trying to reconcile the extant version of Sister Agatha's younger self—lovely, bright-eyed, and intractable—with the decrepit figure she had become. When as a young woman Sister Agatha (the former Catherine Comeau Starr) had come to the convent from Cape Breton—leaving behind, it was said, a broken-hearted privateer who wanted to take her back to his native Barbados—she had painted, in rich tones of sienna, gold, and scarlet, the stations of the cross in the outer chapel and the frescoes on the walls of the classrooms and halls. It was said that she had done the first painting (sinuous figures in a lush Eden) on the wall of her own cell without prelude, without

permission, just after taking the veil. Some years later she had transformed the second-floor corridor with a painting of the martyrdom of
Saint Agatha, the virgin's breasts being borne away on a huge platter
by the Roman soldiers while Agatha hid her loss beneath her arms
and her doubled-over torso. It was one of the school's stories—slightly
revised by each generation of students—that Sister Agatha's own
breasts had been torn from her chest with hot tongs by the priest who
had discovered her first painting. Felice's contribution to the legend
was that her persecutor had been the Abbé Gerard Sosonier, though
that mild-mannered man would have been but a child during Sister
Agatha's early, troubled conventical years that were now robed in
myth.

Though most of the girls chose to see Sister Agatha as comic, Felice
perceived her as unutterably forlorn, mistreated, abandoned. The
wrinkles in her almond-shaped face all pointed down, except when
one of the gleeful smiles Felice watched for illuminated her face. In
contrast to the other nuns' lips, which seemed uniformly trained in
tight lines, Sister Agatha's mouth often worked like a child's about
to cry. Even her black habit looked abject. Her skirt and veil were not
starched, as were those of the other sisters, but lay wilted on her thin
frame, and did nothing to disguise the slight hump of her back nor
the protuberance of her belly. The glazed bonnet of the order, looking
on the other nuns like cheerfully burnt pastries, was in Sister Agatha's
case green-tinged and misshapen with age. The rosary that hung from
her waist was of wide-spaced, urine-colored beads, unlike those of the
other nuns, and did not make an important clatter as she walked. The
other sisters had rosaries of silver that looked, as they clicked busily
down the halls or across the grounds, like glinting crossed knives in
the depths of their dark skirts.

Felice had been in Sister Agatha's Latin and English literature
classes last spring, the nun's final term of teaching. Sister Agatha's
favorite textbook authors were Catullus, Herrick, Marvell, and
Donne, but she also liked to quote the recently published Gerard
Manley Hopkins; he was, she told Felice (whom she had chosen to
read the verse aloud to her after classes), her spiritual brother.

Mother Superior was said to disapprove of the students' being
exposed to modern poetry in the English class; she was also displeased

that Caesar and the Gallic wars, supposed to occupy a major place in the Latin curriculum, had been almost entirely supplanted in Sister Agatha's class by the love poems of Catullus. And although she was, in general, a supporter of Sister Agatha, Mother Superior did not particularly admire the evolution of the nun's teaching style, which had finally come to consist almost entirely of student and teacher recitations. Mother Superior offered to mark written tests for her, but Sister Agatha clung to the oral examinations in which the girls were asked to name their favorites of a given group of poems or poets, the highest marks going to those students whose tastes matched her own. Good marks on final exams, therefore, were easy to come by, but the recitations—also part of the cumulative grade—were more difficult. Sometimes the girls had been tempted to refer to a surreptitiously opened text to help them through, but this was done only in the most extreme emergencies, for it was felt that Sister Agatha—even though she did not say so—somehow knew of these transgressions. Sister Agatha could not only recite each poem word for word, but her hands could find, almost miraculously, it seemed, where each lay in the book. But often she had left the book, and her desk, to recite an impassioned verse while swaying about the platform, so that the suspense of whether she would step too far engrossed the students at the expense of Catullus or Marvell. In Felice's mind, the image of Sister Agatha at the brink of the platform was inextricably bound with her memory of the love poems, and the plaintive, hypnotic voice in which they were recited.

Last May Mother Superior had informed Sister Agatha that it was time for her to retire from teaching. In protest, the aging nun had risen during the next day's mass and stood cruciform before the statue of the Virgin Mary. The spectacle of Sister Agatha trembling before them, her arms outstretched as though in penance, caused such rustlings in the sisters' pews and commotion in the girls' section—where Felice was one of the very few not to giggle—that it had been necessary for Sisters Theodota and Constance to escort the nun out. Soon thereafter she had initiated her practice of spontaneous speeches during meals, a situation that, Sister Theodota had been heard to observe, simply could not much longer be tolerated.

One day near the end of the term, Felice had been drawn aside by

Sister Agatha in the hall and bestowed with the title of "My favorite student, in all these many years." Not long after, when Felice had carried a bowl of gruel to Sister Agatha in her cell, where she was enduring the monthly illness that had abruptly resumed on the day of her retirement (and which condition was not only a sham but likely to disgrace them all, most of the sisters agreed), the nun whispered, "O child, hold this secret: I am not unclean, it is only from my hands that I bleed, only from my hands." And she lifted the hands, pale and trembling, toward heaven before lowering them and taking the girl's hands into her own. "God gave me one last year of teaching," she told Felice, "so that I might know you, and light your way."

Each of the students at the convent had a particular favorite among the nuns, a paragon whose mannerisms and acts were carefully observed and then compared, in friendly rivalry, with those of the other girls' ideals. In this sub rosa contest that continued year after year, Mother Superior, Sister Constance, and Sister Claire were perennial favorites. Mother Superior's following had greatly increased since she had expressed the opinion—out in public, where even the Abbé could have heard her, had he chosen to—that female suffrage, recently approved in Canada, was not only commendable but morally correct. Sister Constance, with her small oval face, her features as perfectly formed as those of a wedding-cake figure, and her short, square teeth perpetually framed by a smile, had long been the standard of female beauty at the convent, but was considered by the present generation of students to be a bit too sweet. Sister Claire, the good-natured music teacher, remained popular even as she aged; Felice, who was considered her best piano student, was officially the current leader of Sister Claire's claque. But, privately, Felice had shifted her chief allegiance in recent months to Sister Agatha, who, other than her protégée Evangeline (lately become a novice, and therefore no longer considered a girl), and other than Felice, had among the girls only detractors.

Thus it was not only because of her custom of attentiveness that Felice fixed every detail of that December luncheon so vividly in her memory. It was also as Sister Agatha's self-appointed champion and protector that she memorized each utterance, gesture, and expression, and in this Felice herself displayed foresight; weeks and then months later she would be able to recapture this day for a circle of admiring friends, and to bask in the shared glory of Sister Agatha's vision.

After Sister Agatha's outburst, though all observers attempted to appear scrupulously disinterested, Felice sensed the congealing of tension in the room, a tension binding them all in an uneasy union. Felice noted how Sister Theodota's left hand, the same one that had grasped Sister Agatha's skirt and pulled her back down to her seat, lay for a moment upon the table, still fisted. She saw the glances exchanged among the nuns, and ceasing to eat, she watched Sister Agatha's struggle against tears. As Sister Theodota made short work of the jelly cleanup—scooping it up in her napkin and setting the napkin at the edge of the table for Soukie—Felice observed the nun's lips, pursed so severely that they nearly disappeared (this, the same expression of disapproval that Felice had experienced in arithmetic class). At the same time Felice was also aware—as the other diners, preoccupied with the cleanup, were not—of the light dawning behind Sister Agatha's face and gradually suffusing it, a light which caused her to lay down her fork and to lift her eyes toward the crucifix on the wall.

When Sister Agatha chanted, *"Gloria in excelsis Deo,"* Felice was expecting speech; Sister Theodota, who was not, jumped, jabbing her fork into her lower lip.

"Lay out the waxed linen cloths, Sisters, my beatification is at hand."

Sister Theodota, fork gripped in midair, glared at Sister Agatha. Then she said in a strangled, saccharine voice, "Yes, dear, we know." Turning her face about the table like a searchlight, the nun focused on Blanche, who cringed, and then on Celeste. "Mademoiselle Rouget, I believe it is your turn to clear?"

Celeste rose, and with an ironical glance toward Felice, lifted the tureen of cod and potatoes and carried it toward the kitchen.

Felice carefully averted her eyes from Sister Agatha, who was smiling in her direction; though the smile was meant to be tragic, it was rendered pathetic by the nun's traitorous upper lip, which retreated high on the shore of her gums, leaving a naked pink expanse above the tea-stained teeth. Felice looked instead at Celeste's curly head, which bobbed up and down as she walked; her deportment was the despair of Sister Theodota, who periodically had the girls glide back and forth across the parlor floor, urging them to move "Like swans, Mademoiselles, like swans." Celeste, Felice decided, looked more like a duck; her feet pointed out when she walked, and with the strain of carrying the heavy dish her elbows pointed out too, forming V's at her sides.

Felice could see from the corner of her eye that Sister Agatha had begun to roll pellets of bread under the fingers of her right hand. When Celeste returned with dessert the nun crossed herself, leaving a bit of bread clinging to her forehead.

"Stewed apples again," Sister Claire reported, peering into the dish Celeste set before her.

"Sisters!" Sister Agatha fairly shouted, causing a hush to fall across the room. "Jesus has given me his ring of betrothal . . ." She held out her hand as though to admire the ring, while bread crumbs snowed from between her fingers. ". . . all diamonds and pearls. My time of glory is nigh, Sisters."

"Such amazing news," Sister Theodota began, in her most acid voice.

"Sisters and girls," Sister Claire said, in a deliberately conversational tone, "did you know that we had a record harvest of Gravenstein apples in Nova Scotia last year? Isn't that interesting? More than one million and a half bushels, I understand, and a quarter of that for export."

Sister Theodota, who considered Sister Claire's outlook altogether too worldly, made a great show of rearranging her rosary in her sucked-in lap before receiving the dessert dish.

" 'Is the shipwrack then a harvest?' " Sister Agatha intoned in English (which made most heads turn, as French, mother tongue of the Acadians, was ordinarily spoken at the convent). " 'Does tempest carry the grain for thee?' "

"Rubbish," Sister Theodota said and turned to look at Mother Superior, who was, at the moment, engaged in conversation with the Abbé.

"No," Sister Agatha said, "not rubbish. Gerard Manley Hopkins, the great Jesuit poet." Sister Agatha's lips turned upward in a little triumphant smile, Celeste snickered, and Felice, as reader of the poems, felt included in this small victory.

"One day," Sister Theodota warned, her voice so low and menacing that all the girls (but especially Blanche, already agog) shivered. "One day, Sister, you will go too far."

"There is evil in this convent," Sister Agatha hissed, turning her head toward Sister Theodota. "Evil, nursed here like the asp in Cleopatra's bosom."

"That's it. You've gone too far." Sister Theodota rose, pulling Sister Agatha upward with her, and cast another look toward Mother Superior, who stood, dabbing her lips with a napkin, and started toward them. Sister Claire and the novice Evangeline rose simultaneously, with twin looks of alarm, as though following stage directions.

"Aren't you ashamed of yourself?" Sister Theodota gave Sister Agatha's shoulders a gratuitous shake as she arranged her in her grasp. "Making a scene before the young ladies!"

The young ladies at all three tables, Felice noticed, were not only attentive but positively delighted. No one but she, Felice thought, saw the pathos in the nun's submissiveness, nor the grace in her outstretched, upcurved hand, the hand like that of a young and beautiful virgin martyr being led away to her bonfire.

That hand brushed Felice's shoulder as Sister Agatha was led through the human corridor that had rapidly formed. The hand then drifted to the chest, and as Sister Agatha turned her head over her shoulder, struggling for a moment at the door against Sister Theodota's and Mother Superior's double grip, she called back, "Persecution! Glory! I have given up my bosoms for the glory of Jesus. The Micmac Indians came in the night to steal away my virginity but my bridegroom . . ." Here Sister Agatha flung her head away from Sister Theodota's hand, which attempted to cover her mouth. " . . . my bridegroom allowed me to suffer this glorious sacrifice instead."

Sister Agatha was pulled through the door and out of sight, but her cries of "Persecution! Glory!" could be heard echoing against the corridor walls and then, more faintly, in the stairwell.

"Quiet, ladies!" Sister Constance had positioned herself in the doorway, her chin raised as though to make herself appear taller than she really was. "Calm yourselves. Perhaps we could ask the Abbé for a prayer?"

The Abbé, who had remained seated, quietly studying the hem of his sleeve, flinched. But he rose smoothly, made a large sign of the cross over the girls and nuns—whose hands descended to their rosaries—and murmured soothingly in Latin. Another sign of the cross from him, and Sister Constance directed the girls to the parlor, "And with composure, Mademoiselles, if you please."

Celeste's fingers dug into Felice's wrist as they exited. She held her just outside the door until Anne joined them and, drawing the three of them into a circle, whispered, "I heard something just *awful* about Sister Agatha—tell you later, after confession." Then the three marched, arms linked, to the parlor; Felice, at the center, could feel the others' suppressed mirth, giggles welling up like slow bubbles in a pot about to boil.

The girls entered the parlor, found their needlework baskets, and arranged themselves in their customary places on the brown-and-yellow–striped sofa. They sat in a circle with the other girls—nineteen altogether—with the dark-eyed, inscrutable novice Evangeline at one end, in a straight-backed chair. Evangeline began the reading, taking up at the third chapter of *Brave Souls: True Tales of French Acadians in Exile,* as the girls worked on separate squares of needlepoint that, stitched together, were to form the new parlor rug. Mother Superior hoped the project would be completed by the time of the Bishop's visit next Easter.

Felice punched her needle through the cloth, but she did not really see the slow accretion of purple stitches that were extending the petal of an iris, nor did she hear—beyond a rhythmic rising and falling—the heroic story Evangeline was reading. She could think only of Sister Agatha. She imagined the nun in her cell, lying disappointedly uncanonized on the narrow bed, still wearing the black shoes neither Mother Superior nor Sister Theodota had thought to remove. Perhaps they would take off her glasses and bathe her forehead with cold water, which would make Sister Agatha screw up her face and splutter. Then Mother Superior might throw open the window, letting in a cold blast of salt air. "Now, that's better," Mother Superior would say, the wind lifting her black veil. "You'll be yourself in no time." Sister Theodota would be moving about the room, straightening the few objects there—the table, the breviary and the small standing crucifix on the table, the wooden crucifix on the wall, the figurine of Our Lady in a niche in the corner. Perhaps the two of them would then kneel by her bed and pray for Sister Agatha, their fingers and voices slipping over the Ave Marias and Pater Nosters too smoothly, while a few translucent tears fell from Sister Agatha's closed eyes into the hard pillow under her cheek. Above the nuns, the vibrantly fleshy Adam and Eve, lightly clad in diaphanous garments, would look out from the green paradise on the wall, their expressions not changed in the slightest since Sister Agatha painted them there some forty years before.

A tear rolled down Felice's right cheek, the side away from Celeste, and fell into her needlework, soaking into the purple flower. She stared down at the rows of stitches, her fingers, the needle, holding herself still, for behind the dam of her held breath was a torrent of sadness. She was remembering her first day at the convent, when she had felt as isolated, and misunderstood, as Sister Agatha in the lonely confinement of her cell.

It had been nearly a year ago—December 8, 1920—that Felice had come to L'Académie du Sacré Sang. As Uncle Adolphe's wagon reached the top of the rise at Nevette, she had her first view of the dark-stone, turreted convent building. It had seemed to Felice like a dungeon in a very bad dream, and she was sure that Mama would not —did not—want her to go there. At the thought of Mama looking sorrowfully down upon her dear little daughter, Felice felt rings of sobs rising from her stomach. "Quiet, Felice," Uncle Adolphe had said through gritted teeth, and his nails bore into her arm. "Be a good girl." He couldn't whip her then, he said, but he promised to make up for it later if she didn't behave herself. After a short tour of the convent building, Uncle Adolphe and her brother Philippe were gone, on their journey back up the rutted highway called the Chemin du Roi to Wolfville, where Philippe would attend the Acadia University and help in the shop. Felice was led by Sister Theodota into the small white chapel, where they had knelt before a statue of the Virgin Mary and said an interminable rosary in celebration of her safe arrival and the Feast of the Immaculate Conception. Having lost track of the prayers, Felice looked at the nun's heavy profile, her closed eyes bulging behind their lids, and at the square, unfamiliar fingers counting the beads. Looking at her own small hands, Felice felt her chest begin to ache.

Later that afternoon, as soon as she could escape, Felice had run away from the convent and the nuns, whose skirts made a cold, windy sound when they walked, to the edge of the bay. She clambered over the low rock wall and scrambled heedlessly down the cliff and cried, leaning against a boulder at the end of the cove, her head against the unyielding rock, remembering the warm curve of her mama's breast as she rocked Felice before the fire and read "La Belle au Bois Dormant" aloud, her voice vibrating against Felice's ear. She also remembered, with terrible longing, her papa busy at his desk with the leather-bound account books and Philippe bringing in the smell of cold with him as he banged and clattered through the door and chunked a log on the back of the fire, making sparks fly out, while she watched from the circle of her mama's arms.

The convent handyman, Jacques, had found her there on the rocks that night, she trapped by the long Bay of Fundy tide, and carried her up to the convent on his back, his lantern swinging a moon of light on the path before them. That night Felice sat in Mother Superior's lap and cried against her black pleated bosom. Mother Superior had always been especially kind to her since that first night—Mother Superior's heart bled for the unanchored souls of this world, which is why, it was said, she refused to have Sister Agatha sent to the sisters' retirement home in Halifax—but sometimes, Felice had found, the superioress' intentional acts of kindness left her feeling more lonely than ever. For instance, Mother Superior had Felice sit beside her at the teacher's desk in history class during her first weeks at the convent school, a practice that increased Felice's difficulty in making friends;

it was only after she made a face back at Celeste Rouget, when Mother Superior was safely occupied at the board, that their friendship had begun. It had been—it cheered her to think of it now—a magnificently grotesque face, eyes crossed, tongue extended, as startling an expression as that on any of the gargoyles on the convent's outer walls, and it had inspired her first appreciative laughter from the girls. When Mother Superior swiveled back, Felice's face was as innocently blank as a freshly gessoed canvas, a transformation that aroused further laughter and admiration from her classmates, but no censure—beyond a faintly suspicious frown—from the superioress.

Mother Superior's most recent kindness had been to arrange—without consulting her—a Christmas holiday in Wolfville for Felice. When Felice, shifting from foot to foot, said, "Oh, but I'd rather stay here, or go home with Celeste," Mother Superior looked confused and a shade disapproving. "But your uncle, your grandmother, your brother—don't you want to see them? I know they would be terribly disappointed if you didn't come."

Felice had nodded, trying to smile, and, bobbing a curtsy, said, "Thank you, Ma Mère." But she had been aware as she went down the hall, her footsteps painfully loud, that Mother Superior was watching her go and wondering, shaking her head.

What Felice could not tell Mother Superior, what she could hardly bear even to think of—and remembering them now, she pricked her finger with the needle and, unconscious of the tiny red stain spreading into the white patch of her needlework, sat gripping it tightly—what she tried to barricade from her thoughts were Uncle Adolphe's whippings. Uncle Adolphe had whipped her for what she could not help, for crying about Mama and Papa. Sometimes she still woke in the night, crying after a bad dream; that was awful enough at the convent, when only fierce imaginings of Mama looking down kept the dark from swallowing her up. But it had been worse at Wolfville; when she cried there, Uncle Adolphe had switched her bare bottom, she bent over his lap, and then he rubbed her with slow, wintry hands. It was a part of her body that had never been exposed otherwise; at the convent, the rule was to bathe in underwear, reaching beneath to scrub, and to dress under a nightgown. Thinking of the rubbing made

Felice's stomach go queasy with fear and guilt; when Sister Theodota abruptly entered the room and announced, "Time for confession, Mademoiselles," Felice jumped as though caught out.

Felice looked down at her needlework and noticed with horror the red stain upon it. For a second—before she realized that her index finger was throbbing—its appearance seemed mystical. As Sister Theodota approached on her round of inspection Felice rolled her square tight and stuffed it into her basket, praying that the nun would not ask to see it. When Sister Theodota had passed, leaving her unscathed, Felice looked down at the offending finger and thought of Sister Agatha's words: "A sign, Sisters, a sign."

When the other girls filed out the door and turned left, on their way to the outer chapel, Felice's feet took her in the opposite direction, toward Mother Superior's office. She hardly thought what she was doing, even after her short knock on the door, Mother Superior's response, and her saying breathlessly, rushing in, "Mother Superior, I am going to be a nun."

Mother Superior's startled eyebrows angled above her spectacles. Her pen halted. "How came you to this decision, dear?"

Felice studied her shoes. Mother Superior didn't really believe in her, never had. To gather courage, she thought of Sister Agatha; Sister Agatha's plan for Felice was much grander than mere nunship. Sister Agatha had whispered one day in her cell that Jesus had singled out the convent for two canonizations. "I saw this truth in a dream. Mark my words, heed the signs."

As a saint, she could join Mama in heaven; they could have tea together, just as they used to, but at a golden table. As a saint, she could work miracles; she could freeze Uncle Adolphe's hands, reaching greedily across the table for petits fours, into claws for everyone to see.

"Are you certain?" Mother Superior was saying. "God calls us individually to this rigorous vocation." Mother Superior was all straight lines: the veil, the severe white edge of her cheek, the fingers, the pen. Felice looked beyond the superioress to her shelf of reference books: the brown leather *Catholic Encyclopedia,* the writings of Saint Thomas Aquinas, the many-volumed *Lives of the Saints* by Alban Butler.

"Yes," Felice said stoutly. "I am certain. God has called me. And I want to stay here at Christmas to strengthen my soul. Someday," she went on quickly before Mother Superior could interrupt, "I want to save my Uncle Adolphe. He is—I hate to say it, Ma Mère—not only an alcoholic, but an, an—atheist."

"Really?" Mother Superior gave her such a personal and interested look that it gave Felice a pleasant bodily shock of warmth. She looked down at Mother Superior's rug, at the blue and brown rings linked together like snakes. "How do you know he is an atheist, Felice?"

"When Mama and Papa died," Felice said, raising her eyes and looking squarely at Mother Superior without blinking, "he would not say the rosary with me and Philippe. And I have never seen him pray, Ma Mère," her speaking voice raised to drown out the inner one which was reminding her that neither she nor Philippe had thought of saying the rosary either, that terrible day.

"You'll have to change your ways." Mother Superior's intonation made her statement sound half question. "You'll have to avoid the detrimental influence of girls like Celeste Rouget."

"Yes, Ma Mère." And before the nun could add further reservations, Felice said, "I'd better go to confession—don't want to be late."

But after Felice hurried down the hall, through the kitchen where she had left her cloak, and out the kitchen door (where Soukie, examining the sky and polishing the lip of a crockery bowl with a dishcloth, said dolefully, "Pleurisy weather, Mademoiselle"), she went first not to the chapel, but to the rock wall beyond the orchard.

Along the wall was a row of pollarded willows, gnarled by age and buffeting winds from the bay. The trees had been planted there, it was said, by the first group of Acadians to resettle the French coast of Nova Scotia after the British-imposed exile of 1755. The girls called them the Evangeline Trees after the Acadian heroine who had made her parting vow to Gabriel beneath the willow trees of Grand Pré.

Felice's particular favorite among these trees, the last and largest in the row, filled the inner elbow of the wall. The tree had a large hollow into which Felice could look at the cracked and faded painting of Our Lady of the Willow, nailed there years ago by Sister Agatha. The Madonna's downcast, forbidding gaze was appropriate, Felice thought, for a protectress; the girl considered Our Lady the guardian of treasures she had found on the beach and stored deep inside the hollow in a secret compartment.

After crossing herself before Our Lady, Felice swung from a low willow branch up to the wall, where she stood looking out at the Bay of Fundy. She gazed long at the water, forcing herself to take in the complete sight of it, as she often did, like a long draught of bitter medicine. The bay was so wide that she thought of it as infinite, and its fierce forty-foot tides as part of her earthly trial. At high tide, standing here, she could hear the waves boom into the rock cave at the foot of the cliff and then suck back out again. Presently, however, the tide was dead low and silent. This afternoon the water was flat and iron-colored, like the lid of a casket, except near the horizon, where the sun had begun to drop below the clouds, throwing upon the water a shallow, unconvincing sheen that looked like amateurishly applied silver plating.

Finally allowing herself to shiver, Felice drew the heavy woolen cape more tightly about her and, dropping to her knees, huddled by the willow. Fingering the soft material of the cape, she thought for a moment of Mama weaving it for her, the shuttle flying back and forth through the dark purple threads while Felice played with her doll, bending its knee joints to make it walk across the hearth.

Then she reached into the secret compartment of the tree hollow —its inconspicuous opening was just inches from Our Lady's right elbow—and drew out, one by one, her treasures. There was an iron fitting from a ship, a piece of sea-glazed green glass, various smooth cobbles that had caught her fancy, and her chief prize, a scrap of heavy red brocade she had found buried in the sand—this was cloth, she liked to think, from some lost lady's dress. She fondled each object reverently, touched the brocade to her lips, and then replaced everything, in the usual order, back in the secret hole.

Felice stood up again and, leaning against the willow, looked out at the bay once more, staring at the half-wafer of sun poking down from the gray mat of clouds until it went out of focus, for the mist in her eyes. Then she jumped down, landing ankle-deep in snow, and ran—late, as usual—through the orchard to the outer chapel, the branches slapping at her face like little whips.

FELICE HAD BEEN PLUNGED INTO A NEW WORLD ON NOVEMBER 22, the Day of Saint Cecilia, for whom her mother was named. To the cruel irony of that coincidence, Felice later assigned various interpretations: evidence of her own sinfulness, heinous enough to warrant this punishment from God; an indication that her mother too was a saint, and taken straight up to heaven; a sign that Felice herself was to be a saint, and this her first real trial.

On the morning of that day, Felice had been snuggled deep under the eiderdown comforter, dreaming about a game she and Mama were playing with brightly colored bits of glass, or jewels, when Seine jumped onto the bed and settled on her neck, purring loudly.

"Oh, Seine, how did you get in here? I was dreaming," Felice complained, but shifted him to her chest and stroked his silky gray fur. His yellow eyes stared into hers, then closed half shut in delight. He purred and arched his back under her hand.

Seine was Grandmama's cat, and her closest companion at Uncle Adolphe's house. Philippe, four years older than she, was treating her with an older-brotherly scorn that had become more pronounced since their coming to Wolfville. He was forever going off to the Gaspereau River with the blacksmith's son, who claimed there were monsters' tracks frozen in stone there; when she tried to go along, Philippe was furious. "Go on back to Uncle's house. Why can't you make your own friends?" Once on the way back from the tutor's house Philippe had pushed her and she'd fallen in a ditch and gotten her best skirt muddy. All because she just teased a little about that prissy Amy Eaton. She planned to tell Mama and Papa about how awful Philippe had been when they came back. Because she wasn't in regular school it was hard to make friends. There was Prue, who lived on the corner in the yellow house that smelled funny; Grandmama made her spend some afternoons there, playing with silly Prue and her dolls. Where she wanted to go was to the Eaton girls' house—Abigail was her age and had a pony—but Philippe didn't like her to go there, and he was the only one who was formally invited.

"Felice?" Bette's white-capped head appeared at the door. "I've been calling and *calling* you to breakfast. You'd better hurry—you know how your uncle is when you're late. I gathered the eggs for you —now, get up." And she disappeared, with a rustling of skirts.

Felice tossed Seine to the floor; he landed with a comfortingly solid sound. She looked in the wardrobe at the dresses hanging there. "Who wants to be worn today?" Felice asked out loud. At one end of the closet was a brown dress that she didn't like; it seemed to cry out that she never wore it. "Oh, all right," she said, "you're dull, but you can't help it, and you don't have many buttons."

There wasn't time to replait her hair. She looked at her reflection in the oval mirror—the glass was so small she could not see all her face at once—and brushed the top of her head as best she could. She hated the color of her hair, plain brown; if only it were blond, or even red like the Eaton girls'. She studied her face, fitting together the whole from the partial sections she could see. It was an acceptable face: clear blue eyes (Papa said that's where the stars stay in the daytime), a nose she thought must be Roman, and, thank goodness, a smooth skin. Suzanne Perin, her neighbor in Yarmouth, had begun to get great red bumps on her face.

"Fe-lice," Bette called from the bottom of the stairs, "breakfast is getting colder and colder."

Felice ran down the steps, skimming her hand along the banister. When Uncle Adolphe was in his shop and couldn't see her, she sometimes slid down the long, gleaming curve. Once Grandmama had emerged from the hall shadows just as she slid into the newel post's high carved pineapple. "Goodness, child, try to act civilized!" she had cried, but without heat.

In the dining room, Grandmama was sitting with her hands folded in her lap. She nodded her head as Felice entered. Philippe was staring at the ceiling. Uncle Adolphe sat in his padded armchair at the end of the table and drummed his fingers upon the mahogany. He glowered at Felice as she walked to her chair.

Elaborately silent, Uncle Adolphe broke open his muffin and applied a thin layer of marmalade to each half. Bette, rustling around the table, poured tea from the Limoges pot.

They ate their herring and eggs without conversation. The only sounds were Bette whistling in the kitchen and Grandmama's juicy chewing noises.

Felice looked past Philippe, who made a face at her, to the naked cockatoo in its cage against the wall. It had pulled out all its feathers after the journey with them here on the train from Yarmouth. Its skin was mottled and raw.

"Grandmama, maybe Pip needs a wife," Felice said.

"You had no business bringing that bird here in the first place," Uncle Adolphe began. "Why you couldn't leave it with neighbors is more than I can comprehend."

"Maybe we'll have a letter from your parents today," Grandmama said quickly, looking at Felice and then at Philippe. "Wouldn't that be grand?"

They both nodded, and Felice fell to thinking of the muff and fur-lined coat Mama had promised to bring her. They had been gone five days now—four days since leaving Felice and Philippe in Wolfville, and one day since boarding the ship in Yarmouth. Felice had marked off the days on one of Papa's business calendars that read "Belliveau's Marine Products, Yarmouth, Nova Scotia" at the bottom of each tear-off month. Papa often went to faraway places like New Brunswick and Paris on business, but this was the first time Felice could remember Mama being away from home. Papa had taken her on this trip to Boston so that she could consult a doctor, a specialist in female ailments. They should be home in at least three weeks; Felice could hardly wait. The plan was to take the train back down the coast week after next with Bette and have the house ready when they arrived.

"That's that," Uncle Adolphe said, rising from the table and taking his heavy gold watch from the small pocket of his waistcoat. "The shop will open late today," he added, letting the full weight of his glare fall on Felice, "thanks to you, Mademoiselle Belliveau." He picked his way across the Turkish carpet with high-kneed steps. If she could have been one of the Greek ladies in the wallpaper Felice would have laughed at him—he looked like a long-legged heron with a round stomach.

"You mustn't mind him too much, Felice dear," Grandmama said after Uncle Adolphe had disappeared from view and gone to the front of the house to the jewelry shop. "He doesn't understand children— but he does care for you." Grandmama blinked at her. "You know he cares for you, dear?" Grandmama had to have peace, Papa said, and he warned Mama of it before every visit—Mama was prone to disagree for the fun of it.

"Yes, Grandmama."

"Well, you run along, then," she said, mollified. "Don't be late for Monsieur Langouste."

When Felice and Philippe returned to the house at noon, Doctor McConnell was walking down the front steps, leaning on his gold-headed cane. They ran from the top of the hill, reaching him just as he had untied Carrot and was climbing into the buggy. The doctor looked down at them with rheumy eyes. He fumbled in his bag—it was stamped with his initials, in gold—for peppermint sticks.

"So you've not heard the news?" he asked, handing each of them a striped candy.

Felice and Philippe shook their heads no.

"Your grandmama has taken a spill and pulled her hip," Doctor McConnell said. He paused. "She'll be up and about in no time," he added in a soft voice, but he shook his head sadly as he looked above their heads toward Cape Blomidon.

He jumped to the buggy seat, agile for such an old man, flicked the reins, and clattered down the street behind Carrot.

Felice and Philippe ran into the house and up the stairs to Grandmama's room. Felice had her hand on the knob when Philippe grasped her arm, holding her back. "Listen," he said.

Felice stopped the rushing in her head and inclined an ear toward the door. There was the sound of moaning, punctuated by the strident voices of Bette and Uncle Adolphe, who seemed to be disagreeing about something.

Uncle Adolphe opened the door suddenly and stormed out, colliding with Felice. She felt the rough wool of his waistcoat and the bulge of his watch beneath her cheek for a moment. He stood back, surveying them. His face twitched peculiarly.

"Come along, then, children," he said, touching their shoulders and ushering them down the steps.

"I am not a child," Philippe protested. "Charles Troop was working in the smithy when he was fourteen."

"True, true," Uncle Adolphe mumbled. He locked the front door to the house. Felice and Philippe watched open-mouthed as he went into the shop, asked the Misses Pudsey to kindly return at a later time (he never turned away a customer!), locked the door, and pulled the blind across it.

Then he pointed to his study behind the shop.

"You children go wait for me in there," he said. "I want to talk with you."

They walked through the shop, past the gold bracelets and watches gleaming on dark velvet inside the glass cases. Felice, her heart beating fast, wondered if Uncle Adolphe had discovered the missing cameo ring. He had a whole jar of them, and she hadn't thought he'd notice the temporary absence of just one. She had borrowed it to try on in her room, and once had worn it to Prue's house. Had Prue told her mother?

"Oh, Philippe," Felice said, sinking onto the horsehair sofa. "I feel awful."

Philippe sat next to her and, breaking his peppermint stick in two (Felice had dropped hers), offered half to her.

"Poor Grandmama," he said.

They sat sucking their candies, Felice thinking of her room and Grandmama's room.

"I wonder if she's dying," Philippe said.

"Grandmama?" Felice felt a pang, thinking of poor Grandmama, her fingers morosely stitching a quilt top. Papa had said to be nice to her, and to be obedient. What if she got gangrene like Grandpapa did and lost her toes one at a time? Felice snapped off a huge piece of peppermint at the horror of it.

Uncle Adolphe loomed at the door. He stood looking down at them for a time. His mouth was pinched, as though he had eaten something sour. Felice began to feel cold. Her uncle pulled a crumpled paper from his trouser pocket, smoothed it, and, after folding it into a small square, tucked it into his watch pocket, all the while studying the floor.

He gave a preliminary cough. "Children, I am not skilled in speech." Felice knew then it was not about the ring. She felt a dizzy spot in her head.

Her uncle was silent a long, terrible time. Felice stared at the indentation in the wrinkled flesh around his left eye, the print of the jeweler's loupe.

"Children," he said finally, "Philippe, Felice," his voice cracking like tiny bones, "you are alone."

Felice's body felt a shock of cold as Uncle Adolphe pulled the telegram from his pocket. "Regret to inform you," he read, "Jean Philippe Belliveau and wife Cecilia drowned in early hours November twenty-second. Ship *Triomphe* caught in hurricane outside Boston harbor. No survivors."

Philippe sucked in air as though he had been punched in the stomach.

"Where are they, then?" Felice said, rising as if to go there. "Where are they?"

"Dead," her uncle said, his face seeming to resound like a long, mournful bell. "They are dead—no survivors." Felice fell back stunned, remembering her mama lying on the parlor floor, bright red flooding from between her legs, and Mama crying, *"Ma petite, ma petite, c'est perdue."* Felice had felt a blow of dark nausea then, thinking her mama was dying. And now she was really dead, she and Papa.

"No bodies or effects recovered," Uncle Adolphe read. "Sincere regrets, Charles A. Matson, chief clerk, Lyon Lines."

Felice looked at Philippe, who was biting the back of his hand, at the gloomy face of her uncle before her, and beyond, at the columns of darkness marching upon her. "But where are they?" she cried. "Where are my mama and papa?" Felice lodged her face in the corner of the sofa, rubbing her cheek against the rough horsehair to keep back the great stabs of pain, but she could not prevent the crying that wanted to burst her body apart.

"Now, Felice, stop," Uncle Adolphe said. "Your mama and papa are in heaven."

Where was heaven? Felice felt her body burn and then go icy.

"Hush, no, no!" Uncle Adolphe was shouting at her. "I can't abide this."

Felice reached out blindly for Philippe and fell, wailing, onto his shoulder. It felt too young and thin.

"Young lady, stop this, stop this." Uncle Adolphe shook her arm. "Look at Philippe—he's not crying. Felice, stop—you're acting like, acting like—After all, he was my brother—I am grieved too, but Felice, they are . . ."

Felice hit at him with her fist. The room was blackened. She could not see his face.

". . . all I can bear of this . . . the limit," Uncle Adolphe was saying, "get a long switch to you . . . lady . . ." when the darkness rolled in like a wave and covered her.

BY THE TIME FELICE REACHED THE OUTER CHAPEL, MOST OF the sisters and girls had already confessed. Sister Agatha, she was glad to see, had been released for the sacrament and was kneeling in a pew in the far corner of the church. Sister Agatha's arms were on the pew before her and her head was buried in her arms, but whether from fatigue or a state of deep contrition, it was impossible to tell.

Felice slipped into a back pew beside Celeste who had, she whispered, just arrived herself. "We were up in the dormitory—where were you?" And she proceeded to whisper—a buzzing noise frequently interrupted by her and Anne's high-pitched giggles (all of which occasioned warning glances from nuns attempting to say their penances in the front pews)—the story that Felice had missed: how Sister Agatha had reached beneath the chemise of a Doucette twin as that girl sat in the bathtub. This because, Celeste ended, with a hiccup that would have been, out of doors, a whoop, "she has nothing of her own there."

Felice, sensing Sister Theodota's eyes upon her, muttered, "Going to say the stations." And she slid back out of the pew, genuflected, and began a voluntary round of the stations of the cross, a self-imposed penance to clear her mind for confession.

The stations of the cross, fourteen chronological scenes of Christ's agony for the sinner to meditate upon, had been painted on the walls of the outer chapel by Sister Agatha in the style, she liked to say, of Botticelli. Sister Theodota regarded the figures, with their elongated limbs and their skin grown more sallow with the passing years, much too ugly for edification; in this, Soukie had told Felice just last week, Sister Theodota had the support of the Abbé, now of a mind to replace the paintings with something more conventional before the Bishop's visit. Felice, who had meant to scrutinize her own soul, found herself thinking of Sister Agatha as she faced the first station. She imagined Sister Agatha spread-eagled across her rendering of the hollow-eyed, scrawny Christ, the nun jerking her head side to side, as though enduring the rhythmic lash of a cat-o'-nine-tails. She envisioned herself leaping forward out of the crowd, shackling her wrist to Sister Agatha's, and fixing upon their persecutor—a priest with the eyes of Uncle Adolphe—a look so noble that the chapel sang with light.

Shuddering, Felice moved on to the second station and stared, unseeing, at it. As she walked to the third station, Jesus staggering beneath the cross, she hugged her arms against the sides of her chest, under her cloak, to feel that her plum-sized breasts were still there.

She glanced down at the Saint Cecilia medallion gleaming between them, just above the barely perceptible swell of her black serge uniform. If Mama had worn the medallion faithfully, it would now be at the bottom of the ocean; no, she corrected herself quickly, in heaven, about her soft white neck. God had given Mama another medallion, though, a matching one, but of finely hammered gold. And a dress of sky-blue silk, cut in the old-fashioned, puffed-sleeve style Papa preferred.

It was more difficult to imagine Papa in heaven; not that he wasn't deserving, but it was hard to think of him staying put anywhere for long. Felice had to strain her mind's eye to find him, a vague form at the edge of paradise, as if he were just arriving from, or departing on, a business trip.

When she said her rosary, Felice devoted all the Paters to Papa and the Aves to Mama; thinking of Papa now, she realized that she had forgotten to say the prayers at each station.

"Pater noster," she began, looking at the painting of Jesus, his mouth an oval lozenge of pain, *"qui es in caelis."*

Jesus' face writhed. A convergence of plaster cracks in His forehead made it look as though He were exploding from within. The cross bore into Jesus' puny back. A ball of mud thrown by the still-outreaching hand of a boy had splattered his straining thigh. How could God allow this torturing of His only begotten son? Felice pushed back her cloud of doubt about God's kindness by superimposing the Yarmouth church's version of this scene over Sister Agatha's painting of it; in the picture at Yarmouth, the sky was blue and Jesus looked already full of gathered glory, even beneath His cross.

The church at Yarmouth, where Felice had attended mass intermittently with her family, shone with joyful ruby and gold lights reflected from the stained-glass windows. This chapel was shadowy and dank even in summer—a haven for spiders—and there was sometimes ice on the walls in the winter. Today it was so cold, in spite of the woodstoves, that Felice's breath made puffs of fog. The austere Abbé was partial to the outer chapel, which he seemed to regard as more his province than the warmer, shell-white Chapel of the Virgin Mary in the convent building; he insisted on holding not only confession here, but every other Sunday mass, Mother Superior's warnings about the girls' taking colds to no avail. He had not even seemed the least ruffled when, one Sunday last winter, the Precious Blood had frozen during communion in the outer chapel, and the nuns had been required to scurry to the kitchen for hot cloths to wrap about the chalice. The waiting Abbé had resembled a sculpture of a priest, his hands folded in prayer so long that they looked like two halves of the same finely chiseled stone. It was said that the Abbé had once intentionally swallowed an ant that had fallen into the chalice during a summertime mass rather than allow the drops of Precious Blood to fall in casting out the insect. Felice wondered if he had swallowed it live, and if it had tickled going down.

Now, stop this immediately, Felice reprimanded herself, pay attention. She thought how it must look to observers in the pews, she not only daydreaming but grinning.

As she moved on to the next station she glanced covertly sideways to see who might be watching. The front-row nuns, she was surprised to observe, had all left, and in the far back corner which Sister Agatha had occupied, there was only uninhabited, dusky air, and the wooden pew-tops glimmering beneath the faint light of the wall sconce.

Felice turned to the fourth station and said a short, fervent prayer for Sister Agatha, who was perhaps at this moment making her way back to the main convent building or going along the corridor to her cell, moving through the unseen world with the silence, and the certainty, of a ghost.

When Felice went to the next station she saw the confessional door open to release Anne, whose long blond hair, washed earlier in the day and still unbraided, hung about her face like a glowing veil. Anne started up the aisle toward the altar, and Celeste, the last but Felice to confess, went inside the upright wooden box, banging the door behind her.

Felice began to hurry from station to station, rolling off the Ave Marias and Pater Nosters inside her head, fingering her beads, and moving as quickly as seemed decent past Christ's red hands, the dark purple sky behind the mountains, and the grieving, blue-robed women beside the rock-plugged cave.

Felice reached the confessional just as Celeste emerged. Her friend walked pigeon-toed up the aisle, her head bowed in a convincing show of reverence. Felice entered the dark box and eased the door shut behind her. "Bless me, Father, for I have sinned," she began, and then hesitated. She'd forgotten to gather up any sins to confess. They had to be bad enough to be taken seriously, yet not so grievous as to occasion a heavy penance. The Abbé coughed; Felice saw him shift behind the barred window of the confessional.

"I talked back to Sister Theodota once. I was late for meals four times." The Abbé's head did not move; it looked bored.

"I almost doubted God's heavenly goodness," Felice said, thinking of the picture of Jesus. "Oh, Mon Père," she continued, inspiration returning, "I have hatred in my heart—for my Uncle Adolphe. It preys on my soul like a hungry snake. He is an atheist, and a mean man, Mon Père, and I don't want him to go to hell—just purgatory —but I do hate him."

"What has he done to make you hate him, my child?"

"He speaks against God. But," she added, her voice dropping lower, "I am going to save him. I am going to be a nun—Mother Superior thinks so too." At this Felice twisted her rosary tight about two crossed fingers, praying for the Abbé to preserve, as was his sacred duty, the sanctity of the confessional.

The penance was three Aves and one Pater. Kneeling before the altar at the prayer bench, her elbows propped comfortably on the armrest, Felice whispered the prayers. She walked out into the failing light of day feeling purified and lighter.

Celeste and Anne ambushed her on the path.

"What took you so long?" Celeste demanded, falling in step.

"Yes—" Anne, Celeste's perpetual echo, said, "what took you so long?"

Felice shrugged, looking beyond Celeste at Anne without returning her conciliatory smile. Anne, she decided, looked about a hundred times better in chapel light than she did out of doors; her neck was thin and gawky, like that of an adolescent water bird, and her small pale eyes seemed lost in the length of her face. Because of her anxiety to please both Celeste and Felice, Anne's face was now oddly contorted by conflicting expressions that worked out to be, in sum, a sort of leer.

That, and the peremptory way Celeste guided her by the elbow, irritated Felice. She pretended not to listen to their chatter about an upcoming oyster roast at Anne's house, where, Celeste declared, she was going to be kissed by a handsome stranger.

Celeste, who had been leading them along the rock wall toward the orchard, made an abrupt detour for the woodpile, where Jacques was stacking wood for the stoves.

A sailor's son who feared water, Jacques Ondy had begun consoling himself with rum when only a boy. When Mother Superior—then known as Sister Marie Thérèse—had come to Nevette fifteen years ago, she had persuaded Jacques to stop drinking and to attend mass, a conversion that marked the first step of her rise in prominence in the convent. Jacques now did all the heavy work about the grounds, tended the chickens and cow, which were kept in a shed beyond the orchard, and in summer managed the garden. He rarely spoke, and when he did his voice sounded creaky, as from disuse.

"Hello, Jacques," Celeste and Anne said in unison. Though making Jacques talk was a game Felice had invented, she remained silent now.

"Good afternoon, Mademoiselles," Jacques finally said, tipping his hat. He smiled, but sidewise, in a futile effort to conceal his uneven, cormlike teeth.

Celeste bolted, pulling the other two girls with her, toward the orchard. "Race you to the Evangeline Trees," she shouted, and dropping hands, they ran across the crusted snow, ducking between the apple trees, to the willows.

Celeste and Felice, panting against the wall, both claimed victory; Anne came in a clear third, the fault, she said, of a branch that caught in her hair.

"You know what?" Celeste said when she had regained her breath. "That man's in love with me." She hopped up on the wall, sitting with her knees drawn up to her chest.

"Jacques? I really don't think we ought to tease him," Felice said. "He's a very sad person, you know."

"What is the matter with you today?" Celeste craned her neck down to look at her. "You sound like Priss-Face."

Priss-Face was Antoinette Mouton, an older girl being groomed for the novitiate; she would be, they all agreed, a Sister Theodota-type nun.

"Priss-Face," Anne simpered, a little too late for effective timing, and pulled herself up on the wall beside Celeste.

"Oh, shut up," Felice said, resisting an impulse to twist Anne's ankle. They were both, she decided, too stupid to understand anything. They certainly wouldn't be able to comprehend the importance of the decision she had come to today. So she said, looking past them at the sun, now blood-red and wobbling on the rim of the horizon, "I just don't feel very well." And she didn't, she discovered, she really didn't; she drew her cloak tight against her body.

"Well, let's go down to the beach," Celeste said. "A walk is what you need."

"It'll be dark soon."

"We won't stay long. And we'll have," Celeste whispered to tempt her, "a conference."

Felice looked at Celeste's gypsylike face. Celeste was fourteen, a year older than either Felice or Anne, and the source of dark knowledge: menstruation, the nighttime activities of married people, and the sexual martyrdom of local saints, those women in the village of Nevette whom Celeste identified as having been forced into wedlock against their wills to burly, hard-drinking fishermen.

"A conference about what?" Felice asked.

For answer, Celeste darted out an arm to Felice's chest and tugged at one of the buttons of her cloak.

Felice jumped back. "Celeste, you are really awful! You ought to hear what Mother Superior says about you." And she turned and started toward the convent.

"I knew I should have asked Françoise to come instead of you. I will next time," Celeste shouted after her. "Come on, Anne."

Felice went on without looking back, forcing away the stabs of jealousy by stamping her black shoes into the snow. She imagined Celeste falling down the cliff, but only, she hastily amended, part way, just enough to bruise her slightly and teach her a lesson.

In the kitchen Soukie was punching down bread dough and squinting at the Yarmouth weekly newspaper propped against the flour bin.

Her lips moved as she read, whether in consequence of having to struggle with French (not the language of her childhood) or whether she had not been properly trained, Felice had sometimes wondered, but never decided.

"Sit down, Mademoiselle," Soukie said, nodding her red head toward the kitchen table. "I'll tell you in a minute—soon's I finish this about the rescue."

Felice sat down because the cozy kitchen was a better place to while away the time before dinner than her cubicle or the study hall, and not, as Soukie assumed, out of eagerness to hear a summary of the latest catastrophes.

Soukie thought that everyone waited with an excited apprehension equal to hers for the weekly news dispatch from the secular world. The kitchenmaid, whose confession was heard first each Saturday so she could get a head start on dinner, received the post while the nuns and girls were in the chapel; to offset the resentment she seemed to feel others must harbor about her having the freshest reports (and also, perhaps, to show off her bilingual abilities, rare in a kitchenmaid, which position she clearly felt beneath her), Soukie acted as convent crier, with the worst of the news being broadcast well before Saturday bedtime.

But what Felice had heard the sisters complain of was not Soukie's having the news first, but her accounts of it, which were interwoven with dire predictions, gloomy self-congratulations on her earlier predictions, and complaints about Mother Superior's ordering only a French-language newspaper. (It was Soukie's un-muffled opinion that she and Sister Agatha, the only native speakers of English at the convent, were quite insensitively treated; she really ought, she had said to Felice more than once, write to the Bishop about it, should she not?) Sister Claire and the few other nuns who read the paper agreed with Soukie that an English-language edition should be ordered as well; though they put forward the argument to Mother Superior that it would be a good educational tool, another motivation, no doubt, was the crumpled, lard-smeared condition in which they were obliged to read the only paper that was subscribed to.

Mother Superior, however, pointed out that most convents did not receive even one popular journal; two would certainly be excessive. She also refused to have Soukie replaced (though she continued to chip away at the servant's unfinished manners), for Mother Superior herself had rescued Soukie from an unfortunate home situation on Digby Neck. Soukie's father, it was whispered, was a ne'er-do-well and suspected wrecker (one of the clan that make their living by luring ships to the rocky coast at night with lanterns), and her mother a profligate, lazy slut (Celeste claimed to have heard Mother Superior use this very word, though of course none but the most gullible believed her) who raised her children in Godless, disorganized squalor. Mother Superior had arranged for Soukie to be educated at the academy, working only part-time in the scullery when she first came, before taking on the full command of the kitchen.

"Well, Mademoiselle." Turning to Felice, Soukie folded her floury hands at her waist, as though giving a class recitation. "There has been a most dreadful shipwreck—now, didn't I predict it, a week ago Wednesday?—just out from Halifax. The bodies are still washing in, and crates of yard goods. There was a honeymoon couple, Scots, isn't that tragic?—but not a trace of them has been . . . Oh, I *do* apologize, Mademoiselle," she said, clapping her hands to her mouth as Felice, an anguished expression on her face, rose, knocking back her chair. "I keep forgetting." And she rushed at the girl, crushing her in a yeasty embrace.

"It's all right, Soukie," Felice said, struggling for release. "I just don't happen to be feeling very well."

"Not dyspeptic, are you?" Soukie pulled down Felice's lower right eyelid. "Noo-oo. But I tell you what, Mademoiselle, you may be taking a chill—you come sit closer to the stove, and Soukie will tell you some *nice* bits of news.

"Now, listen to this," she said, resetting Felice in her own rocking chair and putting the loaves of bread in to bake. "There was a woman in Yarmouth who everyone said was wicked, but when she died last month she left every last cent to the Catholic Church. And guess what?" Soukie went on, when Felice had made no response to this good tiding. "A bluejay pecked at the kitchen window last night while I was washing up."

"A bluejay? In December?" Felice snorted.

"Yes, in*deed.*" Soukie went to the window in question and, rapping on it, nodded her head as though she had just proved her statement. "That's what makes it miraculous—a lucky omen. Something very important will happen, you'll see, Mademoiselle."

Felice sat looking at the dark window—it was now entirely night —and while Soukie, back to her original theme of doom, was recapitulating evidence she had earlier set forth of a perilous winter (berries and acorns thick on the trees, the early southward migration of birds from Brier Island, an ominous greenish cast to the water on certain days), Felice thought of Celeste and Anne, down below the cliff in the dark. What if one or both had slipped on the icy path while struggling back up to the top, and had fallen down on the hard rock below; they might be lying there unconscious right now, and the tide coming in.

Felice rushed to open the back door, looked up at the moonless sky pricked with stars, and then, heedless of Soukie's "What in the world? Mademoiselle, what in the world?" ran through the empty dining room, where set tables awaited the diners, and into the hall. She went first toward Mother Superior's office, but then—driven by what felt like desperate hope—turned and raced upstairs to the dormitory, where she found Celeste and Françoise rearranging Anne's hair. So relieved was Felice to see them that she hugged each one, even Anne, and apologized for having been so disagreeable earlier in the day. When the bell rang, the four clattered down to dinner arm in arm, everything almost entirely forgiven.

4

Felice wasn't her usual self Sunday morning. Her feet didn't want to step into her underwear and her fingers, doing up the chemise buttons, felt tired. Then, as she pulled the nightgown over her head, she was dizzy. She swayed for a moment against the white curtain that separated her bed from Antoinette's. She touched her face, wishing for a mirror; if she could see herself, she would feel better. After braiding her hair (she had learned to straighten the part by touch, like a blind person), she pinned on her veil, took up her missal, and joined the other girls who were wordlessly trooping down the stairs to the chapel. Ordinarily Felice felt hungry before Sunday mass, without breakfast; today she was glad not to have to face the bowl of lumpy porridge.

At the chapel door, she dipped her fingertips in the stoup of holy water; it was cool against her forehead. Felice took her assigned seat between Antoinette and Blanche. She had been permanently separated from Celeste and Anne during mass because their whispering once caused the entering Abbé to lose rhythm with the censer, and the smoking vessel had struck the shoulder of Sister Theodota.

The Abbé appeared, vested in gold and white. With the Asperges, thinking of herself washed in hyssop, being made whiter than snow, Felice began to feel better. She liked communion: looking forward to receiving His Body and Blood into her own and then walking back to her pew, thrillingly pure, gave the Sunday masses a plot that the weekday ones lacked.

"Mea culpa, mea culpa," the Abbé chanted, tapping his chest with his knuckles. *"Mea culpa,"* Felice responded with the others, *"mea maxima culpa."* Missals rustled. Knee benches creaked as the girls

and nuns rose and fell with the litany. During a long spell of prayers said kneeling, Felice felt a bit dizzy again and shifted to lean back against the pew.

The Abbé stood at the rail, and the nuns in the front row rose and went forward. Felice bent her head, studying the reverential sandwich of her hands. At the edge of her vision, the pews ahead emptied and filled, the wave of motion reaching steadily back toward her. As the girls in the row ahead filed out, leaving a cold space there, Felice had her usual dangerous thought: what if she remained in her place when the time came for her row to rise and go forward—what then? Her heart beat faster with the drama of indecision, but, as always, she stood with the others when her time came.

The resistance heightened the joy of giving in. Felice's bowed head felt heavy with repentance; the smooth rail congratulated her wrists. She tipped her head back at the cool rustle of the Abbé's approach, and then she saw, through half-closed eyes, the silver bowl filled with transparent moons. Felice extended her tongue, hoping it wasn't as yellow and furry as it felt, and the Abbé placed the wafer there tenderly. She took it inside her mouth, liking the slight tug of the dry papery Host on her tongue. This is His Body, His Blood, she sang inside herself. She rose and walked, head bowed very low, to her pew, the wafer slowly softening on her tongue, suffusing her body with whiteness.

At the conclusion of mass Felice remained kneeling, her eyes closed against the temptation of noticing others notice her. When she felt the chapel to be empty, she opened her eyes and looked out across the even ripple of pew-backs at the white figure of the Virgin. To Felice she was the very embodiment of constancy, from her gentle, unchanging smile to her graceful feet, with their realistically sculpted toenails (which from this distance she could not see, but remembered from the times when she knelt close and studied those sandaled feet, and the raised little finger of the right hand, and the half-lidded, downcast eyes). The sacred fire pulsed steadily at Mary's feet, behind its thick dome of glass, and threw a rosy glow upward, onto the frozen, fluid movement of her alabaster robe, warming the tips of her fingers.

"O Blessed Root and Gate," Felice whispered aloud, "guide me."

She leaned back slightly, against the edge of the pew and against the contentment that felt solid as an arm. She let her eyes float shut, and asked Mary to be her mother, just as Saint Thérèse had done; then she sat all the way back in the pew and looked around her, feeling, in spite of her dizziness, a comfort like the memory of home. This was what came of her decision to become a nun, she thought, smiling, crossing herself, and looking about at the white walls that held her with such light firmness. This proved, she thought, shifting her legs in pleasure, that her instinct about a religious vocation was correct, in spite of Mother Superior's first reaction. Mama thought so too— she could feel the warmth of her approving attention, and Mama was not at all envious, either, of her devotion to Mary; they would work together, in heavenly collaboration, holding conferences about Felice's health and progress. Mama would be so proud when, at the Bishop's visit next Easter, Felice's candidacy for the novitiate would be announced, just after her confirmation. She would study very hard in the Abbé's catechism class from now on, so that her confirmation would be perfect, and so that he would recommend her for the novitiate. Last year she had been dismissed from catechism class, for drawing in her book.

Felice comforted herself with the thought that Saint Thérèse had probably done much worse things as a young girl. She would tell Mother Superior—perhaps today—that she had taken Saint Thérèse as a model; then Mother Superior would begin to understand. Saint Thérèse, whose name Mother Superior had taken when she joined the sisterhood, had been, as a girl and a young novice, high-spirited, with a runaway imagination and mischievousness that it was her task to tame. Had she not, like Felice, hungered after fine clothes, even when already dressed in black, and had she not, as a novice, gossiped with outsiders through the grille in the convent door? Yet that liveliness, correctly plumbed—Felice had heard Mother Superior say this herself—was the source of profound depths of mystical understanding, a radiant intensity of devotion that Felice thought of as far removed from the experience of humdrum nuns like Sisters Theodota and Constance. Her own life would be, she thought, ecstatic, washed in prisms of fantastic color and sound. She would see and hear things that others could not; but she would, from her rare knowledge, move, and save, others.

When Uncle Adolphe pursued her, she would pray so magnificently that she would turn to pure, fiery light, and he, awestruck, shielding his face with one arm, would jump back. As she moved slowly away, the air would be filled with a subtle perfume of roses, and Uncle Adolphe would gape at his fingertips, bruised a light purple, and finally fall on his knees in a state of contrition and adoration, his soul washed clean.

Felice sat still for one more moment, letting the idea of her own holiness pluck at her a little longer. Then she rose, genuflected, and went down the aisle and into the hall. The dizziness persisted, but it didn't matter now; that was below, in her body. She, and the white walls of the corridor, and the delicate tap of her feet against the floor, were pure soul.

Outside the dining room the odor of fish chowder accosted her. Feeling a bit nauseated, she turned and headed for the stair, thinking to go to her cubicle and lie down.

"It's time for luncheon, Felice. Didn't you hear the bell ring?"

Felice turned to see Mother Superior at the dining-room door, hands planted on her wide hips in a posture of impatience.

Felice opened her mouth to protest, and then closed it. This was an opportunity for her to display perfect obedience. Hands folded before her, she walked back to the dining room, passing humbly beneath Mother Superior's gaze, and when the nun complained, "You are eternally late, Mademoiselle," responded, "Yes, Ma Mère, I am sorry."

The meal seemed to drag on forever: another trial. Felice sat taking tiny sips of the greasy chowder and trying not to listen to the argument between Sisters Claire and Theodota about the tarnished condition of the sconces in the chapel, and whose responsibility that was. Across from her, Sister Agatha was silent today; she listed to one side as though she had suffered some injury, and paddled her spoon dejectedly in her soup, wrinkling her nose and closing her eyes with each infrequent mouthful, as if ingesting some unpleasant tonic. Felice had just decided that she would assist Sister Agatha upstairs after luncheon and talk to her about her ambition, when Sister Claire said to her as they all rose, "Don't forget your practice today, Felice."

So, sighing, but feeling that Mary was displaying a serious interest in her by imposing so many demands, Felice went obediently to the parlor. As she walked, she began to hum just beneath her breath one of the odd tunes that sometimes came, unbidden, into her mind.

She sat down at the piano, lifted the keyboard cover, and blew into her cupped hands to enliven them. Then, imagining Mama and Mary looking down expectantly, she lifted her arms in a grand preliminary flourish and played a scale; her fingers chased one another up and down the keys like playful, lightfooted mice, just as Mama's had done.

After what Sister Claire would have called much too brief a warm-up—but she was doing well to sit here at all, she argued internally—Felice set out the Bach variation she was currently working on. The finished music of Bach aroused in Felice some of her richest spiritual feelings, an experience she had difficulty keeping sight of during the process of learning each piece. She hadn't been able to get past the first eight bars of this variation without Sister Claire's interrupting her with "Watch your phrasing, please!"

So she began carefully, deliberately, moving from measure to measure with a stateliness that sounded appropriate, even though the pace was too slow. She got past the critical bar and soon was deep into the unexplored territory of the second page. It was satisfying to her, the way her fingers did the notes' bidding, almost, it seemed, without her having to think at all. But as she went on, and especially during a very difficult run, her fingers began to feel sluggish and bored. The odd little tune reentered her head. It had a surprising rhythm—slow, quick, quick, like a waltz, but with irregular turns that would have tripped up feet, and it was much too plaintive, besides, for a dance. She tried to keep both themes going—sight-reading the Bach, leaning forward to receive the clusters of notes from the page, while the song in her head dipped above and below. When the two collided in a sour chord, Felice sat looking for a moment at her hands on the keyboard. Then, after turning to make sure no one had entered the parlor, she played the tune with her left hand, bending her body over the melody to keep it from escaping into the room.

There was the sound of paired footsteps in the hall—nuns taking an indoor constitutional. Before someone could enter and ask her to play, Felice shut the keyboard and, armed with the excuse that she felt about to faint, hurried out of the parlor, down the hall, and up the stairs to the dormitory.

She climbed, still dressed, into her unmade bed. If Sister Theodota had made her inspection round yet, she would have collected demerit points for the bed, and for the heap of clothes in the corner, which she refused to look at. She curled up in a circle, hugging her knees, in an attempt to get back the warmth she had felt earlier. She tried to see Mary's face in the chapel, and in heaven, where she sat with Mama. But her mind was blank. Cold, nausea, and loneliness seeped through her limbs, the weight of misery making her inert, unable to move even one finger. She felt like a wide-awake, suffering stone.

When Celeste and Anne tiptoed in and bounced on the foot of her bed, Felice sat up, the relief of company pushing back even the physical malaise.

"Come on," Celeste said, "down to the beach."

"I don't know," Felice said, fingering her nubby counterpane. "I don't really feel too well. Why don't we just talk in here?"

"Priss-Face," Celeste whispered, none too softly, nodding her head at the next cubicle.

"You won't be horrible?" Felice asked, remembering Celeste's fingers pulling at her cloak.

"Just fortunes," Celeste said, her eyes widening innocently.

"That's right," Anne said. "We'll tell fortunes." Today Anne's hair was bound about her head in severe braids; still, it shone like a misassigned halo.

"I haven't asked Françoise," Celeste added. "But I guess I could —she *loves* fortunes."

"All right, I'm coming," Felice grumbled, throwing back the covers. "But I don't feel well at all." She pulled on her cloak and followed her friends numbly down the stairs, out the back door, and across the grounds.

The air was damp, cold, and strangely still, as though the wind were holding its breath. A sheet of clouds hid the sun. Lagging behind,

Felice forced her feet to move across the lawn and through the orchard. She felt as stiff as the figure on Mama's music box, a shepherdess hopping one notch around her circle with each chimed note; in her head her funny tune played over and over, but with a mechanical tone, like the music box.

Celeste and Anne had already climbed the wall when Felice reached the line of willows. She looked into her tree at Our Lady, crossed herself—her fingers, icy on her forehead, reminding her of forgotten mittens—and then pulled herself over the wall, landing awkwardly on one foot. She walked, half-limping, to the edge of the cliff, where Celeste and Anne waited.

When Felice stood by them and looked out, she said, "Oh, no. We can't go down there today." For a low fog covered the water and the shore, obscuring even the lower part of the path from view.

"Sissy," Celeste said, and started down the cliff; Anne, looking back to see if Felice was coming, went next, and Felice, humming her tune for courage, followed them down the path that wound through pitted, sienna-colored rocks to the shore.

They descended into whiteness, as into a cloud. Felice's head was a jumble as she blindly felt her way along the path: her tune, Uncle Adolphe's face advancing and receding, the blood-sister pact she and Celeste had made last spring. When she reached the shore Celeste and Anne were circling in the milky fog, their arms outstretched. "This is what heaven looks like," Celeste said.

"It is not," Felice said. "That's sacrilegious."

"I suppose *you* know. I suppose *you*'ve been there—you and Priss-Face and Sister Agatha."

Ignoring her, Felice walked toward the sound of water and stood watching the waves. She thought of each drop of water as having traveled a great distance, perhaps all the way from Boston. At low tide the waves plopped disconsolately against the shore, as though depleted by a long journey that hadn't been worth it. But when the tide was coming in, as now, the waves seemed charged with competitive energy, each anxious to slap the sand first and be off on the next leg of the race. Felice walked on, watching the wrinkles that tagged with wild rapidity across the water's edge, as if something urgent were being communicated, and looking at the lines graven in the sand at the water's outgoing, an exotic script she and Celeste liked to read when they came here on clear days, just the two of them together.

"Celeste," she called. "Come see what the water has written today."

"Over here," came a voice from the whiteness. "We're telling fortunes."

"Celeste? Anne?" Felice whirled about; she could see nothing but fog. She began to stumble inland. "Celeste?"

"Here—by the cliff." Nothing of the cliff was visible but a jagged rock, high up, that protruded through the fog like the prow of a ship bearing down on her.

Felice took a deep breath. "I will not faint," she said aloud. Clutching her rosary in her pocket, she walked back to the water and followed her own footsteps back up the shore.

Celeste and Anne rematerialized, seated on rocks near the foot of the path. Felice ran toward them and fell onto a low boulder; though the rock was slick with frozen spray, it had the reliable feeling of a familiar body. "I thought I was lost," Felice said, and holding her head in both hands, added, "I feel very strange."

The other girls were engrossed in the hieroglyphs Celeste was drawing in the sand. With a stick she made circles and boxes and triangles, fortunetelling marks. Felice huddled forward, only half-listening as Celeste tossed pebbles and predicted Anne's fate—an early marriage and three sons. She felt chilled one moment and hot the next. She watched the lacy edge of the water appear from beyond the wall of fog and draw back, like a foamy tongue. The sound of water was muted and the convent seemed remote. Even Celeste's voice seemed far away, and her own hands in her lap looked tiny, like doll's hands.

"Felice is going to marry a sailor," Celeste divined, studying the arcane chart she had made in the sand. She turned and tossed a pebble back over her shoulder; it fell on a number.

"Eight children," Anne exclaimed. "Let's see how many boys, how many girls."

Felice reached down to touch the small rock. It seemed that her hand had to travel a long distance before picking it up. It was a flat blue rock, the same color as most of the large cobbles and boulders at the cove, and there was a lightning-shaped line etched across it.

"I don't want to know," she said. "I probably won't get married at all, anyway. I think I'm going to be a nun."

Her friends stared at her. A new expression began to gather in Celeste's face. "And be like Sister Agatha?"

"Felice loves Sister Agatha," Anne said. "She wants to be just like her."

"I do not," Felice said. "I do not want to be like her. She's sad."

Celeste looked down and poked at the sand with her stick. "Sister Agatha doesn't have any breasts," she said.

"Sister Agatha doesn't have any breasts," Anne echoed.

Celeste piled up sand. "Poo-or Sister Agatha, poo-or Felice." Damp sand flew.

"I do not like her—I am not like her," Felice protested, stamping her foot. She felt horribly dizzy; perhaps she should go back to the convent.

Celeste drove her stick deep and threw up a great clot of dun-colored sand. "Then say she doesn't have any breasts. Say poor Sister Agatha."

Felice began to rise, then sat back down.

"Poor Sister Agatha," she said woodenly. "She doesn't have any breasts."

"I know," Anne said, scraping up sand with her fingers to add to the pile. "Let's make breasts for Sister Agatha."

"Yes, let's," Celeste said, throwing down her stick and gathering handfuls of sand. She looked questioningly at Felice.

Felice fell to her knees and began to scrape at the cold sand with her fingers. "Poor Sister Agatha," she said.

"Poor Sister Agatha," Anne repeated, starting a new mound.

"Poor Sister Agatha," Celeste said in a low, sleepy voice that made the words sound magical.

The three dug and patted the sand, chanting, "Poor Sister Agatha, the priests took her breasts, poor Sister Agatha, we'll make her some more."

The mounds rose to points. Celeste searched among the fortunetelling rocks and placed one on the top of each mound. She began to giggle. Anne joined her, falling back on the sand under the force of her laughter. "Poor Sister Agatha," they gasped, red-faced.

Felice tried to laugh, but it hurt. Tears came to her eyes.

Celeste jumped to her feet and began to dance back and forth in front of the sand breasts. Anne imitated her, tapping her palm across her open mouth, the two of them chanting, "Sis-ter Ag-ath-a, Sis-ter Ag-ath-a . . ."

"Come on, Felice," Celeste said, between chants.

"I can't," Felice said, "I don't feel good." Her stomach rose and fell as though she were seasick. The chanting and dancing went on.

"Poo-or Sis-ter Ag-ath-a, poor Fe-lice, poo-or Sis-ter Ag-ath-a, poor Fe-lice . . ."

Felice's head spun wildly and she hugged herself to stay upright.

"Come *on,* Felice . . . Sis-ter Ag-ath-a, Sis-ter Ag-ath-a . . ."

As Felice rose, the rock clenched tight in her perspiring hand, the dizziness spiraled downward in her body, and her legs gave way beneath her. The last thing she knew, falling, was the fog, and then whiteness filled her head.

When Felice regained consciousness, Anne and Celeste were carrying her down the beach, Anne holding her feet and Celeste her arms.

"Ooow," Felice cried, "you're hurting me. Put me down."

They lowered her to the ground, and Anne, dropping her feet, gasped. "She's wounded," she said. "Oh, Saint Anthony, she's wounded."

Celeste knelt beside Felice's legs with such a serious expression that Felice, alarmed, struggled upward. "Maybe she's got *It,*" Celeste was saying as Felice looked down at her legs and at the lacy edge of her exposed underwear. Then on her hiked-up petticoat and her drawers she saw spots of red and, leaning forward, saw a dark, shapeless stain between her legs.

Felice reached to touch the stain, wings of terror beating inside her, and she thought of Mama, and she knew she was dying. *"Perdue,"* she whispered, sinking back. *"Perdue*—oh—Mama."

WHEN FELICE AWOKE, SHE WAS LYING ON A BED IN THE INFIR-
mary, and Mother Superior was sitting beside her. "I thought I was
dead," Felice said, feeling her face to be certain she wasn't.

"Nonsense," Mother Superior said, rising. "You've merely become
a woman."

"How did I get *here?*"

"Jacques carried you." Mother Superior walked to the bureau and
came back bearing a white bundle. She laid it on the bed beside Felice
and said in a prayerful voice, "This is a monthly sickness we must all
endure—it is God's will." Then, clearing her throat, she continued,
more briskly, "Now, Felice, the main thing you must do is keep
yourself immaculate." The nun undid the cloth and held up a harness-
like affair of heavy cloth. "You wear this about your waist," she said,
holding it ludicrously against her own black girth. "And these," she
continued, holding up a stack of cloth pads, "you change very often
—two or three times daily—and send them down in the laundry
chute. Now, is that clear?"

"Yes, Ma Mère," Felice said, closing her eyes, wishing to faint
away.

Mother Superior's clammy hand descended to her forehead. "Poor
Felice," she said. "After you have washed and arranged yourself, you
may remain here, lying down—you are excused from classes tomorrow."

By dinnertime, however, after a visit from Celeste, Felice felt well
enough to go to the dining hall and later, after vespers, she lay on her
own bed, with Celeste, Anne, Marie, Françoise, and Blanche perched
on the sides, the group of them whispering until well past bedtime.

Felice, wearing the deliberately not-pained expression of a saint, described the rigors of womanhood while Anne, Marie, and Blanche asked questions, and Françoise and Celeste, the other two initiates, nodded sagely. Later Celeste, in a husky whisper, told the others about the horrible and mysterious rite of which menstruation was only a part, her tale so laced with adjectives of pain and ecstasy that Marie, burying her face in her knees, said, "I think *I'll* become a nun," and Blanche, to whom the story was totally new, wept.

The next morning Felice awoke feeling as though she were on fire, and she had a deep, painful cough. She was listless at breakfast, only sipping at her tea. "I *can't,*" she said when Sister Claire enjoined her to eat, and began to cough and cry all at once. Sister Claire felt her forehead and went to consult with Mother Superior.

The two of them put Felice to bed in the infirmary, Mother Superior scolding all the while. "This foolishness of running about on the beach must stop," she said, shaking out a blanket. "We are not a nursing order, you know." But her voice didn't sound as harsh as her words, and Felice thought that both nuns looked worried.

"Will I be all right?" Felice asked.

"Of course—you just have a sniffle," Mother Superior said, patting the cover. She and Sister Claire were smiling down at her, their faces fuzzily angelic, as Felice closed her eyes and fell backward into sleep.

For several days Felice lay tangled in a feverish sleep broken by spells of coughing and by the ministrations of the nuns, whose cool hands pressed her forehead, smoothed her hair, and tucked her arms beneath the covers. When the nuns raised her legs to change the pad between them, Felice, in the confusion of half-sleep, thought of the discomfort there as the source of her illness.

Sometimes Felice kicked away the hot covers and lay with her feet against the cool iron bars at the end of the bed. "You must stay covered, Felice," she heard a clear voice say one day, and the blankets were pulled up over her and tucked firmly beneath the mattress, the motion tipping up her body on one side and then the other. Felice could see the long oval face of Sister Claire smiling down at her. "You do look better. Can you sit up a bit and eat this soup?" Sister Claire showed her the picture she had placed on the table by Felice's bed:

it was a fluffy-winged guardian angel hovering above two children who were crossing a bridge.

Felice began to wake more often, but, because the light seemed too bright, she lay with her eyes closed when she awakened in the daytime. At night she could not tell if her eyes were open or shut, or, sometimes, whether she was remembering or dreaming.

One night Felice lay thinking of an island where she had gone as a young child with Mama and Papa in a small sailing boat. It was July, the sky was blue, and the water glittered in the sun. Papa carried his ornithology book and a sketching pad; and Mama, a white wicker picnic basket. Felice left Mama and Papa on the beach and climbed the cliff to explore the center of the island where the gulls nested. "Be careful," Papa had called after her. Beneath her feet were purple Michaelmas daisies and yellow buttercups, of which she picked a bouquet, and wild strawberries, which tasted like summer itself. She put every other one of the berries in her pocket for later.

The top of the cliff was a rolling quilt of grass patch and rock, and was covered with the feathers of gulls, the long white shafts of adult birds and the short fuzzy feathers of the chicks. As she approached the rookery the gulls circled above her, dipping close and crying raucously. There were eggshells in the gullies next to the white rock boulders and a just-hatched chick staggering through the grass. Felice squatted to look at it, stretched to touch its fuzzy head. As she did, a large gull dove and thumped her shoulder, throwing her back. Felice looked up: the sky was dark with the angry, circling birds. "Papa!" she cried out, "Mama!" She scrambled to her feet and ran, the stems of the flowers sticky in her hand, back across the meadow, which dipped and swelled before her. Once she stumbled and fell over a rock. When she got to her knees, she found a sheep by her side grinning meanly at her, its lips pulled back over yellow teeth. "I am dreaming," she said to the sheep.

Felice ran and ran—the going back was farther than the coming— and when she reached the cliff, the sun was lower in the sky. She slid down the rock to the beach, where the boat rocked like a cradle in the soft waves, and the white wicker basket marked the spot of their luncheon. Mama and Papa were not there. She called in both directions, but the wind tore her words to rags. The wind also ruffled the pages of Papa's book and tugged at the sail wrapped about the mast of the waiting boat. Up the beach, a flock of shore birds followed the motion of the water, scurrying on their stick legs as the waves rolled in. A gull dove into the water near the boat and brought up a silvery fish in its bill. Another bird circled, black against the sky. In the distance, Felice heard the vengeful cries of the nesting birds and the truth pierced her: the birds have eaten Mama and Papa. She looked frantically about their picnic spot: there was not a trace, except inden- tations in the sand where they had sat. The blanket was neatly packed away in the basket with the remains of luncheon. She looked up and down the beach and up into the sky. "Mama, Papa," she cried. There was only the sound of birds, and the wind, and the wild, uncaring water. Her hands grasped at herself. There was no one to tell. Mama and Papa were eaten by the birds, she sobbed into her arm, the birds have eaten up my mama and papa.

Felice was biting her arm when she awoke. She turned on her back and stretched out, trembling and cold. It was several long seconds before she separated the weight of the dream from herself. It was dark in the room, with no moonlight to illuminate the objects, but the bed felt as though it were facing the wrong direction. "Mama," she called out, and her hand struck iron. Then she knew she was not in her room at home, in the walnut canopy bed Papa had made, but at the convent, and that Mama and Papa were not there, and she went back to sleep crying, holding the Saint Cecilia medallion tight in her hand.

Another day Felice awoke from a dream that evaporated when she opened her eyes, but her heart was beating fast. In the dim light she could just make out a shape beside her, between the bed and the wall. It seemed to have great black wings that slowly began to move as she stared at it. She screamed, and Mother Superior came running. When Felice told her that she had seen a bird, the nun said she had no doubt dreamed of the Holy Spirit, who was watching out after her.

In the daytime the nuns came to see her in rounds, in accordance with an apparently orchestrated plan. One appeared in the morning and one in the evening, discoursed a few minutes about the progress in classes and the needlework, said a prayer, and departed. The novice

Evangeline, who had trained as a nurse at the order's mother house in Halifax, came twice a day to mix a vial of bitter-tasting medicine, and to feel her forehead. She almost never spoke, and looked generally disapproving of this illness, even suspicious of it. Sister Claire occasionally came in, unscheduled, between classes and, humming, walked about the room, straightening things that didn't need straightening. Mother Superior visited once a day, usually before dinner, when the smells of food were strong from the kitchen, to read to her from the *Lives of the Saints.* The Abbé came twice to hear her confession and to give her communion. He came one other time for a religion lesson, but his questions swam about in Felice's mind like elusive fish, and she was pronounced not yet well enough for catechizing.

In the middle of the day, while classes were in session, Felice's solitude was often relieved only by the noontime entrance of Soukie, who brought her a tray of bland food. Sometimes when Soukie came to retrieve the dishes she would sit and talk; so glad was Felice for company that she did not attempt to deflect the maid from her usual topic. "God has a purpose in everything, don't you agree?" The maid tilted her red head to one side and fixed Felice with a parrotlike stare. "For instance, when the *Aurora* wrecked . . ." (here Felice shut her eyes and burrowed deeper into the covers, trying to concentrate on the inflections of Soukie's voice) ". . . a great load of wood washed up on shore. It was like it was heaven-sent, Mademoiselle, truly, because the men built the Odd Fellows building out of it; they'd had the plans, and the inclination, but not the building material, you see. . . ." Soukie droned on and on, until Felice fell asleep, dropping away from the words. "Other folks say there are wreckers among us, that we tie bells about the sheep and draw the ships in. Now, you know that's not so. . . ." and Felice drifted, seeing Soukie as a red, fluffy sheep with a blue-ribboned bell about her neck, high on the cliff at the island's edge, and Mama and Papa coming home, their ship passing perilously close to the shore. When the tide began to take the *Triomphe,* the prow turning toward the rocks, Felice woke with a start.

Mother Superior had begun to encourage Felice to stay awake longer in the daytime; not only could too much sleep enervate her further, she said, but she was getting behind in her schoolwork. The nun had brought her books and arranged them in a stack by her bed: the catechism, Cicero, arithmetic, the plays of Racine, the history of British America, written in English, and the history of France, which Mother Superior had her students memorize ten pages at a time. But merely opening any of these books made Felice drowsy; she thought she might stay awake reading novels if Celeste could smuggle some in to her, but Mother Superior had outlawed visits from the girls.

During her visits Sister Theodota reminded Felice of the special importance of arithmetic, but when she tried to do the assigned problems the numbers taunted her. She wished Philippe were here to help her; he was good with numbers. She had a letter from Philippe, in which he said he was taking the course in engineering. He said Mother Superior had written to tell them Felice was not well, but mending, and not to worry. Philippe said he hoped she was much better now, and that she would be home for Christmas, which was now only two weeks away. Reading this, Felice decided she was much too weak to travel, and took an experimental walk around the room to prove it. She fell back on the bed, her head buzzing slightly, and smiled as she thought of Uncle Adolphe at the head of the dining table sawing at the roast goose, and her own seat empty.

She picked up Philippe's letter again to read the postscript; it said that Pip had died and that Philippe had buried him in the back, behind the carriage house. Felice fell asleep with the letter in her hand; she dreamed that Uncle Adolphe was examining Pip's stippled body for mites, to see if the bird had infested his house, and then he was examining Felice for insects. He found them, small black ones she had been trying to hide under her sleeves. "Corn beetles," he said, and when he plucked one from her it broke in half and the remaining part dove into her skin. "This is very serious," he said. "I don't know that I can fix it." He held her arm to his ear and shook it like a silent watch.

ONE DAY FELICE HEARD—OR DREAMT SHE HEARD—SISTER AGATHA
shout, in English, through the open door, as another nun went out,
"She is washed in the blood of the Lamb!"

"Even overlooking the sacrilege of that remark," Felice understood
Sister Theodota to say, "that is a Baptist phrase, Sister." Though
Sister Agatha had been converted to Catholicism as a child, and had
later converted her English, Baptist father, her spiritual lineage was
considered a bit suspect by some, a situation that her frequently
unconventional observations only served to inflame.

A small scuffle ensued. "Come along, Sister."

"I want to see the child."

"She is sleeping," Sister Theodota said, slamming the door, at
which noise—in the room, or in her dream—Felice awoke and lay
looking for a while at Sister Agatha's painting of the Assumption
of the Virgin. She floated back into sleep imagining Jesus descending
for Sister Agatha, transforming her black habit to a pearly white
satin gown with one touch of His finger, and she rising in a shaft
of light—her face young and beautiful, having shed its mask of
mortal time—and smiling down upon them all, forgiving those
who needed forgiveness, and blessing all others, particularly
Felice.

Another afternoon Felice awoke to find Sister Agatha in the chair
at her bedside. Felice blinked, surprised; the last thing she remembered was laying down her heavy soup spoon. Now the spoon was
gone, the bowl was gone, the noon light had dimmed, and Sister
Agatha sat waiting.

The nun smiled when she heard Felice stir. "Hello, my dear," she said loudly, as though speaking across a great distance. "I've been concerned about you."

"Hello, Sister Agatha," Felice said. "I've not seen you before, have I?" She realized that she was very glad to see her now; her heart lifted. "How are Celeste and Anne?"

"Those hoydens are quite well, though they wanted not to be. They tried to become sick themselves so they could join you here and miss the winter examinations, but it's hard to fool Mother Superior, you know." Sister Agatha giggled, then coughed. "This is all in the way of saying," she continued soberly, "that they miss you too."

Sister Agatha reached out and fumbled for Felice's arm. "You don't feel hot," she said. "You must be much recovered, though still weak?"

"Yes."

"I've known any number of people who had pneumonia," Sister Agatha said. "In every case, a crisis of the spirit was involved. I've been on my knees day and night, night and day."

"Pneumonia? Is that what I've got? Mother Superior said I had a bad cold, and grippe, with complications."

"Now, I don't wish you to think me insubordinate, Felicia," Sister Agatha whispered, drawing her chair a bit closer, "but Mother Superior either minimizes or maximizes." Sister Agatha looked quite gleeful as she said this. Then she fell silent, her face resettling into its customary downturned lines. "Mother Superior is a good woman," Sister Agatha said, "though her understanding has its natural limits. It's not *just* because of her that I've not been to see you—true, I wasn't included in the rotations—but there were other considerations, too, such as praying for your recovery, and my own meditation. This meditation takes a great amount of time, my dear, and energy. And I'm not as young as I might be, Felicia—ah, I used to be so very young, you know," she said in a heavy voice. She sighed, and then went on, more brightly, "But these days are better, really. I am closer to Him." Sister Agatha crossed herself and folded her hands in her lap. She smiled a small expectant smile, clearly awaiting questions.

"What do you meditate about, Sister Agatha?" Felice turned on her side to face the nun. She didn't feel sleepy at all now.

"I think on the rack and the scourge of life, and the rewards that await us in His glorious mansion. I think of Our Lady, and of my own dear ancestor. . . . How are you, my dear?" Sister Agatha asked when Felice sat up.

"I have been meditating too, Sister Agatha—about becoming a nun."

Sister Agatha's eyes, in the effort to fix more exactly on Felice, oscillated wildly.

"I am going to save my Uncle Adolphe. He is even worse than a Baptist," Felice said, thinking of Sister Agatha's conversion of her father. "He's an atheist."

Sister Agatha mumbled what seemed to be a prayer, in support, Felice thought, of her grappling with the soul of Uncle Adolphe.

But when Sister Agatha spoke again, it was of herself. "I have been much misunderstood, child, much misunderstood. It is my earthly test—which I have passed, you realize, more than passed, excelled in!" Here Sister Agatha's fist hammered her chest until it was gently subdued by the other hand. She laid her head against the chair, looking as though she might have dozed off, but soon continued, in a voice of perfect clarity, "Most of my ancestors were Catholic—on my mother's side, not only French Acadians all the way back but one of the first and finest families to come from France. In 1692, praise God. Now. I want to tell you a story—a very true and important story. I have not told anyone else. But you, Felicia, you are a sensitive spirit. . . ." Then Sister Agatha sat silent a long while, her eyes raised heavenward. Felice hugged the covers and waited.

"Catherine Laurier," the nun began finally, "Catherine Laurier was a most beautiful woman. Of course, you remember the verse 'My love is like a red, red rose'?"

"Yes, Sister."

"Who wrote it, please?"

"I—I don't know right this minute, Sister."

"Robbie Burns! Don't you remember anything from your English literature lessons?"

"Yes, Sister, a great deal. Really. Please go on."

"Well," Sister Agatha said, with a deep sigh, sinking back into her chair. "She was a poetic creature, as I said. A red, red rose. Yes, her hair was black, and her skin was as white as snow but for the cheeks, the beautiful scarlet of late summer roses. She always wore a dress to match those lovely cheeks." Sister Agatha raised one trembling hand to her own left cheek and cupped it for a moment. "She was born in 1720 in Beaubassin—one of the very earliest Acadian settlements, if you remember your history." Dropping her hand, Sister Agatha fixed upon Felice an almost bellicose expression, as though anticipating either some disagreement or impudent lapse of memory.

"Yes, Sister, I remember that very well."

"All right, then. Well, her father had been a fur trader, and her husband was a fur trader too. Her husband was bewitched by her beauty—Catherine Laurier was the most beautiful woman in Nova Scotia, they say—and he never strayed from her side. Do you understand me so far, Felice?" Sister Agatha asked, with her pedagogical frown.

"Oh, yes."

"Very good. Very good. . . . It is a lovely story, but it is a sad one too, so very sad." Sister Agatha stroked her veil as though it were long hair. "If she had resisted, Jesus says, she would have become Saint Catherine—ascended into heaven, and sat at His side. . . . But she *did* resist," Sister Agatha said, jerking her veil so hard that her black bonnet was pulled askew. "God did not help her—forgive me—and she was overwhelmed. There is nothing woman can do against the brutal male, whose strength is so great, greater than all but the Heavenly Host, who must intervene. . . ." Sister Agatha halted. Felice saw that she was trembling, and she thought of Uncle Adolphe, and her terrible task.

"Why didn't God help her?" she asked, alarmed.

"Oh, I am a sinful woman," Sister Agatha moaned, crossing herself. "My faith is weak. Jesus can only do so much, you see—*she* must have been weak, her heart must have entertained lust. . . ."

The nun sat with her hands pressed together in a praying attitude, but Felice could see that she was not praying. She was looking out over her hands into the past.

"What happened to her, Sister?"

"Well," Sister Agatha said, adjusting her bonnet and settling back into her storytelling position, "Catherine Laurier lived in Beaubassin with her devoted husband. They had nine children, five of whom survived infancy. Her eldest daughter was Agatha Laurier—my great-grandmother—and she was the first carrier of this story. She took it to Cape Breton, married Peter Paradis, and passed it on to her daughter, Lucy Paradis Comeau, who gave it to her daughter, Adele Comeau Starr, who begat . . ." Sister Agatha's voice trailed off. "Who begat me, who begat no one." She paused again, her lips quivering. "My unborn child is an orphan," Sister Agatha whispered, "because she has no mother."

Felice considered this for a moment, but decided it didn't quite make sense. "What about Catherine Laurier?" she prodded.

"Well. It was nighttime, a full moon. The Indians were there—a great many Indians. They had come to persuade the French to move on—they couldn't keep the English back, you see. They finally had to drive the settlers into the wilderness for their own protection, but that's ahead of the story. The Frenchmen—including Catherine Laurier's husband—were meeting with the Indians at the church. Agatha didn't want to go to bed—she wasn't the least bit sleepy—but her mother made her do so. Agatha lay in bed, under a pile of furs, watching her beautiful mother sewing by the fire. It was an enormous fireplace, so big three or four people could have sat in it if they wanted to. Well. The baby was crying—that would have been Claude—and the mother, still sitting by the fire, unbuttoned her dress to nurse him. Then two Indians came in the door!" Here, Sister Agatha jumped, and Felice looked at the door, half expecting it to open. Sister Agatha began to pluck at the bodice of her habit.

"What did they do, Sister Agatha?" Felice asked, shivering.

"Awful, awful . . . They tore her pretty dress . . . Agatha saw that much . . . Her mama screamed . . . Agatha hid beneath the covers . . . Oh! Oh!" Sister Agatha hid her face in her hands and cowered, as though beneath blows. Then, whimpering, she sat up and, after several deep breaths, went on. "I told you it is a painful story. Catherine Laurier threw herself into the flames, and was delivered up to God. It is also a very beautiful story. She may be canonized yet, Felice, all the evidence is not yet in."

There was a long silence during which Sister Agatha took jagged breaths and Felice wavered between the desire to close her eyes, so that the nun would vanish, and an impulse to put her arms around the sloping black shoulders. She watched as Sister Agatha crossed herself, removed her glasses, and dabbed at her eyes with a sleeve.

When Sister Agatha had rearranged her glasses and veil, she looked toward Felice. "Mother Superior reads the *Lives of the Saints* to you, does she not?"

"Yes."

"Well, you pay close attention," Sister Agatha said, shaking a finger at her, "and tell me if this case is not remarkably similar." She rose unsteadily. "I must be going back to my cell now, to continue my prayers. Jesus visits me there—He will take my soul to heaven one day soon, and I must be in readiness."

"Goodbye, Sister Agatha." Felice watched her sway across the floor. The nun knocked against a bureau, muttered, and then said, "Father, forgive me," and crossed herself. She fumbled for the door-knob and opened the door, turning back to say, "Bless you, child."

Felice snuggled beneath the covers and had just closed her eyes when the sound of angry voices erupted in the hall. She sat up again, and was watching the door when Mother Superior marched in. She advanced rapidly on Felice, a volume of the *Lives of the Saints* gripped beneath her elbow, her rosary clattering.

"What has Sister Agatha been telling you?" Mother Superior demanded, thumping into the chair that had just been vacated.

"An—an Acadian story."

"Felice, I hope you won't take her stories too seriously. She was a fine scholar, and I am devoted to her—she was especially helpful to me when I came to Sacré Sang, but she has . . ." Mother Superior paused, and scanned Felice's face, "certain difficulties. But she is fond of you, and you must include her in your prayers, as I do."

Mother Superior opened her book and ran a finger down the table of contents. Weekly readings from the *Lives of the Saints* were a regular part of the nun's course in world history.

"Ma Mère? Has there been a saint from this convent yet?"

Mother Superior, flipping through pages, gave her a sharp glance. "Not that I am aware of."

"Then maybe it's our turn."

"This is not an appropriate thought, Felice. Study, emulation—that's what the saints' lives are for—not for games of speculation." She cleared her throat. "Now, here we go. 'Saint Ebba, Abbess, and Her Companions, Martyrs,' " she announced. " 'In the ninth century Saint Ebba governed the great monastery of Coldingham, situated in the Merch, or Marshes, a province in the shire of Berwick, which was for some time subject to the English, at other times to the Scots. In the year 870, according to Matthew of Westminster, or rather 874, according to the Scottish historians, in an incursion of the cruel Danish pirates, Hinguar and Hubba, this abbess was anxious not for her life, but for her chastity, to preserve which she had recourse to the following stratagem.' " Here Mother Superior licked the tip of her index finger and turned the page with it. " 'Having assembled her nuns in the chapter-house, after making a moving discourse to her sisters, she, with a razor, cut off her nose and upper lip, and was courageously imitated by all the holy community. The frightful spectacle which they exhibited in this condition protected their virginity. But the infidels, enraged at their disappointments, set fire to the monastery, and these holy virgins died in the flames, spotless victims to their heavenly spouse, the lover and rewarder of souls.' "

Mother Superior snapped the book shut. Felice flinched, and touched her nose.

"Questions?" the nun invited.

"What was their reward, Ma Mère?" Felice asked, talking through spread fingers, feeling her intact lips and the warm breath against her skin.

"Their pure souls were taken to heaven, as brides of Christ. Chastity is the greatest virtue of woman on earth—and will reap the greatest reward of everlasting life with Him. Now, Felice, I want you to understand that even a married woman can be chaste in her *heart,* and be blessed by God, and taken to heaven. But such women are not called to God's holiest service, nor are they likely to be found among the saints."

"My mother had a chaste heart."

"Yes, dear, no doubt she did." Mother Superior patted her hand and started to rise.

"Saint Thérèse is my model. Was she yours, too, Ma Mère? Is that why you took her name?"

"No. Her name was chosen for me, by my mother superior. Humility, Felice, is the first condition of life for those in God's service." The nun's voice sounded impatient.

"I'm humble, Ma Mère." Felice's voice quavered. "And I'd be happy for any name you gave me, I truly would."

Mother Superior bent toward her. "Are you crying?"

"No," Felice said, blinking back tears.

"I don't think you've been eating properly. Soukie tells me you didn't finish your supper last night." Mother Superior redirected her gaze to the bedside table, where the midmorning cup of molasses-sweetened tea, still untouched, sat in evidence. "Now, drink this," the nun said, handing her the cup. "You need to build up your strength if you're going home at Christmas."

Felice choked on the cold tea, then began to cough. "I *can't* go, Ma Mère—I'm much too sick."

The nun cradled Felice's head in her large, capable hands. "I think you'd better have a mustard plaster, dear. Now you just lie there, very calm, very calm." And with a sigh Mother Superior turned and went out of the room.

Felice sat rigid, the cup handle squeezed tight, and stared at Sister Agatha's paintings of the Virgin. In one panel, Jesus stood over the body of his dead, outstretched mother, gathering her soul into his arms like a cuddled animal. In the twin painting, Mary trod air as robust angels helped her up toward heaven. Mother Superior might not understand, but Mary did, and she was in heaven, body and all, looking down upon her, offering her consolation and strength. She had only to persevere, to purify herself through sacrifice and hardship, and the gates would open.

So when Mother Superior and Soukie returned with the noxious mustard plaster, Felice lay down even before she was asked and without a whimper allowed them to slide it beneath her gown. It was heavy on her chest and stank of sulphur.

"Ma Mère," Felice said as the nun prepared to leave again. She spoke in a low, calm voice that belied the burning pain of the plaster. "I need to speak with you. Privately," she added, as Soukie lingered at the door.

"I'll be right along then, Soukie," Mother Superior said, nodding her out. "Please get started cleaning those fish."

"You'd think a Christian who brought a gift of fish would have cleaned them, wouldn't you?" Soukie said, finding some dishes by the door to delay her. "That's the normal practice on Brier Island."

"Fillet them, too, Soukie, and don't be all afternoon about it." Mother Superior frowned after the maid, and then turned to Felice. "Well, Mademoiselle, what was it?" she asked, gathering the *Lives of the Saints* from her chair.

"When you have time, Ma Mère, I'd like to talk with you again about joining the order—very seriously."

"Of course, Felice, but what is the great urgency? If this is God's will, it will all come about in good time."

"A crisis of the spirit."

Mother Superior stood looking at her. The expression of her gray eyes and pale, doughy face went through several alterations, and Felice began to wriggle beneath the hot plaster. She realized that Mother Superior suspected her of having Unclean Thoughts, the transgression that disturbed her above all others. Finally the nun said, "Do you need to talk with the Abbé?"

"No—yes—I guess so, Ma Mère."

"Perhaps you could get up for confession and catechism tomorrow. I think you'll feel much better, getting out of bed. Get some fresh air. *Ex*ercise." The nun boxed at one corner of Felice's tucked-in blanket, straightening invisible wrinkles. "Don't you agree?"

"Yes, Ma Mère. But too sick to travel," Felice called after her.

The door clicked shut and Mother Superior's brisk footsteps receded down the hall. The room was very still but for the whisper of fire in the woodstove. The light seemed suddenly faint and unreliable—just a thickening of clouds over the sun, Felice told herself. In the dimmer light, the details of Sister Agatha's paintings receded, and white objects—the pitcher on the nightstand, the apron Soukie had left draped over a chair, Felice's hand in the air—had an eerie luminosity. Felice would have risen to light the kerosene lamp but for the mustard plaster, which was now searing her chest. She would have to wait until Mother Superior came back, but that could be a very long time. Felice lifted one edge of the plaster and felt it tug at her skin. What if Mother Superior forgot her—either accidentally or on purpose—for so long that the plaster cleaved to her chest and when it was pulled off, would take her breasts with it, leaving her blank? Felice eased her fingers beneath the loose collar of her gown and felt along the edges of the plaster, raising it slightly on one side and then the other, to let herself breathe.

This is what the fires of hell would be like, no relief ever. And each sinner all alone in her cell, praying for the solace of company. Felice closed her eyes to help her rise above the pain, and thought of the heaven Mary ascended toward. There would be many-windowed houses there, iced in gold. Palm trees, warm breezes, golden streets. A high wall all around, with turrets from which heaven's citizens looked down. Mama was there, watching her through a miraculous telescope, and Mary, and Papa, and Grandpapa. Someday she would be there too, and Sister Claire, and Mother Superior, and Celeste. No, she was not sure about Celeste. Anne and Françoise? Probably too soon to tell. But Sister Theodota certainly, and the two Marys, and Sister Constance, and Sister Agatha. Sister Agatha, robbed of breasts: she would have an exalted place, a golden throne and crown. Philippe would be there too, and Pip, resurrected, in a cloak of soft feathers, and a big room to fly about in. He would be a special helper to the Holy Spirit, and wear a radiant gold bar upon his chest. Felice went to sleep thinking of his profile, one friendly eye focused on her, his head more furry than feathered.

Felice was awakened for dinner by Soukie, who removed the cold plaster from her chest, put more wood on the fire, and then left her alone. She lay listening to the new logs shift like uneasy bones, and waited for visitors. But none came until after she had fallen asleep again, and when Celeste crouched by the bed and whispered, all in a rush, "They found a tongueless man in Nevette, washed in with the tide," Felice at first thought she was dreaming. But when Celeste went on, "He's to be brought here for nursing—right in this very bed, how do you like that? But you're getting out soon, Soukie says," Felice, surfacing through the mists of sleep, thought that this was Mother Superior's scheme to force her out of the infirmary, and home to Uncle Adolphe.

IN THE MORNING FELICE THOUGHT THE TONGUELESS MAN MUST have been a dream, but Soukie, who brought her breakfast, was full of talk about him. So he was real. Was it true, also, that he was to replace her in the infirmary?

"La, Mademoiselle," Soukie said, rolling her eyes. "I'm just the kitchenmaid. All I know is, we're fixing up that storage room next to the kitchen for the gentleman, and Mother Superior said it would be 'for the time being.' Imagine, Mademoiselle, a strange man looking over your shoulder while you cook!"

According to Soukie, the tongueless man had been found on the north shore of the village by Antoine Gentil. That gentleman, Soukie said, had been on his way to the cod-drying house, with nothing on his mind but repairing the leaky roof there, when he spied an odd black form on the beach. "At first he thought maybe it was a big fish —that's what he told Henri the baker," Soukie said, nodding her head with satisfaction at this bit of documentation. "He called out to his mates—they were just a little way behind—and they went to have a look. Well, you can imagine their surprise when they found it was a man, Mademoiselle, sopping wet and nearly blue. They found pieces of a dinghy nearby—it must have wrecked on the rocks there, Antoine Gentil said. At first they thought the man was dead—la, why wouldn't he be, in that freezing water?—but when they bent down close and touched him, he opened his eyes. Antoine Gentil told Henri that those eyes—black, they were—gave him a very shivery feeling. The man opened his mouth like he was going to speak," Soukie said, gripping the end of Felice's bedstead and leaning toward her, "and not a *word* came out—just a wild sound, like an animal. Mademoiselle, can you imagine," Soukie whispered, "he doesn't have a tongue—just a little stump of one. Antoine Gentil thought right away of a cod— that's what he said to Henri—since part of his job is cutting out the cods' tongues and packing them up. Mademoiselle, have you ever heard of anything so peculiar?"

After Soukie left, Felice propped the arithmetic book on her stomach and stared down at it, trying to look studious in anticipation of the morning nun. She read and reread a problem Sister Theodota had assigned; it had to do with the division of thirteen pears and seventeen apples among twenty-one children. At each reading, by the time she had reached the end of the problem she had forgotten the first part, and the meaning of all the words slipped away from her. A picture of the tongueless man kept intruding; try as she might to pull a black curtain across the image, she continued to see the strange form at the water's edge. What if she had found him? She read the arithmetic problem again, trying to force the rows of apples and pears into her mind, and the tongueless man out. But it was no use. The man dove in and out of the water like a porpoise, or a shark, circling a ship. His mouth closed on a small silver fish and he was pulled forward and up, a hook deep in his tongue. She ticked her own tongue against the roof of her mouth to dispel the numbness she felt there. She thought of Uncle Adolphe, his tongue bleeding, a crimson thread zigzagging down his chin. He knelt at her chair, pointing mutely at the herring-baited hook that speared his tongue, and he begged for mercy. She healed his wound by the touch of her saintly hand, and she forgave him, requiring only that he wear a gold replica of the hook on his watch fob, as a reminder of God's omnipotence.

Felice was lying with her eyes closed and her arithmetic book flat on her chest when the door opened and Mother Superior and Sister Claire came in, a pale and limping Françoise between them. Felice picked up her book hastily. The nuns laid Françoise on the bed next to the window. Mother Superior threw the girl's cloak on a chair and pulled the curtains closed around Françoise's bed.

"Go get a pan of hot water, Sister," Mother Superior said, "and some gauze."

Sister Claire emerged from the curtain and looked at Felice, who was sitting on the edge of her bed. "Françoise has a nasty cut on her leg," Sister Claire explained, "but it's not serious—don't worry."

After the nuns had bandaged Françoise, Mother Superior pulled back the curtains with two energetic motions. "Felice, you may get up now and go to your religion lesson," she said. "The Abbé has offered to take time from his busy Saturday to help you catch up."

"And a music lesson?" Sister Claire asked.

"As long as she doesn't tire herself. Now, Felice," Mother Superior said, her arms akimbo. "Françoise. This business of romping about on that beach must cease. That is now against the rules. This academy has always been known for the fine deportment of its young ladies." She looked at Françoise's leg, propped on a pillow, and sighed. "I *knew* someone would get hurt—I'm just grateful it was no worse. I am entirely too busy, young ladies," she said, lifting the pan of water and heading for the door, "to worry about you girls getting killed."

Sister Claire, at Mother Superior's heels, turned back at the doorway to smile at Felice, as though to soften the other nun's words.

"What happened?" Felice asked after the door closed.

"I fell partway down the cliff," Françoise said, with a grimace that only enhanced the delicacy of her profile. Tendrils of hair clung gracefully to her forehead, which was very white and slightly indented in the center. Felice thought her as lovely as a cameo. "Come over here," Françoise whispered, turning to look at Felice, "so we can talk."

Felice perched on the edge of Françoise's bed, a blanket wrapped about her.

"Have you heard about the strange man?" Françoise asked. When Felice nodded yes, the other girl said, "That's why I fell—I was running down to the beach to tell Celeste and Anne about him. My Aunt Febianne saw the Le Blanc brothers putting a pallet on their wagon—they're bringing him. My aunt brought some new underthings for me. See?" Françoise pulled up her skirt to reveal a petticoat edged with a flounce of eyelet and lace.

"Did your aunt see him?"

"No, but her neighbor Beatrice Pinet did. It was Beatrice's brother who kept him last night. She said he has very, very dark eyes, and that he looked *right* at her. Doesn't he sound scary? I hope he never looks at me," Françoise said, smiling with the certainty that he would if he ever got the chance.

There was a sharp rap on the door. "Felice?" Mother Superior called. "The Abbé is waiting."

Felice dressed quickly, shivering, and walked to the classroom just down the hall.

The Abbé rose as she entered and motioned toward the chair beside the desk. "Come sit here, Mademoiselle." Felice felt unsteady on her feet, as though the room were a pitching boat.

Felice recited the assigned parts of the catechism, responding to the Abbé's questions with such smoothness that the sound of her own voice reassured her. She smiled when she finished, and folded her hands in her lap.

"Very good, my child," the Abbé said, "very good indeed. I am delighted that you are making such progress." The Abbé put his pointed black elbows on the desk, interlaced his fingers, and studied her for a moment. "You have an ascetic face, Felice—you may surprise us after all."

Felice looked down at her hands, aware of the delicate curve of her eyelashes against her skin.

"Mother Superior has told me of your strong interest in the religious vocation," the Abbé said. "I encourage you to ask the Blessed Virgin for help—she can give you counsel and guidance."

Felice nodded and looked up into the Abbé's eyes with her humblest expression.

"The Blessed Virgin is closer to God than any other saint is," the Abbé said. "Now, why is this? It is because never, never in her life did she have a lustful thought. Nor was her body ever sullied in any way. Though she is the mother of Jesus Christ, she didn't—that is, God removed Eve's burden from her. From Eva to Ave, as the hymn says. Mary of Nazareth was the purest of all human women ever to dwell on earth, an ideal example for all young girls, whether they are called to God's work or to motherhood."

"I *agree,* Mon Père."

The Abbé gave her a smile, a more perfunctory one than Felice would have liked, and lifted a book from the desk. He pulled the long purple ribbon that hung from the bottom and the volume fell open in his hands, halved. "Hear what Saint Augustine has to say. 'Let us love chastity above all things, for it was to show that this was pleasing to Him that Christ chose the modesty of the Virgin Womb.' "

"I have asked her to be my mother, Mon Père."

"Yes? That is fine, child, fine and wise." She was rewarded with a warmer smile. The Abbé cleared his throat, and was about to continue reading—his finger had found the place in the book, and his mouth was open—when he cocked his head and frowned toward the hall. He closed the book gently, rose, and walked very quietly to the door, as though stalking something.

The Abbé peered down the hall. "Stay back, child," he said, flapping his hand in Felice's direction, though she had not moved. Then he went out, slamming the door behind him.

"What is this?" Felice heard the Abbé shout. "Why have you brought him through the main corridor?" Then Felice heard other voices and the sound of heavy feet. She stood up and tiptoed toward the door. "Do you not realize where you *are?*" the Abbé demanded. "Take him in through the side door."

"Pardon, Mon Père," a gruff male voice said. "Mother Superior sent us this way. She said those side steps are steep, Abbé."

After a moment, Felice inched open the door. She could hear the men's footsteps receding in one direction, and the Abbé's in the other. She slipped out and walked down the hall, going, without thinking why, toward the sound of the disturbance. When she passed the music room, Sister Claire turned from her position at the window and beckoned her in. Felice joined her and looked out at the gray sky and the snow-patched yard.

"They'll be coming along any minute now," Sister Claire whispered.

"Who?"

"The men—with the invalid. Yes!" she said, pressing her nose against the pane. "There they are—look! What a sight!"

Felice caught her breath as a double column of fishermen appeared, bearing a stretcher between them. On the stretcher, which appeared to be made of fir boughs, was a blanketed form. Though Felice could not see the face, she could imagine it—eyes staring up at the sky, the soundless mouth open. The Abbé met them on the walk and trotted alongside, shouting something that Felice could not quite hear. One of the bearers slipped on the icy walk and the stretcher dipped precariously to one side. He nearly rolled out onto the snow, all uncovered, Felice would tell Celeste and Anne; she hoped they were not watching.

The men resteadied their burden and went quickly out of sight. Sister Claire drummed her fingers lightly on the windowpane. "Mother Superior is a courageous woman," she said, "and a persuasive one. I never would have believed," she whispered conspiratorially, as she led Felice to the piano, "that the Abbé would come around. It is highly unprecedented, you realize, sheltering a man in the convent."

Felice took her place on the bench, thinking, as Sister Claire laid open the music, what reactions this gem of information would elicit from Celeste and Anne. "It was either bring him here, or let him die —none of the villagers would have him," the nun said in Felice's ear.

Felice touched the cold, yellowed keys, imagining how jealous Celeste would be when she heard that Sister Claire had talked to her just like a girl friend. "Not a word of this," Sister Claire said, laying a finger on her lips as though she had read her mind, and Felice jumped, sounding a cacophony of notes.

"Now play, dear," Sister Claire said, taking a chair beside the piano.

It was a Chopin waltz, one of Felice's favorites, but her fingers were stiff at first and the lilting melody seemed, under the circumstances, difficult to enter. After several bars, however, her hands and arms relaxed and she began to float, deliciously full of music. She smiled and she hummed, watching her fingers instead of the notes on the page. Mama had often played this piece, her hands bent gracefully at the wrists, her amethyst ring winking in the firelight.

When she finished, she turned to look at Sister Claire. The nun sat with her head against the chair, eyes closed, and she was smiling so blissfully that Felice wondered if she was sleeping. Her long face, which often looked tired, was now rosy and smooth, and Felice noticed an enviable dimple at the corner of her mouth.

"Ummm," Sister Claire finally said, "I forgot where I was." With her eyes open, she looked tired again, like the other nuns; Mother Superior believed in the deprivation of sleep, though not of food, and liked to say that all true spiritualists are insomniacs.

Sister Claire yawned. "That was lovely, Felice, and astonishing, really, that you don't sound a bit out of practice. It sometimes happens, though, that you play your best after a long absence."

Felice did not do so well with the scales, nor with the Bach exercise, but as she was leaving, Sister Claire said, "You really should study at a conservatory some day, Felice. Is there any possibility your uncle would consider it? There is a fine one in Boston—I went there when I wasn't much older than you."

Felice departed, glowing. She decided that she would bring Uncle Adolphe to God with angelic music; he would be transformed into a kindhearted man, ashamed of his former acts, and would show his repentance by sending her to the conservatory. She would become a nun later, and perhaps return to this convent as assistant music teacher.

Later that week there was a blizzard. For a day and a night and the better part of another day, the winds howled at the corners of the convent and whistled beneath the doors, in spite of the draft bolsters. The snow fell so thick and fast that it seemed to Felice like a dream. The storm left the Chemin du Roi impassable and halted all trains, thus making Felice's remaining at the convent during Christmas a certainty. Mother Superior, in a meeting of the entire school, said that only the girls who lived in nearby villages and who could be fetched by sleigh would be going home for the holiday.

Françoise, who cried over novels and was considered very sentimental, whispered to Felice after the meeting that it was fortunate the tongueless man had washed ashore before the blizzard. "Three days later and he would have died," she said, a skim of tears rising to her eyes. Felice, whose delight about the impossibility of going to Wolfville spilled over into benevolent feelings for the stranger, sniffed with her, the two of them sharing a handkerchief during vespers.

During the next few days, rivulets of talk about the tongueless man flowed throughout the convent. It was said that the man had finally taken some broth, that Mother Superior had fed him herself, cradling his head in the crook of her arm, and that he had gagged when he swallowed, much of the liquid running down his chin. Soukie wondered aloud, bringing in Felice's tray, how the man was going to live, eating no more than a bird. But perhaps God was looking out after him, she said, for it was a miracle he was alive at all.

Felice learned from Sister Claire that the Abbé was bent on learning the man's origin; he had spoken to him in French, English, and Latin, and was rewarded only by a glimmer from the Latin, confirming the Abbé's belief that the man was a Catholic, the only reason he had suffered him to come to the convent in the first place. The Abbé had his first clue about the man's religion the day he was found, when the Abbé administered extreme unction. The refugee had put his hands together in a gesture somewhat like praying, the Abbé reported, and had seemed immediately to grow stronger.

Soukie and Celeste—who had boldly walked by his open door for a peek—described the tongueless man as black-eyed and yellow-skinned, with completely hairless cheeks and chin (a feature which Soukie mentioned twice, with raised eyebrows). His hair, long and black, flowed back from a prominent widow's peak. His suit of clothes, according to Anne, who had talked to someone who had spied it in the laundry room, was black and had long folds and tucks in it —not the sort of clothes worn along the French coast, or anywhere in Nova Scotia. He was now wearing a nightshirt reputed to be the Abbé's, a possibility that occasioned much giggling among the girls. Who could imagine the Abbé without his collar, snoring in a nightshirt? Soukie brought Felice reports of the tongueless man every day, though she said it gave her the shivers just to go into his room. "His eyes are so black, Mademoiselle—and just think of his tongue," she said, clucking her own tongue against her teeth and shaking her head.

There were several theories about the missing tongue. Sister Claire believed—and Mother Superior was somewhat inclined to agree with her—that the man might be a survivor of the hellish battle of Verdun, during the Great War; perhaps he had been a prisoner of war, Sister Claire speculated, and had his tongue cut out when he refused to talk. Soukie thought it possible that the man had been misidentified as a wrecker, and punished by sailors who had been told—by some vengeful, Godless party—that the gentleman had lured ships onto rocks at night with a lantern. There was talk, among some students, of his being a pirate whose shipmates and captives had mutinied and, after snipping out his tongue, put him to sea in the dinghy to die a lingering death. Felice, Celeste, Françoise, and Anne favored the idea of his being a pirate's captive, someone who had found a cache of buried treasure, had talked about it, and was snatched up in the night by the pirate, who cut out his tongue for telling the secret. The pirate threw him in the hold of the ship and brought him from Barbados to the coast of Nova Scotia, expressly to cast him into the freezing water and then to rebury his treasure, perhaps somewhere not so very far away.

There was some talk among the villagers that the tongueless man was an incarnation of the devil, or the Antichrist. There were others, Françoise's Aunt Febianne among them, who sensed about him the air of a martyred saint. There were some who felt he was perhaps exceedingly brilliant (the Abbé was the most conspicuous proponent of this view), and others who thought he was probably quite dull, except in the matter of getting himself so well situated at the convent.

Sister Agatha took two distinctly different views of their guest. Her first known reaction was expressed on the Saturday morning when Felice moved out of the infirmary and the stranger moved in. Felice and Soukie, who were carrying the girl's things back to her cubicle, met Sister Agatha on the stair landing.

"Are you going up too, Sister?" Soukie reached for the nun's arm. "We're just resettling Mademoiselle in her room, on account of that mute gentleman. . . ."

"Philomel!" the nun cried, shaking free her elbow. She lifted both arms upward and threw back her head, as though enjoining God to listen. "Philomel!" Her voice reverberated in the stairwell, so alarming two nuns descending above them that they leaned over the banister and stared.

"Philemon?" Soukie gave Felice a puzzled look.

"Philomel. She means the tongueless man."

"The child understands," Sister Agatha said, taking Felice's hand. Felice did understand, and not only the reference to Philomel, who, she had learned in Sister Agatha's literature class, was a misused virgin whose tongue was cut out by her captor but then transformed by the gods into a nightingale so that she might sing in wordless, achingly beautiful melody, of her ennobling pain. Felice also understood, her hand joined with Sister Agatha's (and she therefore sharing the looks of icy disapproval bestowed by Sisters Mary Owen and Constance as they brushed by on the landing), that Sister Agatha identified her own plight at the convent with that of these other martyrs unable to speak themselves of the infamy done them, but then, in a metamorphosis worked by the avenging angels, allowed to sing forth, to shine out.

But that same day, at dinner, Sister Agatha put quite a different interpretation upon the stranger's arrival. She interrupted a discussion about the new parlor rug to say that the girls couldn't be too careful, what with the tongueless man in their midst. "Keep well laced, young ladies," she whispered. "It may be a ripe opportunity for canonization—perhaps God has sent him for one of us." Sister Theodota looked positively dangerous as she passed the bread, which did not prevent Celeste from rolling her eyes, nor from kicking Felice beneath the table. Felice, who had drawn her breath too quickly, felt herself choking on her food; after being pounded on the back by Sister Claire, she regurgitated a sticky mass of fish into her napkin. This disgusting event, Sister Theodota implied by her glances at the girl and at Sister Agatha, was the aged nun's fault; and she later petitioned Mother Superior, the girls heard from Soukie, for silence at meals, as was the norm in "sensible, reverent" convents.

In the dormitory that night, huddled on the floor beside Felice's bed, Celeste speculated aloud to Felice, Anne, Françoise, and Blanche about what horrid things the man would do were he to catch one of them. Blanche, who breathlessly repeated some of the words after Celeste, later told the story to a group of younger students, thus winning an immediate, newfound popularity and getting an invitation for Christmas to the home of the Doucette twins, whose family lived in the largest house in Nevette.

Anne invited Celeste and Felice to her house, but Felice decided not to go. She felt it important, she told Mother Superior, to spend some time in quiet meditation about her vocation. Not only had Mother Superior seemed impressed by the announcement of this sacrifice, but the nun had given her a commending glance as Felice was entering the chapel alone later that day. The warmth of Mother Superior's approval sustained Felice throughout the holiday until Christmas Eve, when, at mass in Nevette, she stood with the villagers to sing "Silent Night" and "O Little Town of Bethlehem." These had been Mama's favorite carols, and she had played them at their last Christmas together, just two years ago. Felice could see the piano so clearly, the grain of the oiled wood and the name of its maker, Hallet & Cumston, inscribed in baroque gold letters above Mama's hands. At the festive convent luncheon the next day Felice could barely eat for remembering the house in Yarmouth, the smells of lemon pudding and goose and fresh-cut balsam, and the roar of a tall fire, and how even the snowflakes against the window had looked cheerful because of the coziness inside. That afternoon Felice lay on her bed, her braids pressed against her mouth to stifle the sound of crying. At supper Sister Claire observed her closely and afterward took her to the parlor, where they spent the evening playing four-handed carols on the piano and eating toffee.

During the remainder of the holiday, Felice divided her time between the chapel and the piano, where she practiced the difficult Bach exercises Sister Claire had chosen for her. The preludes and inventions not only strengthened her fingers but reorganized her soul and invigorated her will. When Felice chanced to think of Mama at the end of a measure, and then of Uncle Adolphe, her courage swelled; she saw herself confronting Uncle Adolphe, he unable to touch her for the band of holy air about her body, and she thus tapped for initiation into the most sacred of all societies.

One night after supper when Felice was practicing alone in the parlor, and the oil lamp was guttering and the wind was moaning like a survivor, she felt a shadow at the open door. Perhaps, she thought, it is the tongueless man, loose in the convent, his dark eyes looking in and seeing me. She shuddered and played more resolutely, watching the brave intricacy of her fingers. After the Bach she went without pause into her own composition; it felt, in its throbbing intensity, like a prayer without words. When she came to the end of the piece, the doorway and the hall were deserted.

8

ONE DAY NOT LONG AFTER SHE RETURNED TO CLASSES, FELICE sat daydreaming during the arithmetic lesson. She stared out the window at the flat, white ground and saw herself riding a beautiful chestnut pony in the snow. The pony's bridle and saddle were festooned with red and gold bells, because she was a princess in medieval France. Instead of her black serge uniform she wore a riding habit of crimson velvet, and soft boots to match. She had trunks full of embroidered silk dresses and a loving mama and papa and no brothers, just a sister like Celeste, and a little baby sister.

Sister Theodota, who had been writing long-division problems on the board, jarred Felice back to the classroom when she said, "Copy these problems and solve them quickly, Mademoiselles." She folded her arms, watching as the class reproduced the problems on their papers. Then the nun erased the numbers, dusted her hands together, and, after a row-by-row scrutiny of the students, sat down at her desk.

Felice tapped a pencil against her teeth and regarded the first long-division problem. She stared at the numbers—7379068166—enclosed by the roof and one wall of the division sign and at the numbers

—3285—that were supposed to go into them. It seemed unkind, somehow, as though the numerals might be splintered by the act. Could numbers possibly have feelings, she wondered, letting the pencil point follow the wooden grain of her desk from paper to inkwell. Just below the inkwell was a burl, like an angry eye; the pencil traced it, bearing down, and the point snapped.

Felice looked up. All around her, the other students were working intently, heads bent. Sister Theodota, who was marking copybooks and frowning, probably had spare pencils, but Felice didn't want to walk all the way up the aisle to ask her.

She tapped Blanche's shoulder. Blanche turned her head sideways and back, like a swimmer taking air, and continued erasing as she listened to Felice's request, her face tight with panic. She shook her head no and dove back to her paper.

Felice inched her foot across the aisle to nudge Antoinette's, but the distance was too great. "Antoinette," she whispered, "may I borrow a pencil?" Antoinette, totally absorbed, didn't respond. Felice noticed with despair that the other girl's paper was filling up with neatly written numbers. She was already on the second problem. "Antoinette!" she whispered louder, brandishing her broken pencil.

Antoinette looked and nodded.

"No talking!" Sister Theodota called out, raising her head just as the new pencil changed hands. The nun leaned to one side to fix Felice, then Antoinette, with her glare.

Felice turned her attention to the problems. She had the first two numbers of one solution—22—and was just bringing down the 6 to divide again when Emma Doucette rose from her desk and went to stand at the side of the room, a smug look on her face for being first. She was quickly followed by Laura Doucette and Antoinette, who glanced down at Felice's incomplete first problem and then at Felice, her face expressionless. It didn't seem to elate Antoinette at all that she was finished; Felice decided that she looked like Sister Theodota already.

Felice bent her head again, working faster, trying to ignore the occasional sound of a student rising and walking to the side of the room. Felice knew that Sister Theodota was writing down their names in order of finishing. Glancing about, she saw that there were only five students still at their desks. She completed the first problem and stared at the second: the figure beneath the division sign looked as long as a train.

Sister Theodota was pacing the floor and looking at her watch. "Time," she said, her voice like chalk on the board, "time, Mademoiselles." Two more girls rose. One of them was Celeste, who looked sympathetically at Felice.

Felice wrote the first number of the quotient, an 8, and then traced and retraced it, feeling herself sliding along its lines, up and down, in and out. She couldn't remember 8 times 3. She tried to think of 8 times 4, 8 times 2, but the entire table had vanished from her mind. She was counting on her fingers when Sister Theodota advanced down the aisle. She and Blanche were the only ones who had not yet finished.

Felice quickly added five more numbers to the quotient and stood up. She would even say she had done it in her head (a practice abhorrent to Sister Theodota), but she wouldn't be the last one at her desk. She brushed by the nun and went to stand at the side of the room, at the tail end of the line next to Celeste.

Sister Theodota stopped at Blanche's desk and tapped impatiently on it with a ruler. "Finished?"

"Yes—no," Blanche said, sounding as though she might cry at any moment. "I'm not sure they're right."

Sister Theodota held Blanche's paper up to the light, and after a dramatic silence, said, "Have you been *chewing* this paper, Mademoiselle?" She allowed a few seconds of nervous laughter from the class, and then said, "Neatness, Mademoiselle, and alacrity are two qualities on which you would be well advised to concentrate. That goes for some of you other young ladies, too," she said, suddenly swiveling to look at the girls near the end of the line. Felice smiled weakly, but Sister Theodota had already turned to march back to the front of the room, leaving Blanche in lonely disgrace at her desk.

"Now let's have the problems worked at the board. Emma, you do the first, and . . ." Sister Theodota's gaze traveled down the line. ". . . Felice Belliveau, the second." Sister Theodota turned to arrange the chalk, and Felice exchanged a look with Celeste. It was only a sidewise look, a split second, yet when Felice started forward to the board, the papers were exchanged.

After class was over, and Felice had escaped unscathed (mercifully, Sister Theodota had not collected the papers), she and Celeste walked down the hall side by side, their little fingers linked.

"Thank you, Celly," Felice whispered outside the door to Mother Superior's classroom.

Celeste squeezed her hand and winked, a gesture she had apparently adopted during the visit to Anne's house. "You would have done it for me—we're blood sisters, remember."

At the beginning of Mother Superior's class there was a review examination on the Canadian Boundary War and the expulsion of the Acadians. Then Mother Superior announced that there would be a quiet study period for the remainder of the hour, while she marked the papers.

"But first," the nun said, "I want to give one of you this representation of Our Lady." She held it up: a small oval of dark blue glass, to which was affixed a flat silver sculpture of the Virgin Mary. It brought a gasp of appreciation from the girls. Because of her position in the convent, Mother Superior was often given devotional objects and, true to her vow of poverty, gave them all away, sometimes as a special commendation to a particular girl, but usually in lotteries. Recent prizes in this class included a standing silver-plated crucifix, a leather bookmark on which was tooled a somber portrait of Saint Elm, patron of mariners (this, the work of a local artisan), several gilded religious cards, and three rosaries. Felice had won the best rosary, a blue-beaded one that glittered like ice. But this blue and silver icon, fashioned to hang on a wall, was clearly the finest object Mother Superior had yet offered.

"The number I am thinking of is between one and fifty," Mother Superior said, lowering herself into the chair behind her desk. "And, as usual, I will write it down." In a moment she raised her head and nodded at Marie, who sat at the first desk on the left side of the room. "We'll begin with you and continue down and up each aisle."

Marie guessed thirteen. Mother Superior, her face inscrutable, nodded at the next pupil.

Felice was the seventh student to guess; she counted those ahead of her and said "six" when Mother Superior called for her number.

"It belongs to you, Felice." Mother Superior rose and held up the figurine. In the light from the window, it shone a deep, rich blue, like the sea in a painting or a dream. "Come and receive it."

Felice walked up the aisle quickly, oblivious to the resentful upward stares of the other girls. Mother Superior gave her the object and, holding Felice's hands between her own, whispered, "Perhaps this is not mere coincidence—perhaps Our Lady is speaking to you." The nun, her face transfigured by a possible communion with Mystery, squeezed the girl's hands so tight that the silver cut into her palm, and Felice went weak with joy and responsibility.

Every few minutes during the study period, Felice peeked inside her desk top to look at the gleaming Virgin. When she held her history book before her, she let her eyes go out of focus and imagined Mary helping her to become a saint. It would happen when Uncle Adolphe was chasing her; to avoid his horrible bony hands she would leap over the cliff, but as she fell she would be given wings in celebration of her chastity. She would fly out over the bay, the brilliant summer water, and then glide back to land, circling above the convent; the nuns and students would look up, amazed, and fall to their knees every one, even Sister Theodota. The Abbé, saying the litany alone in the spidery dampness of the outer chapel, would doubt the miracle when he was first told of it, and as a consequence all his accumulated indulgences would be taken from him and distributed among the girls.

But a little dark spot nagged at Felice, dissolving only momentarily each time she pushed it from her mind. By the time class had ended and Felice was gathering her books together, the worry had taken word form: I have sinned. When the other students gathered around to touch the smooth glass and silver treasure, Felice could not even smile. Saint Thérèse would certainly never have cheated in arithmetic class, nor have allowed Mother Superior to be so fooled.

She took the long way to her next class, past the infirmary where the tongueless man lay. As she paused there, her heart beating unaccountably fast, it occurred to her that his affliction might be a punishment for lying. Once when she was a little girl and had told a fib, Grandmama had held her bird-shaped scissors and worked them in the air, so that it looked as if the bird were talking. "Snip, snip," Grandmama had said. "That's what happens to the tongues of little children who don't tell the truth."

At the afternoon exercise hour, a new prescription of Mother Superior's designed to rid the girls of what she called "gallivanting energy," Felice said to Celeste, in a soft voice, "We must confess."

"What?" Celeste looked at her, startled. The two of them were awaiting their turns in the tag races. Because of the cold weather, the exercises were conducted in the cellar, a long room lined with sacks of potatoes, apples, and dried beans.

"What happened in arithmetic class was a mortal sin and must be confessed," Felice said.

"Well, leave me out of it—what if the Abbé tells Sister Theodota? As my blood sister, you'd better not tell on me." The runner on their team came dashing home, holding out the stick. Celeste grabbed it and leapt forward, pounding toward the dark, far wall beneath the shadows of hanging sausages and hams.

After Felice's turn, when the two of them were at the end of the line, Celeste said, "I guess this is how novices act," adding with her cruelest smile, "I heard somebody say just the other day that you look *very* much like Antoinette."

Their schism lasted several hours, through the rest of the afternoon, dinner, and the gathering afterward in the parlor, during which the girls sang and Felice accompanied on the piano. At bedtime, Celeste went upstairs with Françoise and Anne, the three of them joining arms, without a backward glance at Felice.

After lights out, Felice tiptoed to Celeste's bed at the other end of the dormitory. "Celly, I'm sorry," she whispered, sitting on the edge of the bed. "But you don't want to go to hell, do you?"

Celeste sat up, still half asleep.

"Celeste, do you want to roast in the flames, have your flesh peel away one layer at a time, and have your hair catch on fire, with no water to put it out? Do you want to be pierced in the eye with the devil's pointed stick?"

From Celeste's silence, Felice divined that her words were having an effect. "Besides," she went on, "I can't be confirmed with a blot like that on my conscience. It would send me to hell and you too, probably, because you knew about it and didn't try to save me."

"All right," Celeste said. "I know what. We'll confess it directly to God—right now. Come on."

Wrapped in blankets, the two of them tiptoed down the stairs and through the halls. By the time they reached the chapel, Celeste was fully in the spirit of their mission. "This is the right thing to do," she whispered as they felt their way up the aisle in the dark, guided by the pulsing red light at the feet of the Virgin. "What if we died in the night?"

They knelt, and Celeste said, "You confess your sins, and I'll confess mine."

"Dear God," Felice began hesitantly, as though addressing a dutiful letter. "I wasn't interested in the arithmetic lesson. When Sister Theodota sent me to the board," she said, her voice growing stronger, "I used Celeste's paper instead of mine. For this, Father, I am most grievously sorry. It was a mortal sin."

"God," Celeste said, "I too am sorry for my sin, though I do not think it was a mortal one—in any case, I ask for forgiveness for me and my friend Felice, who will be confirmed this spring, and who says she wants to be a nun."

They decided on three Aves and two Paters as an appropriate penance. In the absence of other light, the sacred flame at Mary's feet burned dark red and threw sinister shadows up into her skirt, looking as if, Felice thought, the Virgin were crossing over hell on a foot-bridge. She crossed herself fervently as they rose, and said a silent prayer of thanks to Mary for saving her.

On the way back through the dark convent they met no one. As they parted, Celeste whispered, "That was fun."

Felice slept peacefully that night, temporarily cleansed of remorse.

The next night it was Celeste who awoke Felice. "Wake up," she said, bouncing on her bed. "Let's go exploring."

Felice sat up groggily. "Is it morning?"

"No—it's night—I haven't been to sleep at all yet."

"What's the matter?"

"Nothing—we're going exploring."

"Why?" Felice mumbled, sinking back into her pillow.

"Because it's fun," Celeste said, pulling the covers from Felice. "And I went with you last night—come on," she said, tugging at Felice's arm.

"But it's against the rules," Felice said, standing and wrapping the blanket around her.

"You weren't too worried about that last night," Celeste said. "Besides, no one will see us, and it's a silly rule anyway."

Felice followed Celeste down the steps, each of them carrying a candle. Her friend strode purposefully through the lower hall and into the kitchen, made straight for the cake tin and cut two huge slices of chocolate cake.

"What if they miss it?" Felice asked.

"Soukie doesn't know or care—come on."

Felice, her mouth full of chocolate, followed Celeste out of the kitchen. "Where are you going now?" she whispered, between bites. "Let's go back."

"No—ssh," Celeste said over her shoulder. "If you don't want to do this, I imagine Françoise will."

They crept along the silent hall, holding hands. Felice could feel her heart drumming in her ears. "Where are we *going?*"

"To see the tongueless man," Celeste said, stopping to readjust her blanket.

"Oh, Celeste—no."

"You little baby," Celeste said in a violent whisper. "You never want to do anything. All right, then, don't come."

When Celeste walked on, Felice followed, holding to her friend's skirt. The candle shook in her hand, and she felt she was scarcely breathing.

They stopped before the infirmary door. "Sssh," Celeste said, and turned the doorknob. "Blow out your candle," she commanded. Felice did, and then, looking back at the dark hall, wished she hadn't.

It seemed to Felice that the creaking of the door was loud enough to wake any sleeper. She held her breath as they inched inside.

It was not so dark in the room as in the hall. Dim light from the rising moon fell through the window and washed across surfaces, suggesting dark forms underneath. Felice could see the shapes of the bureau, an overstuffed chair, and a table where a crucifix stood, casting its shadow onto the moonlit floor.

The beds looked like coffins. Felice closed her eyes, but that was worse: then she saw them rocking in the shadows. She looked again, as Celeste pulled her forward, at the bed nearest the window. There were two sets of grim iron bars against the wall: the headboard, and its shadow. She forced her eyes to move from the wall to the bed, and she jumped when she saw the long form there. When she closed her eyes the form rose up at her, and she gasped.

Celeste pinched her. "Sssh!"

Felice took a deep breath and crossed her fingers. When she looked at the bed again, she stared hard, to keep it down. She looked at the form again, a dark ridge where she herself had lain, and at the head on the pillow, barely distinguishable in the darkness.

She was breathing more easily, thinking, this is really more like a dream than life, when she saw, at the far edge of the bed, in the moonlight there, a man's arm.

She reached for Celeste, but Celeste was not there. For a moment she thought she was alone, and this was a cruel trick—Celeste had locked her in—until she saw the other girl's shadow pass by the far side of the bed.

Felice waited a moment. Nothing happened, so she tiptoed closer.

The man lay so still that he would have seemed dead but for the slight whistle of breath between his teeth. Felice leaned closer, straining to make out the features of his face. At first it seemed there was a beard where Soukie said there was none, and then she realized there was not. Her face was very close to his. She could see the eyebrows, the long nose, the slightly parted lips. She shuddered and drew back. Then she thought she saw him rise, his eyes open, his mouth a round abyss.

Felice turned and fled, bumping against furniture as she went. Celeste caught up with her in the hall. "Slow down," she hissed. "Do you want to wake everybody up?"

"Oh, Celeste—his eyes—did you see?"

"How could I? He was asleep. Sssh." Celeste flattened herself against the wall and pulled Felice to her side. In the distance there was the sound of a door opening, and then silence. They waited several minutes, which seemed hours to Felice; she composed excuses and prayerful litanies begging forgiveness, but then they walked down the hall and up the stairs, and reached the dormitory without incident.

Felice lay a long time without sleeping. She held the Saint Cecilia medallion in her hand and clamped her eyes shut so that bright yellow doughnuts of light grew from the black background. That was how she had kept herself from being afraid of the dark at home in Yarmouth, and it was the only way, now, that she could keep back the image of the tongueless man's face.

The next day at confession, Felice awaited her turn kneeling in a back row, inhaling the musty smell of the outer chapel's pews and damp walls. She felt unusually nervous, and when Sister Theodota tapped her on the shoulder, she jumped.

She closed the confessional door behind herself carefully and knelt. The Abbé's shadow rearranged itself. Her body felt heavier and heavier as she and the Abbé droned through the preliminary sentences and as she confessed to relatively minor infractions, matters of mere envy, pride, and sloth. Then she paused, looking at the Abbé's profile, wondering if he would tell Sister Theodota if she confessed her sin. Maybe Celeste was right—a direct confession to God was probably enough; after all, this *was* an unusual situation. Sister Claire had told her once, after she had first come to the convent, that a direct confession to God was possible in extreme circumstances. Felice had asked her about it after the Abbé told the religion class that unconfessed souls went directly to hell, and she had been worried about Mama and Papa's permanent habitation. Doubtless they had confessed in time, Sister Claire had reassured her, and the lack of an intermediary between themselves and God might have meant a longer stretch in purgatory, she guessed, but nothing more. In Sister Claire's opinion, God was more reasonable than man gave Him credit for being.

The Abbé shifted. Then Felice realized that he had already assigned her the penance, and she was expected to rise. But she could not move.

"Is there something more, my child?"

"Ye-es."

The Abbé waited, and Felice wished she had answered differently. Finally the Abbé said, "Have you had unclean thoughts, my child?"

After a long pause Felice, in a barely audible voice, whispered, "Yes."

The Abbé cleared his throat several times. "I thought as much," he said, "for you are entering the age of danger. Although serious, this is quite to be expected. You must call on Our Lady for assistance. Do you pray to her for help?"

"Yes, Mon Père," Felice said meekly.

The Abbé doubled her penance, and sighed heavily as she rose.

Felice went to the altar, knelt before a field of burning candles, and said her penance with the utmost gravity and concentration. Then, without warning, just as she had finished, she saw Uncle Adolphe. His face was laughing, though she had never seen him laugh. She looked into the offertory flames and thought of holding his hands to them: that made him scowl.

"I will save him," she said aloud, with such firmness that the nearest candles flickered. Her words forced the dark weight of him back.

Felice stood, smiling. Then she hurried, just on the decorous side of running, toward the dining room, for it was rumored there was to be creamed lobster for supper.

9

DURING THE MONTH OF JANUARY THERE WERE OPTIMISTIC RE-
ports about the progress of the tongueless man, or Monsieur, as he
was now known in convent and village. Soukie, whose duties permit-
ted her access to the infirmary, was only too happy to share her
information with the girls. Monsieur was still liverish-colored but had
filled out a bit, Soukie told Felice, and when Mother Superior saw him
sitting up for the first time the other day, the superioress decided he
was going to pull through after all, thanks to the extraordinary nursing skill of the sisters of Sacré Sang. The novice Evangeline had
voluntarily surrendered her position as teachers' assistant in order to
take on the main burden of caring for Monsieur. Soukie, who often
lingered throughout the meals, reported that Evangeline fed him
every mouthful, dabbing at his chin with her own handkerchief, and
that the postulant insisted on changing the sheets every third day, as
if the laundry weren't under enough strain already.

At the Abbé's urging, Soukie said, Evangeline often read to Monsieur from the missal or breviary. It was the priest's conviction that
God, not the women of Sacré Sang, was due the credit for healing the
invalid. Opportunity for full exposure to the Catholic faith, and not
any particular nursing advantage, was God's reason for bringing
the foreigner to the convent: so went the Abbé's widely quoted re-
buttal to Mother Superior's interpretation of Monsieur's growing
strength.

Of course Soukie didn't want to take sides in this disagreement, she
told Felice. But when Evangeline read the Catholic liturgy aloud one
might think from Monsieur's pleased expression—his eyes shut, his
lips almost smiling—that the Abbé was right and the gentleman did

have at least some feeling for, if no literal understanding of, the Latin tongue.

Felice considered Evangeline's undertaking noble, even heroic, and when imagining herself in the novice's position felt a not wholly unpleasant glissando of fear run throughout her body. She thought several times of asking her if she might be of assistance in the infirmary after classes, but hung back. In the halls, at meals, in the chapel, she studied Evangeline. The novice, whom she had earlier thought of as haughty and aloof, now seemed to her almost seductively enigmatic. The milk-white skin of her face, the minute blue veins on her eyelids, the pockmarks on her forehead just above the left eyebrow, and, on those rare occasions when she spoke—as at meals, requesting the butter—her voice, richly damp, as with backed-up tears: all of this, Felice decided, suggested a lifetime of sorrow. She might even be an orphan, like Felice herself, for she never seemed to have a carefully hoarded letter in her pocket, as most of the sisters did. Then, when Evangeline grew up and became beautiful, Felice surmised, she and a handsome man had fallen deeply in love. They had planned to marry. Evangeline's name was entirely apt, Felice thought, for she had certainly experienced—like the Acadian heroine of exile—a cruel parting from her one true love; it was written in her face, her manner. Heartbroken, Evangeline had retreated to the convent for consolation and the strengthening of her soul. But God was going to allow Evangeline to meet her true love once more before she died; this reunion would be, as in the case of the first Evangeline and her Gabriel, a glorious bursting-forth of joy and platonic fulfillment. Then they would both go to heaven, and dwell there together in eternity.

That Evangeline was now concentrating with fervid intensity on her spiritual life seemed obvious to Felice. When eating, when walking down the hall, the novice kept her face turned away, the better, Felice thought, to focus on a compelling inner world. Held askance, her face was like a pale leaf, but when she did look up and into another's eyes —an event Felice often encouraged, with questions, with coughs—the power of her dark eyes was intoxicating.

Felice thought her so lovely that she prayed to the Virgin Mary for a light case of the smallpox, that she might have a similar beauty mark on her own brow. Sometimes as she sat in arithmetic class working a difficult problem, Felice pressed the blunt end of her pencil against her forehead and, when Sister Theodota called on her, took courage from touching the imprint lightly with her fingertips; at such moments she felt a kinship between herself and the novice, though the impressions left by the pencil-end soon faded.

At meals Felice imitated the delicate manner in which Evangeline loosened flakes of fish from its spine and placed each morsel into her mouth with the care she might use in laying a relic in a tabernacle. This simultaneous intake of food allowed her to share the novice's state of mind: pure, serene, strong. One day at luncheon, when Felice managed to catch the other's eye, Evangeline smiled. Felice flushed, looked down at her plate, and spent the remainder of the meal planning her approach to Evangeline: she would ask the novice how she had lost her parents; she would tell her about Uncle Adolphe; they would become confidantes, closer even than sisters. Evangeline would accept Felice's offer to help nurse the tongueless man; together they would heal him, fend off his advances, and bring him to God.

But then, as the diners rose and Evangeline passed by, Felice could not think what to say.

That night, after lights out, Felice gathered Celeste, Anne, Françoise, and Blanche in her cubicle to tell them about Evangeline. She explained about the Gabriel in the novice's past; she told them how Evangeline had retreated here after the tragic parting to recover from grief and to prepare herself for the greater happiness to come. The tongueless man was to be, indirectly, the agent of bliss. For God had specifically given Evangeline the dangerous task of nursing Monsieur, Felice said—and in such a convincing tone that all the girls, including the narrator, forgot that this was mere speculation—so that she might prove her worthiness for infinite joy. Felice even thought, she said, that the glory of virgin martyrdom might be Evangeline's. "Because," she whispered, "have you thought what Monsieur might try to do to her when he gets strong enough to walk?"

"What?" the others whispered urgently.

"First, still lying in bed, he'll try to touch her. Her hair, her arm, her lips. But she won't let him. So he'll get up out of bed and follow her—when it's dark, and there's no one around. . . ."

"Ooooh," the audience squealed.

"She'll run—he'll chase her, catch her. But she won't give in."

"No?" came the chorus.

"She'll choose death, or ugliness, instead. Maybe she'll cut off her nose and lips with Soukie's bread knife, like Saint Ebba did—or plunge the knife into her heart. Either way, Monsieur will finally understand his sinfulness, and be converted—so Evangeline will win that glory too."

"What about Gabriel?" Celeste wanted to know.

"Well, she won't die immediately. He'll be notified, and will come quickly, riding bareback on a borrowed horse, his heart pounding as fast as the horse's hooves. Evangeline will be afraid for him to see her, because she's mutilated, but he'll love her anyway. He'll kiss her forehead, and hold her hand so tenderly. God's voice will be heard —she will die happy, knowing what rewards are to come."

Blanche sobbed so loudly at the conclusion of this story that Celeste clapped a hand over her mouth and hissed, "Shut up. Antoinette will hear you and tell the sisters. Noisy babies aren't allowed here." Celeste had had no patience with Blanche ever since she had deserted them for the Doucettes at Christmas; after the holidays the twins had cold-shouldered Blanche, preferring an exclusive triumvirate with Antoinette, and Blanche had sheepishly returned to this group.

"Leave her alone, Celeste," Felice whispered. "Blanche couldn't help it. It *is* a very moving story."

Two days later, after classes, Sister Agatha drew Felice aside on the stair landing to say that she wished to speak with her about "a matter of some urgency." Felice followed the nun to her cell, where Sister Agatha confided that "the man quartered here is an Indian. I am certain of it. Beware, child." And she pressed into Felice's hands a sheaf of dusty papers which constituted, she said, the first chapters of a Micmac grammar, as yet unpublished, which she had compiled during her missionary work among Indian schoolchildren many years ago. "Speak to the Abbé, child—he thinks I am too old to possess the faculty of reason—but *you* speak to him. Have him read to the stranger from these pages. He will see. It will be proved!" The nun emphasized that Felice should not attempt this reading herself, but have the Abbé do it. This would not only assure Felice's protection, but it might just advance Sister Agatha's cause. Once aware of her superior intellectual functioning, the Abbé would let her resume teaching, Sister Agatha said. It had always been the nun's suspicion that the Abbé was behind her enforced retirement; Mother Superior would not be so cruel.

Felice promised to deliver the pages and departed, her head spinning from the responsibility suddenly placed upon her. She looked through the sheets of faded script; they seemed to be in no particular order, and were filled with lists of odd words. "Piskwa," she sounded out, and "Wee-ge-gi-jik." In a paragraph headed "The Urgent Question," she found written *"Kesalt Sasus?"* meaning "Do you love Jesus?" "It is touching to see," Sister Agatha had written, in English, "with what sweet ardour the Micmac savage is capable of responding, 'Ah, *Kesalt Sasus!*' "

"Kesalt Sasus?" Felice practiced, descending the stairs. *"Kesalt Sasus?"* Maybe she should go to the infirmary, ask Evangeline's permission to enter, and put this question to Monsieur. He would clasp his hands together and fall to his knees; he would be so affected that Evangeline would beg Felice to stay and assist her in this contest between God and the devil.

But instead she went, as directed, to find the Abbé.

The priest was in his classroom, marking religion examinations. Felice timidly placed the papers on his desk. "This is from Sister Agatha, Mon Père. It's a Micmac grammar. She asked me to tell you that you could read to Monsieur from it. She says it will prove he's Indian."

"Does she, indeed? Is Sister Agatha not aware that I would naturally have thoroughly investigated this possibility? Have I not labored in the vineyards of the Micmac people for many years, in spite of the small harvest reaped there?" He glared at Felice as though she were the object of his wrath.

"I'm sorry, Mon Père—I didn't—I just thought—*she* just thought, if you'd only read a bit of her work to him. . . ."

"Don't be impertinent, young lady. Kindly return these amateurish pages to Sister, will you, and tell her we do appreciate her efforts in this matter."

Felice told Sister Agatha a modified account of this incident, emphasizing the Abbé's gratefulness but leaving out the part about her being an amateur.

"Nothing on my own situation, then?"

"No, Sister, I am sorry."

"Never mind, never mind—I am much too busy anyway, as it happens. Preparations," she mumbled. "Now run along, child."

Felice scuffed away quite downcast about the entire episode; she was not much use to anybody, she thought. Her spirits did not revive again until that night, when she told a new version of what her friends now called the Saint Evangeline story, in which the tongueless man was characterized as the last surviving member of a primitive tribe of aborigines.

"That was the best ever," Celeste said approvingly, "the scariest."

On the evening of the second Sunday after Epiphany, Soukie told Felice of a spine-tingling event that had taken place not three hours before in the infirmary. "Monsieur walked," Soukie whispered into the girl's ear. "Evangeline told me so herself. She left the gentleman —sleeping soundly, so she thought—and went outside to the grotto. When she came back, she found him in a heap by the window."

"*Dead?*" Felice set down an ironstone platter with such force that a hairline crack appeared in its border.

"No, sssh, of course not, Mademoiselle. Here, give me that. The poor gentleman was just weary from the effort. He must have taken four or five steps—Evangeline said the Abbé measured the distance after they helped him back to his bed."

Felice sped up the stairs, and in an unusual breach of security called

Celeste, Françoise, Anne, and Blanche into her cubicle before lights out. Whispering very softly to keep Antoinette from hearing, she repeated Soukie's story, adding her own conjecture that of course Monsieur had been attempting to follow Evangeline.

The reactions were so clamorous, and the sudden stillness in the adjoining cubicle so absolute, that Felice had the others write out their questions.

"Is he bruised anywhere?" Celeste wrote on the back of a Saint Simon Stock religious card, and handed it to Felice.

Felice's written response—"I suggest you go see for yourself"—brought on such shrieks and unsuccessfully muffled laughter that Antoinette appeared in the doorway and asked if she might borrow a hairpin.

Felice's account of Monsieur's first walk aroused most of the girls to boldness. Changing classes, going to meals, headed for the chapel, Celeste, Anne, Françoise, and Felice—but not Blanche—arranged their routes through the building so that they passed by the infirmary. Often the door was shut, because of Evangeline's insistence that her patient needed long periods of rest in which to recuperate from the spill. Behavior when the door was open depended upon whether or not Monsieur was attended, and by whom.

The Abbé, who had renewed his attempts to ascertain the tongueless man's origin, did not mind an audience. Therefore Felice and Celeste were able to witness, from the doorsill, the elderly midwife Brunhilde Tareno, who recalled some phrases of German from her Teutonic childhood, questioning Monsieur; and on another occasion they watched a visiting Italian sailor (veeery handsome, Felice and Celeste reported to their envious friends) speaking and gesticulating to Monsieur while the Abbé looked on. Though neither language seemed to elicit a sign of recognition, there were certain sounds Monsieur seemed to prefer, the Abbé told the girls, and he intended to use this as the basis for discovering the man's native tongue.

When Evangeline was seated beside her patient, the girls glanced in but did not stop. Felice dallied past, hoping for the novice to summon her, and scanning the room for details to be used in the Saint Evangeline stories.

If Monsieur was alone, the girls—usually in pairs, or in a group—would linger and cough or shuffle their feet. More often than not, Monsieur turned his head, which sent them scuttling, hands inter-locked, up to the safety of the dormitory. Celeste claimed that she had once gone inside the door by herself and said, "Hello, Monsieur. My name is Celeste Rouget," and that he had smiled *very* warmly, as though to signify he was delighted to make her lovely acquaintance. When Felice passed by unaccompanied, she looked in only from the corner of her eye; once she saw, or imagined, Monsieur reach out his hand toward her.

The tongueless man had made no further efforts to walk. But this did not discourage speculation, at the now regular after-lights-out meetings in Felice's cubicle, about where in the convent Monsieur was likely to be encountered, and with what results.

Felice, the most gifted narrator of the group, was content with stories. But Celeste, tired of listening, wanted action. She proposed bets and dares connected with going inside the tongueless man's room. She taunted them all for being sissy; Blanche, she said, was the worst sissy, for being afraid to go by his door, and Felice, the next worst.

"That's completely unfair," Felice said. "What about that night? And once—I haven't told you about this—I went in alone, when he was awake."

"When?" Celeste demanded.

"A few days ago."

"What happened?" Blanche breathed.

"Well, I wanted to ask him a question in Micmac—*Kesalt Sasus?* It means, Do you love Jesus? So I said, *'Kesalt Sasus?'* His eyes lit up—I held out my rosary to him, and he kissed it, *passionately.*"

"How thrilling!" Françoise said.

"Not true, though," Celeste judged. "It's just a good story."

Goaded by Celeste, Felice came up with a justification for visiting the infirmary. They would go together as an impartial jury, and put before Monsieur the names that had been proposed for him.

Mother Superior preferred Francis, after her favorite male saint, Francis of Assisi. But the Abbé wanted to christen the man Eude, in honor of the Eudists, with whom he had studied at the College of St. Anne when he first came to Acadia as a young ecclesiastic; he had already written to the Bishop asking if His Eminence would do the honor of baptizing Monsieur Eude when he came at Easter.

Discussion of this issue was now convent-wide, with nuns and girls taking sides; in a few instances, long-simmering resentments had boiled up during arguments about the name. It would be a service to the entire community, and not just to the Abbé and Mother Superior, Felice pointed out, if they could help resolve the problem once and for all. And this could best be done, she said, by determining which name Monsieur himself preferred. They would go all the way into Monsieur's room, get his attention, pronounce each name, and gauge the reaction.

The other girls, excited by the prospect, agreed. Celeste was assigned the name Eude; Françoise, Francis; and Felice, in the event of a tie, was to say both names. Anne and Blanche were to be judges; Anne protested that role was too minor, but she was overruled.

They decided to go the next Friday afternoon at three o'clock, when Evangeline and all the sisters would be in the chapel singing their office, and the other students would be doing homework or tidying their cubicles.

At the appointed hour, the five girls met in the hall outside the infirmary. The door was shut.

"Shall we wake him if he's sleeping?" Celeste whispered.

The others merely shivered for answer, and Celeste eased open the door. Felice pushed by Celeste to enter first, and the rest of the girls came behind her.

Monsieur was seated upright in bed, studying his palms. As the girls advanced, on tiptoe, he dropped his hands to the counterpane and looked up, his face startled at first, and then, Felice thought, satanic.

"We're just here to help you choose a name," Felice said sternly, in French and then in English. Behind her there was some giggling and shoving.

They lined up in a row several feet from his bed; he revolved toward them. Felice looked at a point just above Monsieur's head; she could feel his eyes burn her lips, her neck. This was good practice, she thought.

"Go on, Celeste," she said from one corner of her mouth.

"Eude," Celeste said. Monsieur regarded her with interest. "Eu-ude," she repeated, extending her neck and pursing her lips.

"It looks like she's kissing him," Françoise whispered, setting off an explosion of giggles.

Monsieur's eyebrows shot up. He looked up and down the line of girls, then his lips parted in a slow grin.

Giggling nervously, the girls clung together. Felice punched Françoise. "Hurry," she whispered.

Françoise stepped forward. "Fran-ciss," she cooed, "sweet Fran-ciss." Monsieur jerked his head to look at Françoise, and smiled broadly.

"Francis wins," Françoise declared.

"You're not the judge," Celeste said. "Say both, Felice."

"Eude," Felice enunciated carefully. His dark eyes met hers; she forced herself not to waver. "Eude," she said again; he frowned, as though trying to understand. "You," Felice pointed at him. "You, Eude."

"You're saying Eude too many times," Françoise protested.

"You, Francis." Monsieur looked at Felice's extended finger, then at her face. "Francis. Eude. Francis."

Felice dropped her hand. "The same," she said. Monsieur's jaw moved as though he were trying to speak. "Now let's go."

"I agree," Blanche said, clutching Felice's arm. "A tie. And I'm a judge."

Monsieur's eyes veered to Blanche; she went red and covered her mouth with both hands, as though to forestall hysteria.

Felice and Blanche began to sidle toward the door.

"No, wait," Celeste said. "Eude!"

"Francis!" Françoise fairly shouted.

Monsieur looked back and forth, his expression one of puzzlement.

"Augustine?" Anne tried out.

"Ridiculous," Celeste snorted.

There was a silence. Monsieur stirred beneath the covers. Felice stood frozen: he was coming after them.

"Let's go," Blanche whimpered, and took shelter behind Felice, clutching her skirt.

"Sissy!" Felice slapped back at her with a trembling hand. Monsieur leaned forward slightly, his shoulders hunched. He looked thin, pitiably thin, Felice told herself. "Mathusala!" she cried out, in sudden inspiration. It was a good long name, heavy enough to weigh him down. "Ma-thus-a-la," she intoned, raising her hands before her, as though casting a spell. "Ma-thus-a-la." She began to take small steps backward toward the door.

The others moved with her, and, giggling, took up the chant: "Ma-thus-a-la."

Monsieur stared at Felice as though mesmerized, she thought: she could make him change his eyes by widening or narrowing her own.

The girls knotted together, clasping hands. "Ma-thus-a-la," they chanted, drawing out the vowels.

"Just what is going on here?"

The girls whirled about, knocking against one another. Over Blanche's head, Felice glimpsed Evangeline's face, a dark, angry triangle beneath the white chapel veil.

"We were just trying to help," Celeste said, "about Monsieur's name. What would you think of Mathusala?"

"I think it's very silly. I think you girls are acting very silly and immature. Why aren't you in study hall? Now, leave this instant."

All the girls but Felice scampered out. "Evangeline," she said, "we didn't mean any harm."

"Really, Felice, I had thought better of you."

"I *am* better. Truly. I have been meaning to speak to you for a long while, about . . ." Felice heard her voice grow smaller and smaller, "about helping with Monsieur—his nursing and conversion. I think you're very—" Evangeline cut her off with a dismissing wave.

Felice backed out the door: it was closed in her face. Fighting back tears, her cheeks burning with shame, she hurried up to the dormitory.

The others were discussing the possibility of being told on and punished. "What did she say, Felice?" they asked.

"Nothing," Felice said, and taking her rosary, went down to the white chapel to pray. Felice erased all thoughts of Evangeline and Monsieur by saying two rosaries and the entire Litany of the Blessed Virgin before the bell rang for supper.

During the meal, wrapped in the armor of her sanctity, Felice deliberately took no notice of anyone.

After lights out, Celeste, Françoise, Anne, and Blanche went uninvited to Felice's cubicle. "I watched Mother Superior all during supper," Celeste reported, "and she didn't look a bit mad. Evangeline didn't either, really." Françoise, who had placed herself in the superioress' way, said she had received a warm smile and greeting. Celeste concluded that Evangeline wasn't going to tell, and if she did, what did it matter? They had only been trying to help.

So spirits were high during that night's meeting; of the five, only Felice was subdued. Celeste proposed they call themselves the Dare Club, and said she intended to get Monsieur to pursue her; none of the others, she taunted, would do as much. Françoise said she would, and began to describe particulars of the chase; she was interrupted by Anne, who provided what were, for her, some titillating details.

"This is all make-believe," Felice broke in. "I saw something that really happened." In contrast to the other girls' voices, Felice's tone was serious, almost angry.

"What?" the others chimed, already half-convinced.

"This is what happened after you left the infirmary. I stood outside the door. Evangeline only *thought* I had gone." She paused and looked down at her hands clasped in her lap. "This is a tragic story. Poor Evangeline has totally—*totally*"—she looked up—"lost her chance for virgin martyrdom."

"What do you mean?" Celeste whispered excitedly.

"Well, I thought I heard something—strange. So I opened the door, just a tiny crack. And guess what! Monsieur was walking!"

"Oh, no!" Blanche squeaked. "I knew it!"

"Ssh," the others said. "Go on, Felice."

"Walking right toward Evangeline. She was standing in the corner, by the wardrobe. He walked closer and closer, holding out his hands. She just *stood* there."

"Unarmed?" Anne asked.

"Well, she did have her sewing scissors. She unsnapped them from her blouse and held them up toward him, like this . . ." Here Felice stood and demonstrated Evangeline's posture. "Then he touched her shoulder. So she held the scissors to her bosom." Felice moved her fist from midair to her chest. "But when he put his arms around her, she dropped the scissors to the floor, and that was *it.*" Felice sank back to the bed.

"What?" Françoise asked. "That was what?"

"Her last chance at sainthood. *Because* . . . of what she did."

"What?" they all breathed.

"Fell into his arms. She let him—kiss her. She kissed back. Oh, they kissed and *kissed.*"

"What next?" came the chorus.

"Well, I thought I shouldn't look, and I was so *shocked*—so I just quietly shut the door and tiptoed away." Felice's stifled giggle sounded like a hiccup, or a sob.

"How horrible," Celeste said, "wonderfully horrible."

"Horrible but true," Felice corrected.

"Horrible, but true," Blanche repeated, as though in oath.

ONE WEDNESDAY IN LATE JANUARY SOUKIE LEARNED THAT Madame Doucette was dreadfully upset about some filthy stories Blanche Melanson had told her twins. Madame Doucette had every intention of complaining to Mother Superior, the Doucettes' maid

Polley confided to Soukie, who passed on the intelligence to Celeste that very evening, during the washing-up.

As best Celeste could make out, she informed Felice during a private conversation later that night, Blanche had told the stories to the Doucette twins during the Christmas holidays, but their mother had only just found out.

"Evangeline?" Felice cried out, clutching at Celeste with icy hands. "Monsieur?"

"Ssh. No, I don't think so. Evangeline wasn't mentioned. The Private Act, and its results, is what Soukie said. I asked Soukie if she had any idea where Blanche heard such awful talk. . . ."

"Stupid—you shouldn't have done that," Felice whispered savagely.

"Don't call me stupid," Celeste hissed, giving her a little pinch. "It was a natural, innocent question—and we need to know. Anyway, Soukie said no, so it seems like it's just Blanche who's in trouble—unless she tells on us, of course. And if she does, we deny it."

"You deny it, you mean. It was you who told about how babies are made. And what about poor Blanche?"

"Poor Blanche! She's stupid. She's got a big mouth, and I always told you she couldn't be trusted. And *you* were in on it too, don't forget that."

Felice was silent a moment. "The others will have to promise not to talk, too."

"They will," Celeste declared.

"How did Madame Doucette find out?"

"Emma got It, and her mother said she wanted to have a little talk with her and Laura. She said the story she'd told about the Holy Spirit bringing them wasn't the whole truth. Emma and Laura said they knew, and Madame Doucette said tell me, and they did. And when Madame Doucette got so upset, of course Emma and Laura said they'd heard every word of it from Blanche. Now Madame Doucette is coming to see Mother Superior and get to the bottom of things, Soukie said Polley said."

"Shouldn't we at least warn Blanche?"

"Are you crazy? She'd just cling on to us, and we'd all be thrown out."

"Thrown out?" Felice said in a hollow voice.

"It happened before, Soukie said, when she was a student, for the exact same thing."

"But Mother Superior likes Blanche."

"But she hates dirty stories. So swear—to absolute secrecy."

"I swear," Felice said dully.

"We'd better not have any more night meetings for a while—and we have to avoid Blanche. Don't even speak to her. I'll go tell Anne and Francie."

Felice knelt to pray, but could not, for the whirring in her head. She climbed into bed and pulled the covers to her chin. When Blanche tiptoed to Felice's cubicle a little later, Felice clamped her eyes shut and took long breaths, in imitation of sleep. After the other girl went away, Felice lay for a long while staring up into the unfriendly dark.

Icy drafts accosted Felice when she climbed out of bed the next morning. Teeth chattering, she pulled on an extra layer of underwear and her thickest stockings, but she was still shivering when she entered the dining hall for breakfast.

At the head table, Mother Superior, scolding Soukie for burnt bread, looked normal. Throughout the room there were the reassuringly familiar sounds of chairs scraping into place and cups rattling against saucers. As Felice took her seat, she glanced at Evangeline; she too wore her usual expression, one of such remoteness as to suggest that her physical presence here was the result of mere chance.

At Felice's table, the nuns were discussing the weather. Sister Claire predicted seven inches of snow; Sister Theodota said ten inches, and a heavy blow at sea. Sister Agatha cheerfully said she was expecting "a blizzard, or worse." Evangeline, one hand to her throat, turned to gaze at the threatening sky.

"If we had a blizzard, no one could get to the convent," Celeste said.

Felice, looking at Blanche innocently stuffing her squirrellike cheeks, kicked Celeste under the table. For all her talk about discretion, Celeste was really very careless.

"Can anyone tell me what is worse than a blizzard?" Sister Agatha asked in her schoolteacher's voice.

"Two blizzards," Sister Theodota said, with a honk, and then turned rather pink.

"A holocaust. I'll give you another chance. Can anyone name the world's most prolific, and varied, poet?"

"Yes—Shakespeare," Felice said confidently.

Evangeline gave her a close look, and Felice looked away immediately, down into the gray mud of her oatmeal. What had Evangeline meant by that expression?

"Wrong again," Sister Agatha crowed. "For a hint, I will sing you one of his—or her—best-known works of the middle period. 'Western wind, when wilt thou blow,' " she warbled, laying down her spoon and clasping both hands to her chest, " 'that the small rain down shall rain. Christ, that my love were in my arms . . .' "

"Contain yourself, Sister," Sister Theodota snapped.

Sister Agatha unfolded her arms and returned her hands, trembling slightly, to the bowl and spoon. Felice smiled across the table, hoping the nun would perceive her support. Sister Agatha did not look toward her, but Evangeline did—again, a hooded, yet critical, gaze.

Making herself as small and noiseless as possible, Felice tried to eat. She felt that the novice was still staring at her; her own swallowing sounded very loud to herself. Felice imagined that Evangeline was thinking how forward, brazen even, this student was; the novice was probably realizing she should report Mademoiselle Belliveau's unseemly behavior in the infirmary to Mother Superior. Felice stole a glance upward; Evangeline was looking elsewhere, or pretending to.

Any chance Felice might ordinarily have had to explain away the infirmary incident would probably be rendered impossible by a much worse accusation against her. Blanche—here Felice cut her eyes toward that girl, who was obliviously hacking her fried egg into small pieces with her knife—Blanche, when confronted, would tell the sisters about Felice's scandalous Evangeline story. Felice would try to deny it, but no one would believe her, not even Sister Agatha or Sister Claire; there would be too much evidence piled up against her. Her sin was even more heinous than

Blanche's; she had impugned the reputation of a novice, and she would have to go. When Uncle Adolphe came, Mother Superior would give him permission to whip her all he liked: "She has behaved most deplorably, Monsieur; we are all shocked and disappointed."

After breakfast, Felice drew Celeste, Françoise, and Anne to the parlor and said she had a confession to make. "Someone else actually told me that story about Evangeline—someone else who saw it herself."

"Who?" Françoise asked.

"I can't say—I promised."

"Uh huh," Celeste said sarcastically. "Sure."

"It's the truth," Felice insisted. "I wouldn't make up anything that horrible."

"You're a good storyteller, Felice," Celeste said, "but a terrible liar."

Felice stared down at the floor. "But if Blanche tells on me, about that story . . ."

"*We* never heard it," Celeste said, "did we, Anne and Francie?"

They all shook hands with the secret grip of the Dare Club, and hurried off to class.

Felice felt somewhat relieved until arithmetic, when she took her seat behind Blanche. Blanche turned around to smile; Felice, following instructions, gave her only the coolest nod of recognition. Looking as though she had been slapped, Blanche whirled back around and feigned absorption in her arithmetic book.

Felice stabbed at her hand with her pencil. Poor Blanche, poor Blanche; this was the worst wickedness of all. She hoped Mama was not watching her right now.

She studied Blanche's head, the fat braids divided by a center part that was as straight and white as a shaft of bone. Above her imperfectly pressed collar, Blanche's neck was pudgy and unnaturally white, a sacrificial neck, like the picture of Saint Lucy in the *Lives of the Saints.*

Blanche gave off a faint cheesy odor, and there was a light sprinkling of dandruff on the shoulders of her dark uniform. One of her five buttons was only half done, and when Blanche's arm shot up in response to a question put by Sister Theodota, it popped all the way out, exposing a swatch of undergarment.

"Incorrect, Mademoiselle Melanson." Sister Theodota made a mark in her grade book. "Mademoiselle Belliveau?"

Felice stood up. "Sister Theodota, I want to confess that I did not do my homework last night, and I have absolutely no excuse. I am sorry, Sister."

Taken off guard, Sister Theodota blinked for a few seconds at Felice, and other students turned to stare. For Felice to confess to not doing homework was unusual, but for her to offer no excuse was unprecedented.

"I see. A zero for the work then, but an A for candor." The nun recorded the grades in her book. "Exemplary candor," she added, bobbing her head in the direction of several of the other more facile-tongued students, one of whom—Celeste—crossed her eyes at Felice as she sat down.

Her head sheltered beneath one arm, as though from further blows, Blanche glanced back at Felice. From the other girl's expression, which was at the same time accusatory and pitiful, Felice understood that Blanche considered the homework confession another hostility against herself. You are wrong, Felice wanted to shout, wrong, *wrong*. But she carried with her throughout that day, and many more, the image of Blanche's eyes, flashing with unshed tears, bright like tiny mirrors.

That afternoon at piano practice, Felice's fingers found all the wrong notes. Sister Claire sat patiently by as the girl returned again and again to the beginning of the Mendelssohn song and stumbled forward a few bars. Behind her, Felice could feel the heavy gray sky refusing to snow. That meant Madame Doucette would come, and the confrontations begin.

"That's enough for today," Sister Claire finally said. "We'll try it again tomorrow."

"Please don't give up on me, Sister," Felice wailed.

"What? Don't be melodramatic, Felice," the nun said, pinching her cheek in affectionate reprimand.

By day's end, when Felice and Celeste met in the deserted outer chapel, there had been no sightings of Madame Doucette.

"Maybe she won't come after all," Felice said.

"She could have been here already," Celeste pointed out. "We couldn't have spies watching every second."

"I've been thinking, Celly," Felice said, shifting on the bench, where they knelt side by side, rosaries in their hands, "that it might be best to stand by Blanche—after all, she's our *friend*. And she might be less likely to tell about other things."

"Like what other things?"

"The Evangeline story."

"Oh, that. No one will believe her. And we couldn't keep her from telling if she's forced—she's a sissy, you know: she'll give under pressure."

"The sisters have seen her with us anyway," Felice argued, "so our avoiding her will only make things look suspicious."

Celeste shook her head and stood up. "If you want us to back you up, you'd better do what we agreed on."

"I'll talk to Anne and Francie myself, then," Felice muttered as Celeste went away. Felice sat back in the pew and let the rosary fall into her lap. She could go back to Blanche on her own and warn her. If Blanche wouldn't protect her about the Evangeline story, they would just have to go down together. That way Felice would at least atone for her sins, and God would probably forgive her.

When the dinner-bell rang, Felice walked slowly back to the convent, her stomach aching with something other than hunger. Throughout the meal, she avoided Blanche's eye, and realized she would continue to do so: she was a coward. Every bit of food weighed upon her sinful tongue like further sin; every mouthful swallowed increased the store of blackness inside her.

In arithmetic class the next day, Blanche's seat was empty. Felice and Celeste exchanged looks; this, then, was it—Blanche must be in Mother Superior's office. Felice sat staring up at Sister Theodota as though engrossed in fractions, but waiting to be summoned.

The bell rang. Felice and Celeste walked together to the weekly student evaluation meeting that took the place of history on Fridays.

Blanche was not there either. The Doucette twins were, however, and looking smug, Felice thought; it seemed to her that Emma Doucette glanced significantly in her direction.

Felice's heart pounded as she took her seat and looked up at the semicircle of nuns on the platform. Since her crime was worse than Blanche's, they were going to make a public spectacle of her.

Mother Superior stood and called the girls forward one by one to receive the slips of paper that summarized each student's performance that week.

"Felice Belliveau!"

Felice walked forward—she did not know how—and took from Mother Superior's outstretched fingers the slip of paper. She did not look at it until she sat at her desk again. *Très bien,* it read. She could not believe it: the words swam and then reshaped before her eyes. *Très bien.* She was saved.

"Celeste," she whispered, bending forward and waving the paper at the other girl two aisles away, *"très bien!"* Celeste, who had never received that highest evaluation, smiled ruefully.

Celeste was called forward, took her slip, and returned to her seat. *"Assez bien,"* she mouthed to Felice, and shrugged as though she didn't care.

Then Mother Superior advanced to the edge of the platform. Her face was grave. "Mademoiselles," she said in her coldest, most official voice, "I have something very serious to tell you. Blanche Melanson has been dismissed from L'Académie du Sacré Sang for disgraceful, shameful conduct."

There were surprised gasps from the students. Felice dared not look at Celeste. Holding her breath, she stared fixedly up at Mother Superior.

"Blanche Melanson, by her own admission, has been using reprehensible language and telling indecent stories to young, innocent girls," Mother Superior said, her hands gripping the rosary at her waist. "We cannot condone this sort of behavior; it has a harmful effect on other inhabitants of the convent, and when carried beyond its walls, may sully the unblemished reputation of the order. Let this be a warning to you, Mademoiselles. If there are sinful thoughts in your hearts, consult with one of us or with the Abbé—do not follow the example of Blanche Melanson."

Mother Superior sank wearily into her chair. The girls remained still, their eyes upon her; finally Sister Claire stepped forward and excused them.

Felice and Celeste found Blanche in the dormitory. She was sitting on the floor between the bed and the bureau, her head on her knees, sobbing. The bureau drawers were open and their contents were heaped on the bed. "Blanche?" Celeste said.

Blanche looked up. Her face was so swollen and red that Felice felt embarrassed for her. She watched uncomfortably as Celeste knelt and put her arms about Blanche, an embrace that was tolerated but briefly. Blanche suddenly sprang back, pushing the other girl away. "Get out of here!" she screamed. "Get out—it's all your fault, anyway."

"Well, you didn't have to be so stupid," Celeste said, tossing her head and standing. "It was stupid to tell anything to the Doucette twins. You have a big mouth—that's your problem."

"Not so big," Blanche retorted. "I could have told on you but I *didn't,*" she said, her voice rising to a higher pitch. "The Abbé wanted to know who else, and I should have told him but I didn't—now get out. . . ."

"What did you say—what did he say?" Celeste demanded, gripping Blanche's arm.

"None of your business."

Felice clutched the bed rail, woozy at the sudden prospect of being sent in disgrace to Wolfville, and looked out the window. The expected storm had not materialized; there was only the chariest skim of white on the ground. "Did you—did you mention Evangeline?" she asked.

"No—*no*—now let go of me, Celeste. Get out, get out!" Blanche shouted so loudly that Felice and Celeste fled, for fear someone would come to investigate.

After luncheon, Felice and Celeste waited in the parlor and watched the stairs until the disgraced girl had left. She was fetched by her father, a shambling man whom Blanche very much resembled, and departed after only a brief, public interview with Mother Superior. Satisfied that Blanche had had no further conversation with the nuns, Celeste nevertheless insisted on a conference with Felice, Anne, and Françoise. They met after classes in the basement, where, seated on bags of apples, they rehearsed their surprised denials should the accusations ever be forthcoming.

For her part, Felice did not care about the scheming; she felt remorseful, haunted by Blanche's miserable face, and so full of guilt that she would have gone straight to Mother Superior with the whole story were it not for Celeste's persuasive reasoning that it would not save Blanche anyway. Looking out at the bay from her window, Felice thought of the inexorable roll of waves upon the shore, and of having to go back to live with Uncle Adolphe. If she did, she would drown herself. Then she thought of Mama, her face clouded by disappointment, and she resolved to pray harder, for herself and for Blanche.

Blanche's expulsion focused attention as much on the crime as on the punishment. Mother Superior's announcement provoked intense private discussions among the students about exactly what lurid details had been passed on by Blanche to the Doucettes; in this activity, the twins were not loath to cooperate. Celeste, Françoise, and Anne took part in some of these secret gatherings; Felice did not.

This shared illicit preoccupation might have continued for days or weeks, had it not reached a public climax Saturday night at supper.

That evening, Mother Superior forbade mealtime conversation. The novice Evangeline, seated at the lower end of the room beneath the crucifix, read from the Book of Job while the nuns and girls, eyes fixed on their plates, ate baked cod.

In the silence at their table, Felice was aware of Sister Agatha's open-mouthed chewing, the scrape of her fork against the crockery plate, and her frequent deep sighs. Felice was looking at her—as was Sister Theodota, who was frowning—when Sister Agatha laid down her fork and, placing her hands flat on the table, moaned, *"O Adam, quid fecisti?"*

"Ssssh," hissed the other nuns at the table, like a nest of disturbed snakes.

At the other end of the room, Mother Superior rose halfway from her chair and stared at their table. She sank back slowly, still watching.

Sister Agatha began to eat again, and general silence was restored. For a time, the only sounds were of eating, and of Evangeline's dovelike voice murmuring lamentations. Suddenly Sister Agatha jumped, upsetting her teacup with a crash.

"Do you know your grammar, Mademoiselles?" she demanded, ignoring her spilled tea. "*Amo, amas, amat.*" As Sister Theodota moved to take Sister Agatha's arm, saying, "Let's go rest, Sister," Sister Agatha leaned forward, the lappets of her neck and headdress quivering, and said, looking right at Felice, "Do you know what men use for it? They use their watering sticks, but receive a great deal more pleasure in this, I vow." She ran her tongue across her lips quickly as a skink's, and began to laugh.

She was still laughing as Mother Superior crossed the floor—the laughter and the staccato of footsteps the only sounds in the hushed room, Evangeline having ceased reading—but as Mother Superior and Sister Theodota pulled her upward, Sister Agatha's laughter stopped abruptly, and her face sagged. "This is no way to treat me," she whined as the nuns pushed her forward. "I am Agatha." The stunned diners sat motionless as Mother Superior and Sister Theodota took her out the door and down the hall, cries of "I am Agatha" resounding in the hall and against the stairwell.

Sister Agatha was not present at mass the next morning. She did not appear for luncheon; her plates had been removed, but no mention was made of her absence or her whereabouts. Felice searched for her in the halls, in the outer chapel, on the grounds. Early Sunday afternoon Felice tapped once on the door of the nun's cell, but there was no answer. A few hours later Felice returned to the cell and, after knocking, opened the door. She was shocked to find it empty; the bed, the chair, the table, icons, even the crucifix—all were gone. The small chamber was completely bare, with no reminder of Sister Agatha's habitation but for the painting of Eden. Felice stood for a moment before the fresco: Eve gazed mournfully back at her through the green tangle of branches.

Felice ran to the kitchen, where Soukie was peeling potatoes for supper. "Where is Sister Agatha?" the girl cried, pulling at Soukie's skirt. "All her things are gone—is she dead?"

Soukie laid one finger over her lips. "Now, not a word of this, Mademoiselle. I swore to Mother Superior I would not speak of it. But I will tell you, since you are her special friend. Sister Agatha is still with us, though I believe there were some who wanted to send her away. She is in the turret—for a nice long rest, Mother Superior says."

THE LAST DAYS OF JANUARY WERE WINDY, AND THE SEAS WERE high. When the nuns looked out the dining-room windows toward the choppy, white-capped bay, they crossed themselves, and their lips moved silently. Travelers at sea were remembered in nightly prayers, at the Office of Compline. Candles were lit in the front hall beside the niche of Notre-Dame de Bon Secours, a blue-robed madonna cradling a delicate miniature ship in her lap. Her outstretched hand, worn paintless and smooth by generations of fishermen's wives and sweethearts—and in the last decade, by women of soldiers fighting the Kaiser—now seemed to shine with a special poignance in the flickering light. As the winds continued, sightings of phantom ships were reported from Nevette to Pointe l'Eglise, the specter first appearing as a ball of fire on the water, then gradually taking shape as a vague, three-masted schooner.

There were no sibylline predictions of disaster from the kitchen, as was usual in bad weather. Soukie now wore two scapulars outside her apron, and a lugubrious expression, but that was the extent of her comment, for she—like the other residents of L'Académie du Sacré

Sang—had been enjoined to strict silence following the disgraces of Blanche and Sister Agatha.

The Abbé patrolled the downstairs hall of the convent, constantly exhorting both nuns and girls on the virtues of silence. In the hall, in religion class, after confession, the Abbé was always prepared with admonitions from the holy fathers against unnecessary speech. "He who guards his mouth protects his life," was a frequently intoned reminder, "Proverbs 13:3." He made a habit of arriving late at his classroom and even if there was no whispering he might say, "An undisciplined tongue reveals a dissolute disposition," or, "The tongue is a restless evil, full of deadly poison." To Soukie he often gave the baleful warning, "As Saint Augustine said, it is not without reason that the tongue is set in a moist place, but because it is prone to slip."

According to the new rules of the convent, no talking was allowed among the girls at bedtime, during meals, or between classes. The daily hours of the Grand Silence, normally reserved for nuns and confined to certain periods, were now general, total, and applied to all, both girls and sisters. In order to occupy the students' minds, which were evidently all too idle (Mother Superior said during a meeting two days after the banishments of Blanche and Sister Agatha), each girl was to memorize set passages from Saint Thomas Aquinas and the Psalter each day, and to be quizzed on them after dinner. Imperfections in the recitations would occasion additional assignments, and any degree of gallivanting or gossiping among the girls, the nun warned her hushed audience, would be cause for expulsion.

For a time, nuns were stationed outside the girls' dormitory at night, to ensure order, and during the day the downstairs halls were watchful and still. The entire convent seemed muffled, as though under a spell. The nuns' new practice of collective meditation contributed to this illusion of enthrallment; each morning and evening they circled the convent in a swaying black line, their murmured prayers strung together on one continuous rosary of sound by the bass tone of the sea.

Felice was terrified by the silence about her. She imagined her sins surfacing in the unaccustomed quiet, much as dark objects become visible, and even seem to rise, in clear water. But she dared not speak, either, for fear of punishment, so she kept to herself, and when Celeste tried to catch her eye, Felice moved away.

Mother Superior's sterner self, sitting in command at her office desk, marching down the hall, presiding grim-faced over meals without conversation, was always in Felice's consciousness. Even when the nun was out of sight, in another part of the convent, Felice was acutely aware of her existence, a dark rod subtly inclining in the girl's direction, drawn magnetlike to guilt. It was almost a relief to sit in Mother Superior's class, beneath her actual gaze. Then, should the superioress take action—having been told of, or suddenly divining, the girl's true character—Felice would at least know at once. The other hours of waiting were agony.

At night, Felice lay tightly curled in her bed, not wanting to shift an arm or leg into the hostile region of cold sheet. She thought that she could hear, in the tall silence above her, the sound of pacing. She tried to imagine Sister Agatha's face, but was not always successful; sometimes the black-clad, restless figure wore Blanche's features, grotesquely distorted by endless crying, or her own face, a pale, vague, lost face.

Several times a day Felice knelt in the outer chapel to say voluntary prayers of contrition: this gave her body shape. But when she emerged alone and looked at the dark bay and the steel-gray lid of the sky, fear rushed back, filling her limbs like water, leaving her tired and blurred. She stood alone in the frozen orchard, or by the Evangeline willows by the wall, trying to shiver every bit of badness out of herself. Sometimes she walked to the rim of the cliff and, looking out over the cold infinity of water, considered her dilemma about confession.

If she confessed her sins to the Abbé, she might be expelled from the academy. But if she didn't confess, there was the prospect of hell; already she could feel the distance from Mama, and heaven. She thought of going to see another priest, but the closest one she knew of was in Digby; getting there would require a train ride and an absence from school she could not figure out how to explain. She could go disguised as a housewife to the Abbé's village confession, but of course as soon as she described the particulars of her sins, the priest would guess who was speaking.

Then, on the Feast of the Purification, Felice had an inspiration. It came to her during the blessing of candles in the white chapel, as she knelt, slightly light-headed from the day's fast, at the feet of the Virgin: she would continue to fast, and her sins would wither inside her, turn to dry stalks and then to dust. Felice crossed herself and looked up into Mary's face; the Madonna smiled approvingly back down upon her.

Felice then rose and went with the other girls up the aisle for the Candlemas procession around the convent building.

Felice stepped outdoors, into a night that seemed charged with importance. A mixed incense of balsam and salt perfumed the frigid air, and the golden sphere of the full moon, as if on cue, was just rising above the evergreen forest across the road. The light from the girls' candles illuminated hands and patches of cheeks and forehead, and sculpted dramatic hollows of shadow elsewhere. With a thrilling sense of participation in Mystery, Felice started down the path in the direction of the bay.

As she rounded the corner of the building, Felice looked up to the turret where Sister Agatha was sequestered. She thought she could see the very faintest of lights, like that of a firefly shining with growing disconsolation in a cage fashioned by some thoughtless child, or like the weak light of a foundering ship far out at sea, that fading beacon its only hope.

Poor Sister Agatha. Felice let the wind sting tears to her eyes. Misunderstood, unfairly treated, a martyr, really, in her prison. And she, her trusted friend, too engrossed in her own selfish concerns to have given her any real thought. She would fast not only for herself, but for Sister Agatha as well. Her firm resolve quickened her step and gave her courage to pass alone beneath the tongueless man's room.

Later that night, in the dormitory, Felice took her figurine of the Virgin Mary down from the wall, and holding it in her hands, knelt by her bed to pray. From the other cubicles—even Antoinette's— came the sounds of crunching, as girls ended the day-long fast with hoarded cheese and heels of bread. Felice concentrated on the Litany of the Blessed Virgin, and on the memory of Mary's smile, a soothing smile so like Mama's. When Celeste looked in, Felice did not turn around. Then there was giggling outside the door, and Celeste's distinct voice: "Let's not bother *this* Priss-Pot." Felice held tight to the figurine until the footsteps melted down the hall.

Felice climbed into bed and put the Madonna on the pillow beside her. Stroking the silver and the smooth blue glass, Felice did not feel at all hungry or lonely. Thinking of Mary now lying upon her back, floating on the deep blue as on a placid summertime bay, Felice fell into a wide blank sleep.

The next day Felice ate no breakfast or luncheon; at supper she gorged herself, then felt ill. At breakfast the next morning she tasted the oatmeal—stickier and less appetizing than usual—and spent the remainder of the mealtime rearranging the food in her bowl, dipping her spoon to the bottom, and bringing the bottom layer to the top. This activity caught the attention of both Sister Theodota (who frowned) and Sister Claire (who inclined her head quizzically); obviously, Felice thought, she could not proceed in such haphazard fashion.

That afternoon, kneeling alone in the chapel, the perfect form occurred to her. Since the fast was devoted to the Virgin, she would model it on the rosary. At each meal she would take ten bites of food —one for each of the Ave Marias in a decade of the rosary—and she would recite an Ave per mouthful. One swallow of liquid would be allowed at the beginning and end of the meal, in representation of the Pater Nosters dividing the segments of the rosary.

But at supper she found she had to drink more water, to prolong the time spent in consumption. By interposing a sip and a Pater between every two mouthfuls and Aves, she finished the meal when her tablemates did, and thus, she congratulated herself, kept her degree of sacrifice secret.

The next day, February 5, was Saint Agatha's Day. When she awoke that morning, Felice prayed for Saint Agatha to intercede for her imprisoned namesake, and for herself.

Descending the stairs, Felice felt thinner from her fast, and slightly bleached within. She decided to eat only white foods—the dingy gray breakfast porridge was a concession to circumstance—and to let no particle of food touch her lips.

By luncheon, she was feeling euphoric. She even dared to watch Evangeline as she rose from her reading of the Penitential Psalms to feed the woodstove. Though the novice did not look back at her, neither did she seem to be avoiding her in any premeditated way, Felice thought. Antoinette, who had been shifted to their table after the departures of Blanche and Sister Agatha, was eating like a pig, Felice noted with satisfaction. Celeste, from whom the veneer of contrition had completely worn off, was even worse: smacking her lips, clattering her spoon, making faces across the table at Françoise. When Celeste caught Felice looking at her, she stuck out her tongue, to which a paste of chewed beans still adhered.

Wrinkling her nose in disgust, Felice turned away, took a clarifying draught of water, and sat with her hands arranged in her lap for the rest of the meal.

"Are you feeling unwell?" Sister Claire asked as they rose.

"Quite well. Weller than usual," Felice replied, and slipped away.

That day following classes Felice felt drawn to the outer chapel, there to say a round of Sister Agatha's stations in honor of the saint's day. Because she sensed some divine purpose in this mission, she slipped the figurine of the Virgin into her cape pocket; Mary wanted to be of assistance.

Giddy from anticipation, and fasting, Felice stepped into the cold air and began to walk toward the chapel. She looked very closely at everything as she passed. The rock façade of the convent building, like the rough hide of some huge animal, the small knives of frozen grass, the tips of the tree-limbs tender as nipples beneath the caps of ice: all of the world's details sprang out at her with an unearthly clarity.

Inside the chapel, Felice glided from fresco to fresco. Each familiar prayer rang in her mind with new-minted freshness; Sister Agatha's colors and forms were more vivid than ever before. At the final, cathartic painting—women drooping like willows by the sealed tomb —she dabbed her eyes; then, after liberally dousing herself with holy water, she went out the door.

Beneath the vast, scudding clouds Felice felt small, but cherished. For she was living out her humility and devotion, and Mary must be very pleased with her. The other members of the heavenly family must also be aware of Felice's contrition, her surrendered will; together they would guide her to the heart of things, offer her a sign.

With a sense of mounting climax, Felice went to the back of the chapel, climbed the wall, and walked along the edge of the cliff to the lookout point. Stepping into the fierce, unimpeded wind on the tree-less promontory, Felice held tight to the silver and blue Virgin in her pocket.

The water was turbulent, flecked with whitecaps as far as Felice could see, to the thin line that was Digby Neck. Shipwreck water, Soukie would say. Spears of ice, broken loose from boulders, boiled in the surf; Felice could hear them shattering like glass as each line of waves crashed onto the shore. She remembered walking with Mama along the beach at Yarmouth on such a day as this. The curved, dark line of frozen seaweed left by the high tide had crackled beneath their feet; Mama had been inspired by the tide-line to scallop the hem of a dress with black velvet.

Suddenly as cold as though she had been pitched into the icy bay, Felice took the figurine of the Virgin from her pocket and held it to her chest. Warmth and calm spread throughout her body. She closed her eyes, praying again that her sins be forgiven, and there appeared, as if in answer, a wonderfully clear picture of Mama. She was spinning at a golden wheel, her fingers nimbly gathering yellow threads, her blue eyes smiling down at Felice.

The image faded. "Thank you, Mary," Felice whispered, and slipped the figurine back into her pocket.

Felice turned and ran to her willow tree. Climbing the wall, she glanced up at Sister Agatha's turret window glinting in the sunset. As Felice stared, the window seemed to catch fire and blaze. She jumped to the ground, her eyes still full of light, and looked into the hollow of the tree at Sister Agatha's painting of Our Lady of the Willow. She anticipated a transformation, and was not disappointed: Mary's ordinarily jaundiced face shone, a brilliance that grew by degrees, darkening the orchard, the air. When the light reached a white-hot incandescence, Felice fell to her knees. *"Ave Maria,"* she whispered, embracing the tree. *"Benedicta tu in mulieribus."* Pressing her cheek against the trunk, she heard deep within it a faint but perfect harmony, like a carillon of cathedral bells across a wide landscape.

The music flowed away. When Felice opened her eyes, the light was the usual gray of a February afternoon. She rose unsteadily and looked back up at Sister Agatha's window. A strangely pleasant dizziness drifted over her. It was most significant, she thought, that this mystical experience had occurred on Saint Agatha's Day; it quite likely meant that she and Sister Agatha shared a holy destiny. She, Felice Belliveau, was not only forgiven, but highly favored.

Then, trembling at the edge of faintness, Felice hurried back to the convent.

FELICE ATE A HEARTY SUPPER THAT NIGHT; SHE FELT SHE DE-served it. Also, she reasoned, continuing to fast might call undue attention to herself and prompt the nuns to question her. Since she was determined to reform her lying tongue, a close quizzing might force her to reveal the mystical experience which was meant to be, she thought—at least for now—private. She had probably gone too far in asking Mother Superior, as she was leaving her office with two borrowed volumes of the *Lives of the Saints,* what age the humble Bernadette had been when Our Lady appeared to her at Lourdes. Fourteen, Mother Superior had said, looking at her curiously. Because Felice felt the nun glance her way several times during supper, the girl emphasized her ordinariness, not only eating but overeating, and sitting slouched in her chair.

Felice savored the scallop chowder, and the contrast between her outer and inner selves. Beneath a disguise of flesh lay the afternoon's revelations: Mama at her wheel, the music, the brilliant apparition of Our Lady. But to Sister Theodota, Sister Claire, Celeste, Françoise— to everyone with the possible exception of Mother Superior, in whom a seed of awe had inadvertently been planted—she looked unchanged.

That evening, her voice muffled by the sounds of washing-up, Felice asked Soukie about Sister Agatha. Was the nun well, Felice wanted to know, and had Soukie heard how long she was to be confined?

After looking over each shoulder and edging closer to Felice with her dishtowel and plate, Soukie whispered that she was most concerned about the dear sister. She was eating almost nothing, Soukie said, and had fallen off dreadfully.

"A holy fast!" Felice exclaimed.

"Do you think so, Mademoiselle? She eats only fruit, and peels the skins with her own fingernails. She says she is being poisoned, in spite of my reassurances that no one—*no* one but me touches her food. Mademoiselle, wouldn't you think that she could trust Soukie?" And Soukie tipped her head sideways like a sorrowful spaniel.

"I'm sure she trusts you, Soukie, don't worry. Some divine purpose," Felice mumbled, lowering bowls into the dishwater.

Felice stared down at her busy hands as Soukie described the conflict over Sister Agatha's future. Because Mother Superior wouldn't hear of the nun's being sent to the retirement home—"It would kill her, Mon Père," Soukie had overheard the superioress say —the Abbé and Sister Theodota were looking for a relative or other suitable person to take her in. The priest was anxious to have the move accomplished before the arrival of the Bishop, as the nun's eccentricities, he felt, would reflect badly upon the whole academy. Mother Superior and the Abbé had exchanged some harsh words over who was to blame for Sister Agatha's irregular behavior—the priest charging Mother Superior with leniency, and the nun accusing the Abbé of insensivity in handling the matter of her retirement—but in

Soukie's opinion the whole problem boiled down to Sister Agatha's being English, like herself.

As Soukie was launching into an explication of the similarity between Sister Agatha's and her own mistreatment, Felice interrupted her with a question. "Did she say—or report—anything unusual today, Soukie?"

"Noooo, Mademoiselle. I don't think so. Why?"

"It's Saint Agatha's Day," Felice said into Soukie's ear. "*Very* significant. I can't say any more," she added, when Soukie's eyes widened. "But pray for her," she whispered, leaving.

That night Felice read, by the light of a candle blessed during the Feast of the Purification, the stories of Saint Agatha and several other virgin martyrs. When Sister Mary Owen frowned into her cubicle and demanded to know why Felice was still awake, the girl replied that she was beginning an intense study of the saints' lives, and that in this she had Mother Superior's approval.

"Oh," the nun said, and backed out as Felice slid to her knees.

On this and several successive nights, Felice followed her reading with prayers, which she directed to Sister Agatha en route to heaven. Sister Agatha's unfair punishment was a cruel but necessary part of her martyrdom, like Saint Agatha's or Saint Catherine's time upon the rack, and would one day be justified. The revelation about Sister Agatha's holy character would most likely be made through her, little Felice Belliveau of Nevette, to whom Our Lady had already appeared once.

Felice daydreamed through classes. She thought about the fourteen-year-old Bernadette, and the little shepherd children of Fatima to whom Our Lady had made a series of appearances only four years ago. She anticipated her daily visit to the tree, imagining classes being over and herself there, lapped in golden light. She once fell into such a profound reverie in arithmetic class that she did not hear Sister Theodota summon her to the board; she was then sustained throughout fifteen minutes of standing in the dunce's corner by fantasies of the miracle to come that afternoon.

But later, when Felice went to her tree and stared into the hollow at Our Lady, willing the face to glow, nothing happened. She knelt and pressed her cheek against the rough bark of the tree. She was able to reproduce, though palely, the picture of Mama at her spinning wheel, and she could remember the melody she had heard here. These she thought of as gifts from Mary, and promises that she would return. After all, other apparitions had occurred at intervals of days, or months.

Nevertheless, she began to worry. Perhaps hers hadn't been a real vision at all, but a trick of the devil. She skipped some of the afternoon pilgrimages to the tree; if she were meant to see an apparition, she would be guided there, she thought. She started to fidget during classes, and to draw grotesque faces in her notebooks.

As the memory of her experience grew fuzzy, Felice became lonely. She made contact with her friends; together, they would help Sister Agatha. "I had—a revelation," she whispered to Celeste, in the privy. "Don't ask me to talk about it. But it concerns Sister Agatha—and we are to form a Sister Agatha Liberation and Protection League."

"Who?"

"You, me, Anne, and Françoise. With me as president."

"You?" Celeste protested. "Why you?"

"Because I was chosen. Listen, Celly, we'll have special codes, won't that be fun? And meet at night. . . ."

"*Late* at night?"

"Oh, yes—and we'll pray and read stories devoted to Sister Agatha, and make plans to help her."

"Maybe we could visit her," Celeste said. "Break down the door, and free her!"

"I'm not too sure the Virgin intends that—it might not work, and we could all be expelled. But it's probably safe just to meet—because if Mother Superior did discover us, what harm could she find in the adulation of saints?"

"Well, all right—but what's this priss-pot Virgin experience you keep talking about?"

"Nothing—I can't tell."

"You can't tell because it didn't happen—and you haven't thought up a good enough story yet."

"Please don't say any more about that, Celly—I shouldn't have spoken—and please come tonight. I need you, especially."

Celeste needed no further persuading, and the other girls were more enthusiastic about the League than Felice could have imagined. Not only were they glad to be reunited, but Sister Agatha's cause appealed to them all. Never before a favorite among the students, the incarcerated Sister Agatha was now enormously popular; the nun's punishment (and, less consciously, her crime) struck empathetic chords in each girl.

"Poor Sister Agatha's being so unfairly treated," Françoise said during the first meeting in Felice's cubicle. "Like *me*—Mother Superior made me stay after class today because she thought I was whispering something bad—but it was just about history! So I had to write, a hundred times, 'Excessive talking darkens the mind.' Wasn't that mean and unfair?"

"Yes!" Anne concurred. "Mother Superior doesn't trust us at all —she wouldn't even let Celeste come spend the night with me last Saturday—she said she didn't want any more of that filthy gossip!" Anne looked all injured innocence.

"I hope Mother Superior doesn't catch us here," Françoise shivered, and looked at the candle's long, tongue-shaped shadow leaping on the wall.

"Sissy," Celeste hissed.

"Ssssh." Felice held up one hand. "There is no need to worry or fight. We'll be divinely protected, like the Christians were in the catacombs. Besides, Mother Superior knows I read the *Lives of the Saints,* and approves it. Sister Mary Owen, too. And remember, this is for Sister Agatha—we are meeting for her." Felice crossed herself; the others did the same. "She's probably a saint—because she's a martyr, and she has the prophetic gift, too. Do any of you remember how when Blanche upset the jelly, Sister Agatha predicted what would happen to her?"

The others looked awed; no, they hadn't.

"*I* noticed, and *I* remembered," Felice said. "And I knew even before then that Sister Agatha was likely to become a saint—even when other people laughed at her," she added, with a glance at Celeste. "That's why I'm president of this League.

"Now," she said, picking up the *Lives of the Saints.* " 'The Life of Saint Agatha of Catania, Virgin and Martyr.' " As Felice recounted

Agatha's resistance first of Aphrodisia, then of Quintianus, the other girls bent forward, their eyes shining. Felice occasionally looked at the ceiling, toward Saint Agatha in her turret; her audience did likewise. The girls clasped hands as Felice told the climax: Saint Agatha's being stripped, lashed, her breasts ripped off with iron hooks, but she revealing throughout a dauntless heart. "She is now living in heaven," Felice whispered, "clad as a bride of Christ, willing to intercede for miserable sinners." There was sniffling about the circle as the girls took out their rosaries and spent several minutes in silent prayer. After they all vowed to keep watch during the day and to meet each night, Felice dismissed the gathering, and the other girls stole away to their separate cubicles.

During the day, Sister Agatha's champions dared exchange whispered confidences under the guise of passing a dish of food or borrowing a book. A representative talked with Soukie each evening to gain news of Sister Agatha's physical and emotional condition. Soukie said that the nun's melancholy had lightened considerably when told of the girls' support, but she was still refusing to eat normally. The League members wrote cheerful notes for Soukie to carry to her, and sent small gifts of handkerchiefs and scapulars. The power of the girls' collective, concentrated preoccupation was such that it began to seep throughout the convent, a subterranean trickle as quietly incessant as ground water.

The girls soon became aware that sympathy for Sister Agatha existed throughout the academy. Some of the other students began to tag along after Felice and Celeste, in attempts to wedge themselves into the group. The League considered several potential new members, but most were voted down for being too prissy, having loose tongues, or—at Celeste's insistence—not yet getting "It." Marie Herbin was invited to join, so that there were now five members of the society that convened nightly in Felice's cubicle.

In addition to the story of Saint Agatha, Felice read aloud the lives of several other saints each evening. Though the girls had heard about most of these martyrs in Mother Superior's history class, their stories underwent such profound transformation in these new circumstances that it seemed—Celeste said it, and the others concurred—they had never really understood these tales of persecution until now. Instead of Mother Superior's monotone and the ordinary light of day, they now had Felice's much more expressive reading style—indeed, she even acted out some of the more dramatic scenes—and the frail candlelight that barely held back the dark, and the damp hands of friends to hold during descriptions of torture.

Felice read to them of Saint Catherine of Siena, who could smell the stench of sin where it lay hid, and whose head, after her death, was carried home in a golden bag of pure silk; of Saint Macarius, who, after thoughtlessly killing a gnat that could have been used for the mortification of his flesh, spent six months in the marsh, his body exposed to gigantic flies that pierced even the skins of boars, and returned so disfigured that he was known only by the sound of his voice; of Saint Pelagia, Virgin Martyr, who threw herself from the top of a building when pursued by filthy-minded men, and though she died, it was not the mortal sin of suicide, according to the author, for one "might lawfully expose her life to some danger for the preservation of her chastity."

When Felice read of Saint Agnes, who used a stone for a pillow, subsisted on bread and water, and died at thirteen for refusing to part with her virginity, she could not conceal her emotion. "Just our age," she concluded, her voice breaking, and when she crossed herself fervently, the others followed suit.

Felice wept when reading of Saint Cecilia, who converted her husband both to a *mariage blanc* and to Catholicism, and who lived two days and three nights after a would-be seducer slashed her neck. The virgin's body remained unputrefied after death, Felice read, because of "the whiteness of her purity, the freshness of her conscience, and the sweet odor of her good renown."

Another emotional chapter concerned Saint Thérèse, who lost her mother at age twelve, had visions in which she saw her mother in heaven, and was sometimes rapturously lifted into the air. Felice read all the parts about Saint Thérèse's struggles against the material and sensual pleasures of this world with great feeling, but skipped over the paragraph about the saint's being afraid her visions and voices were tricks of the devil.

Françoise liked to hear about Saint Opportuna, virgin and abbess of Montreuil, whose right arm and rib now rest in Paris, the great part of her head at Moussey, her left arm and part of her skull at Alménêches, and one jaw-bone at L'Isle-Adam.

Anne often requested the story about the triple saints Speusippus, Eleusippus, and Meleusippus for the sounds of their names. Celeste was partial to Saint Arcadius, who was, she observed, just the opposite of the tongueless man; when tortured for being a professed Christian, his head was not cut off immediately, but his fingers, arms, shoulders, toes, feet, legs, and thighs were severed—everything but the tongue, which kept saying "Lord, teach me wisdom," and, to his bloody parts, "Happy members, now dear to me, as you at last truly belong to God, being all made a sacrifice to him."

Saint Syncletica, the beautiful virgin who went into a retreat like her blind sister and whose mouth and jaw were eventually eaten away by cancer, wrote movingly on spiritual subjects. One of these passages Felice liked to read aloud on stormy nights, when the noise of the surf rose up to them, and she copied it out and kept it propped on her bureau: "A ship sometimes passes safe through hurricanes and tempests, yet, if the pilot, even in a great calm, has not a great care of it, a single wave, raised by a sudden gust, may sink her. It does not signify if the enemy clambers in by the window, or whether all at once he shakes the foundation, or if at last he destroys the house. In this life we sail, as it were, in an unknown sea. We meet with rocks, shelves, and sands; sometimes we are becalmed, and at other times we find ourselves tossed and buffeted by a storm. Thus we are never secure, never out of danger; and, if we fall asleep, are sure to perish."

13

ONE NIGHT DURING THE SECOND WEEK OF THESE GATHERINGS, just after Felice had finished reading what was always the evening's final, climactic story, "the very sad, very true life of Saint Agatha, Virgin Martyr," Celeste said they must do something more for Sister Agatha. Reading wasn't enough, she declared.

Felice proposed that they establish a white fast for Sister Agatha, with one girl following her rosary-inspired diet each day. By rotating the duty they would avoid notice, Felice said, and thus intensify the holiness of the act.

This seemed to placate Celeste for a few days.

Then Françoise called an impromptu meeting at recess to accuse Celeste of cheating. She had just discovered a private tin of food under that girl's dresser, she said.

"Fasting was a stupid idea anyway," Celeste said. "It can't help Sister Agatha."

"It certainly can," Felice said. "It could convince the Virgin to intercede." She vowed to herself that she would abstain from all food, beginning immediately, to prove it.

That night, at the League's regular meeting, Celeste interrupted a story about Saint Agnes. "Let's try to visit Sister Agatha—maybe we could get the key from Soukie. It would cheer Sister up more than anything to see us."

Françoise, Anne, and Marie nodded, but dubiously, and looked to Felice.

"It's a stupid idea," Felice said. "Dangerous. It might get us all expelled."

"We could be martyrs, then," Celeste said, "along with Sister Agatha."

"You don't mean that, Celeste," Felice said. "Besides, if any of us are going to be martyrs we don't want to be *that* kind—a *small* kind —just by being expelled. Do we?"

"No!" Marie, Anne, and Françoise chorused.

Celeste frowned. "What kind, then?"

Felice closed her eyes and raised her arms. "We must emulate the saints," she whispered, thinking of the willow tree and her apparition.

"Walk naked before Monsieur?" Celeste giggled. "Cut off our breasts?"

Felice shuddered and dropped her arms. "Stupid! Of course not. You are totally . . ." She glared at Celeste, trying to think of the worst possible word. "Unspiritual." Then Felice crossed herself, and after a silent prayer to Our Lady of the Willow, said, "We must be patient, and wait. Then a miracle will be revealed. By the Virgin Mary, I think."

But the next afternoon, when Felice made her pilgrimage to the willow tree after a day-long fast, she was thinking more of Monsieur than of the Virgin.

A light sleet was falling, making the crust of snow slippery to walk upon. The sky was dark for midafternoon, and there was no one else in sight as Felice gingerly picked her way across the ground. Every few steps she looked behind her, and once—certain she heard steps —whirled around and nearly fell. In the orchard she went faster, holding to steadying limbs. What if Monsieur were to surprise her here, in this thicket of branches?

She hurried to the safety of the tree; Mary would protect her. But when she looked into the ice-rimmed hollow, the face of Our Lady seemed dark, thin. The eyes looked away and down, offering no solace. All about were lonely sounds: sleet stinging the branches, balsams creaking in the wind. Felice put her arms about the willow and squeezed tight, yearning to hear the chiming melody. And then she heard it, clear and delicate as the Angelus. She stood back, swaying with a revelation. Mary had given her this wordless music to take to Monsieur: it would captivate him, shield her, and work a miracle. A miracle celebrating the power of holy virginity, a miracle in honor of Sister Agatha.

Felice went directly to Mother Superior's office. "Ma Mère," she announced, standing before her desk, "the Virgin wants me to assist in the conversion of Monsieur."

"What do you mean, child?"

"I cannot say exactly—some private experience I am not to speak of. By the way, Ma Mère . . ." Felice looked soulfully at the nun. "That is why I may have seemed inattentive in class—worrying, waiting. But now I know I am to take music to him, to Monsieur— to Monsieur Francis," she said, emphasizing Mother Superior's preferred name for the man.

Mother Superior acknowledged this show of support with a brief smile. "What is it you have in mind, exactly?"

"Sacred music—I could play it on the piano for him."

"Moving the piano doesn't sound very practical, dear, and of course he cannot walk to the parlor."

"I could hum to him, or sing. 'Ave Maris Stella,'" she added, naming Mother Superior's favorite song, "and other hymns and anthems." She paused, thinking of her own music, and decided against mentioning it. "Even if he didn't understand the words, the melodies might affect him greatly—since they sound like what the words *mean*. Don't you agree, Ma Mère?" Felice's voice crescendoed as she spoke; she leaned forward, gripping the desk.

Mother Superior rose and came to stand beside her. "I can't see that vocal music would do any harm," she said, placing a calming hand on the girl's shoulder. "Permission is granted."

"Thank you, Ma Mère." She could not curtsy or turn to go, as the nun held to her arm. Felice returned Mother Superior's gaze, subtly adjusting her expression to match—deeply serious, with a hint of a smile.

"You are becoming very steady, very intense," Mother Superior finally said. "I think you really may have, after all, a vocation."

"Thank you, Ma Mère." Felice managed to withdraw from the room sedately, but once in the hall could not restrain herself from skipping. She went to the kitchen, where she wolfed down a slab of bread smeared with butter, and then walked down the hall that led to the infirmary.

She opened the door to the sickroom, which was warm and humid from the tub of bathwater heating atop the stove. "I am to join you," Felice called through the steam, and Evangeline, who was sponging the invalid's brow, jerked up her head, her eyes as startled, as wild, as those of a doe surprised in the depths of the forest.

That evening Felice went to the parlor, thinking she might try out her melody on the piano. Sister Claire was in one corner reading a newspaper; Sisters Constance and Mary Owen sat on the sofa just behind the piano bench, skeining wool.

Felice looked up and down the silent keys that held her secret. She touched, very softly, one chord: that wasn't quite it. Yet she could hear the music even now, very distinctly, in her head. This must mean, she thought, that the melody was only for the tongueless man's ears. She would hum it to him when they were alone; for the times Evangeline was in the infirmary with her, she had best have other pieces to sing. She shuffled through sheet music in the bench and found "Ave Maris Stella" and several anthems. Using the piano top, she knocked the sheets into a neat stack; none of the three sisters, absorbed in words or wool, made an inquiry, or even looked up, as Felice departed.

Armed with sheet music, Felice went to the infirmary the next afternoon. The convent was even emptier than was usual for a Saturday. In preparation for Lent, all the sisters—but Sister Mary Faith, abed with a cold, and of course Sister Agatha, still confined—had gone to the Abbé's house in the village to prepare his ecclesiastical and personal linens. Most of the girls had gone home for the day. Anne had asked for and received Mother Superior's permission to invite Felice to her house. Even though flattered by the nun's confidence in her in allowing the visit, Felice had refused the invitation, saying she needed to study and to meditate. When Celeste sneered, "Well, Saint Prissandra!" Felice had consoled herself by thinking of the surprise she would have when they all returned.

Felice had not slept well the previous night, for imagining this day's event and later conversions and miracles. Sleepiness gave her a giddy sense of unreality; her own knock upon the door and Evangeline's "Yes?" might have been sounds in a story she was reading.

She entered, blinking, as onto a brightly lit stage, and smiled in Evangeline's direction. "I have come to sing," she said. "Did Mother Superior tell you?" She did not look at Monsieur.

Evangeline, measuring out tonic in a glass, nodded to a chair by the wall. Felice backed up to it and sat down. Staring at the window, which framed a bleak sky and frozen orchard, she listened to, but did not watch, the dispensing of medicine. She felt that Monsieur's eyes were constantly upon her, even as he was choking down the tonic. It seemed that he preferred her looks to Evangeline's; this thought made breathing difficult.

She watched Evangeline as she moved about the room, dusting and straightening. Felice wondered what Mother Superior had told her of Felice's present mission and her vocation. The novice's face was, as usual, closed, giving no hint of her emotion. Perhaps she was jealous.

Evangeline walked near the invalid to straighten his covers; Felice let her eyes unfocus.

"Well—do you want to sing now? I'm going to get him another blanket."

Felice nodded, looking straight ahead, seeing only the blur of shaken-out covers, and then of Evangeline's form in motion. She reminded herself how pleased Mother Superior would be with her, and Sister Agatha, too; she would send a note about this visit to the turret via Soukie.

There was a sound from the direction of the bed. Felice hummed one note, then tried frantically to recall her melody. But her mind was blurred too, like the surface of wind-agitated water. She stared down at the top sheet of music in her lap. The notes looked wobbly and odd.

There was another noise, and she looked up. Monsieur was walking.

With slow, purposeful steps, he walked to the end of the opposite flank of the bed and rounded the corner. His long fingers slid over the bedstead as he advanced.

Felice pressed back, scraping her chair against the wall, as he hesitated and seemed to lean toward her.

She stood, her legs gelid beneath her, and turned to look at Sister Agatha's painting of the Virgin ascending. *"Kesalt Sasus!"* she shouted. Her intonation made the words sound like a command rather than a question, and the authority in her own voice reassured her. *"Kesalt Sasus?"* she said again, in a more musical voice. *"Kesalt Sasus?"* she sang, this time to his back.

For he was going out, leaving her behind, and just as her melody was ebbing back.

Felice walked to the door and stood dazed, watching his progress down the hall. Below his nightshirt were dark ankles and the steady flash of white soles. It had been a narrow escape, she told herself. She touched her forehead, then her chest, beginning a sign of the cross in thanksgiving. Her forearm touched her breast and remained there. Divine intervention, she thought; and in honor of her courage and purity.

Halfway down the hall, Evangeline emerged from the linen closet, flung down the blanket she was carrying, and sprinted after Monsieur. When he moved out of sight, Felice began to run too. As she neared the end of the corridor, she heard a male voice cry, *"Mon Dieu!"*

Sheet music pressed to her heart, Felice peered around the corner, expecting to witness Monsieur suddenly struck with speech, kneeling in a shaft of light. Instead she saw, on the far side of the dining-room entrance, three men holding paintbrushes, standing open-mouthed as the tongueless man moved toward them. Felice stared, trying to organize the scene into comprehension; this was stranger than dream.

She recognized the three men as villagers. One was Antoine Gentil, and another his half-wit cousin. Monsieur, his arms extended like a sleepwalker's, circled the men; the half-wit turned with him, holding up a dripping paintbrush as though it were a demon-exorcising crucifix.

Felice tiptoed forward to stand with Evangeline. The novice was gazing reverently at the action, as at the ritualized movements of a mass.

"Evangeline," Felice whispered, "what . . . ?"

"He is saving the painting," Evangeline said in a hallowed voice. "I had thought he was just following me—but look—Sister Agatha's painting."

Felice looked to the wall beside the men, at the fresco of Saint Thérèse and the ant. The saint's torso had been obliterated; one arm reached out from a jagged line of whitewash.

"The Abbé must have hired them," Evangeline added, "while Mother Superior was away."

Felice gaped at Monsieur. Certainly he did look like a wrathful, but holy, agent as he recircled the men. Antoine Gentil's cousin apparently thought so: as Monsieur paused before him, the moron yelped and dropped his brush, which fell into the bucket and was swallowed up by paint. Monsieur turned and drifted back up the hall toward Felice and Evangeline. As he passed he looked directly at Felice and smiled. Tingling from the smile, Felice followed Monsieur a few steps and then stopped. Leaning against the wall for support, she watched giddily as Evangeline herded her patient back to the infirmary.

In Felice's first recounting of the Great Walk, she included the moment when the tongueless man had smiled at her. His expression had been profound, she told Celeste and Francoise the next afternoon, even mystical. She had tingled with a sudden awareness of Mystery, and its paradoxes: God could even use an evil force, if He so chose, to do good.

"Wasn't Monsieur converted?" Françoise asked.

Felice hadn't considered that; she had forgotten until now her original mission of conversion. "It's too soon to tell for certain," she said. "Maybe he was. But, anyway, I had a very important part in the miracle—or miracles—and God let me know that through Monsieur's smile. It was like a translation—a *mysterious* translation—of God thanking me for my action."

"Huh? What action?" Celeste asked.

"Singing to him—confronting him so bravely."

Because Celeste and Françoise jeered at this—though enviously, she judged—Felice omitted the smile and her explanation of it from her next telling of the tale. But no one in her audience—which included Soukie and all members of the Sister Agatha Liberation and Protection League—could deny that she had predicted a miracle.

Soukie took news of the painting's salvation and Felice's omniscience to the nun that very evening. She reported Sister Agatha much enlivened by the wondrous event. "But do pray, Mademoiselles, that this will encourage her to eat—she's as thin as a bird's leg."

By the end of the next week, details of the Great Walk were known and marveled over in the village and beyond. Soukie characterized the tongueless man as a figure of supernatural importance, and she herself, like the little orphan girl Felice Belliveau, prematurely aware of his true character. Even Antoine Gentil and his compatriots, Soukie reported back to the League, were convinced of Monsieur's otherworldliness, and the Abbé would not be able to enlist their support again (though Soukie doubted that the priest would dare attempt another whitewashing, given Mother Superior's wrath over what the nun termed "Abbé Sosonier's craven act"). Mother Superior, already concerned about Sister Agatha's self-imposed diet, was more sympathetically disposed than ever toward the enfeebled nun, Soukie said.

Soukie's description of the attack upon the paintings, and their miraculous salvation, recast Sister Agatha's public image. She began to be thought of in the village as a much-abused, sainted visionary. A few townspeople even came to the convent to request a viewing of the Holy Frescoes.

The sight of outsiders in the hall, standing in awe before the partly reprieved Saint Thérèse, intensified Felice's pride about her catalytic role in the Great Walk. Though she hadn't sung the holy melody, she had embodied it; as shown in all the stories of virgin martyrs, purity of intention was the invincible weapon.

AT SATURDAY LUNCHEON EXACTLY ONE WEEK AFTER THE GREAT
Walk, Felice entered the dining room to find that Sister Agatha's
place had been restored to the table. "Another miracle," she whispered to Celeste, and nodded toward the black dishes as they sat
down. Other diners, too, eyed the dark pottery cup and plate, which
stood out against the white cloth with an accusatory poignance, and
the empty chair that had been returned to the circle. Soukie, bringing
in the platters of halibut, winked at Felice as she put the food on the
table.

The diners sat looking at the fish ringed with rosettes of potatoes.
Finally the Abbé said grace and then Mother Superior raised her fork,
setting the meal in motion. Evangeline, seated by the woodstove,
commenced her reading from Saint Thomas Aquinas, but kept one
eye on the door.

Pretending to eat, Felice listened to Evangeline. When the novice
broke off in midsentence, Felice spun around and saw Sister Agatha
poised on the threshold. The nun's fingers were entwined with her
amber beads, and there was a demure smile of triumph on her lips.

Felice rose halfway from her seat as Sister Agatha made her way
across the room, walking slowly, victoriously, head held high. The
silence was profound. Celeste and Felice rushed to pull out Sister
Agatha's chair; Felice won. The nun slid into place, and Felice returned to her chair.

Sister Agatha did not begin to eat at once, but sat smiling about her.
Then she inclined her head toward Felice. "Good afternoon, Felicia,"
she said, her voice ringing distinctly throughout the dining hall. "I do
hope you are well."

"Yes, Sister," Felice said. She carefully avoided looking at Celeste, who stared at her as if it were her fault, and not Sister Agatha's, that she had not been included in the public greeting.

"We are observing silence, please, Sister," Sister Theodota said in a tinny voice. "But do allow me to observe that you are certainly looking well, Sister Agatha. Well and rested."

She looked, in fact, quite gaunt, Felice thought. The folds of her lower face hung in papery wattles, and her skin was an unearthly shade of white, like the pages of a new missal.

"I have been much too busy for idle resting. Praying for *you,* Sister." Sister Agatha gripped the black plate with her left hand; the fork, in her right hand, descended and brought up a dot of potato. "And I have been fasting as well. Water, three mouthfuls of bread, and the juice of masticated apples—this has been my daily portion."

Sister Theodota made a disgusted noise deep in her throat.

"Like Saint Catherine of Siena!" Felice exclaimed, and then clapped a hand over her mouth. "Sorry, Sister," she mumbled to Sister Theodota.

"Correct, child," Sister Agatha said. "In my case, abstinence was a mortal necessity, but no matter—'twas credit accrued all the same." She took a morsel of fish, chewed ruminatively, and spat into her napkin. "Tastes a bit off to me," she pronounced, and scraped the fish to one side of her plate.

Looks were exchanged, but no words. At a nod from Sister Claire, Evangeline resumed her euphonious reading. No one else spoke until Soukie brought bread around.

Sister Agatha reached into the basket, felt a roll, and said, "I mean no offense, young woman, but no thank you." Holding her hand out over the floor, she snapped the crumbs from her fingers.

"Let me remind you once again that we are preserving silence at meals," Sister Theodota said. "It is part of our general effort to remove certain—blots."

Sister Agatha returned to her half-consumed potato rosette. "It's very hard to poison potatoes, I'm told," she said, speaking louder than before.

At this, Sister Theodota looked to the head table for witnesses. The Abbé had fixed upon Sister Agatha an exaggerated, dutiful frown, like that of a parent attempting to communicate the limit of his patience. Mother Superior, however, was ostentatiously preoccupied with the business of eating.

Sister Theodota turned back around and, crossing her arms on her chest, aimed at Sister Agatha a more lethal version of the Abbé's expression. Everyone else at the table but Felice looked away, or down; Sister Theodota's eyes flicked toward Felice, who, in a reflex developed during long hours of group prayer, glanced down just in time.

For the remainder of the meal, Sister Agatha attended to her food, but she ate with such small sips and bites, with pauses in between for assessment of flavor, that she was the last to finish. The others at her table waited—some more patiently than others—during her cycle of chewing, reflecting, and chewing. Finally she swallowed the last particle of potato and patted her lips with a folded napkin.

Sister Agatha bowed her head. "Dear Lord, we pray that the divine disrelish practiced by a faithful few of us may purge our conventical body of venom."

Sister Theodota noisily crossed knife and fork on her plate. She and several other sisters stood, just before Mother Superior managed to ring the bell of dismissal.

"My bridegroom," Sister Agatha said, raising her voice against the clamor, "my bridegroom thanks each of you who has joined me in holy fasting. Mademoiselle Belliveau, will you assist me to my cell?"

The room was quiet while Felice, blushing, walked around the table. As Sister Agatha rose unsteadily in the girl's grasp, Sister Theodota said, "Careful, Sister. What if you were to lose your balance on the stairs?"

"Here is a husky lass," Sister Agatha said, reaching out for Soukie, who had come to clear the table. "I'll put her to starboard."

Felice and Soukie steered the nun across the floor. The way was crowded with spectators, including Celeste, who glowered, and Anne, Françoise, and Marie, each of whom looked more hurt than angry. To the latter three, Felice gave apologetic smiles.

Sister Agatha halted before the door to declare, "As Saint Catherine says, the very *going* to heaven is heaven." Then she squeezed

Felice's elbow, as though the two of them together had executed this parting shot.

The trio paced slowly down the hall and up the first steps. Sister Agatha ascended like a child, placing one foot squarely on a step, then bringing the other foot next to it before attempting another step. "There you go, Sister, there you go," Soukie said encouragingly as each step was mastered.

Sister Agatha was silent, absorbed in the work of climbing. Felice, overwhelmed by being in the nun's physical presence after so many weeks of imagining her, could not think of any appropriate topics of conversation.

They reached the landing and were nearing the top of the flight when Soukie suddenly turned and blurted, "I think we have a harder time of it, Sister, don't you, being English?" In the heat of her remark, Soukie loosened her grip, and Sister Agatha swayed backward. Felice pulled forward, and they all stumbled up the last few steps.

They went down the hall past the fresco of Saint Agatha's martyrdom. "Such a beautiful picture, Sister," Soukie said. "And the miracle about your other picture—I knew all along. I expect it was because I was born with a caul, don't you, Sister?"

"I knew too," Felice muttered.

"Oh, yes," Soukie said, swinging her head forward to beam at Felice. "Mademoiselle Felice, she knew everything. And all of Digby County knows about the whole affair now—I have made that my business, Sister."

Neither Felice nor Sister Agatha, who was still wheezing from the climb, responded. At the door to the cell, Felice put an arm all the way about Sister Agatha, pried Soukie's fingers from the nun's right arm and guided her inside. "Thank you, Soukie," Felice said in a tone she had heard her grandmother use. "Sister Agatha needs to rest now —as you can see, she is quite tired." Pouting, Soukie backed away and stamped down the hall.

Felice helped Sister Agatha to her bed, but when she tried to ease her down, the nun resisted. "No!" She shook her torso like a petulant child. "Sit!"

Felice stood looking at Sister Agatha slumped at the edge of her bed. "Sister, are you all right? Is there anything . . ."

"Sit!"

"But you *are*, Sister. You are sitting." It was not until the nun fumbled for the straight-backed chair near the bed and pounded its seat that Felice understood that the nun meant for her to sit.

"Yes, Sister." Felice sat. "I'm sorry I misunderstood." She bent her head to get a better look at the nun. Sister Agatha's entire face was alarmingly slack and her lower lip hung loose below her teeth, as though it had come undone. "May I get you something, Sister— water?"

"No—no—just minute," Sister Agatha managed to whisper. "I'll be right in just minute. Then, talk."

"Wouldn't you like to lie . . ."

The nun flapped her head so vehemently that her bonnet slipped sideways, laying bare a patch of bony skull lightly sprigged with gray. Sister Agatha bent forward to peer into Felice's face. Her eyes, enlarged by the thick lenses of her spectacles, made Felice think of the bits of fern and insects trapped in the nun's amber beads. "I'm so glad you're back, Sister," she said, uneasily shifting her gaze to the painting above the bed. Dark-haired and lithe, Adam and Eve looked back at her from their leafy Eden. Their hands nearly touched, the fingers separated by one exquisite inch. Above their still-innocent heads was the red globe of the apple, proffered from the snake's jaws like a gift.

Sister Agatha had leaned so close that Felice could smell the sourness of her breath, and the girl drew back slightly.

"Weeds!" Sister Agatha cried, in English. " 'Long live the weeds and the wilderness yet!' "

"Sister?"

"Gerard Hopkins," Sister Agatha said, resettling her headdress with palsied fingers. "*Saint* Gerard, I should say. He finds this place a hothouse of festering lilies, Felicia. No room for weeds. Weeds yanked up by the roots, kicked aside, trampled, *spat upon!*" After this outburst, Sister Agatha's face crumpled. She seemed about to cry.

"Sister—Sister—we, the League, really *care*. Soukie told you, didn't she, about how we met and prayed every night?"

"Yes, child, it was a great consolation." Sister Agatha fumbled for Felice's hands; the girl took both the nun's hands and squeezed them.

"And especially me, Sister. It was my idea to do that. And there were miraculous visions and sounds, Sister. . . ."

"Likewise, in my prison. Felicia, my child, I have learned much. Saint Gerard came to me, and the Subtle Doctor, Duns Scotus. We sat at a small table and conversed. My bridegroom"—here Sister Agatha smiled, and patted her veil—"my bridegroom was not the least envious—in fact, he sent them to me."

Felice sighed, impatient to continue with the description of her vision.

"Don't you wish to hear?"

"Oh, yes, Sister."

"Only you shall I tell, child, so attend closely. Saint Gerard and the Doctor nourished me with words, so that I need not eat—they thus showed me two paths to freedom."

"I fasted too, Sister, for you. Did Soukie tell you?"

"Yes, child. That helped greatly. Now, listen to my revelation, dearest child." Sister Agatha leaned forward again, and whispered, "God is the dappler, and the dappled! Do you comprehend?"

"I'm—I'm not sure, Sister. Not really."

"Do you want to see God, Felicia?" Sister Agatha rose unsteadily, holding to the iron bedframe. "Go look upon a fish, its rose-mole all in stipple! Look upon a mottled stone! Let the thrush song rinse and wring your ear!" The nun fell back to the bed. "All these are dappled," she went on in a voice exhausted by shouting. "All woven of light and shadow, God's chiaroscuro. And I am dappled, Felicia, and thee. We are not innocents, nor white devils, child—Beware the white savages, Felicia." Sister Agatha shook a finger at the girl. "We must employ cunning against them, as I have lately learned, and done. . . . But you are silent, child, why?"

"Our Lady appeared to me on Saint Agatha's Day!" Felice burst out. "Did you sense that?"

"Perhaps, dear, but you describe it." The nun smiled and closed her eyes.

"I went to see your frescoes in the outer chapel—guided there, I think."

"Mmmmm. Yes."

"Then I went to the willows by the wall—the willow where you put the painting of Our Lady—do you remember?"

"Very well indeed."

"The painting—your painting—blazed with light. Oh, I forgot—your window blazed first."

Sister Agatha crossed herself. *"Deo gratias."*

"And there was music—I cannot describe how wonderful it was."

"No, you cannot."

"Do you think she was really—*there,* Sister?"

"In the eye, or in the air—'tis the same, the work of God. Now, let us give thanks for these gifts to us, Felicia." The nun carefully pressed her fingers together two by two. *"Pater noster,"* she began, *"qui es in caelis . . ."*

Felice joined in, though reluctantly at first, frustrated by being interrupted once again.

At the end of the prayers, Sister Agatha opened her eyes, looking quite refreshed, as from a long nap. "My bridegroom," she said in explanation, when Felice remarked on the improvement. "My bridegroom gives me these transfusions of his love. Do you understand?"

"Yes, Sister. . . . What do you think about my experience? I haven't told Mother Superior about it in detail, but *she* can sense something —she said I have a vocation."

"I think you are a weed. A *rare* weed," she added when Felice did not respond. "An exotic, flowering weed!"

"What do you think about its being Saint Agatha's Day, and Our Lady appearing to *me*—don't you think that we have . . ." As Felice's voice was beginning to quaver, she stopped speaking and took a deep breath. "You know about the Great Walk, don't you, and how I not only knew about it, but had another part—a *courageous* part . . ."

"Child, child. You feel unknown. But I have ever been aware that we are of the same species. Species *and* family."

"Really?"

"Yes. Our father is the Subtle Doctor, the great Duns Scotus, that weed in the prim theological patch. Now. Child. I have something for you."

Pushing her feet against the floor and propelling her body along in little hops, Sister Agatha worked her way up to the head of the bed. Her hand fumbled beneath the mattress and she brought out a small flat box. She edged her way back down the rim of the bed and gave the box to Felice.

"You may inspect it," she said.

Felice unhooked the latch and opened the box so that it lay flat. An oval painting no more than two by three inches was set into the right side of the box. It was a dark-haired woman in a scarlet dress, seated on furs and holding an infant. A tomahawk hung suspended in the air above her head, angels hovered at her shoulders, and she wore a crown of thorns. At her feet were segments of a varicolored snake. The woman's heel rested squarely on the serpent's head.

"It is Catherine," Sister Agatha said. "Saint Catherine, my great-great-grandmother, so cruelly used by the Indians."

"Oh," Felice said, admiring the delicate brushstrokes of the hair-line. "She is beautiful."

"Yes, she was." A few tears leaked from Sister Agatha's eyes and were lost in the creases of her face.

Felice reached out and awkwardly patted her hand.

Sister Agatha blotted her cheeks against her shoulders. "Forgive me, dear child. Now," she said, going on more cheerfully, "I painted this portrait of Saint Catherine myself, many years ago, before you were born. And now it is for you—your legacy."

"For me? Oh, Sister . . ."

"Conceal it well. Nothing is safe."

Felice snapped the painting shut. "Yes, Sister."

"Put it in your bosom," the nun whispered.

"My . . . ?"

Sister Agatha's fingers reached toward her, and Felice hurriedly unbuttoned her blouse before the nun could help her, stuffed the painting beneath her chemise, and rebuttoned herself again.

"Good," Sister Agatha said, her fingers opening and closing on air. "Now, do you know where to keep it?" She spoke with the same anticipatory lilt that had in the past characterized such standard oral examination questions as, Now, who is the superior poet, Alexander Pope or Andrew Marvell?

Felice knew the answer. "In the willow," she said brightly, "the hollow below the painting."

"Good, good. Take it there without delay—I wouldn't be at all surprised, child, if Our Lady visits you again this afternoon and gives you her thanks. Now I must rest."

Felice helped Sister Agatha recline and spread a blanket over her. "Would you had known me in my salad days, child, when I made that painting," Sister Agatha whispered. "I was very lovely, you know, and had no need for glasses at all. The curate . . ." Here Sister Agatha closed her eyes and smiled, clearly in reminiscence. Felice waited, but Sister Agatha said no more. The nun touched her tongue about the edges of her mouth, as though to taste the smile still lingering there.

The girl stood and tiptoed toward the door.

"Felicia?"

She looked back. The nun had raised her head and was frowning sternly in her direction.

"Yes, Sister?"

"You will never betray me?"

"Never."

"Do you promise?"

"I promise."

"Then go, dear child," the nun said, turning onto her right side. "I will sleep." And then, quite abruptly, she was snoring.

Felice went to the dormitory to get her cape. She thought of asking Celeste to go with her, but decided against it; this was her secret, hers and Sister Agatha's. She went quickly down the steps, thinking how much more responsible she was than Celeste, even though a year younger. She went through the dining room and out the back door, slamming it behind her.

The Abbé, who was on the back steps regarding the heavens, jumped at the noise. "Who is that?" he said crossly, narrowing his eyes at her, as through the shadows of the confessional. "Now, what if I had slipped and fallen, Mademoiselle?"

"I am sorry, Mon Père," Felice said, dipping an awkward curtsy. She wondered if he could see the outline of the painting beneath her cape.

"You young ladies are all so rambunctious. Well, tell me, Mademoiselle," frowning as though this were a question that might—or might not—redeem her, "do you think it will snow?"

Felice looked up at the white, low sky. "Perhaps, Mon Père."

"Perhaps, eh? Not much of a prognosticator, are you?" But this seemed to have been an adequate response, for he gazed upon her somewhat more indulgently. "By the bye, Mademoiselle," he finally said, "do you remain interested in our poor invalid?"

Felice nodded hesitantly, thinking of Sister Agatha, and braced herself for an interrogation or a lecture. It was not until he had pulled some papers from his sleeve and said, "He has been attempting to communicate—most extraordinary," did Felice realize he was referring not to the nun, but to the tongueless man.

"Maybe about the Great Wa—" Felice stopped herself, suddenly remembering the Abbé's role in that event.

Fortunately the priest seemed not to have heard her. He was smoothing the sheets of paper with the same care he might take in turning the pages of a holy book, his fingertips brushing away invisible motes of dust. He arranged them in an even stack, which he held up for Felice to see. The top page was covered with odd black markings that looked like sticks, some joined and crossed, some solitary lines. "I don't believe it is any sort of Indian hieroglyphic."

"What is it, then?" Felice asked, squinting at the pages held out to her.

"That is the question, Mademoiselle." The Abbé returned the papers to his sleeve. "I am in hopes that the learned Monk Justin in Brittany, a linguist from whom I received the inspiration and strength to come to this land of Acadia as a young man, can answer that very question." He looked up at the sky again. "No, I am sure it is not Indian. I have asked the lad in my charge—sad case, that one—just to confirm, as it were, my own opinion. There are some who are not aware of the breadth of my knowledge. . . . Well, Mademoiselle," he said, looking down, "that's none of your concern, but I did remember your interest in our poor Monsieur Eude."

"Yes, Mon Père, thank you."

The Abbé bowed slightly and headed down the path toward the outer chapel.

Felice walked quickly toward the orchard as a group of nuns emerged from the building on the way to confession. She paused under an apple tree, looking back to see if the sisters had noticed her, but they were already halfway to the chapel, and too intent on the state of their own souls to be concerned with hers.

Felice went on toward the willows. The soles of her shoes felt very thin on the solidly frozen snow, and the cold manacled her ankles, making her shuffle along with the wary stiffness of a novice skater. She felt strangely empty of inspiration, the result, she speculated, either of the Abbé's interruption or the extreme temperature. At the wall she extricated the painting, now warm from her body, and laid it on the icy stone. With numbed fingers she unlatched the box, and stared in at Saint Catherine. The painting was dominated by the brilliance of the dress, a red as clear and shocking as fresh blood. Feeling a bit dazed, like a character in a play who has temporarily forgotten her part and is fumbling for the right gestures, Felice closed the box, turned to the tree, and, crossing herself mechanically, said, "Our Lady of the Willow, pray for us."

Mary's features were muddy and sad. Felice stood waiting for the transformation Sister Agatha had predicted. When she reached in to touch the face, a bit of paint flaked loose; she stared for a moment at the tiny scar she had inflicted on the Madonna's cheek, and then reached inside the secret chamber to the left of the painting and drew out, one by one, her treasures. She laid them—glass, iron, bit of cloth, cobbles—on the wall beside the small painting, arranging and re-arranging them in different groups. She smoothed the brocade, tracing the ornate pattern of the scarlet threads beneath her fingers as though it were Braille.

Felice picked up the cloth and blew on it, and rubbed it against her cheek. She held it against her cape, the red against dark purple, and whispered, looking at the cape's frayed edge against her wrist, "Mama wove this for me." She summoned up the picture of the loom, the firelight, the wooden doll, and herself on the hearth. But Mama was dim. She could not see her face. She closed her eyes, trying to find Mama at her spinning wheel in heaven.

At first there was nothing in her vision but a red blur, from holding her eyes so tightly shut; then she saw a luxuriantly blossoming, snapdragonlike plant, each red flower unique and marvelously detailed.

"You are a rare weed, Felicia." Sister Agatha's words, so puzzling when spoken, now lay upon her like a benediction.

When Felice opened her eyes again, a light snow had begun to fall. She carefully replaced the iron, rocks, and glass in the hollow. With a new sense of certainty about each motion, she wrapped the painting of Saint Catherine in the cloth and gently laid it on top of the other relics. Then she skipped across the grounds to the outer chapel and confession, humming her willow-tree melody, catching snow petals on her tongue.

15

"A FULL STOMACH IS THE SEED PLOT OF LUST," THE ABBÉ TOLD his religion class. He placed a flawless scarlet apple on his desk and stepped back, hands cinched at his waist, to gaze upon it. "As Lent approaches, Mademoiselles," he said in a mournful tone, "I advise you to fast scrupulously, and to quell *all* your appetites. Think upon Eve, with her appetite for forbidden food—and knowledge. And remember Blanche Melanson." The priest raised his head and scanned the rows of students; Felice winced when his eyes met hers. "Remember poor Blanche Melanson in your prayers—may God and the Holy Virgin forgive her."

That same Monday, at luncheon, Sister Agatha demonstrated the Saint Catherine of Siena fasting technique that had sustained her during imprisonment. "Come up for judgment, you miserable sinner!" she suddenly cried, and vomited up a bit of cod tongue that had slipped past the nave of her throat.

Nuns began to notice a decline in student appetites; by Tuesday, most girls' plates were being returned to the kitchen half or even three-quarters full. Mother Superior, disturbed by this trend, blamed the Abbé's pre-Lenten lecture. The Abbé contested, however, that Sister Agatha's behavior at meals had upset the young ladies' delicate digestive systems.

Soukie, who reported to Felice and Celeste on Mother Superior's concern about the girls' universal pallor and the disagreement between the superioress and Abbé, ended by pleading, *"Please* eat, Mademoiselles. Don't you like Soukie's cooking any more?"

The girls reassured Soukie about her cooking, and though they could have enlightened her as to the origins of the fast, did not. For while both incidents Soukie named had contributed in a general way to the current fashion for abstinence, Felice and Celeste felt themselves to be largely responsible for the highly competitive fast in which the entire student body was now engaged.

At a League meeting Sunday night, Felice had boasted that her intensive fasting and general devotion to Sister Agatha had brought about the miracle not only of the Great Walk but of the Great Release.

Celeste challenged her, saying that she had heard Sister Agatha was freed because she had nearly starved to death, and Mother Superior had convinced the Abbé this would look very bad to a visiting bishop. Celeste said she had this information from the Doucette twins, who had been told it by their mama.

The Doucette twins! And what did Celeste mean by talking to *them?* Those big-mouths, those traitors! Celeste had no conscience at all, Felice said, and had never really been serious about the Sister Agatha Liberation and Protection League. Celeste hadn't even been able to keep a tiny little fast for her.

Ha! She certainly had, and could eat less than Felice any day. Celeste then proposed a white fast of thanksgiving for Sister Agatha: they would just *see* who was the holiest.

After Felice and the other League members accepted this challenge, Celeste also extended it to other girls, including, in her description of the fast, jibes about individual piggishness and descriptions of the pew in hell assigned to gluttons.

Though Felice felt she set the pace in abstinence, Antoinette Mouton was the first to faint, during a handkerchief-hemming session on

Thursday. An epidemic of blackouts followed, some genuine, some improvisational.

Felice was often woozy, but she did not actually faint, a strength in which she secretly took pride. For Our Lady of the Willow—whose face glowed back at her from the hollow on Thursday afternoon—was giving her divine sustenance as a reward for her earlier fast, she decided.

By the end of that week, Mother Superior was scurrying about like an anxious brood hen, sponging girls' temples with lavender water, tempting them with mints. She caucused with her closest confederates among the sisterhood and mapped out a battle plan against the fast.

Her first step was to persuade the Abbé to give an addendum to his appetite lecture, urging moderation. For what would the Bishop think when he came at Easter and saw the girls' ghostly faces?—using a line of reasoning, as Mother Superior told Soukie, and Soukie, the girls, already proven to be effective against the Abbé. (See? Celeste jeered to Felice, *See?*)

The superioress' next act was to call together the sisters and announce that mealtime was now exempt from the Grand Silence, as pleasant conversation was an aid to digestion. And she implored the nuns to eat with gusto, or at the very least, temper their pre-Lenten and Lenten fasts, for the sake of the dear children in their collective care.

Sister Agatha, with whom Mother Superior had spoken prior to this meeting, was the most enthusiastic seconder of the superioress' motions. Sister Agatha herself told this to Felice in a private conversation during which she urged the girl to eat more.

"But we have been fasting for you, Sister Agatha," Felice protested. "All the League has, but especially me."

"You need to keep the bloom in your cheeks." Sister Agatha patted the girl's face. "Even the saints can be lovely, you know—think of Saint Catherine."

When Mother Superior made her next move—so improving the menus that even weekday luncheons were feasts—members of the League were among the first to capitulate. Celeste succumbed on the first day of the new cuisine, when partridge, duchess potatoes with cheese, yeast rolls, and apple pie with whipped cream were served. Even Felice sampled a bit of every dish, and by the next day, seduced by the aromas of chicken fricot and poutine à trou filled with cranberries, ate double helpings.

Mother Superior's final ploy in her campaign against gustatory abstinence was the Doucette twins' birthday party. This great event, engineered by Mother Superior, Sister Claire, and Madame Doucette, was to take place on Shrove Tuesday, the last day before the beginning of Lent. The party was to be held at the Doucettes' house in Nevette, Mother Superior announced at a specially called general meeting, and the girls were to have a holiday from classes all that afternoon.

For two days before the event, the convent kitchen was redolent with special treats being baked for the party—raisin cream pies, velvet kisses, and potato candy. Girls helping at the washing-up were allowed samples of the latest delicacy from the oven.

As party clothes were to replace uniforms for the day, the girls were in a dither over what to wear, and neglected their studies in considering the alternatives. Emma and Laura Doucette were going to dress in pink satin and lace. Even Antoinette, usually above such vanities, showed off her ivory-colored chiffon. Felice was ashamed of her only party dress, of blue silk; there were tea stains on the skirt and it was really too small in the shoulders. She thought of asking Françoise if she might borrow her second-best dress, a brown taffeta, but was too proud.

When the afternoon of the party arrived and Felice put on the blue dress, she found that it was even smaller than she had thought, and she considered, for a moment, not going. She didn't really feel all that well, anyway, she told herself, and this would be a good opportunity to visit Our Lady of the Willow in privacy; lately she had been worried that Celeste might try to tag along. But when she heard the other girls talking in the hall and clattering down the stairs, and Celeste stuck her head in to say, "Come *on,* molasses," she changed her mind. Throwing on her cape, she hurried down the stairs after the others.

Although the nuns were not to attend the party—and this was, to the girls, one of the chief features of the affair—four of them escorted the students down the hill. They walked double file, two nuns in front, then the girls, then two nuns bringing up the rear. As they walked, all of them, nuns and girls, sang "Sur le Pont d'Avignon" and then "Frère Jacques," Sister Claire beating time with energetic flourishes of her arm.

The air was brisk, but not as cold as it had been, and the sky was a clear blue. Felice's spirits rose; she was very glad now that she had come. She breathed deeply, inhaling the odors of woodsmoke and salt.

They reached the bottom of the hill and marched singing down the street. A woman sweeping her steps and two men stacking lobster pots called out, "Good afternoon, Sisters." Faces appeared at some windows of the small frame houses. Madame Tareno, the semiretired midwife who enjoyed her reputation as witch and soothsayer, mumbled some incantation as they passed by and spat into her handkerchief.

The procession continued down the street, past the pier that angled in an L out into the bay. There were a few boats at anchor, rocking and creaking in the waves. Slabs of ice knocked against the sides of the boats and the legs of the pier.

They went by the blacksmith's shop, another clump of small houses, and then neared the Doucettes' house, on the bay side of the road. It was a large white two-story house with blue shutters, one of the few in the village that was painted. There was a wide front porch facing the street, where in summer Madame Doucette served raspberry sorbet and invited her guests to remark upon the Model-T Ford, the village's only automobile (which could traverse the roads only a few weeks of the year, in finest weather), and to admire a more common spectacle, the wine-colored hollyhocks in her garden. Now the car was shrouded in protective burlap, and the garden was covered with much-walked-upon snow. At the corner of the house, a boy was chopping wood and tossing sticks up to the porch. As the procession went up the steps, he glanced at them briefly, then returned to his work.

After greeting Madame Doucette at the front door and reminding the girls to be on their best behavior, the nuns left for a round of visits with village housewives. The girls wiped their feet on the mat of fresh-cut spruce branches and went in. Madame Doucette led them down the hall to the large back parlor that looked out over the bay. With woodstove and fireplace ablaze, and the sunlight pouring in through a row of windows, the room was warm and cheerful. There were brightly colored braided and hooked rugs on the floor, which was painted yellow, and fresh white curtains at the windows. In a corner of the room was a table of refreshments, with a large chocolate birthday cake in the center.

The Doucette twins, who had come ahead of the guests, entered, their dresses rustling. They showed off their birthday presents—silver-fox muffs and new pairs of ice skates—while Madame Doucette handed around cookies. Felice sat in a ladder-back chair in the corner, her shoulders sloping forward so that the tightness of her dress wouldn't be so evident. But when Madame Doucette suggested singing, and Felice was called forward to play the piano, she forgot the condition of her dress after the first round.

After the songs, they played button, button. When Françoise won, a button iced with blue sparkles was given to her. "This is it!" she exclaimed. "My touch button." The others squealed and shouted, for after a girl had collected exactly one thousand buttons, the next boy who spoke to her would be her true love.

Refreshments followed—Felice ate three kinds of cake and several cookies and candies—and then a game of hide-and-seek. When Felice was it, she decided she was tired of playing in the house. She tiptoed quietly down the front hall and, after taking up her cape, went out the door. She went around the front porch, where the boy was still cutting wood, and ran across the flat ground and then over a row of small dunes to the shore. She hid behind an overturned dory and waited, shivering, pulling her cape tightly about her.

It was not very long before Celeste found her. "I knew you'd come here," she crowed as she cleared the dunes. She waved to the other girls who were trooping toward the shore.

Celeste declared she was tired of games and suggested that they tell stories. Some of the girls went back to the house, accompanying the

Doucettes, who didn't want their dresses to get dirty. But the others
—not only Felice, Celeste, Anne, Françoise, and Marie, but a few of
the impressionable younger students—pushed over the boat and sat
in it, huddled together for warmth.

Anne told the story of the ship *Marie Celeste,* which had been
found floating in St. Mary's Bay on a summer afternoon some years
before. It was empty, all its crew mysteriously departed. Dinner had
apparently been in progress when the sailors left, for the dishes and
the food—lobster stew, according to Anne, who said her father had
been one of the search party—were found on the table. Anne's theory
was that the ship had been boarded by pirates, and the crew all made
to walk the plank. Françoise wanted to know why the pirates didn't
eat the food. They were too busy, Anne said, with the tortures, and
they left the food as a warning. "I heard," Celeste said, "that there
was *one* survivor—a man whose tongue was cut out as a warning
against double-crossing the pirates. I think," she whispered, "that it
was you-know-who."

"That's just a *story,*" Françoise said. "I know who the tongueless
man *really* is." All the girls leaned closer. It actually happened,
Françoise said, just a few years ago in Saulnierville, where her mother
grew up. A stranger passed through the village one Sunday in June.
He had a foreign appearance, and dark, dark eyes. Her mother had
seen him herself, Françoise said, and it was her mother's closest friend
to whom the man had talked and given the strange pear.

"My mother's friend's mother cut open the pear for her, and guess
what—there was something so very strange inside."

The other girls held their breaths.

"A picture—of a spider," she whispered. "And it was just lucky she
didn't bite it, because if she had she would have been bewitched, or
died. And do you know—that man looks like Monsieur—my Aunt
Febianne said so."

"I've heard that story before," Marie said, "about somebody in
Cape Breton."

"That just shows you how he moves around."

"Yes, but the story I heard happened a hundred years ago. So it
couldn't have been him."

Felice was then asked to tell her story about Monsieur and "Not-

Saint" Evangeline. Though she hesitated, she might have begun the tale had it not been for the appearance of Emma Doucette, who came to invite them in for hot lemonade and cake. "Mama thinks you're being very rude," she said, and then flounced away, holding her pink dress high above the sand. Watching her go, Felice was relieved that Emma had not caught her telling that story, for she was a famous tattletale; it was Emma who had told on Blanche Melanson.

Celeste, who said her legs had gone to sleep, was hopping about the sand. "Wake up, legs, wake up."

The other girls began to jump also, giggling and falling about for the fun of it. Felice had just joined in too, rather half-heartedly, when Celeste suddenly froze. "Look!" she shouted, pointing, "an apparition!"

The others turned their heads. The boy who had been chopping wood by the front steps was now walking straight toward them.

"That's terrible, Celeste," Felice said, reaching to pinch her. "Shut up that kind of talk."

Celeste shook her arm free. "It's an Indian," she whispered. "Françoise, you'd better run—your touch button—what if he spoke to you. . . ."

Françoise shrieked and, gathering her skirts, ran for the house, making a wide circle around the boy. All of the other girls but Felice and Celeste followed. Felice had begun to walk away when Celeste caught her arm. "Would you dare to talk to him?" and, when Felice looked at the house, said, "No, I guess you wouldn't, sissy."

"I would so," Felice said, crossing her arms and putting one foot on the boat. "Why not?"

The two of them stood like statues; the approaching boy, if he looked—and Felice thought he did—would have seen their silhouettes against the bay, the late afternoon light falling softly on their young faces, catching the glints in their hair. The boy cut across the dunes to the left of the girls. He wore a heavy fisherman's sweater and woolen trousers held up with a piece of rope.

"Let's go, Celeste," Felice said as the boy started down the beach.

But Celeste was already running after him and, after a second, Felice followed.

"Hello!" Celeste called.

The boy stopped and turned around so suddenly that Celeste nearly ran into him—an incident that, Felice well knew, Celeste would delight in exaggerating later.

Felice reached them, and the two girls stood looking at the silent boy.

"Well," Celeste said, glancing at Felice and stifling a giggle, "where are you going?"

"To the wharf," he said, looking fixedly at the space between the girls. Everything about him seemed deferential—his bowed head, his posture, his voice—but when he glanced at Felice she saw that his eyes were not shy. Dark brown, nearly black, they seemed to take in, instantly, everything about her. The power of his gaze held her; Felice felt helpless to do anything but look back at him. When he lowered his eyes Felice felt released, and then uneasy, for he seemed to be staring at her chest.

She pulled her cape more tightly about her as Celeste said, in a slightly disdainful tone, "You're an Indian, aren't you?"

He nodded, dropping his neck lower, and looking, Felice noticed with relief, at the sand.

"You live with the Abbé? You're an orphan? You work for Monsieur Doucette, at the shipyard?" The boy nodded after each of Celeste's questions.

"Well, we've heard about you," Celeste said, in a final kind of tone. "Haven't we, Felice?"

"Umm hummm." Felice looked over her shoulder at the Doucettes' house, but she felt anchored to the sand, just as the boy seemed to be.

"Do you have a girl friend?" Celeste asked, with a sly look at Felice.

"I know about Glooscap," Felice said hurriedly. "He lived on Cape Blomidon—my brother told me about him—he has an Indian friend." Felice's voice sounded leaping and foolish to herself.

"Who?" Celeste said.

"Glooscap—the man-god of the Micmacs—he was a very wonderful . . ." The boy's glance flashed up at her, quick and definite as a pirate's sword. "Wonderful . . . man-god," she finished lamely.

The boy was smiling slightly, a friendly, ironic expression.

"Glooscap walked the shore below your convent," he said. "I could show you his footprints. Would you like me to, someday?"

Felice opened her mouth to speak, but no words came out.

"Felice is an orphan too. You two have a lot in common, I think."

"Shut up, Celeste." Felice turned her head so quickly that her braids flew out. One of them grazed the boy's arm. She gathered the braids together and tugged on them like ropes.

Though she meant not to, she glanced up at the boy. He was still looking at her, and his expression seemed to have softened. She felt incapable of moving, or of looking elsewhere, even when Celeste said, "Felice *likes* Indians—she's told me so, many times."

The boy glanced at Celeste—rather haughtily, Felice thought—and then toward the road. "Here come the sisters," he said.

Felice looked beyond the small dunes at the nuns advancing toward the house, their habits billowing like black sails.

Celeste was already running toward the house. "Hurry, Felice," she called back over her shoulder.

Felice half-turned, but his eyes held her back. "My name is Remi," he whispered, and offered his hand. His lips were thick and looked swollen, as though by desire.

"Remi," she repeated, "Remi." She touched his outstretched hand, and fled.

Celeste was waiting at the back door. "Felice has a boyfriend," she said, in a singsong.

"I do *not*. You are ridiculous." But Felice crossed her fingers as she followed Celeste inside the house, already worried about what the others would say, and whether the nuns had seen.

The nuns were entering the house by the front door just as Felice and Celeste went to the back; everyone was too distracted to notice the girls. Felice took a handful of candies from the refreshment table and, sinking into a corner chair, devoured them greedily. She ate without tasting, thinking only of the boy's eyes and the touch of their hands; her entire body tingled. As the party crowded back into the parlor, Felice's excitement began to ebb and was soon replaced by a feeling of shock, as though she had escaped some grave danger. When Mother Superior, cup and plate in hand, came to sit beside her,

Felice's heart began to pound; what if the nun had seen her? And what had there been to see?—for a moment, she could not remember.

Felice thought Mother Superior looked at her closely once or twice over her cake-filled fork. She squirmed, not knowing where to look or what to do. Everyone else in the room seemed to be involved in some definite activity—carrying away plates, talking animatedly about some particular subject—that she did not know how to join.

"Time to go, Mademoiselles," Mother Superior said, rising and brushing at her skirt. Then she bent to whisper, "I'd like to talk with you later, Felice. Please come to my office after dinner."

Numbly, Felice went with the others to the hall, dipped her curtsy to Madame Doucette, and took her place in line. Celeste gave her several significant looks, which she ignored. They were soon on the porch, then on the wooden steps, and, all too soon, the road.

Felice walked slowly, leaving a gap between herself and Marie, who walked ahead, and causing Antoinette, behind, to poke her in a most un-nunlike way and say, "Step up, Felice." There was no singing or talking. Felice studied the carriage of the nuns' heads and shoulders; she thought they looked stern, offended. She could not bear to look toward the shore, where they had seen her. She had stood too near him—from this distance it would have looked even closer than it was —so close that their touch might have seemed a kiss.

"Remember Blanche Melanson," the Abbé had warned. Felice would be dismissed too, for something worse than mere talk. Uncle Adolphe, crumpled telegram in hand, would meet her on the front steps. He would point silently to his study door, ajar at the end of the dark hall. When she tried to run away, she would falter, the floor thin as spring ice beneath her feet.

Felice's hands grew clammy. She looked at the houses, which passed by too quickly; she prayed that time could be stopped here, in front of this cluster of outbuildings, where something was being burned in a pit, or there, in front of the porch being swept by a grandmotherly-faced woman.

They went by the blacksmith's shop, before which stood a knot of men; from their midst came a sudden piercing whistle of admiration, a whistle to which Françoise and Celeste each immediately laid exclusive claim, to judge by the looks that passed between them.

Then they neared the shipyard, where workers paused to watch the procession. One of those male faces, Felice realized with a jolt, was Remi's. She was so amazed—amazed by the way his eyes scanned the line of girls, and found her, and smiled—that she forgot her earlier fear and smiled back, shyly at first, then recklessly. She even turned her head as she passed by, and as she did, saw that Celeste was staring back over her shoulder, her expression a mixture of disbelief and vast amusement. But Felice was much too excited to heed Celeste at the moment, or even the watchful nuns behind her; for she had just seen that the eyes of several men had picked her out from all the girls.

Climbing the hill, Felice was giddy with her discovery. "I am really very pretty, then," she told herself, feeling the tight, cold cheeks of her face with both hands. Her elation lasted throughout the walk to the convent and her attempt at a private prayer session in her cubicle. It was only when she entered the dining room, and felt Mother Superior's eyes upon her, that her excitement turned to nausea.

She stared at her food, thinking she shouldn't have gone to the party at all; she ought to have stayed here with Sister Agatha, who now sat gazing like a clairvoyant into her teacup. Besides her sinful behavior on the beach, Mother Superior had probably seen the way she returned the lustful glances of Remi and the men at the shipyard. She should use this fork, Felice thought, to scrape welts across her face. Instead, she mashed her peas into a flat gray-green field and stabbed at her roast mutton. When she sensed Mother Superior glance her way again, Felice forced herself to take several bites of meat.

Mother Superior received Felice in her office and gravely motioned her to a chair; the girl felt her stomach turn. The nun sat in the chair opposite Felice.

"This afternoon, in the village," Mother Superior began dolefully, "we received some news that affects you."

Felice began to shiver.

"Perhaps you know already," the nun said. "By your expression,

I think it may be so. Your grandmama, Felice—God has called her to Him. You will go to Wolfville on the train tomorrow. Come, child," Mother Superior said, holding open her arms, "come to me, my poor motherless child."

Felice, stiff-legged, fell forward into Mother Superior's lap and, as the nun stroked her head, crooning, "It is God's will, it is God's will," the girl tasted, very urgently, a mixture of chocolate and mutton.

Felice struggled to sit up, but Mother Superior held her more tightly. "My poor dear child," she said.

"No!" Felice said, pushing against Mother Superior, "I must . . ." and before she could disengage herself, she had vomited.

"Oh dear, poor dear," Mother Superior said, holding Felice out from her and looking at the splattered skirt of her habit. Reaching wildly about for a handkerchief, she shifted Felice to one arm, so that the girl lay across her lap, and Felice vomited again.

Mother Superior sat Felice in a chair, with the wastebasket at her feet. "Poor dear, such a shock—use this—towels—I'll get towels," she said, and flew out the door.

In a few moments Soukie appeared with wet towels and a glass of water. She applied a towel to Felice's forehead and, clucking her tongue against her teeth, said, "La, la, Mademoiselle. Too many sweets."

16

AT DAWN THE NEXT MORNING, THE SOOTY CROSS OF ASH WEDNES-day upon her forehead, Felice boarded the train for Wolfville. With her rosary in her pocket, a new missal at her side, and her mind crowded with Mother Superior's last-minute exhortations, Felice felt girded to do battle, like Joan of Arc. For it was the thought of Uncle

Adolphe, and not Grandmama, that brought tears to her eyes as she gazed out the window for one last view of the station. She raised her hand in farewell as the Abbé, his face puckered with concern, made the sign of the cross over her, and the train began to move forward.

She leaned back against the red plush seat as the train gathered steam and the lamps hanging from the ceiling began to swing like pendulums. Mama had said those lamps were like metronomes, and putting one arm around Felice, had rocked her in cadence: "Click, clock, click, clock."

Felice closed her eyes. Do not cry, she commanded. She squeezed her eyes shut until lozenges of light appeared. "Mary, give me strength," she murmured, pressing her rosary against her thigh.

When she looked out the window again the station house was gone and she could see, across the marsh, the first light of morning on the windows of houses and beyond them, the great gray expanse of bay. There was the wharf, reaching out into the vast water like the fragile antenna of an insect, and the Doucettes' house, larger and brighter than the others. The shore where she had met the Indian boy was not visible, but she could imagine it, and herself still there. Her skin prickled as she remembered, and quickly pushed away, the boy's standing so close. The line of houses receded, carrying with it the tainted beach. The village seemed to be pulling away from her, rather than she from it, and holding captive, sealed, like flies in Sister Agatha's amber rosary, a scene she was powerless to undo.

"This may be God's task for you," Mother Superior had said this morning when Felice confessed that she didn't want to go to the funeral in Wolfville, for fear of Uncle Adolphe.

"But he's an alcoholic, Ma Mère, and an atheist, and he—he—beats me."

"There is no better time than bereavement to bring a soul to God —I think you know this from personal experience, Felice? Conversions are milestones in the careers of ecclesiastics, and even in the lives of saints. I will be praying for you hourly, my child." Mother Superior had bent to kiss her cheek, and pressed the new white missal into her hands. "Your uncle may be surprisingly receptive, Felice. Read to him from this. Now, run along and get dressed, dear—I think you will gather strength as you go, and find this a most significant journey."

The train rattled over a bridge; Felice looked out at the frozen river that snaked through the snow-covered marsh to the bay. She thought of the dark water running beneath the glittering epidermis of ice, and of the fish and other creatures living there. Many years ago, it was said, some of the village children had skated on the river, during spring thaw; the ice had cracked and one boy had fallen in. His body had been found at the edge of the bay, so the story went, supported by a chaplet of fish.

The Gaspereau River near Wolfville would be frozen now too. Felice imagined Uncle Adolphe, having refused to say the rosary with her unless she sat in his lap, and enraged at her refusal, chasing her to the high bank above the river. She would look down at the ice, the sheet of it shimmering like heaven, as Uncle Adolphe lunged, his hands spread like octopi. She would float down like a petal. The ice would melt to receive her, and then close again above her head. Later, she would be found on the riverbank, the ground beneath her verdant and mossy, an oval of eternal springtime in the snow. It would be known as the Miracle of the Gaspereau. All the nuns and girls would come for the funeral. The apparition of Our Lady of the Willow would descend and hover above Felice; though She would appear only as brilliant light to everyone but Sister Agatha—who would see the true face—all would understand the significance of the moment.

The conductor had to ask twice for her ticket, for Felice was crying into the plush armrest, in mourning for the lovely young girl outstretched in the coffin. "Mademoiselle?" When he touched her shoulder, Felice started. Through her tears, the man's eyes had a sinister gleam. "I am so sorry, Mademoiselle, but I need your ticket, if you please." She blinked and the face was transformed; distressed gray eyes behind spectacles, and cheeks like blancmange.

She produced the ticket and the conductor punched it, making bowing motions all the while and occasionally touching his hat, as though uncertain whether or not he should remove it. "May I offer my condolences, Mademoiselle? The good priest at Nevette has told me. Is there something I might bring you—broth, a pillow?"

"No, thank you."

"Anything that the Fundy Railway Line can do to be of service. . . . Is this your first train ride, Mademoiselle?"

Felice shook her head. She had been once with Mama, another time with her whole family just before Mama and Papa left for Boston. The train had been crowded on that last trip to Wolfville, and Philippe had had the window seat most of the time. Her tears rose again as she thought of that injustice.

The conductor mumbled something, touched his hat, and moved on, exercising the puncher in midair. Across the aisle a lady in a feathered hat leaned forward, evidently about to speak, her features arranged in a smile.

Felice echoed the expression, wanly, and turned to the window. She pulled her rosary from her pocket and began a decade of Aves, pressing the blue knops tightly between her fingers. She tried to concentrate on the prayers, saying them for Grandmama, but the words seemed to catch in the rhythm of the turning wheels. Felice summoned up a few appropriate tears as the plaintive whistle sounded. "Poor Grandmama," she said softly, lips against rosary, but she could not really imagine her dead. Sick, and very tired, but not dead. She could not imagine heaven either, at the moment, nor anyone in it; she felt too tired.

She stared out at the dense forest of evergreens whizzing past, trying to separate one and then another from the blur until she felt dizzy, and then she closed her eyes. "Remember thou art dust," the Abbé had said, grinding his thumb into the pot of ashes. The chapel had been cold and dark this morning. He had marked Mother Superior, then Sister Claire, with the penitential Lenten cross. Then he had stood above her. His thumb had felt angry against her forehead. "And to dust thou shalt return."

"Ave Maria," Felice began again, rubbing a smooth bead between her fingers, *"benedicta tu in mulieribus . . ."* The words made a steady, lightly drumming sound. She settled herself in the crook of the seat and let the beads fall through her hands, the smooth, cool ovals like

preserved tears or solid drops of rain. The words made a sound like rain, and beneath her, the wheels were musical.

Felice awoke several times, briefly, when the train stopped and the conductor came through, calling "Weymouth," and "Plympton," and "Annapolis." She could hear the thump of valises and the sound of people settling themselves. Once she opened her eyes to find the feather-hatted woman leaning over her; she seemed to be talking about luncheon. Felice was too tired even to shake her head; she turned, holding the pillow that had materialized from somewhere, and reentered her dream; it was a painting, like Sister Agatha's, that she could walk about in.

The conductor roused her a few miles outside Wolfville. "Pardon, Mademoiselle, but I thought you would like to wake up now."

Felice struggled up and looked groggily out the window. They were traveling through apple country, the fertile valley that the Acadians had diked against the Fundy tide. The apple trees were now venerably hunched and knotted; their twisted limbs reminded Felice of sufferers in purgatory. Between orchards there was an unimpeded view, beyond the dip and swell of prairie, of Cape Blomidon. The red cliffs glowed in the last light of afternoon, looking as magical and spirit-inhabited as they were said to be. The far edge of the Cape protruded like an Indian-shaped nose into the frozen Minas Basin. Felice imagined the mouth of the face below ground, the lips thick, slightly parted. Involuntarily, she crossed herself. Uncle Adolphe's head, strangely elongated, swam before her, and she turned, relieved, when the feather-hatted woman said, "Excuse me dear, are you from the convent? Now, don't let me interrupt you if you are saying your prayers."

Felice listened to the woman talk about her earlier temperance work and the spiritual delights of delivering a man from the bondage of King Alcohol as the train gradually slowed. She did not look out at the farmhouses nor at the houses on the edge of the village. She stared at the woman's pupils, remembering how she had sometimes seen a tiny image of herself reflected in Mama's eyes. Around them in the car, people were stirring, reaching for belongings. "Wolfville, Wolfville," the conductor proclaimed. There were loud metallic noises; a window or door was opened; cold air and smoke gusted through the car. "You can't imagine, dear . . . thrilling . . . a man surrounded by his happy family . . ." There was a long squealing sound and the train, after several jerks and shudders, stopped. There was a sudden, thick silence. It sank into Felice's arms and legs and she felt for a moment peculiarly cold, as though she were naked. She glanced down at herself—her clothes seemed normal, though creased. When she looked beyond the woman at the platform outside the window, her fear laid a haze across the people waiting there.

"Are you being met, dear?"

"My uncle." Felice's eyes refocused on the woman. She counted the green plumes: eight. "He drinks."

"Oh, my." The feathers trembled, as in a breeze. "Goodness. Shall I—shall I have a word with him? How long does the train stop here? Porter—Porter—If only my sister weren't expecting me. Poor thing, her husband just died, and she has a swollen foot. . . . Porter . . ."

With what she felt to be an ironic smile, Felice stood up. She brushed at her skirt and gathered her things together while the woman offered phrases of distress and advice.

Felice made her way up the aisle slowly, dallying, the valise bumping against each seat as she went forward, glancing against the shoulder of an elderly gentleman who looked up angrily and rattled his newspaper.

The train steps were very steep. The conductor helped her down and stood holding her elbow as Felice looked about. It was growing dark and a light snow was falling. There was no sign of Uncle Adolphe. Maybe he would not come until everyone had gone, Felice thought, and then they would be all alone here. She began to feel faint.

"Has no one come to meet you? Shall I go inquire?"

"No, I can go alone," Felice said in what sounded to herself a brave voice. She began walking toward the station house crouched at the end of the platform.

"Goodbye, Mademoiselle," the conductor called. "God bless you." His words melted behind her like flakes of snow.

Then Felice saw Philippe. He was loping toward her, grinning his lopsided grin. And he was alone. Felice began to run toward him, her bag banging against her knee. Then she dropped her things and plummeted at her brother. He swung her in a circle and, when he set her down, surveyed her with mock seriousness and said, "Can this *really* be my little sister?" Felice clung to his arm.

They walked past the station house to the wagon. "How are your studies? Are you passing anything?"

"Oh, Philippe, you sound just like Papa." Felice looked up at him; he smiled like Papa, too, and had gotten very much taller than she.

She did not think of Uncle Adolphe again until they reached the wagon and he was not there. "Why hasn't Uncle come?"

Philippe jumped into the wagon, then held out his hand to help Felice scramble up. "He is not very well," Philippe said shortly, and snapped the reins against Blackie's haunches.

Felice felt she should not inquire further. He must be very sick, she thought, perhaps dying.

"How did you get so pretty?" Philippe looked at her again with his new seriocomic expression. "I thought you were always going to be my mean, bratty little sister."

"You were the mean one," Felice protested. "You never once let me go exploring with you."

"Before long you'll be having suitors."

Felice was silent a moment, looking out at the dirty rime of frost at the road's edge. "Mother Superior says I would be a very good nun," she said. "Maybe even a saint."

Philippe laughed—Felice hated him for a second—and then jumped down to lead the horse up the slippery hill.

Felice lifted her face to the light sting of snow. She imagined her uncle lying in bed, hopelessly ill. She would pour a cup of medicine for him; he would blink up at her and say, "An angel?" She would sing the "Ave Maris Stella," and then read from the missal Mother Superior had given her. He would confess before he died, a repentant, humble sinner. Thank you, he would whisper, closing his eyes and reaching to touch Felice's hand. You have saved my immortal soul. As a last rite, Felice would hum the willow-tree melody, with the harmonizing voices of angels in the background. Philippe would stand gaping, astounded.

At the top of the hill Philippe vaulted back into the wagon. They rode a while in silence, both of them looking at the winking and bobbing ears of the horse. "You will be glad to know that Grandmama died peacefully," Philippe said.

Felice sucked in cold air. How terrible she was to have forgotten. She thought of how Grandmama had looked when she said goodbye last fall, her head turned to look at the rain outside, her hands laced across her large, defeated body.

"It was Saturday morning—I was at the library, but Bette was there —Bette said she went peacefully, no pain—Bette has been wonderful. . . ." Philippe sighed. "She's the only one who can handle Uncle."

"Really?" Felice said weakly, looking away. There was Prue's house; she thought of Prue's wax doll, and the strange smell of the parlor.

"He won't come out of his study. No one can go in but Bette—she takes his food in on a tray." Though the street was empty of people, Philippe lowered his voice. "He had Grandmama in there with him all day Sunday—Uncle Edmond and I and Doctor McConnell finally got in at dinnertime and carried her out. It was a struggle."

"He stole her?" Felice saw him, one-hoofed like the devil, long fingers reaching out from the dark cave of his study. The picture was so horrible that she giggled, a sort of sputter.

"What? It's not funny, Felice," Philippe said sternly.

They had reached the house. The chimneys looked like ears against the pale sky. In the yard and in the street it was dark. Philippe helped Felice from the wagon. She staggered; her legs felt frozen. Philippe reached for her bags. "I guess I shouldn't have told you. I thought you were more grown-up than that."

"I *am* grown-up," Felice said, jutting out her chin. "I *am,*" she said to his back, as she followed him up the walk. Ahead, the house gathered like a silent wave. "I got the highest mark—a *très bien,*" she said. "I had—apparitions," but Philippe did not turn around.

The door opened; there was a chorusing of relatives. Aunt Rose pushed through the cousins to her and Felice collapsed against her bosom, which was soft as a feather pillow, and smelled of damp babies.

FELICE WAS SHEPHERDED DOWN THE HALL TO THE KITCHEN. TO Great-Aunt Charlotte, who rasped from the parlor, "Let me see her, let me see Jean's child," Aunt Rose said, "Later, Aunt. The child is tired—she must eat." Aunt Rose settled her at the kitchen table, shooed out the small cousins, and, after giving Bette instructions about next day's funeral dinner, left.

Felice ate a few spoonfuls of tepid stew and nibbled at the bread, which tasted of ashes. Then she sat stirring the spoon in the depths of the bowl, watching the pieces of potato rise and sink.

In the pantry, Bette had begun to whistle. From the direction of the parlor there was a drone of subdued voices and an outburst from a young cousin, quickly stifled. Felice wished Aunt Rose hadn't sent the cousins away; she wasn't the least bit hungry, and there was a terrible stillness all about her.

"Bette," she called. Her voice sounded profanely loud to herself, but Bette apparently did not hear, for the whistling and the clinking of jars continued. "Bette," she said again, this time in a hoarse whisper.

Felice laid down her spoon and, propping her elbows on the table, pressed her hands over her eyes and forehead. "Mother most admirable, virgin most prudent, mystical rose," she murmured. But the silence leaned against her; she could not remember the litany. "Damnation," she said, and then horrified, crossed herself twice. What if Mother Superior had heard that? Mary probably had, and Mama. She was a wicked girl, and should—would—be punished.

"Felice?" Bette looked down quizzically, her arms embracing jars of marmalade. "Are you unwell, duck?"

Felice shook her head. She picked up the spoon and began to eat. "Where is Grandmama?" The steadiness of her voice calmed her.

Bette looked at the ceiling. "In her room," she whispered.

"And Uncle Adolphe—where is he?"

Bette set the jars on the far edge of the table. "In his workroom."

"What is he doing?"

Bette glanced at her sharply. "Now how would I know, *chérie?*"

"Philippe says you're the only one who goes in there." Felice hesitated. "Is he—is he drinking?"

"Duck, I put the tray down and go. I don't stay to chat or look about. No, Mademoiselle. If your brother didn't need a housekeeper . . ."

"How does he look? Sick?"

Bette furrowed her brow and puckered her lips in a pretense of disapproval. Her mouth was red and moist as fruit. "You ask too many questions, child. Now I must go—would you like some pie? It's mincemeat. There's the table to be set, beds to be turned down." She started toward the door just as Aunt Rose entered, carrying a hiccuping baby.

"I was coming to find you, Bette. Let's arrange the table, shall we? Felice, you've never met Moulie, have you?" She passed the red-faced infant before the girl. "Not hungry, dear? Do try to eat a little something."

"I'm fasting," Felice said, but Aunt Rose was already leaving.

Felice pushed away the bowl and replaced it with her missal. She drew the rosary from her pocket and arranged it in a coil on the table. Then she opened her missal. *"Kyrie eleison, Christe eleison,"* she whispered. She turned a few pages; the paper was very thin, nearly transparent, and smelled of the convent. The heading for the funeral mass was printed in Gothic letters, making the words look bristly and dangerous: *"De profundis clamo ad te, Domine,"* she read. Her voice seemed too loud in the silence.

Felice sat quite still, her fingers growing damp on the page. She could hear the muffled clatter of dishes being set out in the next room, and Aunt Rose's mild commands. Beyond, she could just hear—or imagine—a mumble of voices in the parlor. But the clink of china and the voices were tiny sounds, flotsam on a flood of silence. Felice listened so intently to the quiet that it pulsed in her ears. It was in the unlit spaces of the house, the rooms beyond the kitchen and parlor and hall. At the other end of the house, in the shop, the bracelets lay on velvet, in the dark, and the watches ticked nervously above the stillness. Somewhere in the workroom, where the silence lay like a dark fog, hidden among the shadowy forms of chairs and cabinets, was Uncle Adolphe. His secret shallow breathing seemed to come from every corner. Felice pressed her rosary to her forehead. *Pater noster, qui es in caelis . . .* She would not be afraid.

But she could not help thinking of the space above, and the silence there, washing about the massive tester beds and wide-planked wardrobes and chests. She thought of the room where she usually slept, now empty and dark, and Uncle Adolphe's room, and Grandmama's room, where the silence was deepest. Grandmama lay on her bed, and the dark pressed against her eyes and nose and mouth, and against the laced fingers that were beginning to loosen on the sheet. Felice thought of how Sister Syncletica had looked when she lay in her coffin last year, the shadow of hollyhocks across her face like a sentence, the bones of her mouth rising against the flesh. Did Grandmama look like that? Felice thought fiercely of a sunny afternoon in Grandmama's room, and Mama with her, looking at the bureau where the rose-patterned clock stood, and the white china cat that Felice was allowed to touch but not pick up, and the figurines of a dancing shepherd and shepherdess that Papa had brought Grandmama from Paris. But the picture was thin, it faded, and Grandmama was in the dark room, all alone. Filling the room, lapping about Grandmama's bed, rising to the ceiling, was the silence. A dark, terrible silence, like that at the bottom of the ocean.

Felice squeezed the rosary tight. Your parents are not in the ocean, Mother Superior had told her, over and over, last year. They are in heaven. And Grandmama was in heaven too, or on her way to join Grandpapa. Felice arranged the rosary carefully in her hands. She would tell Uncle Adolphe about Grandmama's place in heaven, console him; the consolation would bring him to God.

Suddenly it seemed very easy. She put the rosary in her pocket and briskly arranged a tea tray. She placed her own pot of tea on the tray, and a fresh cup and saucer from the drying rack, and a cut-glass milk pitcher, Grandmama's favorite.

She carried the tray across the room, past the pantry, where a row of cakes stood on the shelf, and into the hall. Bette and Aunt Rose were ascending the spiral stairs above her—she could hear the light click of Bette's heels and her aunt's heavier tread. They had left open the closet door beneath the stairs; Felice had played there when she was a young child.

She looked down the hall in both directions, then scurried across. She knocked on Uncle Adolphe's door before she had time to stop herself. "Tea, Monsieur," she called brightly, just as Bette would have done.

There was silence. Felice tried the door; it was locked. "Tea, Monsieur," she called, less certainly. She did not hear him come. The door was opened suddenly, startling her. She looked down at the cup clattering in its saucer.

"Eh? Felice?" The voice was slurred, tired.

She did not look at him, but marched past, brushing against the limp sleeve of his coat. She carried the tray to the worktable, where the room's only light burned. On the table were scattered tiny silver springs and wheels, like the entrails of a mechanical animal. She put the tray on the edge and pushed, shoving back instruments.

"Watch what you are about, young lady." He was coming toward her. The jeweler's loupe rose from his forehead like a horn.

"Some nice tea, Uncle," she said, pouring with a shaking hand. She pressed against the table to feel the rosary against her thigh. As the cup filled, tea leaves rose to the surface; she chased them with one finger.

Uncle Adolphe leaned across the table and rearranged the instruments, pincers and tweezers of various sizes, and miniature screwdrivers. Felice imagined herself shackled to the wall, Uncle Adolphe choosing a pair of pincers, turning toward her. . . .

"I am very busy," he said irritably.

"Uncle . . ." Felice's voice was reedy.

"Don't cry, child, don't cry." He leaned heavily against the table, staring dully at the field of silver parts. His fingers descended and chose a tiny stem. He held it up to the light.

"Grandmama—it's so sad." Felice touched her rosary. She remembered—too late—the missal. She looked about for signs of drinking. The room was dark, and she could not see beyond the table.

Uncle Adolphe circled the table and sat down. "Just run along now, Felice. Tell them I'll be there shortly." He pulled the loupe over his eye, grimacing as he adjusted it. He pried open a pocket watch and bent to examine its inner workings. Felice could hear the rapid, frightened-sounding tick of it. She shifted from one foot to the other. He seemed to have forgotten her.

"Have you prayed, Uncle?"

The way he looked at her made her feel the question was ridiculous. He snorted and returned to his work. "Go, go." He waved his hand at her.

Felice pulled out the rosary. The cross swung and struck the milk pitcher, making it ring.

"It's the mainspring," Uncle Adolphe muttered, picking at the mechanism with a long needle.

"I will pray for you, Uncle. *Ave Maria, gratia plena . . .*"

Uncle Adolphe raised his head and stared. "What is the meaning of this?"

"It is God's will," Felice said, smiling slightly. She wished Mother Superior could hear her; perhaps she could. "*Ave Maria . . .*" The beads swung in the lamplight.

Then they were gone, jerked from her hand. Uncle Adolphe had thrown the rosary into a drawer and slammed it shut before she realized what had happened.

"My rosary," Felice wailed. "Uncle . . ." Her fingers held air. "Uncle, give me my rosary." She reached for the drawer, but he pushed his knee against it. She touched his leg and drew back.

Uncle Adolphe did not look up. "Go along, now," he said. He began to hum tunelessly.

Felice looked at the brass drawer-pull, held her hands out, and dropped them. "Uncle . . ."

"Go," he said, slamming his fist, making silver parts jump in the lamplight.

Felice went, quickly. A ruler of light showed her the door; she ran toward it and spun out. Uncle Adolphe crossed the room then; she could hear his footsteps. He would pull her back in, take up the pincers . . .

The key turned in the lock.

"Uncle," Felice called, trying the knob and knocking. "Let me in . . . you must listen."

Footsteps, and then silence. Felice rattled the knob and released it. Holding her empty pocket, she crouched by the closet; she felt robbed, and naked. When Aunt Rose found her there a few minutes later, Felice could not explain.

That night, Felice and her cousins Elizabeth and Francette told stories beneath the covers in Felice's bed. When it came her turn, Felice said she would tell the true story of how Uncle Adolphe stole Grandmama if they would promise never, never to tell. They promised, and grew quite still.

"It was the day she died," Felice whispered. "He put her on the wagon beside him, propped up."

"Dead?" Elizabeth sounded skeptical.

"Yes—cross my heart."

Felice told how Uncle Adolphe had driven Grandmama down Main Street, past the train station, and through the orchards and over the dikeland to Cape Blomidon. He built a fire there and made tea for Grandmama. A search party was sent out, but they were never found. "Glooscap took Grandmama to heaven," Felice said. "But he didn't want Uncle. He threw him over the cliff and he was drowned."

"That's not true," Elizabeth said. "Uncle is here—Grandmama, too."

"Have you seen them?"

"No, but my parents did—Papa talked to Uncle Adolphe today—and I heard him the other day—I did—he was shouting."

"Me, too," Francette said.

"That was only Uncle's ghost." Felice bit a corner of the quilt to keep from giggling. "It will walk around unhappy for years before he goes to hell. But all of Grandmama is in heaven—her body, too."

The younger girls were quiet; Felice could feel them considering the truth of this. She crossed her fingers to cancel out the lie and she wished for Celeste. "Let's go see—I'll prove it," she said, sliding out of bed.

"No," Francette wailed, in a whisper. "Not in the dark."

"Sissy." Felice tiptoed across the room, opened the door quietly, and leaned out. There was silence but for a distant, feathery snore.

Felice led the way; she didn't feel the least bit frightened. Elizabeth and Francette followed, holding hands, at a distance.

Grandmama's door was locked, as Felice had known it would be. Elizabeth put an ear to the door. "Mama says she's in there."

"She may be, tomorrow. The angels will probably bring her body back," Felice whispered. "But she's not there now."

"How do you know?"

"Sssh, come on." Felice felt for the banister and started down the steps. It was very dark; she went slowly and quietly, feeling her way along the wall. Though she could not hear Elizabeth and Francette behind her, she was certain they would come. A vague plan about frightening Uncle Adolphe began to take shape in her mind. But first, she thought, they would go to the kitchen for cake. They went the long way, through the parlor and dining room, to avoid passing Uncle Adolphe's study. Felice, in the lead, bumped against the sofa and the edge of a table, sending Great-Aunt Charlotte's sewing basket to the floor. She picked it up, spilling spools of thread; the three girls fumbled for them in the dark, then went on.

It was easier to see in the dining room, for the light beneath the kitchen door. "Sssh," Felice whispered, tiptoeing forward. Elizabeth and Francette hung back, gripping chairs.

Felice eased open the door, her eye to the crack. The hinge creaked, and at the far edge of her vision there was sudden movement. Before she slammed the door shut she saw Philippe and Bette, springing apart. They did not see her.

Felice ran, bumping into Elizabeth.

"Ghosts?" Elizabeth whispered.

Felice pushed at her. Her ears were ringing.

"Is it ghosts?" Elizabeth and Francette asked, pulling at her skirt.

"Be quiet," Felice muttered savagely, racing up the stairs.

When she leapt into the bed it rocked sickeningly beneath her, and her ears buzzed, as with flies.

THE AFTERNOON SUN SLANTED THROUGH STAINED GLASS, SPAN-gling the mourners with amethyst and ruby streaks of light. With the final cold strains of the organ still echoing in the high timbered ceiling, the priest began the introit of the funeral mass. His voice was a thin stream, barely audible even to Felice, who sat in a pew near the front of the church. Beyond the outflung, white-robed arms of the priest was the coffin, banked with sprays of balsam.

Felice had seen Grandmama in her room early that morning. Her face was gray and her mouth hung open at one side, as though she had been hit. Felice had turned away, but Aunt Rose held her head, forcing her to look. "That is your grandmother," she said, "and she has been here all this time, right in this house." Where did she get such ideas and stories? Aunt Rose wanted to know. Surely she hadn't learned them from the nuns? When Felice confessed, in a quavering voice, that she had only been teasing, Aunt Rose proclaimed herself shocked. "Elizabeth and Francette are impressionable young girls. Whatever possessed you?"

"She's just like her mother," Uncle Edmond said, his indulgent expression so much like Papa's that it hurt. "Always up to some mischief."

"Uncle stole my rosary," Felice had burst out.

Her aunt and uncle looked at each other above Felice's head and said nothing, but before they left for the church, Uncle Edmond drew her aside. "Don't bother your Uncle Adolphe about praying right now," he whispered to her. "He just doesn't understand. But I am sure he is sorry that he took your beads." He held out a loose fist and dropped the rosary into Felice's hands.

It was now twined about her arm, and glittered in the bracelet of reflected violet light that lay across her wrist. Felice moved her arm back and forth, making the rosary beads wink and bleed color. Uncle Edmond and Aunt Rose didn't understand, either. They thought she was just a mischievous child. But it was usual for people doing God's work to be misunderstood; the stories of the great Christian martyrs proved that. Felice touched the beads to a pool of crimson light on her skirt, turning the rosary a brilliant deep purple. When Felice's true nature was revealed, and she was taken into heaven, the sky would be just that color, staining onlookers like ink. They would fall to their knees, Uncle Adolphe, Uncle Edmond, Aunt Rose, the cousins, and all the nuns and girls. Philippe too, and Bette; they would prostrate themselves. One handsome boy, a prince or a knight, would scoop up her rosary, hold it to his heart and then his lips. Never have I seen such a beautiful girl, he would say; I pledge my life to your service.

Felice rewound the beads about her fingers, making rings, until Aunt Rose nudged her. She raised her head and watched the priest shake holy water into the coffin. His movement was rhythmical, and businesslike, as though he were salting a fish. She looked away from him, at the back of Philippe's head; she hated that sanctimonious head, so lately pressed to Bette's, and this morning bent close to Felice as he asked what made her act so childish, telling such stories. She stared for a moment at the crease in his neck, hating it, and at the revolting little hairs that grew along its banks.

Philippe was flanked by Uncle Edmond, whose left cheek twitched slightly, and by Uncle Adolphe. Doctor McConnell sat on the other side of Uncle Adolphe, by the aisle; he had come to the house this morning and himself ushered the grieved eldest son to the church.

Each time Uncle Adolphe shifted in the pew, the doctor gave him an alarmed sidewise glance as though afraid he might bolt.

A blade of crimson light lay across Uncle Adolphe's jaw, emphasizing the gaunt, underfed character of his face. Felice imagined for a moment that it was blood, a wound inflicted by her follower the handsome prince. Then she remembered that she was supposed to feel sorry for him, because he was pathetic. She had overheard Aunt Rose and Great-Aunt Charlotte say so. And Bette had said so to Felice this morning in the kitchen. "You and your brother didn't take on half so much as he does," Bette had whispered—his voice was then audible through two closed doors—"and you lost *both* your parents, all at once." Bette had reached out her hand, but Felice backed away from it into the hall. Uncle Adolphe was emerging from his study on Doctor McConnell's arm. Her uncle's face was drawn, the eyes screwed shut like those of an infant about to cry, but he did not cry.

Now Uncle Adolphe was staring toward the front of the church, blinking continually. Though Felice looked very closely, she could see no moisture. Felice was thinking about that day of the telegram—the way Uncle had unfolded and smoothed it, the way he had glared at her—when she saw him rise from the pew. She gripped her rosary, startled. But everyone else was rising, too, all around her; Aunt Rose pulled her up by the elbow.

They turned toward the aisle, Elizabeth, behind her, pressed close. Felice turned with a look that made her step back. "Tattletale," Felice muttered without moving her lips, just loudly enough for her cousin to hear. Felice wished Elizabeth would be sent to school at the convent; the other girls would make up names and stories about her, just as they had about Antoinette and the Doucette twins.

As she left the pew Felice saw for a moment the pitying, curious eyes of people seated across the aisle. A woman in a feathered hat craned her neck to look; for a moment Felice thought it was her acquaintance from the train. She drew herself up, proud and straight, as she walked forward, her gaze fixed on Aunt Rose's back. She pressed her hands together, as she did when going up for communion. She glanced once toward the empty pew where she had been sitting, at the red and violet bands of light now falling against wood, and at the roseate window above the pew. Through the border of the window, a cloudy white glass, she could see leafless trees, their many-branched limbs like the delicate bones of fish.

Felice ascended the steps into the candlelight and incense. The smell was like Candlemas. Before she had time to think, she was at the coffin. She had meant not to look, but it was too sudden; she forgot. There was Grandmama, her eyes so terrifyingly closed, her mouth askew. Felice stood staring, unable to move her feet or eyes. Grandmama's dress was black and shiny like oil, and had the iridescence of oil in water. Her arranged waxen hands made Felice think of how a candle flakes when scraped at with a fingernail.

Aunt Rose took Felice's hand and tugged, dislodging her. As she passed by, Felice looked at Grandmama's feet; they pointed straight up, absurdly, like a doll's feet. They looked so much like they couldn't help it that Felice wanted to cry out.

Uncle Adolphe stood at the head of the coffin, his face and body contorted like one of Sister Agatha's martyrs; the procession flowed around him as around a rock. Felice stumbled past the priest, who reached out starchily, too late, and went stiff-legged down the steps. Aunt Rose's arm encircled her as she walked.

When Felice touched the pew, she had a sudden, sharp picture of Mama's face, crumpled, ashen; there was a brief, bewilderingly fierce stab of pain and then she felt suffocated, as though a hand were pressing over her mouth and nose.

They sat again, as other people came and went. Felice slumped against the pew; she felt the way she sometimes did just before the morning bell, when she was dreaming but thought she was awake.

The organ began again, and then the procession from the altar. The crucifix went past, and the coffin; Felice could feel their shadows. Though she did not look, the coffin seemed to go by very fast. She imagined horrible grins on the faces of the pallbearers as they rushed the box toward the graveyard.

She was on her feet again, pulled and pressed forward. Somewhere a baby cried—had someone brought Moulie? Rows of heads turned, like waves; Felice thought of a boat cutting through water, and of the riffled pages of a book. She pressed her missal against the pain in her chest.

The round window at the end of the church was a large red sun, with purple teardrops set in a wheel. When she stopped to stare at it, someone took her out the door.

Felice gazed up at the sky. The sun looked pale, almost transparent, in the white sky, like a dim moon, she thought, or like a communion wafer. Felice walked where she was led, looking up at the sky and the trees. Here and there, a few stubborn brown leaves wagged on their branches. Felice thought of Mama and Papa. It was not possible that they had gone and left her here.

They approached a knoll, its rise covered with gravestones; some were rounded at the top like stiff tongues. Felice looked out beyond the crest at the frozen Minas Basin. When Mama and Papa had left, the water had been blue and the sun had shone on it. They would come back. They promised.

Felice was pushed into line between Philippe and Elizabeth. There was a big hole before them, like a trough, and the corners of it going down looked very sharp and hard. Frozen clots of red earth lay piled at the other side; as Felice watched, a piece of it slid and fell out of sight. She backed up, but the legs behind her made a fence. Then she saw the coffin, and the priest. There was a bald spot at the back of the priest's head the size of a biscuit. Other people closed in, making a dark circle around the hole. Felice tried again to escape; faces came down at her like weapons, and hands held her back.

The box was tied up. The sound of creaking ropes made Felice's skin hurt. She thought of Grandmama's absurd feet, shut away. It was not right. It was not true. Aunt Rose was here, Philippe was here, and Uncle Adolphe. She looked at her hands, opened and closed them in the winter air.

The coffin was lowered, groaning. It went slowly, and then it was gone. Felice tried to faint, but could not.

Uncle Adolphe pressed close to the grave. He looked as though he might dive in, but men's arms held him back.

Dirt began to rain in the hole. It sounded hard at first, then softer. Though Felice closed her eyes, she could still see it, curving up from

the pitch of the shovels, then falling in broken red waves. Grandmama, in the box, was at the bottom. It must be very heavy falling
on her, and dark as the ocean.

Felice thought of Mama's feet, in the fashionable little boots Papa
had brought her from Paris. She thought of them limp, fluttering, as
Mama drifted near the bases of rocks. She thought of Papa's feet,
shoeless, the nails green, black.

Felice screamed. She felt the sound coming out; it would not stop.
She opened and shut her eyes, seeing patches of dull light and darkness. She was carried away; she kicked and hit against air. There were
voices, blurred and foreign, like an unfamiliar language. She did not
care. She thrashed and wailed. She was pulled, then carried, bouncing
up and down. "They left me," she cried, "they leeeft me."

There were the sounds of doors opening and closing, and scuffing
feet. Someone held her. It smelled like Aunt Rose. Felice cried and
cried, holding on. She heard sheets pulled back and she felt herself
being lifted. Then she felt the pillow, cool against her cheek, and it
was easier to breathe.

When Felice awoke it was late afternoon. A pale column of light
slanted across one wall, illuminating the fat pink roses in the wallpaper. She lay staring at the wall a long time, at the cold, mean light,
and at the roses that reminded her of cabbages. "I hate cabbage," she
said aloud. She hated it so much, for an instant, that she could smell
its vile odor, cooking, and the thought of how much cabbage she had
had to eat in her life brought tears to her eyes.

Below, in the lower regions of the house, she could hear voices, and
someone beating on a pan—Bette, probably, or perhaps one of the
little cousins playing drums. In the street there were sleigh bells and,
briefly, shouts. The sounds made her feel sick; she turned and put the
pillow over her head.

When she moved, her body found cold spots in the bed. She wriggled her feet and, when she did, realized someone had taken off her
shoes and stockings and put on her flannel nightgown. She turned her
feet round and round; from the ankles she could see them, pretty,

delicate feet, and she could see herself, too. Poor, pretty Felice, she thought, hugging herself, poor, pretty Felice, and kicked angrily at the quilts.

There was a pounce, and a heaviness on her legs. Felice sat up, throwing back the pillow. "Seine!" He was on his haunches, batting at her feet with first one paw and then the other. He looked so comical and friendly that it made her cry again. She reached out and pulled him to her; he struggled at first, still playful, but when Felice stroked his head and said, "Nice kitty, nice kitty," he relaxed on her chest, warming it.

Felice lay on her back, stroking Seine, looking up at the shadowed ceiling. Mama and Papa were gone. She had never felt before how utterly gone they were. They would not be back. She let just her fingertips rest on Seine's back. The loneliness was terrible, terrible. That she was still here, alone, was terrible, but it was interesting, too, that they could be so completely gone, and she could be here. The feeling of interest lasted only a moment, pushed out by nausea. She was not enough, she would be blown away, uprooted, scattered, with no one to care.

Pushing Seine back, Felice rose and walked across the room to the oval mirror that shone like water in the dim light. She leaned forward and looked in. Her face was pale, but substantial; she tested it, touching cheeks and nose and chin. Her eyes looked huge and mysterious against the pallor of her face. She touched the long curve of cheek and chin, and the graceful line of her throat. She thought of Saint Cecilia's throat, white and delicate beneath the rough hands of her executioners; she shivered, thinking how Saint Cecilia had not flinched. And she would not, either. She smiled at herself; her own face was so full and pretty and young it brought tears to her eyes, and would to anyone else's, too.

Felice dressed quickly and brushed her hair. She did not braid it, but let it hang long and loose, framing her face like a veil. She took up her missal and rosary, and after one last smile at herself in the mirror, went to find Uncle Adolphe.

She went slowly, gracefully, down the steps. On the landing, she paused. There were voices in the parlor. The dinner would be over, then, and most of the guests gone. She wondered what they had said about her. For a moment her face burned, and then she tossed her head. It didn't matter. Let them say their worst. Head high, she continued down the stairs and went into the parlor, where there was a cluster of relatives around the fireplace. Uncle Adolphe was not there. When Great-Aunt Charlotte called out, "Felice, dear, you have heired the porcelain cat," she just nodded and went on into the dining room.

The remains of the funeral dinner lay on the table: meats carved to the bone, half-consumed dishes of vegetables, serving spoons lying at disconsolate angles. On Grandmama's Limoges cake stand there were chocolate crumbs and a smear of dried icing.

Seine rubbed past her, curling his tail around the leg of a chair and then against Felice's skirt. He meowed and Felice picked him up. Pressing his furry head against her cheek, she went into the kitchen. Bette and Philippe looked up from the table—guiltily, Felice thought —and Bette rose. "You must be hungry, duck," she said.

"Not in the least. Where is Uncle Adolphe?"

"In the yard," Bette said, sighing. "The poor gentleman."

"Why do you want to know?" Philippe asked as Felice reached for her cape, which hung by the door. "I'd stay away from him, if I were you—he needs to be left alone."

Felice smiled her most angelic smile at Philippe and went out the door. The cold air nearly took her breath away. This is God's will, she whispered, this is truly God's will. Seine squirmed and Felice set him down. She watched him trot across the snow toward the shed, his tail straight up in the air.

Uncle Adolphe was at the side of the yard, near the picket fence. He was bent over and he seemed to be hitting the ground. When Felice walked closer, clutching her missal, she saw that he was digging. He had made a small wound in the earth.

Felice rubbed her fingers against the pebbly grain of the leather missal. The rosary was safe in her pocket. She remembered her face in the mirror. When Uncle turned, he would see that angelic face.

"Uncle," she said softly. She walked around to the side, where he could see her.

Uncle Adolphe's jaw worked, and the cords of his neck stood out as he thrust the shovel. It rang against the frozen ground, and brought up a chunk of earth no larger than an egg. Felice saw that he had cleared away a patch of snow, leaving a rind of ice around the cut in the ground.

"Uncle, may I read to you? Will you listen?"

He wriggled the spade beneath a small rock. When it jumped free, he stood back, staring down at the pock it had left in the ground. Uncle is pathetic, Felice thought. Poor, pathetic Uncle.

She opened the missal. *"Exsultabunt Domino ossa humiliata,"* she read. Her voice was too high. *"Miserere mei, Deus,"* she continued in a lower register.

Uncle Adolphe nudged at the hole with his foot. He set the shovel an inch behind it and brought his heel down, stamping the blade in.

"Uncle, if you listen, it will help you."

He glanced at her; his mouth was furious, the lips drawn completely in.

"Would you rather read it yourself, Uncle?" She held the missal out to him. "You may have it, if you like. A gift."

Without turning his head he spat, sideways, into the snow. Felice thought he must be drunk; she would get to that later.

"Here, Uncle," she said, making a plate of her joined hands. "It is for you." He swatted and the book fell. A holy card twirled down like a leaf.

"Oh, Uncle, you should not . . ." Felice stooped to pick up the missal, brushing at the pages that had touched ground. She looked at the blade of the shovel, and then up at her uncle, huge above her. "Please don't hurt me, Uncle." Her voice quavered, and she dropped the missal. "I was only trying to help you." Her fingers scrabbled against ice. "Don't you want to go to heaven?" She struggled up. Uncle Adolphe was very near. She could see his nostrils open and close. "Uncle?" She opened the missal.

Uncle Adolphe grabbed the missal with both hands. The shovel clanged and slid on ice. There was the sound of ripping paper. Felice stood, not breathing, as he wadded up pages and stuffed them in his mouth. He chewed furiously, watching her.

"No."

He spat, and ripped more pages.

Felice leapt forward, reaching for the missal, and he dropped it. He held her wrists. She wriggled in his grasp. "Don't whip me, Uncle," she whispered.

His jaw made two long circles and he spat again, over her head. Then he let her go and pushed the missal toward her with his foot.

Felice bent slowly, watching the shovel. She snatched up the missal and jumped back.

Uncle Adolphe began to chop at the ice with the round blade. His face looked finished with her.

"Uncle? Will you . . ."

He continued digging. Felice stood for a moment, watching. She opened the missal, and closed it. Then, feeling foolish, and utterly exhausted, she walked slowly back to the house.

19

THE DAY AFTER THE FUNERAL, FELICE AWOKE ANGRY. SHE WAS glad she was leaving tomorrow for the convent, where she was appreciated. Some day everyone here would regret not taking her seriously, Uncle Adolphe especially, and Uncle Edmond and Aunt Rose, who had looked at her so strangely last night during dinner, and Philippe, and Bette, whom she had heard tell Aunt Rose that "the poor little girl is too closed up in that convent." And she might take Seine with her, she thought, feeling the snug warmth of him against her back; she was the one he loved best.

Later that morning, while playing fox and hounds with her cousins, Felice found Pip's empty birdcage behind the carriage house. The forlorn sight of it rusting there, half buried beneath the snow, sealed

Felice's decision to take Seine: what if they were to let him starve? "I won't let anybody hurt you, little cat," she whispered to him that night, tucking him beneath the quilt next to her.

At breakfast the next morning, a Saturday, the day of her departure, Felice announced that she was taking Seine with her. To her surprise, Bette, who was serving the herring, said it was an excellent notion; she didn't intend to stay on herself, and then who would there be to feed the poor animal? Philippe, who was seated at the head of the dining-room table, turned on Felice. Felice was not entitled to the cat, he said, it was as much his as hers, and it was just like a silly little girl to imagine that the train conductor would allow it, or the sisters either, for that matter. Aunt Rose, at the other end of the table, said she wanted no more bickering, absolutely, do you understand?

"Take the damned thing," Uncle Adolphe said, brandishing his fork. A clot of scrambled egg fell into a dish of strawberry preserves, making some of the cousins—though not Felice—smile. It was his only comment during breakfast, which marked his first appearance at the table since the funeral. He had been closeted in his study the last day and a half; Felice had not seen him since the afternoon she accosted him in the yard. He now sat opposite her, straddling the leg of the table leaf; but for his one outburst, he was taciturn and listless throughout the meal. Felice watched him surreptitiously as he ate, his thin shoulders drawn up toward his ears, his hands trembling, and she felt almost sorry for him. She had offered him a chance, a golden opportunity, and he had scorned it.

Great-Aunt Charlotte, who had been studying Felice, tapped a spoon against her water glass. "It is appropriate that you have Seine," she pronounced, fixing Felice with her watery gaze. "In light of your inheritance. I refer, of course, to the white china cat. Now, that is a fine piece of porcelain, Felice, not a toy. Remember that."

"Yes, Aunt."

The old woman continued to look at her. "Isn't the child pretty?" she said at last, her voice cracking on the last syllable. All heads turned. Felice could feel the blush rise from her neck.

"Just like her mother," Uncle Edmond said, winking at her, and smiling until Felice did not know where to look. "Poor Cecilia," Aunts Rose and Charlotte murmured in unison.

After breakfast, Felice packed her bag, nestling the porcelain cat in a corner swaddled in newspaper and her flannel nightgown. She decided, as she examined her reflection one last time, that she would take the oval mirror with her also. Grandmama would want me to have it, she told herself, reopening the valise and sandwiching the mirror between her chemises and her best dress. Grandmama had put the mirror in the rose room especially for her; she had said the delicate carving was suitable for a young lady.

Felice thought the others would probably agree she should have it, but just in case, she wriggled the nail from the wall and hid it beneath some linens in the bottom drawer of the bureau. The mutilated white missal was already there, beneath a quilt that was rarely used. Felice had wanted to throw it away, but that didn't seem right, and she couldn't take it back to the convent.

Felice's relatives gathered at the front door for her departure. Great-Aunt Charlotte lowered her downy, rouged cheek for Felice to kiss—it felt and smelled like a much-used powder-puff—and told her to be a good girl. Aunt Rose gave her a thorough hug and whispered, "Now, don't study so hard, Felice. You can stay with us, you know, if you get tired of that convent school."

"I'm not ever going to leave the convent," Felice announced. "I have a vocation there."

Aunt Rose drew back, blinking. Felice rather liked the expression of mixed bewilderment and awe she had produced upon her face. Looking about, she saw a circle of duplicate expressions—except on the faces of Uncle Edmond, who was frowning, and Uncle Adolphe, who kept his gaze fixed on air at a point safely above Felice's head.

"Goodbye, Uncle Adolphe." Felice boldly reached to take his hand and pressed it. "God bless you," she said, just as Mother Superior would have done, and then, "God bless you all." She smiled, crinkling her eyes at them—it felt like a new and not very successful arrangement of her features—and let go Uncle Adolphe's hand, which fell to his thigh with a little slap. Uncle Edmond took her arm and escorted her out to the wagon, where Philippe was already waiting.

Though she preserved her confident, ascetic departure expression throughout the process of settling into the wagon, Felice, waving back over her shoulder, felt a moment of panic. The house, with its snout-like porch, taunted her with failure; she thought of the torn missal in the drawer, Uncle Adolphe in his dark, private world, Mother Superior perhaps even now on her knees in the convent chapel, offering up futile prayers. She would be cruelly disappointed when Felice described her efforts with Uncle Adolphe.

Philippe, in the seat beside her, appeared lost in thought, and as depressed as herself. Their ride through Wolfville was silent; neither spoke until they were at the train platform. "Goodbye," Philippe said, "please write to me once in a while." His eyes were as mournful and innocent as a bereft child's. Felice clung to him, thinking it might have been better if they had been on the ship with Mama and Papa, and all gone down together. Only the sight of the conductor—it was her friend from the previous journey—smiling and reaching down his hand to her kept her from bursting into tears.

When Seine was handed up after her, the conductor did not reject him, as Felice had feared, but laughed. "A cat in a birdcage! Now there's a novel arrangement. Don't worry, sir," he said to Philippe, "we'll take special care of this young lady."

The conductor showed Felice to her seat and inquired if her traveling companion would care for some cream. As the train jolted into motion, Seine, whose ears were already plastered to his head from fear, began moving his mouth in piteous, barely audible protests. Felice bent close to his yellow-green eyes, looking at the black vertical lines of his pupils. "It's all right, kitty, it's all right." Then, since the conductor clearly didn't mind, she unscrewed the bottom of the cage, pulled Seine out, and arranged him on the seat beside her. She managed to restrain him until the train rounded a sharp curve, and the whistle screeched. The cat thrashed against Felice's grip and then vaulted out over her into the aisle. The conductor, just reentering the car with his ticket-puncher, shut the door as Seine streaked toward it. He reached out with the puncher, and Seine bolted sideways, scrambling up the sides of seats to the luggage rack, accompanied by exclamations—including squeals from one woman who held her ears —from the passengers.

The conductor eventually coaxed Seine down with a piece of

smoked fish, and he made a ticket for the cat which he insisted on punching at every stop. Enveloped in all this activity and attention, Felice hardly noticed that her sadness had melted away.

Passengers from other cars came to see the famous cat, and two sisters—girls about Felice's age—invited her to come sit with them. Felice and Seine moved, with the help of the conductor, to their family's quarters two cars ahead. The mother and father asked questions about her trip, and about the convent; the girls' older brother, a handsome, nearly grown boy with light hair and blue eyes, smiled at her over his newspaper. During lunch—the Comier family had brought a picnic and insisted on Felice's sharing it with them—the boy (his name was Robert) asked if she preferred a ham or turkey sandwich, in such a solicitous tone that Felice felt quite confused and said, "I don't know—both." When everyone laughed, Felice drew Seine onto her lap and stroked him to hide her embarrassment. The cat yawned, showing his tiny, needlelike teeth.

In the afternoon the girls played cards, and Robert smiled down at them. Occasionally his eyes met Felice's. The time passed so quickly that Felice was surprised when the conductor called out, "Nevette." The girls exchanged addresses, promising to write and to visit. Robert helped her with her bag and the basket. "Goodbye," he said with his perfect, dizzying smile.

Descending the steps, Felice felt the boy's eyes on her, and she squeezed Seine so tightly beneath her elbow that he yowled.

Jacques, reaching up his hand to her, looked startled. Not until that moment had Felice considered what sort of reception the cat might find at the convent. She held her breath and crossed her fingers when she saw the Abbé right behind Jacques, but he said only, "Welcome back, my child," and lapsed into a preoccupied silence that lasted throughout the bumpy ride up the hill.

The halls of the building were empty. Behind the closed doors of the classrooms, students were studying for the Monday examinations. The nuns were closeted in Mother Superior's office; when she heard the drone of their voices Felice felt she had been gone no time at all.

Felice took Seine to the kitchen, where Soukie was stirring soup. The kitchenmaid smiled and nodded with an air of great solemnity. "A cat is just the thing, Mademoiselle," she said. "Our other puss is getting to be a real dawdler—the mice just rule that cellar."

After Felice had fetched some milk for the cat and set it on the floor, Soukie whispered, "Now, don't tell a single soul, Mademoiselle, but I have some exciting news!" She beckoned the girl closer. There was a breviary on the table; Soukie tapped it with her middle finger. "Just look at me," she said, one hand on the breviary and the other clutching the soup spoon. "Well, Mademoiselle—don't you see? I'm going to become a nun!"

"Really?" Felice tried to imagine Soukie's chin above a starched collar, her red hair tucked away beneath a wimple.

"Monsieur," Soukie whispered. "Didn't I always tell you he was sent here for more than one special purpose? I had a dream, Mademoiselle, and—just imagine this!—Monsieur *spoke.*" Soukie paused for dramatic effect, the soup spoon dripping at the edge of the pot. "He spoke, Mademoiselle, I vow he did—and in Latin—yet *I* understood it, every word. And, Mademoiselle Felice, he said very distinctly that I should be admitted into the novitiate right away"—here Soukie struck her chest with her spoonless hand—"He said it was God's holy will."

Although Soukie had made her promise not to say a word about her revelation, it was soon obvious to Felice that it was known throughout the convent. Before dinner, when the nuns sang their office in the white chapel, Soukie joined them from the kitchen in a tuneless, brassy voice that penetrated the halls. Felice went downstairs with Celeste, Anne, and Françoise to see that Seine was properly introduced to the cellar. They sat on sacks of apples and listened, giggling, to Soukie cheerfully trumpeting out mispronounced Latin litanies above. The other girls told Felice that Soukie had entered this new phase in her campaign for nunship quite unexpectedly, on Ash Wednesday; that the Abbé was furious at Mother Superior for having raised Soukie's expectations, but Mother Superior said she had done no such thing. Soukie's only champion, the girls reported, was Sister Agatha, who was said to be writing to the Pope on her behalf. At

Sister Agatha's suggestion, Soukie had been praying in the kitchen, kneeling by the stove when she should have been preparing meals, and Mother Superior herself had to finish cooking dinner last night.

"She's a terrible cook, too," Celeste said, wrinkling her nose. "It's no wonder she never married."

"Ce-leste!" the others said.

"All Lenten food is boring anyway," said Anne, always a loyal defender of Mother Superior.

"She was probably so furious she couldn't cook," Françoise said. "She has been looking so mad—have you seen her, Felice? She looks like this." Françoise drew her pretty face into a grimace.

Françoise said that her Aunt Febianne had told her yesterday the Abbé was inquiring in the village about placing Monsieur under the care of a Nevette housewife. "Aunt Febianne said the Abbé said he's well enough to leave the convent now," Françoise reported, "but Auntie's afraid of him—especially after what you saw him do to Evangeline, Felice."

"What! That's a secret story!" Felice's heart pounded in her eyes, and she could barely see. "You promised never to tell."

"Did I?" But Françoise couldn't keep her face solemn, and she giggled. "No, I didn't tell."

"Why should she?" Celeste said. "Since it wasn't true anyway?"

"I'm tired," Felice said. "Leave me alone."

"We prayed for you in Mother Superior's class every afternoon," Celeste said, with a trace of a sneer. "Did you save your poor uncle?"

Felice looked down at her shoes. She wished she hadn't even bothered to come back. "I don't know," she said.

Celeste put her hands together in mock prayer, and looking up through her dark lashes, said, "Oh, Sister Felice, hallowed be thy name. . . ." She ducked, laughing, as Felice threw an apple at her. The apple bounced along the floor; Seine jumped and stilled it as though it were a mouse.

"Felice can't be a nun," Françoise said. "You still get It, don't you, Felice?"

"Umm humm."

"Well, Antoinette doesn't—hers stopped."

"That's right," Celeste said, sitting up. "She told the Doucette twins it showed how pure she is, that Mother Superior said so. Now they're pretending they don't get It either."

While the other girls speculated as to whether or not emancipation from menstruation was requisite for becoming a nun, Felice sat looking into the dim space beyond the lamplight where Seine was batting the apple across the floor.

"I met a boy on the train," she announced.

"*You* met a boy?" Celeste said.

"What color eyes does he have?" Françoise wanted to know.

Felice told them his name was Robert Comier, that she expected to see him soon, that he had begged her to write, and she produced, for evidence, the address from her pocket. She answered questions about the color of Robert's hair and skin and jacket, his height and the shape of his nose and chin. As Felice was describing the parting smile, Celeste interrupted her. "Wait till Monsieur hears about this —he's going to be heartbroken!"

Everyone but Felice screeched with laughter; the best she could manage was a strained smile.

Celeste held up one hand for attention. "Ssh. Let me tell you something about Monsieur—something I heard him say. Well . . ." Widening her eyes, Celeste looked around the circle. "You know his door's been closed lately, but do you know *why?*"

"Why?" the others—all but Felice—chimed.

"Because he's been in mourning—missing Felice." Felice scowled; the others giggled expectantly. "Anyway," Celeste went on, "I tiptoed by the other day and heard him crying out a name. Fee-leece! Fee-leece!" Celeste made her voice sound strangled. "Come back, Saintee Fee-leece!"

After the laughter had died away, Felice said, "You're just jealous, Celeste, because you haven't got a real boyfriend like me and Françoise."

"I do, too."

"Who?"

"Can't tell."

"Ha!" Felice turned to Françoise. "What did Emile say to you the day you walked on the pier with him, Françoise? You never have told us—not me, anyway."

Françoise curled a tendril of hair about her finger and smiled mysteriously.

Anne was beginning to recount the story of her sister's romance— a story the girls had heard several times before but never tired of— when the dinner-bell rang. When they rose, Seine trotted toward them. "Let's take this kitty to the dormitory first," Celeste suggested. "I think he'll be lonely down here."

Felice, looking toward the darkness beyond the pool of light, agreed, and she scooped Seine up into her arms. Leading the way, she hurried up the stairs.

In the kitchen, Soukie was carrying out dishes of food while Mother Superior watched, her fists planted on her hips. Felice curtsied, off balance, as Mother Superior turned to look at her. The nun's eyebrows arched up. "What animal is this?" was her greeting.

"I brought him, Ma Mère," Felice said. "He needed a home. My uncle . . ."

"And where are you taking it?"

"Upstairs," Felice said in a smaller voice. "He can sleep under my bed. He's very clean."

"Looks like a good mouser, too," Soukie said, returning for a pot of tea.

"Felice, you surprise me," the nun said. "Put that cat in the cellar and go wash up for dinner—all of you." And without another glance at Felice, Mother Superior took up a tureen of split-pea soup and headed toward the dining room, her skirt swinging like a bell.

20

"WELL, FELICE?"

Felice stared past Mother Superior, who was seated at the desk in her office, at the *Catholic Encyclopedia*. One of the volumes, L–M, was upside down; Felice could not imagine how it had happened.

"Felice?"

"Yes, Ma Mère?" Felice ducked her head, as she had done today in history class when Mother Superior had called on her to recite. And now the nun was waiting for an account of the miraculous conversion of Uncle Adolphe.

"I . . . it was very sad, Ma Mère. My Grandmama was buried in the snow . . ."

"The Lord's will."

"Yes." Felice made a sign of the cross in unison with Mother Superior, then looked down at the hand which had acted. Its nails were black beneath the rims and the knuckles were grimy. She covered the nails with her other hand and squeezed until it hurt.

"And your uncle?"

Felice raised her head. Mother Superior looked huge behind the desk, and permanent, as if the space she filled would always be filled.

"I wish *you* had been there," Felice said, in her most dovelike voice. "It was very hard to know what to do—but you could have advised me."

Mother Superior's eyelids flickered slightly.

Felice took a deep breath. "Uncle Adolphe drinks terribly." She shifted her gaze from Mother Superior's eyes to her forehead. "Terribly. My cousin and I found a big pile of rum bottles in the carriage house—and that wasn't even all of them, Bette said. I met a lady on the train, going there . . ." Felice's voice trailed off as she looked at Mother Superior's face: the expression had not softened. "He stole Grandmama," she blurted out.

"Stole?" Mother Superior's eyebrows jumped.

"Yes, Ma Mère." Felice nodded emphatically. "It's lucky she was even buried. He put her on the wagon and took her to Cape Blomidon —she got a nasty cut on the forehead."

Mother Superior pursed her lips and looked sideways at Felice.

"He *did* steal her, Ma Mère—he's a terrible man."

"Did you tell him to pray to God for forgiveness?"

"Uncle is pathetic—he cannot . . ."

"His pathos is his distance from God, Felice."

"Oh, yes, Ma Mère. I told him that. I prayed for him, with him. I prayed for him *constantly,* Ma Mère," Felice said, her eyes filling with tears. "Constantly. But he was terrible. He stole my rosary, and when I gave him the missal . . ."

"Your rosary too?" Mother Superior sounded incredulous.

"He *did* steal my rosary, Ma Mère. Like this." Felice pulled the rosary from her pocket. "I was praying, like this," she said, letting the beads cascade over her fingers, "when he reached out . . ." Here Felice extricated one hand from the beads, and in a swift motion jerked the rosary away and stuffed it in her pocket. "Like that—then he threw it in the drawer."

"Then he has it yet?"

"No—no—it was *this* rosary—I thought he should not have it— well, I didn't know—my Uncle Edmond got it back."

"He did?"

"*Yes,* Ma Mère, I promise."

"I see. And the missal? Did you read it to him?"

"I tried, but he threw it on the ground, Ma Mère, and *stepped* on it. He even . . ." Felice stopped; she could not bring herself to tell the rest.

"Beware of coloring the facts, Felice."

"I'm *not* coloring the facts, Ma Mère, I *didn't* color them." Tears started to her eyes again.

"Perhaps not intentionally."

"I wish . . ." Felice looked down at her clenched hands. "I tried to do what was right—I tried very *hard,* Ma Mère," Felice said, her voice breaking.

There was silence. Felice glanced up through wet lashes at Mother Superior, who was observing her closely.

"Can I still be a nun, Ma Mère?"

"What do you mean, Felice?"

"Don't nuns have to make conversions?"

Mother Superior cleared her throat. "There are many different ways of serving God. Teaching the young, for example."

"Or being a missionary? I would like that, Ma Mère."

"At present, Felice, I would advise you to concentrate on the here and now. Be studious, obedient, kind." Mother Superior ticked off the virtues on her fingers. "Say your prayers faithfully. Be punctual—you have improved in that regard, Felice, I commend you." Mother Superior folded the counted-off fingers into a fist and wrapped her other hand about it. "But you must subdue that imagination of yours, Felice."

"Ma Mère, I . . ."

"The life of a nun is not adventurous, Felice," the superioress said, rising and circling the desk. "At least not in the popular sense. It is a life of routine, obedience, and denial. The rewards are great, but so are the sacrifices." She patted the girl's head. "You may go now."

Felice rose. "But that's the kind of life I *want,* Ma Mère. Routine, obedience . . ."

"That will be all, Felice. Go get ready for supper."

"Yes, Ma Mère." Felice curtsied and then rushed out of Mother Superior's office and into the hall, where she collided with Sister Theodota.

"Watch your step, please!"

"I'm sorry, Sister," Felice sobbed. She hurried down the corridor past Notre-Dame de Bon Secours and the open door of a classroom, where Sister Constance sat writing at her desk. The nun glanced up in surprise as the girl clattered by. "Mademoiselle?" she called after her.

Felice sprinted up two flights of steps, watching the frowning faces of her shoes as she went. She clung, panting, to the rail on the landing. Mother Superior was right; she was terrible, hopeless. She would never be a nun, never get to heaven. Hanging over the railing, she looked into the depths of the stairwell. Across the shadowed floor glided two nuns, darker shadows, like the shapes of fish seen from the cliff high above the bay. Felice stared at the empty space the departed nuns had made. Here she was, uselessly alive, when Mama and Papa, so much better than she, were gone, gone. The darkness throbbed in her eyes and, for a moment, she thought she would fall into it.

But with the sound of voices above, Felice's head cleared and she began slowly to climb the stairs once more. Antoinette and the Doucette twins, all three wearing the good-conduct ribbon, passed by. Antoinette nodded. The Doucettes, clattering behind like handmaidens, were too absorbed even to glance at her. Felice stuck out her tongue at their backs and stamped up a few more steps.

Then she saw Sister Agatha, unattended, above her. The nun descended smoothly, without holding to the rail, the crucifix of her rosary in one opened palm, the amber beads gleaming in the dusk. "Sister!" Felice cried, and ran up the steps to greet her.

"Felicia?" Sister Agatha said as the girl touched her arm. "Where have you been? I've been looking everywhere for you." Her mouth fell into a pout.

"In Wolfville—at my grandmother's funeral. Didn't anyone *tell* you?"

"Oh, yes. But it seemed such a long while."

"I had to—talk with my uncle—bringing him to God. But he's a very bad man, a . . ."

"A savage," Sister Agatha said matter-of-factly. "Well, come along, child," she said, taking Felice's elbow. "Let's get to work."

"What work do you mean, Sister?" Felice asked, going with her down the steps.

"I am to write a history of my life and privations, and *you* are to record it. My bridegroom has made himself clear on both of these points."

"Do you really hear His voice, Sister?"

"Ah, yes." Sister Agatha paused, one foot extended, and her head cocked, listening.

"And He spoke—about me?"

"He did." Sister Agatha moved on, taking Felice with her. "Only *you* are to be trusted with this project. He was adamant about that. And I think you will find it an instructive project, too, Felice. In the matter of your savage, for example."

"Mother Superior didn't really believe me about Uncle Adolphe—about how terrible he is."

"Mother Superior is something of an innocent."

Felice smiled, imagining Mother Superior confronted with Uncle Adolphe in one of his black moods: *then* she would understand.

They reached the second-floor landing and started down the hall to Sister Agatha's room.

"There are three orders of man- and womankind, Felicia. Weeds, innocents, and savages. Weeds, you understand. Innocents are unconscious weeds: sweet things, but overly domesticated. And savages are brutally divided weeds; they have sliced out all their light, or all their shadow, and are thus of two sub-orders—dark savages and white savages, both very dangerous. There will be a chapter on this, with examples."

They entered the nun's cell. Felice helped Sister Agatha sit on her bed, which was littered with papers.

"What are all these papers, Sister?"

"Documents, evidence. You will want to study them."

Felice sat on the chair by the bed and picked up a sheaf of pages: there were sketches, marked Latin examinations from years past, letters.

"This is a nice drawing, Sister," Felice said, peering at a faded pencil sketch. "This girl combing her hair."

"That odious word—nice! I had rather hear clumsy than nice."

"I'm sorry, Sister," Felice drew back, stung. "I didn't mean . . ."

"It has my own particular . . . *flavor,* wouldn't you say?"

"Yes, Sister."

"As will my autobiography. The color of Saint Thérèse's writings, the passion of Siena's Catherine, the poetry of Saint Gerard—but utterly—unique. Now. Let us start."

"Do you have something I could write on, Sister? And a pen?"

The nun patted her hand over the nearest papers.

"I could go get mine."

"No, no, never mind. Commit it to memory." Sister Agatha folded both hands in her lap. "That will be safer for now. So," she said, straightening, "the epigraphs. 'Long live the weeds and the wilderness yet!' and 'Glory be to God for dappled things.' Put those into Latin, please."

"Me? Now?"

Sister Agatha nodded. "You may use bucolics or Georgics."

"Well, let's see—*Longus*—um—*vivere*—"

"You intend to use the infinitive?"

"Ah—no—*vive?*"

"Who is your Latin instructress now, Felicia?"

"I have none, Sister."

"I thought as much. You see—my retirement was out of season. There will be a chapter on that, too."

"Maybe you should get someone else to help you, Sister—someone smarter."

"*No!* You are the only one I trust. And furthermore, you were designated. Never mind about the epigraph for now—we'll go on to the dedication." She cleared her throat. "This humble volume is respectfully dedicated to the Subtle Doctor Scotus, and his doctrine of *Haecceitas*. . . . You know its meaning, of course?"

"No, Sister. Sister, I think the supper-bell just rang."

"Thisness!" Sister Agatha shouted, slapping her thighs. "Do you understand?"

"No, Sister," Felice said in a small voice, "not quite."

"Thisness!" Sister Agatha waved her arms about the room. "Me-ness!" She clapped both hands to her chest. "Thee-ness!" she cried, opening her arms to Felice. "Now do you comprehend?"

"Yes, Sister," Felice said, utterly bewildered. "Would you like to go down to supper now? We are already late, I think."

Sister Agatha grumbled, as they descended the stairs, about the declining standard of education in the convent. Felice was feeling depressed, thoroughly out of favor with everyone, even Sister Agatha, until the nun halted on the final landing and, squeezing her hand, whispered, "Saint Catherine of Beaubassin has spoken to me as well, child. She doesn't want my life to pass into obscurity as hers has done. And she said specifically—and quite independently—that you were the one to help me. We will be twins in glory, Felicia—her very words."

"Twins in glory?"

"Yes, child, twins in glory."

They entered the dining room. Grace had been said and everyone was waiting. Felice could feel Mother Superior's icy gaze upon her as she and Sister Agatha walked to their table. She guided the nun to her place and then took her own seat; the chair scraped horribly in the silence.

After looking back and forth between Sister Agatha and Felice, Sister Theodota raised the carving knife and aimed it at the haddock.

The cooling fish lay in a runoff of juices that had already softened the curls of dried dulse lining its flanks. In spite of the mystical black spots on its head, where Christ was supposed to have picked it up (therefore making haddock, in the Abbé's opinion, the holiest flesh for consumption during Lent), this particular fish had a flabby passivity about it. Felice stared at the cooked white eye as Sister Theodota's knife clanked against the plate and cracked into bone. A large chunk of its lower portion was soon set before her, making her stomach turn.

When Felice added a dollop of potatoes to her plate, Sister Claire, Mother Superior's chief assistant in keeping up Lenten appetites, enjoined her to take more.

Then Sister Claire began a conversation about Ford motorcars; when that topic languished, she offered embroidered altar cloths, and the need for fresh ones at Easter. Sisters Claire and Theodota soon said all they could about the linens, and then lapsed into the silent consumption of haddock.

Idly stirring her potatoes as she looked about, Felice thought there was really no need for appetite-stimulating conversation anyway. Of all the diners, only she and Sister Agatha displayed the indifference to food normally extolled during Lent.

Sister Agatha's fork descended and ascended with slow, hypnotic regularity. Sometimes her fork brought up a tiny morsel of food, sometimes it brought up nothing; the nun chewed each mouthful endlessly, whether fish or air, and occasionally touched her napkin to her lips.

The others were eating without restraint. Sister Theodota, as usual, had started at one side of her plate and worked methodically toward the other; it was already more than half cleared. Sister Claire, whom Felice suspected of making faces with her food, rearranged dots of potato and fish on her plate while she chewed, studying the effects like an artist, her head turned slightly to the side. Evangeline's eyes looked glazed; though her arm moved in a steady rhythm from plate to mouth, the fork's aim was not always entirely accurate, giving her the appearance of an invalid being force-fed. Celeste was eating with her mouth open, but the nuns at their table were too distracted to give her a look.

At the other tables, too, heads were bowed over plates. Even Antoinette, recently shifted back to the middle table, was busily chewing. Felice smiled, remembering the day Antoinette had been reciting in religion class, her oblong, slightly pouty mouth opening and closing like a fish blowing bubbles, and Celeste had whispered, "She looks just like a pollock."

Felice realized that Mother Superior was staring at her. She ducked her head and began to eat, stuffing a huge forkful of potatoes into her mouth. When she looked up again, after a few more bites, the nun had turned away.

It was Felice's and Marie's turn to help with the washing-up. As they passed her on the way to the kitchen, Mother Superior said, "No mischief, young ladies." Felice turned her most wide- and damp-eyed look on Mother Superior, but she had already turned away, talking to Sister Mary Faith. Felice clenched her jaw and swung through the kitchen door.

Soukie, wearing a kerchief pinned to her hair, novice-style, chattered about her strategy for getting out of the kitchen and into the order. Felice closed her ears and scoured pots with a vengeance. Soukie finally took the soup pot from her. "You're going to wear it out, Mademoiselle. Look, here's your friend to see you."

Felice looked down at Seine, who rubbed against her legs and meowed. "You would not believe how that cat gets around, Mademoiselle," Soukie said. "Today, while you young ladies were in class, I found him up on the fourth floor. And it's a good thing, too," she said, hefting a dry platter back to its place on the shelf. "Plenty of mice up there as well."

When Seine followed the girls up the stairs, Felice did not try to turn him back.

They found Celeste, Françoise, and Anne before Felice's mirror, pinching their cheeks and lips to make them red.

"Look at Françoise's hair," Celeste said. "Turn around, Francie. Doesn't she look like a lady? Now, turn around again, let them see the back."

Françoise's long hair was swept up in a chignon; beneath the cloud of dark hair her neck looked as delicate as the stem of a flower.

"Let's do yours like that, Felice. Wouldn't she look pretty with her hair up, Françoise?"

"Yes," Françoise said, admiring herself in the mirror. "Those braids make her look like a child."

"Sit down, Felice," Celeste commanded, picking up her brush. She and Françoise undid Felice's braids while Marie and Anne watched. "I think it would look good in a swoopy sort of knot, don't you, Françoise?" Celeste shook out Felice's hair and began to brush it.

Felice closed her eyes. She forgot Mother Superior, Sister Agatha, and everything else. She floated, conscious only of the soft touch of fingers on her head, the hum of her friends' voices, and the warmth of Seine in her lap.

"There, now," Celeste said finally. "Look at yourself, Felice. It's good, isn't it?" she asked the others triumphantly.

"Beautiful," Anne breathed.

"She looks like Sarah Bernhardt," Françoise said.

But Felice, leaning toward the mirror at the face beneath the piled-up hair, thought she looked a little bit like Mama.

21

DURING THE THIRD WEEK OF LENT THERE WAS A BLIZZARD. FOR three and a half days the snow fell so fast and thick that it made a white veil about the convent building. Looking out the windows, Felice could see only the swirling white flakes; the outer chapel, the orchard, and even the closest trees were hidden from view. The wind battered the building with such ferocity that Felice could imagine, with all landmarks obscured from view, that the convent was being blown about in space, and might come to rest in some other part of Nova Scotia, or perhaps in France, or Boston, when the storm was over. No one ventured out of doors, even for snow cream, everyone heeding Mother Superior's warning that if they stepped out even a little way they might become confused and not find the way back, ever. (It had happened not many years ago to old Père Herriot, at the College of St. Anne, Mother Superior told the girls and sisters during a specially called meeting the first day of the storm; he had not been found until spring, in a melting bank of snow at the foot of a ravine, his fingers frozen to his rosary.) All communication between Sacré Sang and the village was severed. Not even the Abbé ventured up the steep hill from Nevette, for, as Soukie said, he would have been as imperiled as a storm-tossed ship without compass or rudder. "La, Mademoiselle Felice," Soukie said, pummeling a great mass of bread dough, "if he should lose the road, I shudder to think . . ." Neither Jacques nor the usual few visitors came either, with their news from the villages, so that for a time the convent seemed the entire world, moored alone in a vast opaque white universe.

For Felice, the sudden isolation produced a transformation that was comforting rather than frightening. With the out-of-doors grown so perilous, the convent took on a homelike security. And everyone seemed to rise to the occasion with cheerfulness, and even a certain gaiety. Discords and minor feuds dissolved; the girls were united in their excitement; and the sisters were lenient, even friendly. Mother Superior radiated energy and warmth, directing both routine and emergency convent activities with evident relish. The absence of the Abbé, Soukie remarked to Felice and Celeste, as they helped her cut out cookies one afternoon, had done more for Mother Superior's humor than she would have believed possible; she hadn't scolded about yesterday's scorched bread, and had even come in the kitchen to tell her, Soukie marveled, that if she weren't approved for the novitiate, an assistant would be found to help her with the worst scullery chores.

Mother Superior called Felice into her office on the second day of the storm. She smiled warmly upon the girl, her irritation about Felice's account of Uncle Adolphe now apparently a thing of the past. "I have been thinking, my dear," the nun said, "about your confirmation name. It is your own choice, of course, but it would please me if you took Marie Thérèse—not just because this is my name in religion, but you are rather like her, I think. An overactive imagination, yes, but a spiritual gift as well." Felice, glowing with pleasure, agreed; her own preference, Cecilia—her mother's name—was temporarily forgotten.

In her happy eyes, the physical interior of the convent took on a new beauty for Felice. The snow brightened the air and lent an ethereal glow to objects inside the building. In the chapel, the white pews and embroidered altar cloths held the light, and the Lenten cloths that shrouded the crucifixes and the statue of the Virgin shimmered a rich, deep purple. Every detail—the nautilus-shaped holy-water stoup, her prayer beads, her own slim fingers riffling the gold-edged pages of her missal—seemed to have an enhanced clarity and preciousness. Stoves poured forth warmth (in the Abbé's absence, the rationing of wood was suspended), delicious steaming soups and hot muffins were served at meals, and readings from Dickens were substituted for the usual Acadian history or religious works at sewing hour. Felice thought the climate of the classrooms seemed trans-

formed, camaraderie replacing the aura of vague threat and anticipation of failure. She found the memorization of history paragraphs and
the multiplication of fractions—usually so dreary—now positively
cozy activities.

Felice's sense of security extended even to the infirmary where the
tongueless man lay. That door stood open most of the time now, and
there was a regular stream of sisters going in and out, carrying in
stove-wood and fragrant hot chowders and tea, for Mother Superior
and Evangeline were determined that their patient not take cold.
Felice reestablished herself in the chair by the inner wall, and spent
an hour or two there in the afternoons, reading to Monsieur from the
missal or psalter.

Felice continued this practice of sitting in the infirmary even when
the snow had ceased to fall and the girls went out after classes to
throw snowballs and to build icy effigies of their favorite nuns. Soukie
let her carry in Monsieur's dinner, and Evangeline sometimes let her
keep watch alone, so that Felice felt a firm sense of importance with
regard to the tongueless man, and in the workings of the convent in
general. Initially she felt safe from him too, and met his gaze with
serenity, though she was aware that his eyes were often upon her. She
preceded each visit with a session before the mirror, combing and
rebraiding her hair, sometimes letting it hang loose, tied back with a
ribbon. To Mother Superior and Evangeline (and to the Abbé, when
he returned) she gave reports on the man's spiritual progress, noting
every reaction, every nuance of expression when she said this prayer
or that, when she sang the "Ave Maris Stella," when she pressed her
rosary into his hands. For her part in this holy work, Felice felt
blanketed by the warmth of the entire sisterhood.

Partly to offset any envy they might feel because of the nuns'
approval of her, but mostly for the sheer delight of it, Felice gave long,
after-hours recountings of Monsieur's activities to her friends. These
stories were of a decidedly different flavor than the reports to the
sisters, with emphasis on seduction (his looks, sighs, and even winks)
and on danger, elements that Felice emphasized more and more as the
days passed, both so the other girls' interest wouldn't wane, and
because these aspects—whether in reality or in her own mind—were

gradually intensifying. There was a deeply pleasurable tension between the spiritual and the sensual that Felice was vaguely conscious of as she sat on the edge of her chair, letting the rosary beads fall one by one through her fingers, making her voice mellifluous, glancing up occasionally at the man's eyes smoldering at her from the pallor of his face and the pillow.

Celeste and Françoise appeared in the infirmary twice, and on another occasion Celeste came alone. During these visits they walked ostentatiously about the room, made faces at Felice, and, before they were well out into the hall again, erupted in fits of giggling. They were able to report to Anne and Marie that Monsieur did indeed leer and stare, though, Celeste and Françoise contended, he had directed most of that attention toward *them*.

"Of course you would say that," Felice countered majestically, when Celeste said Monsieur much preferred her looks to Felice's. Then Felice went on to describe the most recent horrifying event: she had been reading aloud from her catechism book, she said, and had been so absorbed in it that before she had known what was happening, he was up out of bed and by her side. "Before I could move," Felice whispered, "he had touched me."

"Where?" they all wanted to know. "Where?"

Felice pointed at her left breast.

"Ooooh, I bet it left a mark," Celeste said. "Let's see."

"You're crazy, Celeste," Felice replied, pushing her off the bed, starting a noisy, free-for-all wrestling match that brought two nuns to the door.

"Sssh," Sister Claire said, shaking her head and frowning.

"Don't you young ladies remember this is Lent?" Sister Constance demanded.

"Yes, Sister."

"Then be quiet, or I'll have to report you to Mother Superior."

This mild rebuke was the only chastisement Felice suffered, and did nothing to mar her general feeling of security and contentment during the time of the blizzard. She liked to look out her window, now that the snow had stopped falling and the convent had stayed right where it belonged, at the shapes of the outer chapel, the back wall, and the willows, reassuringly familiar beneath the beautiful heavy white cover. In the distance beyond the wall, the balsam trees looked like ruffled white sentinels keeping watch over the bay. She felt that she was a cherished member of a large family, and wrote to Philippe that she expected Sacré Sang would be her permanent home before long. Even Seine, she could not resist adding, was happier than he had been in Wolfville, much sleeker and fatter.

After she mailed this letter, Felice found that Uncle Adolphe, recently forgotten, now loomed up out of the depths of her mind at surprising moments. She encountered his angry face in dreams and once, terrifyingly, in the tongueless man's room, when the invalid opened his mouth in what turned out to be nothing but a protracted yawn.

The general conventical good will embraced even Sister Agatha, who, as the eldest member of the community, was given spare blankets and was respectfully deferred to in all conversations about historic snows of bygone years. She flourished under this new variety of attention, and after giving a well-received guest lecture to Mother Superior's history class, confided to Felice that she might yet stage a pedagogical comeback. At Mother Superior's request, the subject was eighteenth-century literature; though Sister Agatha made it clear that she held the writing of this period in low esteem, with the notable exception of William Blake (from whose *Songs of Innocence and Experience* she chose several recitations), the superioress sat smiling throughout the lecture. And after class, Mother Superior effusively thanked the other nun for a lecture that was "not only edifying, but entertaining as well."

Late afternoons found Sister Agatha in the parlor, talking to a group of students about legendary personalities in an earlier era at the convent, and about her own history there. Felice, whom Sister Agatha introduced as her hagiographer, sat by her side and took notes. The nun spoke with particular animation of the summer she had spent studying in Italy with "the great masters," and how her aesthetic training had been interrupted by a call from God to her true vocation —the education of young ladies, and, when she was still up to it, missionary work among the Micmac Indians, and—most important of all, of course—"a sacred marriage to Christ, that most exacting and satisfying of all bridegrooms."

Even when Sister Agatha had what Mother Superior referred to as "one of her little spells," she was treated with tolerance. One night Felice found her on the third-floor landing, pressing her face against the icy pane of a north window, and muttering, over and over, "that savage, that savage." Felice managed to dislodge the nun and lead her to her cell; all along the way Sister Agatha mumbled about a dark savage who was loose, roaming the convent grounds, and hungering to mutilate her. As Felice tucked her in bed and tried to console her, Sister Agatha replied, "Don't worry, child, all will be made right," and signed a cross on her forehead, above the red imprint of the frosty window. At breakfast the next day the print was still visible, the reddish-brown of a birthmark. Sister Agatha's fingers returned again and again to the mark upon her brow; she complained of a severe burn. Most of her tablemates looked at her sympathetically, and Sister Theodota—though she shook her head, and made a little whistling noise in her teeth—even refrained from making her usual recommendation for Sister Agatha's removal.

That morning the Abbé climbed the hill in snowshoes, bearing a basketful of eels and a letter from Bishop Chrysostom. The eels, which Antoine Gentil had wrested through holes in the ice at Bonaventure Pond the day before the storm, were served fried on toast at luncheon. The Abbé rose after the meal to say that he had been terribly concerned about the nuns and girls being all alone during the storm, and that he would spend the afternoon on his knees in the chapel, thanking God and Saint Eude for their deliverance. Next, he read the Bishop's letter aloud: it expressed, in rather florid language, His Eminence's great anticipation about meeting the nuns and girls of Sacré Sang, and about participating in the events of Easter. Then, removing his spectacles and smiling benevolently, the Abbé said he had several important announcements to make. These were: the confirmations of Felice and three other girls to take place at Easter (no surprise, this); the final profession of postulant Evangeline Gericault (again, no surprise); acceptance into the Sacré Sang novitiate that same holy day of "the outstanding student Antoinette Mouton" (an announcement which brought Antoinette coos of congratulations from the nuns, and wry looks from Felice and Celeste). On Holy Saturday, the Abbé went on, there were to be two baptisms, one of "the stranger whom God has placed in our hands," and the other of "the half-breed Indian lad who is now living with me." At this, Felice felt Celeste's foot upon her own. "Your boyfriend," Celeste mouthed silently.

"Savages shouldn't *be* baptized," Sister Agatha muttered, striking the flat of her hand against the table so hard that the teacups jumped. It was an outburst that the sisters and even the Abbé did their best to ignore.

"This Easter will be an especially momentous one for all of us," the Abbé continued, with a cough. "I challenge you to redouble your austerities, in preparation for these sacred events, and for this great holy season."

Even with the Abbé's return, life at the convent retained its dream-like quality, at least until the snow began to melt some two weeks later. His reentry into their sphere altered the focus of the nuns' and girls' activities, with more emphasis on spiritual, and less on homely, pursuits, but it did not, for a time, disrupt the cohesion bred of shared solitude and peril.

Perhaps because they felt cooperative, perhaps because they were ready for a change of pace, both nuns and girls took up the Abbé's appeal for asceticism with a zeal and a vengeance that exceeded his expectations. Prayers were voluntarily increased, even by the most recalcitrant girls, and all faces shone, as with a collective beatitude. Even Soukie was relatively silent, though persisting in the unsanctioned wearing of her kerchief, and after a rebellious clanging and battering of pots in the kitchen, following the Abbé's announcement that she was not scheduled for induction into the novitiate at Easter, she asked every quarter-hour, as penance, that the Lord "set a watch before my mouth, and a door round my lips; that my heart may not incline to evil words to make excuses in sins."

Mother Superior suggested in history class that each girl do one silent penance devoted to a sinner unable to help himself. In response to this, Felice put a pebble in her shoe (it was a small, pretty one she had gotten from the shore last fall) and did her best not to hobble as she walked; it made a satisfying round bruise on her instep, and accrued, she thought, to Uncle Adolphe's small capital in heaven. She also committed a daring act in the tongueless man's room, kneeling by his bed when Evangeline was gone to say the rosary. With her head bent, neck exposed, she suffered great anguish and fear both times she did this, but she restrained herself from telling the other girls.

By the end of a week, the spiritual temperature in the convent had risen to fever level. Voluntary penances increased and so did speculation. It was rumored among the girls that Sister Theodota had spent three nights sleeping in a tub of cold water, saying the Penitentials all the while, and that Evangeline was habitually making her bed on a pallet of pine cones laid on the drafty floor of her cell. There was talk of hair shirts and flagellation, and Celeste claimed to have seen a row of scourges hanging from pegs in the sisters' vestment closet. "That explains, then," Françoise said, "the awful noises I heard in Sister Agatha's cell yesterday morning."

"Poor Sister Agatha," Celeste whispered, looking toward the ceiling in the direction of the nun's quarters. "She will be rewarded."

The others agreed, and murmured in unison the credo of the Sister Agatha Liberation and Protection League: "Fie to her detractors, death to all traitors; all hail, Agatha!"

It was Celeste who proposed that members of the League flagellate themselves with the prickly branches of balsam. She broached the subject on the Sunday of the Golden Rose, when the five of them were gathered in her cubicle just before Compline. After mass that morning, Celeste told the others, she had gone into Antoinette's cubicle to borrow a needle and thread and had found Antoinette naked to the waist, scourging herself with a length of packing rope. Antoinette had turned, scourge in hand, Celeste reported, and she had seen the welts on Antoinette's breasts.

"That's even more than nuns do," Anne said in awed tones.

"No, it's not," Celeste said, "and I know. My cousin was a nun for several years, you remember."

"If Antoinette can do it, we can," Felice said with a toss of her braids, and that decided it.

"She is just about completely flat-chested," Celeste could not resist adding as they parted.

On the fourth Monday of Lent all the girls but Marie (who pleaded the illness of Monthlies) gathered again. From beneath her bed Celeste drew out the balsam boughs that she and Felice had cut that evening while the nuns were at vespers.

"Let's just hit our backs," Anne said, shivering as she unbuttoned her blouse.

"I agree," Françoise said. "It would be sinful to damage our bodies. What if we had babies and they couldn't eat?" She turned, slipping her embroidered camisole over her shoulder.

The other girls turned away to undress and, at the signal from Celeste, began to strike their backs in unison.

"Three and four," Celeste said, making it a song. "Four and five, five and six, six and seven . . ."

The sharp points stung Felice's back and she hit harder. In just a few minutes, she thought, she would not notice the pain. But it did not happen; her back began to burn, and she shivered, feeling the cold against her skin. She looked out at the snow, palely luminescent in the moonlight, and thought of Uncle Adolphe. She had prayed for him all afternoon, as it was a day marked for concentration on the conversion of sinners. She imagined him dead and struck herself so hard she thought she must have raised blood. She backed up to the mirror to see. Her shoulders were a blur in the dim light. She reached to touch herself, and as she drew her hand away, dry, her eyes met Celeste's in the mirror. She turned quickly to face her, covering her chest with her arms, but Celeste stood motionless, shameless, smiling, her breasts full and white, the nipples astonishingly dark. Above her revealed body, Celeste's face seemed transformed—older and rather sinister.

"Keep counting, Celeste," Françoise said, slowing the motion of her arm.

Anne looked over her shoulder at Celeste and Felice. "They've stopped, Françoise," she said.

Françoise dropped her bough and turned slowly, her lips curved in a coquettish smile. Anne turned too, holding the fir branch over her chest, but after a moment, as they all stood silent, regarding one another, she lowered the branch to her side so that her breasts, too, were exposed.

Felice felt distant, as though this were a dream, but her breasts tingled. "It's too cold," she said, looking down at the puckered tips of her breasts.

Celeste began to giggle. "Françoise's look up, Anne's look down, but mine and Felice's look right out." The other girls laughed too, nervously, and reached for their blouses. They dressed and parted in silence.

Once in her cubicle, Felice wanted to cry. Instead, she knelt by her bed, intending to stay awake all night saying the Penitentials and the Office of the Dead. But in the morning she woke to find herself in bed and awash in the memory of a dream in which she, her chest bruised and bandaged, was laid as a sacrifice before the altar, and the tongueless man, vested in white and gold, advanced toward her, bearing the oil of chrism in a golden cup.

22

FELICE'S SERENITY SEEMED TO MELT WITH THE SNOW. FOLLOWING the period of unusual intimacy, everyone about her grew irritable, and the atmosphere of the convent—paradisiacal during the blizzard—turned sour.

The Abbé and Mother Superior fretted about Easter and the coming of the Bishop; their storm-engendered truce dissolved. The teaching nuns gave surprise examinations and graded them harshly. Members of the League withdrew from one another, and for a time suspended, by mutual, unspoken agreement, their meetings in Felice's cubicle.

Felice began to avoid the tongueless man's room, going in to fulfill her reading obligation only when he was accompanied. Even with Evangeline or one of the nuns present, however, Felice tried to keep her eyes and mind upon the missal as she read, for she felt that

Monsieur's gaze was constantly upon her, ferreting out every tiny thought.

Mother Superior came in during one afternoon's reading to help Evangeline turn Monsieur's mattress. "Don't leave, Felice," Mother Superior said, waving the girl back to her seat. "Monsieur Francis will particularly appreciate your kind office after this—it tires him so." She and Evangeline helped the invalid to a chair, where he sat—Felice dared to glance—with his eyes closed. She thought that Monsieur looked more playful than tired, like the searcher in hide-and-seek who keeps his eyes shut for thirty seconds while the hiders scatter.

The Abbé entered, waving a letter. "Our first post since the snow —and it brings wonderful news. From the learned Monk Justin, my father confessor in Brittany."

"Indeed." Mother Superior stripped off Monsieur's sheets in three deft motions.

"Justin says—and he has quite a reputation as a linguist, though he modestly disavows it—Justin is of the opinion that Monsieur's language is one of the ancient Coptic dialects."

"And how would *he* know?" Mother Superior snorted, pummeling and kneading Monsieur's pillow.

"Do you not recall those samples of Monsieur's writing which I sent to Brittany? Perhaps *you* do, Mademoiselle," the Abbé said, turning his head in Felice's direction.

"Yes, Mon Père," she said, too late: the Abbé had already whirled around and was reading aloud to Mother Superior.

" 'And I think I can agree with you, my dear son, that the Coptic characters signifying Hermas are inscribed at the end of this curious manuscript. My opinion is offered in all humility, however . . .' " The Abbé read silently for a moment. "And so forth and so on," he concluded, folding the letter.

"So, Sister," the priest went on brightly, "I must admit I was in error with the name Eude. Monsieur will be christened Hermas. I will write to His Eminence immediately. After all, it is apparently Monsieur's own appellation, and quite a worthy one—consider the Latin Penitential of Saint Hermas. Well, Sister," he continued, after an empty pause, "what do you think of it?"

"Francis is much more suitable. He *looks* like Francis. And all the sisters prefer it."

"Looks like Francis! That is no way to select a christening name!" The Abbé opened the letter again and scanned it, as though hoping to find further support there.

Felice stole a glance at Monsieur; he seemed to be attending to the nun and priest with interest, his quick, foxlike eyes darting back and forth between them.

"Hermas is an uncommonly distinguished name," the Abbé said, noisily refolding the letter. "Surely you don't dispute *that,* Sister."

Mother Superior, one of whose most effective weapons was her use of well-timed silences, merely raised one eyebrow, causing the Abbé to splutter on, "After all, Sister, *I* will be doing the baptism. *I* am his spiritual guardian."

Mother Superior and Evangeline flipped Monsieur's mattress; the springs shuddered and emitted several distinctly different squeaks and twangs, like orchestral instruments tuning up.

The Abbé turned to the tongueless man and bowed. "Monsieur Hermas Sosonier. As a catechumen, you will attend your first mass on the Feria of the Great Scrutiny, here in the chapel of our beloved convent." The Abbé extended his hand; Monsieur reached out, smiling, to touch it.

"You see, you see." The Abbé pumped Monsieur's hand. "He understands, and approves—it is confirmed, Sister." And he strode from the room.

"He's not walking to any mass," Mother Superior called after him. "He's much too weak." She snapped out a fresh sheet. "Hermas, indeed," she grumbled.

Evangeline glided about, tucking in corners, not speaking to or looking at anyone until Mother Superior said to her, "What *is* it about a name that makes some people act so foolish?"

"I do not know, Ma Mère," Evangeline murmured. But then she turned to smile insinuatingly at Felice, and Felice was suddenly shocked into memory of the titillating, name-gauging episode with Monsieur. Had Evangeline ever told about that? Would she? Then other, formless, guilts engulfed Felice, and for a moment she could not breathe.

While Mother Superior and Evangeline helped Monsieur back to his bed, Felice rose and sidled out. She could not bring herself to return to the infirmary again; this she interpreted as failure of her spiritual will, and she began to have doubts about her vocation.

There were still moments when her course seemed as steady and certain as ever: the almost physical thrill she felt after a fervent Act of Contrition; a sense of harmony induced by segments of the mass, the peace she could sometimes recapture, kneeling alone by the willow tree before Sister Agatha's painting of the Virgin, who smiled down upon her with the serene conviction that doubters of Felice's character were wrong.

For most of Felice's reservations about joining the sisters of Sacré Sang took the form of imagined rejection—by Mother Superior, the Abbé, or the Bishop, any one of whom might pronounce her unsuited. Though she did not, during this time, put the question to Mother Superior, her sense of the nun's rejecting her for the novitiate was so strong that she felt it to be as good as spoken; she began to think of appealing to the Bishop, who might overrule—or concur with— Mother Superior's decision.

But even her letter-perfect mastery of the catechism, on which the Bishop himself was to review each candidate for confirmation, did little to mitigate her fears. She came to dread her turn to help with the washing-up, for Soukie, who was optimistic about the Bishop's approving her own petition for nunship, could talk of nothing else. One night, as Soukie was marking on the kitchen calendar the demise of yet another day, Felice sprang a private catechism quiz on herself and found that the entire ritual had vanished from her mind. She stared at the rows of red crosses marching toward Easter; if she should stand thus gaping before His Eminence, unable to answer his questions, he would surely say that Felice could not be admitted to the sisterhood. Indeed, he might rule that a student unable to learn the rudimentary articles of faith be required to depart from the convent school immediately. The butter-dish Felice was drying slipped from her hands to the counter top and sent a saltcellar crashing to the floor.

"Mademoiselle! You'll bring me bad luck!" The kitchenmaid squatted to flick some spilled salt over her left shoulder. "Bring me that broom." She stood and began to sweep at the shards so vigorously that Felice edged toward the door. "Yes, go on, Mademoiselle," Soukie said, making a sweeping motion toward the girl, "and don't come back till you quit your mooning—You're going to break everything in this kitchen, and Mother Superior will blame it on me, and give His Eminence a bad report."

Felice fled to the parlor, and to music, the only haven from her growing anxieties during the latter part of Lent.

Felice now practiced twice a day, for she found that working on new passages was a satisfying and diverting occupation. When playing the Bach pieces she had already mastered, she felt entirely secure, enclosed within the amber-lit rooms formed by the music. Caught up as she was in the fluid forward movement of notes, it seemed to her that time had stopped; this motion seemed infinite, and when the invention or variation ended, she could start over and be there again, enclosed in the clarity of pure sound.

Felice was playing so well that Sister Claire said her pupil had reached a new plateau, and would undoubtedly impress not only her listeners at Easter, but other, less partial audiences—even the very exacting instructors at the conservatory Sister Claire had herself attended. On the days when she felt particularly inspired, Felice sat down to the practice as to a performance, imagining a spotlit stage, drawn velvet curtains, Mama in the front row, and a silver-haired man extending his hand, saying, "And now, ladies and gentlemen, we give you the amazing and lovely young Mademoiselle Felice Belliveau, toast of America and the continent!"

On such a day as this, when Felice's gracefully arched hands descended to the keys and began to produce music that surprised even herself, Sister Agatha slipped into the parlor to listen.

The girl was not aware of her presence until she turned, at the completion of Bach's Two-Part Invention in B minor, to find Sister Agatha applauding.

"Sister Claire, we are harboring a musical genius!" Sister Agatha crowed.

Felice sat grinning until Sister Claire said, "Well, genius, shall we be allowed an encore?"

Encouraged by her success, Felice played not the variation next on her program, but a work of her own composition. Though the style of the piece was reminiscent of Bach—with the top hand engaged in counterpoint, and occasional grace notes—it was set in a rhythm and key more favored by the romantic than the baroque period.

"One of the great Lieder?" Sister Agatha guessed, at the conclusion of this work. "Schubert?"

"No, Sister." Felice glanced at Sister Claire, whose head remained tilted in its listening pose. "Mine. And it's—it's an anthem, not a secular song."

"What did I tell you, Sister Claire! A rare performer, *and* a composer! The child has received the creative blessing."

"It was very nice," Sister Claire said in her polite, dinner-table voice. "And now could we have the variation, Felice?"

At the end of the rehearsal, Sister Claire revealed her intention to ask the Bishop what possibility there might be for the convent's acquiring a small organ. And not just for the enrichment of mass, she told Felice and Sister Agatha, but so her protégée might learn to play it. Pleasant though this sounded, Felice felt a sense of anticlimax; much of the enthusiasm of her response was produced in Sister Claire's behalf. After daydreaming all through that day's classes, and the next's, about the ovations and tossed roses that would follow her performance, in a magnificent Parisian hall, of her own First Piano Concerto, Felice announced to Sister Claire, with tentative boldness, her intention of becoming a composer.

The nun gently restored her to reality. "I don't think I have ever *heard* of a female composer, dear. There have been a few excellent interpreters, of course—but *very* few, remember that. I'd beware, if I were you, of underrating the teaching of music. What finer way to spread joy throughout the world, and to please God?"

Felice sought out Sister Agatha, hoping to engage her in further conversation about music. But she found the nun now sunk in silent morosity, unresponsive to her questions and leading statements.

Sister Agatha's changed mood, Felice learned from a conversation with Soukie, had been brought on by the Abbé's just-launched campaign to make the nun more presentable for His Eminence. The kitchenmaid had herself heard the priest command Sister Agatha to attend catechism class, so that she might refresh herself on the tenets of the Catholic faith, from which she had "so willfully wandered."

The nun did appear once in Felice's confirmation class, and listened in silence until the end of the lesson, when she arose to announce that the Subtle Doctor had this moment revealed to her the Immaculate Conception of several female saints in addition to Christ's mother. She was not invited back to class, but could sometimes be seen, in various niches of the halls and grounds, tête-à-tête with the Abbé. Mother Superior was said to be strongly opposed to these private lessons, and, according to Soukie, had several times implored the priest to "leave the poor woman in peace, for all our sakes, Mon Père."

Felice one day came upon Sister Agatha sliding along the second-floor corridor wall toward her cell, her fingers moving spiderlike across the painting of Saint Agatha's martyrdom.

"Sister," Felice whispered, touching the nun's arm, "we won't let your paintings be hurt—don't worry."

The nun turned to the wall, and rested her forehead on a Roman soldier's arm.

"Sister Agatha? Are you ill? Here, let me help you to your room." Felice took the nun by one elbow and tugged her free. Leaning heavily upon Felice, Sister Agatha allowed herself to be guided into her cell and onto her bed.

"Sister, we could work on your autobiography. Would you like me to take notes now?"

"Felicia?"

"Yes, Sister?"

Sister Agatha touched her rosary crucifix to her lips and then to her forehead. "I am to be martyred," she whispered, "in the name of freedom."

"What do you mean, Sister?"

"A savage—of the white variety—has thrust, and thrust . . ." The nun began to lean to one side.

"Do you want to lie down, Sister? You want to go the other direction, then." Felice gently pushed her up away from the bed rail; the nun then eased slowly to the mattress.

Felice took off Sister Agatha's glasses and laid them on the small table. "Wouldn't you be more comfortable with your head on the pillow, Sister?" The nun panted as Felice tried to pull her higher on the bed. "I'm sorry, Sister, I can't get you any further." Felice pulled the coverlet over her. "I'll go get Soukie."

"No. Privacy. My bridegroom comes." Sister Agatha drew her veil over her face.

Felice patted the nun's shoulder and tiptoed away to call an emergency meeting of the League.

But the girls, exhilarated about meeting once again, were more giddy than helpful. Proposals for aiding Sister Agatha ranged from writing to tell the Abbé's mother how mean he was to old ladies, to concealing a mousetrap in the Abbé's lectern missal; the climax of this latter scheme, Celeste said to the accompaniment of nervous giggles, would be the mousetrap's springing out when the priest opened the book during mass and neatly clipping off his tongue. Then he could not speak to, or against, Sister Agatha.

"Stop it, Celeste," Felice protested. "This is serious."

"You're the great biographer," Celeste said crossly. "*You* think of something."

"I will," Felice said, jumping up from her bed. She went to the chapel, where she made a resolution to follow Sister Agatha everywhere, like Saint Jerome's lion.

The next day, the Feria of the Great Scrutiny, Felice broke the seating rule at mass to take a place beside Sister Agatha. The other nuns, aflutter over the tongueless man's rumored attendance, took no notice of Felice's move.

"Hello, Sister," Felice whispered. Sister Agatha, who sat with her eyes closed and her folded hands tucked beneath her chin, seemed not to hear.

Mother Superior entered late, strode down the aisle, and thumped upon her kneeling bench. Then the Abbé appeared in the doorway, one arm supporting Monsieur. Girls and sisters—all but Sister Agatha —craned their necks to look; Sister Constance, three pews ahead, leaned all the way out into the aisle for a better view.

The Abbé's prize catechumen was still dressed in his nightshirt and wore one of Mother Superior's afghans draped about him like a shawl. On his feet were shoes that Felice guessed to be the Abbé's castoffs, for he shuffled, and winced at each step; Monsieur seemed almost ordinary, Felice thought, compared to the barefoot, and infinitely more graceful, creature of the Great Walk.

But she flinched when Sister Agatha touched her arm. "Savages, Felicia?"

Sister Mary Faith looked over her shoulder. "Sssh!" She patted her lips with one long finger.

"The Abbé, and Monsieur," Felice said, from the corner of her mouth. "*Ave Maria, benedicta tu in mulieribus . . .*" she chanted softly, thinking to calm Sister Agatha.

" 'I am gall, I am heartburn'!" Sister Agatha said, loudly enough that nuns and girls three pews deep were diverted from the main spectacle.

As Monsieur was settled in the front pew, Sister Agatha gripped Felice's arm. "Help me to leave this place, Felicia. The hour of my martyrdom is heavy upon me, and I must lay out my wedding raiment."

"Ssh, Sister. I'll help you upstairs in just a little while—right after mass."

"Now!" the nun shouted, standing.

"Ssh," Felice said again, rising to support Sister Agatha. The Abbé was signaling, with chopping motions of his head, for Sister Theodota to remove the recalcitrant nun. "Come on then, Sister." Felice propelled her out of the pew and up the aisle, setting her jaw against faces that turned toward them. "Hurry," she whispered, "so we can go alone."

But Sisters Theodota and Constance caught up with them in the hall. After brushing Felice aside, they manacled the old nun's elbows with white-knuckled hands and led her off between them.

"Fear not, daughter Felice," Sister Agatha called back, from the corner. "A pound of glory outweighs a pound of pain."

Felice returned to the chapel, knelt in a rear pew, and, burying her face in her hands, said a silent, passionate prayer for Sister Agatha.

.   .   .

That night, after lights out, Felice tiptoed to Sister Agatha's cell, feeling her way along the wall; the plaster was like gooseflesh beneath her fingers. Heart pounding, she eased open the door, afraid of what she might find: an empty room, and Sister Agatha banished; or—even though reason argued against it—Sister Agatha martyred, bleeding, stretched in some grotesque pose.

But Sister Agatha stood by the window, holding her face up to the starlight and pressing a crucifix to her chest. She was naked except for her veil. Felice stared at the fact of the nun's revealed body: it was like a withered child's except for the sac-like breasts that hung over her belly. Pendulous, wrinkled, veined, they were not the breasts of a martyr, in spite of the crucifix held between them. Nor was Sister Agatha's hopeful, squinting face that of a martyr, but achingly, embarrassingly human.

Felice stood there a moment longer, tears in her eyes, as an ecstatic smile bloomed on the old woman's face. The smile faded, and Felice tiptoed away, ashamed to have watched.

WHEN IT GREW LIGHT THE NEXT MORNING, A GENTLE RAIN WAS falling. At the very early hour when Mother Superior and the novice Evangeline walked down the hill to the village, before Felice awoke, there was no wind, and the rain fell straight down, each line of water like a long hand-stitched seam. The white frozen land was loosening, the rain pocking the crust of snow and forming pools beneath the trees. On the cliff, ribs of basalt shone through the snow, and on the shore below the convent, the water inside the cave was thawing, so that at each forward rush of the tide chunks of ice rang and echoed against the inner walls.

A little later in the morning a wind began to blow from the water, slanting the rain against the cliff and the bay-side windows of the convent. When Felice began to wake, the murmur of the rain against the window and the clouds of dream through which she rose and fell made her feel as though she were being rocked.

When the bells began to sound—first in the distance, at the village church, and then from above, in the tower of the convent—Felice thought it was Sunday, and she was late for mass. Beyond the white partition she could see the shadow of Antoinette, moving about her cubicle as she dressed. Just one minute longer, she said to herself, and, closing her eyes, began counting to sixty, curling her body to savor the warmth of the bed. When she woke again, after a dream of a brightly colored landscape, the bells were still ringing. Still she did not move at once, but lay listening to the rain. There was a rhythmic thrumming against the window, and beyond, an uninterrupted sluice of water. The sound of it made her whole body feel liquid.

Turning on her side, she looked at her mirror, with its irregular silvering like a skim of ice; the white curtain was reflected in the mirror and the air, which was a soft gray, seemed caught there too. She could see on the bureau the top part of the white porcelain cat, whose sleepy eyes seemed to be looking toward her, and the rim of the gold frame that held the picture of Mama and Papa. She couldn't see their expressions from this angle, but she knew them by heart: Mama with the suppressed smile that made the dimple by her mouth, and Papa, hands folded on his knees, his eyes at once kind and distant.

Felice got up and smiled good morning to herself in the mirror, then dressed quickly, putting on the pale blue blouse and dark blue skirt Aunt Rose had sent her as an early birthday present—she would be fourteen next week. She unbraided and brushed her hair; it was crinkly, like Irish moss, from having been too tightly plaited. The color of the blouse made her eyes shine bluer, and she leaned forward to admire their sparkle, and the lashes that framed them. She turned her head this way and that, marveling at newly discovered angles and expressions, and comparing herself with the picture of Mama. Only when she had pinned on her veil, studying its effect against her wavy hair, and thinking to herself, I must hurry, I am already late, did

Felice remember it was not Sunday. It was Saturday, because yesterday there had been classes. Tomorrow was Passion Sunday, when they would all go to the village for mass.

The tolling, which had momentarily ceased, began again. It was, Felice suddenly realized, the death knell. As the truth of this slapped her she stared, frozen, into the mirror at the fuzzy-haired stranger, the mouth an O. The convent bell rang in solo now, a remorseless monody that said to her, *van*-ity, *van*-ity, *van*-ity. She imagined herself bound to the iron tongue of the bell, each gong bearing her closer to death and to eternal damnation.

The final peal sounded an emphatic punctuation; Felice could feel its vibration in the room, in her body. There was the noise of rapid footsteps in the hall and on the stairs: an exodus to the chapel, in which sanctuary huddled-together survivors could pray for the newly dead. Felice suddenly thought of Sister Agatha.

"Sister Agatha!" she cried aloud and, clapping her missal to her chest, rushed out into the now-empty hall and down the stairs, continuing to moan as she went, "Sister Agatha, Sister Agatha."

Felice entered the chapel door and the low, sibilant hum of prayers being said in unison. The Abbé was not present; Felice could distinguish Sister Theodota's voice directing the not-quite-unified recitative. Felice thought she could detect a triumphant edge to the nun's voice; her knees shook as she genuflected. She knelt and forced herself to look at Sister Agatha's place, expecting to find it empty. But there was the nun's unmistakable form, the limp veil falling so close to her head and shoulders it looked wet, the body swaying slightly side to side.

Then, looking anxiously about for Sister Claire, she knelt in the back pew beside Adele. "Who died?" she whispered.

"Some lady in the village—I don't know who," Adele murmured.

"Ave Maria," Felice whispered fervently. She pulled out her beads, and spent the remainder of the hour saying a rosary of thanksgiving.

There was a respectful hush at breakfast. Mother Superior and Evangeline returned halfway through the meal, their faces arranged in expressions of concealment. Everything about their carriage insinuated that they were bearers of privileged information.

After the dishes were cleared, Mother Superior rose to make the announcement. "Madame Suzanne Gentil, wife to Antoine Gentil, just after bringing into this world her seventh child, a daughter, has died." She looked more disapproving than grieved, Felice thought, though whether for the woman's having gotten herself into the maternal state, or for abruptly abandoning it, it was impossible to guess. "There will be a meeting of all sisters now in my office—I will want some of you to go with me to prepare the body. You girls are on your honor today—tidy your rooms as usual, and do your studies. Take time to say a prayer for the soul of poor Madame Gentil. The Abbé will come in the afternoon for confession, and afterwards you will be taken for a constitutional. You must stay healthy," she added rather fiercely, as though this were now more important than ever, this death an infectious virus to be warded off with prophylactic exercise.

Feeling strangely exhausted, Felice climbed the stairs. She avoided Celeste, who wanted to continue their conversation about boys. Last night Felice had told a long adventure about her future romance with Robert, the boy from the train. Though she denied any interest at all in Remi, she had drawn on her experience of his expression and eyes in the climactic moments of the story about herself and Robert: the troth, the parting, and the joyous reunion many years later. Now the thought of the subject made her very tired.

She lay down on her bed, wanting nothing but to sleep and to be left alone. She put her head beneath the pillow, to block out the sound of Antoinette opening and closing bureau drawers, and when she did not fall asleep at once, began counting slowly to a hundred. She lay what seemed a long time in a mindless, but miserable, state between waking and sleep. Finally she sat up and spent the rest of the morning trying to study, staring at pages of equations that made no sense at all.

By early afternoon, the rain had ceased. The convent was even quieter than usual. All the nuns who had not gone to assist Mother Superior were praying in the chapel or in the privacy of their cells. Girls tiptoed in the halls and whispered when they spoke.

Felice left the parlor, where she had been sewing—she had taken out as many stitches as she had put into her dishcloth—and went looking for someone to talk to. Soukie was not in the kitchen (she was, Felice later learned, "setting the Gentils' house to rights") but Sister Agatha was there, eating cold mashed potatoes with her fingers.

The nun jumped when Felice entered. "Who is it?" she asked, one outstretched hand feeling the air.

"It's Felice, Sister."

"*Deo gratias.*" Sister Agatha crossed herself, marking the gesture with four white smears of potato. "On my way to prayer in the outer chapel, I saw the Gentil woman going up through the air, in a winged boat. Bodily, Felice, bodily, her younger body too, up toward heaven. It proves that I am right and the Abbé is wrong—the Virgin Mary's Assumption will some day be understood, and made dogma." Her voice rose higher as Felice backed away. "This is a sign to me. My bridegroom wanted me to see it."

"Goodbye, Sister, I have to go now," Felice said, easing out the door.

Felice found Celeste, Françoise, and Anne in the basement. They were discussing the Gentil baby and wet nurses. Felice didn't want to hear about that, either, and she left quickly, after extricating Seine from Françoise's lap. She carried the cat up to the dormitory, but the sound of Antoinette saying the rosary in the next cubicle drove her from there too. She put on her cape and went down the stairs again, and out the back door. She would take Seine to the cove, she decided, and show him he need not be afraid of the water. Maybe he could learn to sit on a rock and fish.

Outside, she put the cat on her shoulder—a position she was trying to train him in—but in the orchard he jumped down and began trotting back toward the convent, lifting his feet high in the slush, his ears flat against his head. Felice could not coax him back. She felt so lonely that her chest began to ache.

She went on beneath the dripping apple trees, picking her way along the soggy, white-patched ground to the Evangeline willows. She looked in at the dolorous face of Our Lady, whose askance gaze refused to meet hers, then climbed the wall and walked quickly through the dark balsams to the cliff.

St. Mary's Bay was sullen this afternoon, and its horizon lost in mist. Felice thought of Mama and Papa, somewhere in the far ocean, deep down in the dark, rags of cloth and flesh rolling about in the currents. Shut up, shut *up,* Felice said to herself, and started down the cliff.

The path had not been walked on since the blizzard, and though much of the snow had melted in the warming air and washed away in the rain, there was a treacherous layer of ice on the rocks. Felice slipped her way along and once fell several yards, saving herself by gripping a small thorny bush.

The huge plates of rock at the base of the cliff, having been constantly rinsed at high tide, were not so icy, and she managed to walk to the edge of the water without difficulty.

The close sound and smell of the water cheered her somewhat, and she bent to look at the jewellike rocks exposed by the receding tide. She would find one best rock, a really beautiful, special one, she decided, and add it to her collection in the tree. Right away she found a circular black rock, flat at the base, with golden stripes circling its outer circumference. Held on her palm, it reminded her of a turtle. Next she found an oval stone, speckled salmon and blue, like some huge bird's egg. She put the turtle and the egg in her pockets and walked on along the shore, occasionally stopping to pick up and discard rocks. Then she saw, wedged between two larger rocks, a small red stone. She picked it up: it was perfectly smooth and round and flat, and just fit into the center of her palm. Its only imperfection was a small indentation that was just the right shape, Felice discovered, for her thumb. She stood rubbing it; the stone grew warm quickly, and was silky beneath her skin. She returned the turtle and the egg to the water; each landed with a thunk and a shower of icy droplets.

Holding the red stone against her cheek, she stood looking out at the bay. It seemed friendlier than it had from above. In the distance the gray water was flat, but within the arms of the cove there were gentle swells. The low waves fell quietly, almost politely, on the shore, making necklaces of foam. This seemed consoling, even personal, to Felice, but her chest still ached as though a chunk of ice were lodged there.

She walked further down the shore, toward the large boulders. Lately covered with a rime of frozen sea spray, the huge rocks were now wet and looked, Felice decided, like a family of sea otters resting together. She leaned against her favorite boulder, looking down at the lacy pieces of ice washing about at the edge of the water. The waves lapped at the other side of her boulder, tickling it with spray, some occasionally leaping up toward her and dampening her face with mist.

Felice suddenly remembered a moment she had not thought of for a long, long time, perhaps not since it happened: a summer afternoon when she and Mama had walked together by the churn, a place on the shore near Yarmouth where the water thundered against the rocks and was flung high into the air in great arcs. The spray had glittered in the July sun, but Mama had been sad, blinking back tears. When Felice asked why, Mama sank to a bench and covered her face with her hands. "Your papa has been gone so long," she said. It was later that summer, when Papa was still gone, that Felice had come upon Mama lying on the parlor floor, a red stain spreading on the rug beneath her. Her mother's cry of *"C'est perdue"* ringing in her ears, Felice had to run for help. When she saw the expressions of the neighbor women who came back with her, Felice's legs went so weak she nearly fell. She sat outside the bedroom waiting, while Mama called, "Jean, Jean!" in a voice Felice had never heard before. The neighbor women would not let Felice go in. "You were going to have a little baby sister, but now you are not," one of them told her.

Felice looked down the shore, and behind her at the cliff and empty sky. When she tried to imagine the arms of the cove holding her tight, tears began to slide down her cheeks. She put her face in her hands, half aware even as she did that it was a gesture like Mama's, and cried quietly, for a long while, until the ache in her chest was gone.

When she wiped her face with her hands, smelling and tasting the salt, she felt better. She looked out at the bay, at the edges of waves, and the foam, and the mingling of currents, the lines standing out on the surface like veins; all the details were wonderfully clear. She leaned over the boulder and looked at the field of small rocks on the other side: they shone and winked up at her. You are alive, they said to her. You are alive.

She took a deep, long breath and looked all about her, at the water and sky and rocks. Her eyes seemed to have an appetite for looking, and there was so much that seemed important to see: the grain of the big rock, the mat of rockweed on the other side with dark mussels gleaming beneath, the clouds moving slowly across the sky. A line of birds, at this distance like a strand of dark beads, gave her a little pang of pleasure. She rubbed her hands against the boulder again and then against her face, patting, stinging herself wider awake. The delicacy of her eyebrows and the curve of her cheeks felt like Mama's. "Cecilia," she said experimentally, "Felice. Felicia. Cecilia."

She walked back down the shore, holding the smooth rock in her hand, her thumb snug in its place, and looked down at the rocks and sand and bits of thick-fingered dulse. Even the sand seemed more sharply focused now. The sight of her footprints there, going in the other direction, toward the boulders, made her heart swell with affection for herself.

Because she was watching the ground and humming, she did not see or hear him walking toward her. Not until she reached the end of her footprints and looked toward the cliff was she aware of his presence. And then she was so shocked she could not move, or cry out. It was some seconds before she realized that this figure was Remi, and that he was smiling at her.

"Hello, Felice."

Her heart was beating wildly.

"I came to show you Glooscap's footprints," he said, pointing toward the base of the cliff. "It is said he walked there when he was an old man—you can even see the marks of his cane, and the footprints of his dog."

Felice stared at him.

"How long have you been here?"

"A little while," he said, shrugging. "I was sitting up there." He pointed to a spot midway up the cliff.

"You were watching me," she said. Prickles rose from the base of her neck.

His gaze shifted out to the water. "Do you know how to find clams in winter? I could teach you."

"I already know," Felice said, looking at the profile of his face. There was an irregularity in the line of his nose that made her think of the indentation in the rock. "My papa showed me how."

"Oh. Well . . . would you like me to show you how to make a fish net, then?" He turned toward her, smiling nervously. His skin was coarse, like sand viewed close, and one of his front teeth was chipped. Felice thought that if he stepped closer, she would scream. But there would be no one to hear her. She began to edge toward the cliff.

"I'm building a boat," the boy said, kicking at a pebble, sending it clattering toward the water. "I could take you for a sail when it's finished."

"Oh, I don't know. It wouldn't be allowed." It seemed to Felice that it was growing darker. She looked up at the sky. "I think I hear the bell. I have to go now." She turned and hurried toward the cliff, her feet slipping inside her shoes.

"Will you come back tomorrow?" he called after her.

She began climbing up the path, but it was very slippery beneath her thin-soled shoes. She slid at every step. Panicked, she fell to her knees and began to crawl upward, holding to rocks. She grasped a loose rock, and it rolled down the hill. She lost her balance and went tumbling after it. She reached out for steady rocks, but she was falling too fast: everything cut and burned.

Remi helped her up. "Are you all right?" He held her tightly by the arm. She could not bear to look at him. "Are you all right?" he asked again.

She nodded.

"Then let me help you—hold on." He took her hand, and started up the path.

Felice followed obediently, letting him pull her steadily upward. Whenever she slipped, he paused and held tighter. "Just a small step," he would say encouragingly, and start off again after she had steadied herself.

When they reached the top, Felice looked back down the sheer rock and began to tremble. He was still holding her hand. "Move further away," he said, pulling her toward the balsam grove.

Felice tugged free, and began to run toward the trees.

"Felice?"

She turned back and saw how surprised he looked, and hurt.

"Goodbye, Remi," she called, "thank you."

"Will you come tomorrow?"

She turned and hurried on into the trees. She had the feeling he was pursuing her noiselessly, but when she looked back over her shoulder, she saw him still standing by the cliff, looking after her. He lifted his arm slowly and waved it back and forth.

Gripping the stone in her pocket, Felice stumbled on through the trees. When she reached the clearing on the other side, her heart was pounding furiously again. She ran to the wall and scrambled over it. She laid the red stone in the hollow, on top of her other treasures, but that made her hand and pocket feel empty, so she took it back. Then she flung her arms about the tree, holding on so tight she could hear her pulse against the trunk. She stayed there, embracing the tree, until her breathing was slower, and the bell began to ring.

Celeste accosted her outside the dining room. "What have you been doing? I was looking all over for you."

"Nothing," Felice said. The secret made a warm spot inside her, and as she sat down at the table and shook out her napkin there was an odd little smile on her face.

All through the meal Felice thought about Remi. He had come just to see her, and he had been so kind when she fell. His hand and arm were so strong. No doubt he was in love with her, and wanted to marry her, but he was an Indian, and he knew it would not be possible. But perhaps his father was a French nobleman—the Abbé had said the boy was a half-breed—perhaps Remi would be sent for, included in the royal family. By the end of supper, Remi's face had been transformed in Felice's mind so that he resembled Robert, and variations on Robert, as much as Remi.

That night Felice went alone to the parlor and sat at the piano. She played a Chopin étude, the opening of a haunting Brahms concerto, and an old French love song she had learned from her mother. Then she played, in almost seamless succession, her willow-tree melody and all her other wordless songs. She played with such passion that several people were attracted into the parlor, and Sister Theodota, who said the noise interrupted her meditation in the chapel, later petitioned Mother Superior for a moratorium on every composer but Bach during Lent.

24

DURING PASSION WEEK, THE CONVENT WAS IN A STATE OF FEVERish preparation for Easter and the arrival of the Bishop. With only two weeks left before the Great Event, cleansing, both physical and metaphysical, took precedence over all other activities. Even the girls' scholarly pursuits in English, history, geography, and mathematics, normally given such emphasis at the academy, were set aside in favor of catechising and rearranging bureau drawers.

The Abbé, master of the spiritual realm, and Mother Superior, of the physical, each went about with an increased air of busyness and self-importance, attending to projects in which they occasionally found themselves at cross-purposes.

Because Easter was to mark the first visit of a high church dignitary since the convent was consecrated in 1853, Mother Superior directed the cleaning with more than customary vernal zeal, and she enlisted sisters and girls in scrubbing the building from top to bottom. On sunny mornings coverlets were hung out of every upstairs window like lolling tongues. All the linens were washed and starched and ironed, and the kitchen pots were given a ruthless polishing and set on the steps in the sun to sweeten. Soukie, whose work load was increased so drastically that she hadn't time to read accounts of shipwrecks in the weekly paper, nor, she complained, to write letters to her family in Brier Island, was inclined to agree with the Abbé that spiritual matters were being seriously neglected.

The Abbé now had charge of the girls much of the day, putting them through their paces in the catechism and dogma so that they would shine for the Bishop, but it was his conviction—voiced more plainly as the week progressed—that the nuns were not only shirking their share of the responsibility with regard to the young ladies, but they were also neglecting their own souls. When the Abbé broached this subject, however, he was sometimes ignored or even shouldered aside by nuns wielding dust mops or hauling out rugs to be beaten. Wandering about the areas of the convent where this grand-scale spring cleaning was in progress, the Abbé looked, with his slightly bewildered but altogether put-out expression, like any ordinary male householder in the village, but one with a plethora of wives.

The tongueless man's very body became a battlefield in the contest between the spiritual and the secular. As a special surprise for His Eminence, the Abbé was intent on teaching Monsieur to make both the large and small signs of the cross. In this he had already achieved some success, though some observed that the gentleman still seemed to have no notion of appropriate timing; the Abbé's staunchest supporters, however, argued that these apparently spontaneous gestures perhaps had to do with the man's private spiritual thoughts of the moment. The project occupied much time, and often collided with Mother Superior's schedule for feeding, medicating, and exercising her patient.

If Monsieur were going to walk regularly, it would be best accomplished under her careful supervision, Mother Superior decided; the Abbé's interest in the invalid's mobility was altogether too fitful, she told Soukie. Soukie, Jacques, Evangeline, and Mother Superior herself were chief instructors in the walking lessons, and every hour or two during the day the invalid could be seen leaning on the arm of one of them, in a prescribed stroll through the building or about the grounds. When the hours for signing and walking happened to coincide—as was often the case—there were violent storms in the area of the infirmary. But Sister Claire was finally able to work out a schedule, which, after lengthy negotiations between the priest and nun, had a generally pacifying effect.

The greater visibility of the tongueless man had an influence on several occupants of the convent that was not altogether in keeping with the emotions of the liturgical season. His presence escalated Sister Agatha's preoccupation with virgin martyrdom, and with bodily assumption into heaven, not only by the Virgin Mary but also by the lesser female saints. She went about telling Felice, and anyone else who would listen, that the Assumption was the primary message of her frescoes and recent visions, and that she had no doubt her opinion would one day be legitimized by the Holy See.

The nun also made some private comments about Monsieur to Felice and her friends, with inflammatory results.

The most provocative of these remarks was made on the day that Mother Superior collected uniforms and habits to be laundered for Easter week. After depositing their skirts and blouses in the proper hampers, Felice, Celeste, and Françoise set out together for confession. On the path to the outer chapel they encountered Sister Agatha, who grumbled to them about the musty, ill-fitting habit she was being forced to wear.

"Soon you'll have a fresh habit," Felice said. "Won't it be nice to have it all clean and starched?"

Just then Soukie passed before them, leading Monsieur. "Isn't he looking fit, Mademoiselles?" she called. "He can go a long way under his own steam now." And to demonstrate, she released his elbow, and Monsieur, smiling back at the girls, proceeded smoothly toward the orchard.

"And who has been bathing *him,* I would like to know?" Sister Agatha hissed. "Which of my sisters has reached beneath his garment and bathed his male arrangement?"

Choking back giggles, the girls managed to guide Sister Agatha into the chapel. Then they raced down to the beach to discuss this aspect of Monsieur's care, which had never been considered at all before, not even by the very boldest.

Though neither Celeste nor Françoise had any clear idea of what the male arrangement looked like, each of them drew fantastic sketches in the sand of what they claimed to have heard about, or seen, on one occasion or another.

A story began to take shape in Felice's mind. "Remember the day

you didn't know where I was, Celeste?" she whispered. "You know
—the day Madame Gentil died."

"Yes? Where were you?"

"I came out to the beach—and guess who followed me?"

"Who? Who?" Celeste and Françoise asked, clutching hands.

"Monsieur!"

The girls leaned closer. "Tell," Celeste urged.

"Well," Felice began, "he tried to kiss me, but of course I wouldn't
let him. But—guess what next."

"What? What?"

"He decided to take a bath—right there at the cove."

"Oh, no," Françoise moaned, covering her mouth with both hands
and looking out at the water.

"What happened?" Celeste asked.

"Well, he just had his nightshirt on, you know. And—and—he
raised it up."

Françoise and Celeste squealed and covered their eyes.

Celeste, peeking out between her fingers, whispered, "How far?"

"Up to his neck."

"What did you *do?*" Celeste bounced up and down on her rock seat.

"I just stood there and looked," Felice said, her tone suddenly
casual. She admired her just-trimmed nails while Françoise and Celeste squirmed. "And then I told him to behave himself," she concluded, with a little yawn.

"You wouldn't *dare,*" Celeste said. "You wouldn't have the nerve
to so much as look him in the eye."

"Certainly I would."

"Prove it then, prove it."

That very day, after confession, Felice persuaded Mother Superior
to let Celeste and herself assist in Monsieur's walking regimen. While
Françoise, Anne, and Marie watched from the dormitory window,
they led Monsieur out the back door and guided him in a wide circle
across the soggy ground. Felice and Celeste were beset by giggles, so
that they staggered more than walked, their charge wavering precariously between them, craning his long neck down to peer first at one,
then the other girl. When he looked down at her, Felice, emboldened

by Celeste's presence, bestowed her most seductive smile upon the man; he responded with a curious arching of the eyebrows and a smile which Felice later described to a breathless audience as "simply horrid."

On Palm Sunday the nuns and girls went to the church in the village for high mass. It was unusually warm for April and so close inside the crowded church that the door was left standing open during the service. Felice could feel the slight breeze against her neck moving the locks of hair that had escaped from her chignon. She had shortened her veil with hairpins, and imagined that the sight of her graceful neck must be the focus of all male eyes behind her. She knew that Remi, seated on the other side of the church, two pews back, paid more attention to her than to the liturgy, an intuition that was later confirmed by Celeste, who had no compunction about turning around to look.

As the Abbé talked about this Easter's being an even more joyful event than usual, because of their very special visitor, Felice imagined the Bishop at the altar, and herself approaching. As he looked down upon her—she in the becoming white confirmation dress Sister Claire had made—his eyes would soften, and his heart might even beat a little faster. Later, he would ask her to please consider becoming a holy sister, because beauty kept chaste is especially pleasing to God. At this point, Antoinette nudged her and they went forward to receive the blessed willow branches. After Felice had kissed the Abbé's hand and taken her freshly sprinkled and censed green sprig, she smiled up at him so fervently that his pontifical expression wavered a moment, and she returned to her seat feeling sublimely powerful.

That afternoon, after a luncheon that had been delayed by some sort of excitement in the kitchen, and after a compulsory letter-writing session in Mother Superior's classroom (Felice wrote to the two girls she had met on the train, with special regards to their brother Robert), Felice went alone to sit by the Evangeline willows. Because she wanted to think about Robert, she had avoided Celeste, Françoise, Anne, and Marie. If she saw them coming, she decided, she would jump over the wall and hide behind a tree until they had gone down the cliff. If Remi went to the cove, he would of course be very disappointed—heartbroken even—that she was not there, but as Françoise said, it was best to keep a man in suspense. Not that he was really a proper suitor for her. After all, even if half his blood was royal, half was Indian; even though sisters and girls with partial or total Indian heritage came to the convent, actually marrying an Indian was not ever considered. Not only did most people think of them as having a lower social position, but there was a general impression that they embodied an uncivilized passion of the sort that only Sister Agatha dared describe.

Felice was settled on the wall facing the balsam grove, her head against her willow, thinking about the letter to Robert's sisters and how he might be moved to come for the confirmation she had so casually mentioned, when she heard a sound behind her in the orchard. She flinched with irritation, thinking it was Celeste, who had already seen her, and went on to finish out Robert's smile on first seeing her. Then she stretched, and opened her eyes, looking up at the porcelain-blue sky. "Celeste," she said, "don't you know when to allow a person her privacy?"

She swung her legs around, expecting to see not only Celeste but the other girls too, creeping toward her with mock-Indian stealth.

Instead there was the tongueless man, standing not ten yards away, staring right at her. Felice froze. It even seemed that her heart stopped. Her mouth opened, but made no sound. Her feet and legs, dangling over the wall, instead of jumping and running, went rigid.

For several seconds—it seemed an eternity to Felice—they stood gazing at each other. The man's eyes seemed smaller than Felice had remembered, and puckered all about with tiny lines. Instead of his nightshirt he was wearing the black suit of clothes in which he had first appeared. He made the sign of the cross twice—a gesture that evidently signaled greeting—and with a slow, paralyzing smile, walked forward.

Felice slid down from the wall. She looked wildly in all directions —she could dash past him, toward the convent, or could run to the right, to the field and the barn, where she might find Jacques. Too late, she thought of running through the balsam grove and down the cliff. Her heart was knocking in her ears and eyes, but then, as he came closer, and reached out to her, she did not flinch, as she thought she would, or try to struggle free. When he touched her head, she felt hypnotized. A sensual calm sank through her body, through her head and chest and limbs, and she felt rooted to the spot by a profound curiosity.

His fingers traveled lightly down her forehead, her cheek, and lingered at her lips. Then his hand traced the line of her neck—Felice thought frantically of Saint Ebba, Saint Cecilia, Saint Agatha, and how she should resist, how she should offer a knife—but she did not move. His other hand moved slowly through the air, with a sure grace, just as though this were an act in a timeless ritual that he—and she —knew by heart. Felice held her breath, waiting; when the hand cupped her breast she gave a little cry. As both hands moved down her body, following the lines of waist and hips, Felice backed up against the tree and closed her eyes. She was partly aware, even as this happened, that she was evil, evil beyond description, but she could not help herself.

Only when Felice felt her skirt being lifted did she resist. She slapped at the man's arm. He dropped her skirt, and stepped back, almost politely, as she slid away. He made no effort to pursue her as she ran through the orchard, first toward the convent, and then, realizing she could not face the nuns, doubling back through the trees toward the barn. She cleared the south wall and began to race across the boggy, snow-streaked meadow. As she ran she glanced back occasionally, expecting to see him lifting his long legs over the wall, setting out after her, but she was not followed. She saw no one as she looked back one last time before entering the barn, but the shoulders and turret of the convent building seemed to rise higher, looming reproachfully above the apple trees.

Neither Jacques nor Soukie was in the barn. A few chickens pecked about on the straw-littered floor, and the cow looked up, munching, whiskers of hay protruding from both sides of her mouth. The sheep to be sacrificed for Easter luncheon bleated in its stall.

Felice climbed into the loft and pushed down the ladder. It landed with a great clatter, sending the chickens fluttering and squawking, and eliciting a moo of protest from the cow. But with the ladder down, Felice thought, burying herself in the hay, she would be safe, for no one could climb up, and it was a short enough distance that she could jump down, either into the barn or outdoors, through the window. If Jacques came, she would say she had been chased: there was certainly no way the man could deny it.

Felice lay there all afternoon, reliving the episode over and over. She put her hands where the man's had been, following the curves of her body, remembering his eyes and the tree at her back. Then her fingers went where his might have gone, and pressed there. She felt an urgent prickling, and when she held her thighs tight together, went deliciously liquid all over.

Afterward Felice lay stunned in the cooling, darkening air. She had let the devil take her over, soul and body. For punishment she rubbed her cheek against the rough straw, then took a handful of it and ground it against her thigh until it raised welts.

Felice sat up and looked at the dim silhouette of the trees and the convent tower. She had just ruined her entire life. Mother Superior, the Abbé, Sister Claire, and all the others would be waiting for her, lined up in the hall. "And where have you been?" Mother Superior would demand. She would be sent away at once, bundled heedlessly onto the cart, victim of the angriest, most dramatic scene ever to take place at L'Académie du Sacré Sang.

There seemed but two choices: she could throw herself over the cliff, or she could run away. But after she jumped down from the loft and went outside, she began to walk slowly toward the convent. She devised a story as she went: she had been chased, held down, tied by strangers wearing masks. There had been nothing she could do.

When she entered the back door, long after supper was over, no one noticed her disheveled appearance or her nimbus of guilt. Mother Superior had not even observed her absence from dinner, so preoccupied was she—and all other inhabitants of the convent—with the other startling events of that Palm Sunday afternoon.

25

FELICE WANDERED INTO THE KITCHEN, HOPING TO FIND LEFT-overs from supper. Soukie, who had been chief protagonist in one of the day's dramas, bombarded her with talk.

"Mother Superior was right all along, Mademoiselle. God didn't mean for me to be a nun, but a mother. Just think," she said, holding a feather duster to her bosom, "seven little orphan children to take care of. What could be more pleasing to God and the Holy Virgin than that? And besides," she went on, winking at Felice, "he is so *charm*-ing, Mademoiselle, and a proper gentleman, don't you think, coming to ask Mother Superior and the Abbé for my hand? He looked so nice in his suit, and just a little bit shy, but not *too* shy . . ."

"Who is it?" Felice smeared butter on a muffin and took a bite of it. Her fingers, she noticed, were trembling, and she felt very cold. In an effort not to think, she stared at Soukie's freckled face.

"Antoine Gentil, of course." Soukie gave Felice a hurt look and made a great show of dusting a cake plate, but returned almost immediately. "Providence works in strange, strange ways," she said in a dreamy voice. "Why, if he hadn't been the one to find Monsieur we might never have become acquainted—But it is tragic, isn't it, Mademoiselle, that Monsieur is gone? Gone for good, if you want my opinion."

Felice coughed, spewing out crumbs. "Monsieur?" she piped. "Gone?"

"You didn't *know?* Mademoiselle, where have you *been?*" Soukie rolled her eyes, but didn't pause for a reply. "I was the *first* to know —the last to see him, and the first to know," she said with evident pride. "When I took in his lunch, he was there—and that was the last time he was seen. I didn't notice anything unusual, but then I was pretty excited on my own account, you know." Soukie smoothed her hair and gave Felice a conspiratorial smile. Felice, who was gripping the table edge and holding her breath, did not respond. "When I went back to get the dishes, the bed was smoothed out—as smoothed out as a man can make it, that is—and the nightshirt was folded up on the pillow, and his suit was gone, and *he* was gone—not a note, not a sign."

"Does anybody know what happened?" Felice managed to ask.

"No—no. The Abbé hoped he just went visiting in the village. But he doesn't really think so, I guess, because he is just frantic about what to tell the Bishop if he comes and the man's not here for baptizing. And poor Mother Superior—her heart is broken. . . ."

"They don't think he'll come back?" Felice asked, crumbling an entire muffin into her plate.

"Antoine is looking for him, leading the search—if anyone can find him, *he* can. Do you know what he said, Mademoiselle? I heard him through the parlor door. That I would make an *ex*cellent wife—he noticed that the day I went to help set his house to rights, the day poor Madame Gentil died, rest her soul." Soukie made a long face and crossed herself, then went on hurriedly: "Not that he hadn't noticed me before, but that's just between you and me and the privet hedge. He was a married man then. Why, Mademoiselle, where are you going?" she asked as Felice stood up and headed for the door. "Want some fricassee? I could warm it up for you—better enjoy Soukie's cooking while you can. Madame Girrard—she's to replace me, poor thing—Madame Girrard had a mighty puny little husband—she won't be much of a cook for growing girls, I'm afraid."

Felice heard this last through the closed door. She walked down the hall past the parlor and the offices, where whispered conversations were taking place, and then, turning in the other direction, went up the stairs to the dormitory.

She lay down on her bed and put her hands over her eyes, but scorching images of the tongueless man and of the barn drove her up again. She lit her candle and looked at herself in the mirror. There was a piece of hay caught in her braids: how awful if that had been noticed. She took her hair down and gave it a ruthless brushing, then changed all her clothes, bundling the dirty ones under the bed. She looked at her reflection again, touching her nose and cheeks and chin. Did it show, would other people be able to tell? She touched her neck, remembering. She imagined Remi's hand there, then Robert's.

She caught sight of herself in the mirror: the sleepy, half-lidded expression shocked her. She slapped her cheeks until they burned, and she leaned forward to glare at her reflection. "What a wicked person you are. Wicked. Do you hear me?" Her drawn-up eyebrows looked like furry caterpillars and her eyes were piercingly mean: it was satisfying to see herself look so ugly.

Felice turned and dropped to her knees on the hard floor. The pain in her knees was also satisfying, for a moment; perhaps, she thought, the bones were broken and she would never be able to walk again. It would be a just punishment, and she might become well-known all up and down the coast for how sweetly she bore her affliction. But as she began to whisper the Ave into her palms, she tentatively stretched one leg and then the other to be sure they still worked. It should be a worse punishment than that anyway, she thought, interrupting her prayer. God had sent her a test, a trial, and she had failed. Failed miserably. And not only that, she had lost every possible hope of saving the man. She had done the opposite: sent him on the path of doom and sin.

Even if it was his own fault, really. She hadn't actually *done* anything. Had she?

Yes. Everything. Like Eve, she had lured him. She allowed his touch. And then—worse.

Grinding her teeth together and digging her nails into her scalp, she considered possible alternatives: she could go into the desert somewhere, strip herself naked and expose herself to hosts of blood-sucking flies, as Saint Macarius had done. She could shave her head and powder it with ashes, and become a missionary among the heathen. When they scoffed at her, imprisoned her, she would allow them to cut out strips of her flesh without complaint, let her breasts be pinched and twisted and tortured, even sliced off, without a whimper.

Feeling slightly ill, she cradled a breast in one hand. Perhaps one of the heathen would admire her naked body as it was tied to the rack and, to spare her from mutilation, would buy her for his slave.

Swaying with nausea, Felice stood up and examined her pale tongue in the mirror. She was sick, perhaps very sick. She had better go confess before it was too late.

She would stop in to see Celeste first, she decided. She tiptoed down the hall and paused outside Celeste's cubicle.

When she knocked there was a scream and then a muffled gargling sound, like someone drowning.

Felice opened the door. Forms were thrashing about on the bed beneath the coverlet.

"Celeste?"

A face appeared: Anne's. "It's just Felice," she said.

The cover was thrown back, revealing Celeste and Françoise. Celeste was clutching a pillow.

"Francie thought you were Monsieur!" Celeste said, jumping onto the floor.

"So did you." Françoise kicked out at Celeste. "And you nearly smothered me to death."

Felice began to back toward the door.

"Where were you anyway, Felice? Why weren't you at supper? We thought maybe you had run away with him," Celeste said, giggling.

"I'm—sick," Felice said. "I'm going to see Mother Superior and get some paregoric."

Antoinette, pressing a rosary to her bosom, appeared in the doorway. "Mother Superior says everybody should come to the white chapel. We're saying the stations for poor Monsieur."

Poor Monsieur: Felice had a sudden image of him sprawled motionless on the shore. Perhaps he had tripped and smashed his head against stone. "Is he dead?" she whispered.

"Well, let's *hope* not, Felice. We're saying prayers for his safe return." Piously lowering her head, Antoinette moved on.

"Priss-Pot," Celeste said. "She's probably got him hidden under her bed."

They went down to the chapel, Celeste, Françoise, and Anne whispering and poking one another, and Felice hanging back.

The ritual had already begun. At the head of the line were Mother Superior and, leaning against her, the grief-stricken Evangeline, a wadded man's-sized handkerchief pressed to her mouth. A string of nuns and girls followed them from station to station, murmuring Aves and Pater Nosters at each stop.

Sisters Claire and Agatha stood near the door. Sister Claire held Felice back and nodded for the other girls to go on.

"Look, Sister, here's Felice," Sister Claire said. "Why don't the two of you go around together?" To Felice she whispered, "Sister Agatha has been worried about you—I *told* her she was being silly."

Felice took Sister Agatha's right arm, and together they walked unsteadily to the first station.

"No one of us is safe," Sister Agatha whispered in Felice's ear.

Felice stared up at the framed, lackluster print of Jesus starting out on his final journey. "No, Sister," she said weakly.

"Take extreme precautions."

"Yes, Sister. I will." Felice guided Sister Agatha to the next station. *"Agnus Dei,"* Sister Agatha murmured.

Felice tried to move on.

"No—we haven't prayed." Sister Agatha jerked her right arm free and crossed herself. *"Agnus Dei."* She crossed herself again, and then again and again and again. Her hand flew, slapping forehead, chest, left shoulder, right shoulder.

"Sister—that's good enough. Let's go on." From the corner of her eye she could see Sister Theodota watching from across the chapel. She caught Sister Agatha by the elbow; the nun began to flap her arm violently.

"Be careful, Sister, they might put you in the turret again."

"Yes, yes—Lock me in, safe from . . ." Sister Agatha suddenly went still, clutching her right hand with her left. "My ring!" she wailed. "I am robbed!"

"Ssh, Sister." Felice glanced at Sister Theodota scuttling sideways through the pews, with Mother Superior close behind.

Felice prized Sister Agatha's hands apart; the silver band that symbolized eternal union with Christ was really gone.

Sister Theodota bore down on them. "What is this uproar?"

"Sister Agatha lost her ring—it must have slipped off," Felice explained. "Her fingers are so thin now."

"Her fault entirely. I saw her flailing about."

Mother Superior was soon there, and Sisters Constance and Mary Owen, and then a crowd of nuns and girls. Felice stood against the wall with Sister Agatha while the others searched beneath the nearby pews for the ring.

"All is well," the nun began to chant. "All is well, all is well."

Felice closed her eyes; soon this would be over and she could go to her cubicle, and escape into sleep.

"O praise Him!" Sister Agatha suddenly cried, and sank to the floor.

"Sister!" Felice stooped, thinking the nun had collapsed. But Sister Agatha was kneeling; as Felice touched her, she lifted both hands into the air.

"Sisters! I am eternally chaste! He has brought me the most precious ring of all!"

"Here it is!" Halfway across the chapel, Adele Surette emerged from beneath a pew and waved a hand in the air. "I've got it," she shouted.

"Don't worry, dear, it's found," Mother Superior said, patting Sister Agatha's head.

"Jesus has betrothed Himself to me in the most final manner. When He was circumcised, just so much as a ring of flesh was taken from His holy body. Sisters!" Sister Agatha cried, her voice rising to descant, "He has given it to me and me alone—His ring of holy flesh."

"Sssh—ssh—ssh," the nuns went, a sound like scalding steam.

The silver ring was passed from sister to sister and finally to Mother Superior. "Here it is, dear, your *real* ring." She grasped Sister Agatha's hand and pushed the ring on her finger.

"No! I do not need this ring. I have His ring of flesh!"

"But as a sister of Sacré Sang . . ." Mother Superior began, in her most soothing voice. She looked up. "Sisters—girls—why don't you move on." She nodded in the direction of the next station.

But the company stood, transfixed. For as Mother Superior was speaking, Sister Agatha had snatched off her ring. She put it in her mouth and then, before anyone could cry out, she swallowed it.

There was a general gasp; Felice held her own throat and swallowed hard.

Sister Agatha closed her eyes, crossed her arms across her chest, and smiled.

Mother Superior and Sister Theodota hit Sister Agatha on the back, to no avail.

"Blasphemy," Sister Theodota muttered. "Blasphemy."

Mother Superior stood erect. "You young ladies are dismissed. Run along to study hall. Immediately," she added, clapping her hands.

Felice went out with the other girls, but she did not join her friends as they raced down the hall and up the stairs. She lingered outside the door until Sister Claire emerged with Sister Agatha.

"Where are you taking her?"

"To her cell—now, run along, Felice." Sister Claire's averted face was stiff, making Felice feel she was angry with her. Perhaps Sister Agatha's outburst was her fault, for not having done the stations properly.

Felice went to the parlor and sat at the piano. She stayed there a long while, staring mindlessly at the mute keys.

"Poor Sister Agatha, poor Felice." Celeste's chant from months ago sounded in her mind. "Poor Sister Agatha, poor Felice."

Felice slid to her knees and planted her elbows on the piano bench. "Dear Mary," she whispered, "intercede for me and for Sister Agatha. Tell God that neither of us meant any harm."

There was no answering voice.

Felice screwed her eyes shut tight. "*Do* something with me, God. Punish me, show me a sign." Half expecting blindness, she opened her eyes. But the softly lit parlor was still there in all its detail. The sofa, the chair, the oil lamps, the sewing baskets: everything looked quite usual, even ordinary.

Felice stood up, on legs that were not crippled, and went to the cabinet for tung oil and steel wool. Then, scrubbing as furiously as though it were her own tarnished soul, she polished the piano until it shone.

26

FOR SEVERAL DAYS FELICE LIVED IN FEAR THAT MONSIEUR WOULD return and take further action against her: either exposure of her wickedness or another attack on her person. But as days passed and nothing concrete was learned about the stranger, Felice began to hope that he might never reappear. There were rumors: he had been found stowed away on a ship at Digby; he had stayed the night at Maxwellton, where he changed water into wine; he had bought a buggy and a team of chestnut horses from a rich farmer near Bear River, paying with a sack of gold coins. All these stories were eventually discredited. The only account that persisted and gradually calcified into legend was that which Soukie heard in the village and reported to Felice, who confirmed it in a dream. According to Soukie's sources, no fewer than three north-bound travelers on the Chemin du Roi had passed a gentleman of his description walking south, and an innkeeper in Port Maitland, Soukie also learned, had seen him on early Good Friday morning, hurrying along the road, on foot, in the direction of Yarmouth. In Felice's dream, she had watched the black-suited stranger recede into the distance, until he was only a dark speck on the road, and then suddenly he was gone, as a mote below water. Felice told this part of the dream to Soukie, for general broadcast, but not the next part: that in the farther distance, he waited by a curve, an evil smile upon his face, and eyebrows that sprang out like horns.

Felice was occasionally diverted from her own worries only by concern for Sister Agatha, who had sunk into crisis after the ring incident. Palm Sunday night, and all day Monday, Sister Agatha said that she herewith intended to refuse all food, as it was tainted with mortality. Monday night, she called out for Holy Communion.

Mother Superior, fearing the worst, sent for the Abbé. His eyes bleary and his cassock awry, the Abbé trudged up the dark hill carrying a vial of oil for the sick. When he reached the nun's bedside he found her prone, fully dressed, her mouth open to receive the Viaticum.

To the Abbé's astonishment—which he communicated shortly afterward to Mother Superior, and Mother Superior to Sister Claire the next day, and she to Felice—the nun refused to confess. She would prefer, the Abbé supposed, that the iniquity of her sins transport her to hell before she would ever admit any wrongdoing in the matter of the ring-ingestion. In spite of her resistance, the Abbé had administered Holy Communion and extreme unction, for, as he said to Mother Superior, he would not want to have it on his conscience if she were to die without the sacraments. Then, the Abbé reported, as he was leaving her cell, Sister Agatha had called out for more altar bread. "She cried, 'Please, I am starving,' " the Abbé said, crossing himself in the dark vestibule. "Sister, in my opinion, it is a sin of sacrilege—I have a feeling the Bishop may recommend exclaustration."

Mother Superior sat by Sister Agatha's bedside all through the night, and Tuesday morning she escalated the battle against the aged nun's fast. Not only did she care about Sister Agatha ("She was like a mother to me when I first came to Sacré Sang," she told Sister Claire, who told Felice), but she could not bear to see Sister Theodota's expression of smug triumph when she asked after "the poor dear's health."

Mother Superior was afraid the nun would die, and, she was convinced, the Abbé was afraid that she would not. "He even went so far as to say," she told Sister Claire, "that perhaps it would be best if the poor woman were out of her agony before the Bishop came. The Abbé said it would be 'simply tragic' if His Eminence recommended excommunication, 'not knowing her as we do.' " Mother Superior mimicked the Abbé in falsetto as she reported this last utterance; Sister Claire told Felice she had never seen her look so thoroughly apoplectic.

"Poor Sister Agatha," Felice said. "I wish I could help her."

"Maybe you can," Sister Claire mused. "Let me talk to Mother Superior about it."

Tuesday afternoon Mother Superior called Felice into her office. Sister Claire was there too, and smiled at the girl as she entered.

"Felice," Mother Superior said, "as you are no doubt aware, I am terribly concerned about Sister Agatha. She simply won't eat." The nun rubbed a fist against her furrowed brow. "Sister Claire has an idea you might be able to persuade her. I know she is especially fond of you, and I'm certainly willing to try—but I don't want you to be too discouraged, dear, if it doesn't work—she is presently *very* crotchety."

It was agreed that Felice should go with Mother Superior, Sister Claire, and Soukie to Sister Agatha's cell at dinnertime. Mother Superior was determined to try her hand one more time.

"Here we are, Sister," Mother Superior called out gaily, entering the room behind Soukie, who bore soup, milk, tea, and custard on a tray. "Suppertime."

Mother Superior went right to work, sitting on a chair by the nun's bed, while Sister Claire, Felice, and Soukie stood by watching.

"Heeere we go, dear," Mother Superior said, prying open the stubborn jaw and shoveling in a spoonful of custard past the nun's teeth.

Sister Agatha gagged and spat. "Poisoned," she said. She glared at Mother Superior, and at the others lined up behind her.

"What *will* you eat, Sister?" Mother Superior said, in an exasperated voice.

"The body of Christ," she replied, turning her head to the wall.

"She's been saying that all morning, Ma Mère," Soukie said. "Perhaps she should have some—there is nourishment in the flour . . ."

Mother Superior took one of Sister Agatha's hands into her own and rubbed it. "You have just taken communion, dear. If you do not eat, you will die."

"The Lord's will," Sister Agatha said, crossing herself.

"I think not," Mother Superior said sharply, rising. "I think it is Sister Agatha's will." She motioned Felice toward the chair. "You can try if you want to, but it's hopeless, I fear. She just wants to be stubborn."

"Why don't we go," Sister Claire said, tapping Mother Superior and Soukie on the shoulder, "and let Felice stay and talk to Sister Agatha? She doesn't have to eat, but she might just enjoy her company." And with a wink at Felice, Sister Claire led the way out of the room.

Felice sank to the chair and looked at Sister Agatha. The nun was dressed in a white nightgown and a linen cap. Her hands were clasped tightly together on her chest and her eyes seemed implacably shut.

"Sister Agatha," Felice said, touching the nun's arm. The loose, papery feeling of the old woman's skin surprised her. "Sister Agatha —it's me—Felice."

The nun's eyelids flickered. Her parched lips stuck together, and she extended a white tongue to moisten them.

"Please don't die, Sister," the girl said, gripping her wrist tighter and shaking it. "Please don't die."

The nun's eyes slowly opened. Without the spectacles, her eyes looked small and painfully vulnerable, like those of an animal that lives underground. "Felice?" she whispered.

"Yes, Sister," Felice said, taking the nun's spectacles from the table. "You need these." She tucked the curved wire ends between the cap and the soft, hairy ears. "Now, isn't that better?"

Magnified, Sister Agatha's eyes leapt forward, dominating her face. She looked like a somber, malnourished little child.

Felice took the bowl of custard in her hand. "Now try some of this, Sister," she said, holding a spoonful to the nun's mouth.

Sister Agatha shook her head. "No, child," she said, tears welling up. "I must be in readiness."

"For what, Sister?"

"My death—and resurrection."

"Sister Agatha," Felice said, crossing her fingers. "If you had a vision about this it must have been a false one. For I had an apparition just this morning—Saint Catherine by the willow tree—who said your time had *not* come, that you must live on . . ."

"Truly, Felicia?"

"Yes, Sister—and that I should tell you this. But that we should keep this secret, and tell no one else," she whispered.

"How did she look? What in particular did she say?"

"She was wearing a red dress. She was very beautiful, and there was brilliant light all about her. She told me that you are *needed* here, Sister, for your wisdom."

"She said this?"

"Yes, Sister." Felice held a spoonful of custard before the nun's lips, which parted and allowed it to enter.

"Good," Felice said. "Now, another bite."

Sister Agatha swallowed noisily and turned her eyes toward Felice. "I have not been appreciated here, you realize, child. Forced to retire. Excluded from meetings, maligned, im*pris*oned."

"Maybe that is part of your martyrdom, Sister? And you are appreciated by many, Sister—especially me. You have so many admirers here and in the village—your paintings . . ."

"Yes, my paintings . . ." And while Felice continued to feed her, Sister Agatha told once again the story of her apprenticeship to the great masters of Italian art, and then being called by God to this vocation instead. "And He warned me then, child, you are—you are quite right—that I would not be appreciated, not *seem* to be appreciated."

"Yes, Sister. But you are. Will be." As Felice rose with the empty tray the nun was nodding agreement and drifting toward sleep, a smile upon her lips.

Felice returned the tray to the kitchen and scanned the table tops for leftovers: as Good Friday approached, the meals were getting sparser. "Soukie?" she called. No answer.

There was a bowl of eggs soaking in blue dye on one table and a nearly dry kettle gasping on the stove. Felice took the kettle off and refilled it from the stone jug. She stirred the blue eggs with her hand, liking the sound they made knocking against one another. Felice held up a dripping blue hand and made it look like a claw. If Monsieur came back, she would pinch him with it.

The kitchen door flew open and Soukie charged in. Mother Superior was right behind her, puffing, her wimple and veil flapping like the wings of a frantic grounded bird.

"What's wrong?" Felice cried, grasping her throat.

"They think they've seen a light on the shore, at the cove," Soukie said. "Maybe it's him."

Mother Superior grabbed up the water jug and took two rolls from the bread tin. "The poor gentleman," she said, "will no doubt be famished."

They rushed out again. Felice went to the door and watched them running toward the orchard, a lantern bobbing between them. They were soon consumed by the fog.

Felice ran down the hall. There was a bevy of nuns and girls in the parlor, looking out the window. Felice joined them, her eyes pounding as she stared into the mist. Don't let it be him, she prayed.

"Jacques thinks he saw a light," Marie explained. "He and the Abbé have gone down to the cove to look."

They waited in anxious silence. It was not very long before Soukie and Mother Superior returned with long faces. "Perhaps it was just a ship," the nun said, shaking her head.

The Abbé and Jacques came back soon after. "To bed, to bed," the Abbé said, waving his hand at the girls. "Who knows, he may come back during the night. Whatever, I'm sure God is looking out after him, and knows best." In spite of his brave words, the Abbé looked deeply distressed, and, Felice later heard from Sister Claire, he spent all night circumambulating the building in the hopes he might see the lost man's lantern gleaming through the fog.

That night the wind blew hard, shaking the convent building in its very foundations. Some nuns walked the halls all night, fingering their beads as the wind whistled and moaned. Felice lay wide-eyed, staring into the dark, listening. Somewhere a loose board banged in the wind. She put a pillow over her head to muffle the sound of the wind, but she could hear it yet, an eerie, hollow sound.

The next morning was still, but the fog was thicker than ever. The Abbé and Jacques went out to search once more, but the fog swaddled them like wet wool, and they could see no better than the night before. The Abbé was near despair, for the Bishop was scheduled to arrive that very afternoon. "Maybe his train will be delayed by the weather," he said wistfully to Mother Superior, and then, in spite of her admonitions about the dangers of walking about in it, plunged back into the fog. He continued to search throughout the morning, reappearing periodically to see if there was news from other quarters. "Perhaps God will deliver him back to us later, when we least expect it," Mother Superior said, consoling him with a cup of midmorning tea.

"Perhaps, Sister, perhaps," the Abbé said, patting her hand. Sister

Claire, who was present, later told Felice how touching it was to see them unified in their time of trouble.

The Abbé feared that Monsieur had blown off the cliff in the wind, and at noon, when the fog began to thin, he sent Jacques to look on the shore below. Mother Superior said even before Jacques set out that it was hopeless; she had had a dream he was gone for good. By the time the disconsolate Abbé went to the train station, the fog had largely blown off, with only swatches of it caught in the trees like white, rent veils, and still Monsieur had not been found. Some of the sisters were grieving, and not a few were hurt.

"After all we have done for him," Mother Superior said, chin trembling, as the nuns and girls waited in the vestibule for the Bishop's arrival.

"He will never be found," Evangeline said, burying her face in her hands.

"Now, now, never lose hope," Mother Superior said with renewed vigor, as if suddenly remembering her position.

Felice crossed two sets of fingers, and prayed that Evangeline was right.

BISHOP CHRYSOSTOM'S TRAIN ARRIVED AT 3:12 ON THE AFTERNOON of Maundy Thursday, punctual to the minute.

"Remarkable, considering the weather and the general reputation of the Fundy Railway Line," the Abbé said after introductions in the convent vestibule.

"Fine trains in this diocese," the Bishop replied, rubbing his hands together, *"fine* trains."

Felice thought that the Abbé and Bishop had probably been

through exactly this conversation before, on the railway platform. And the Bishop's remarks to Mother Superior, about the sunshine and his anticipation of a particularly fine Easter day, also seemed rehearsed.

"Come into the parlor, Your Eminence," Mother Superior said. "We will have some tea. You girls," she said, smiling stiffly in the direction of the inner hall, "run along to your studies now."

"Let them come, let them come," the Bishop said. "I want to become acquainted with each and every one. Such well-behaved-looking girls, and smart too, I should imagine."

They all went into the parlor, Mother Superior directing the Bishop to the best seat, and the nuns taking the places previously assigned. The girls stood around the edges of the room, near the wall. Mother Superior looked a little nervous, as there were not enough teacups to include the girls, but relaxed when the Bishop seemed to take no notice of this.

After his first cup of tea, which he praised extravagantly, the Bishop drew from his bag a handsome leather-bound copy of the latest edition of the *Rituale Romanum* and a relic of Saint Eulalia gloved in red plush. He presented these to Mother Superior and the Abbé jointly, as gifts to "the holy community here and at Nevette," and the nun and priest beamed at him and at each other. Even as they exchanged smiles, however, Felice thought she could sense the beginning of a new controversy over the resting places of that book and bone.

Felice stood on one foot and then the other as the adults drank cup after cup of tea and exchanged pleasantries. The girls, after the initial invitation, appeared to have been forgotten, but it was interesting to have this opportunity to study the Bishop at close range. A silver-haired, well-nourished gentleman whose pink cheeks glowed with health, the Bishop exuded confidence and apparently inspired it in others. After half an hour of tea and conversation, Mother Superior, who had been anxious lest some rat of dust or other imperfection of the convent reveal itself, had relaxed visibly, and some of the other sisters were even making mild jokes. The Abbé still had a trace of a frown and clutched his saucer rather too tightly, Felice thought, but even he looked relatively lulled by the prelate's soothing presence.

The Bishop admired the Haviland china, the new needlepoint rug with its squares of roses, orange blossoms, and irises, the view of the orchard, where the fog had lifted and the reddening tips of the trees shone in the mild light of late afternoon. After he had praised everything in sight, Mother Superior proposed a tour of the building.

The Abbé, Mother Superior, and Sister Theodota, in the lead, took the Bishop through classrooms, offices, and the white chapel. The other nuns followed in twos, and the girls, not having been directed otherwise, tagged along at a respectful distance. The Bishop smiled continually, interjecting, "Very fine, very fine" at appropriate intervals in Mother Superior's monologue. His approval, like a fine oil, seemed to make the rooms and furnishings glow; and for Felice, seeing it anew through his eyes, the convent was momentarily transformed into an exceedingly elegant place.

In the corridor outside the dining hall, the Bishop stopped short and, pulling an eyeglass from his breast pocket, stared at the fresco of Saint Thérèse with a close, hard attention he had not shown before.

"Begging your pardon, Your Eminence," the Abbé said, wringing his hands. "I have tried . . . but the sentiment of some sisters . . . er, villagers . . ."

"Amazing," the Bishop said, stepping closer to examine the brushstrokes. "Whose work is this?"

"One of the sisters," the Abbé said, coughing behind his fist.

"Amazing—primitive technically, but the force—the expression— I have not seen anything like it outside Padua, Siena . . . a sister, you say? . . . But what happened here?" he asked, running his fingers down the ragged line of whitewash that had amputated Saint Thérèse's left arm.

"An accident, Your Eminence," the Abbé mumbled. Felice and Celeste pinched each other to keep from laughing out loud.

"A very sad case she is," Sister Theodota said, very loudly. "Quite ill. Just last Sunday . . ."

"There are other paintings," Mother Superior broke in, "all intact. Would you like to see them?" The Bishop said he certainly would.

Mother Superior led the way to the pantry, where Saint John the Baptist looked out over shelves, to Sister Agatha's former classroom, where Our Lady of the Snows dominated the space behind the platform, and to the infirmary, where the scenes of the Virgin's Dormition and Assumption faced the now-empty bed.

The Abbé placed himself squarely in front of the Virgin ascending, in an unsuccessful attempt to hide her: the face and one hand, reaching up through wisps of cloud, rose above him. "Irregular, from a theological point of view," Felice understood him to say. "Done well before my time."

The Bishop backed off a few feet from the Dormition, then moved forward, nodding, apparently pleased by each perspective. "Quite inspired, I would say, quite inspired. May I congratulate you, Sister, and you, Father. Aren't you fortunate to have such an artist, a visionary, in your midst. But you say she is indisposed?" he asked with a little frown of concern, and suddenly glanced about the room as though—since this had been introduced as the infirmary—he expected to find her within.

"In her own cell . . ." Mother Superior said.

"Not really *physically* ill," Sister Theodota put in.

"We had here," the Abbé said, extending his hands in his calming gesture, "the gentleman of whom we spoke earlier. We are each of us bereaved, and especially for Your Eminence's sake, as we did so want you to meet him." He looked to Mother Superior, who nodded at him reassuringly. "We thought, perhaps, Your Eminence, with your superior command of languages . . ." the priest continued.

"Not at all, not at all."

"And your, er, other gifts—you might have helped us learn something more of Monsieur's origins." The Abbé looked sadly down at the bed.

The Bishop followed his glance, and then bent to touch the bed, apparently attempting to fix upon the reality of the departed invalid. "Here, you say, and then—gone? No word, no message?"

"He had no—faculty of speech, as I believe I mentioned to Your Eminence. Some unfortunate accident, I assume, perhaps in the service of his country," he said, with a nod toward Sister Claire, and her prisoner-of-war theory. "Though neither French nor English was his native tongue—something resembling the ancient Coptic is my best guess—he seemed to have a definite spiritual understanding, and to have learned . . . he was to have been a catechumen, you may recall." The Abbé's voice wavered and then stopped.

"Yes, I see. Unfortunate." But the Bishop's expression was placating, suggesting the polite indulgence of a fantastic delusion. Mother Superior patted the pillow—defensively, Felice thought—and the Abbé searched his inner pocket, perhaps for the cryptic writings.

Felice looked at the smooth coverlet, the nightstand bare but for a carefully placed breviary, the sunlight touching on the solid fact of the iron footboard; the Bishop's apparent skepticism helped her for a moment to imagine that the tongueless man had not been real at all, but a figment of the convent's collective imagination.

Felice carried Sister Agatha's tray to her cell rather early that evening, and, quite as she had hoped, Mother Superior and the Bishop appeared as she was feeding the nun and telling the life story of Saint Eulalia.

When the superioress and the Bishop entered, Felice stood up, curtsied, and backed modestly toward a corner of the room. "No, go on, go on, child," the Bishop said, looking approvingly at her and then at Mother Superior.

"A fine girl," the nun murmured. "Sister Agatha," she said, "look who is here to see you—His Eminence!"

Felice had advanced with the custard again, but Sister Agatha was put in such a flurry by the Bishop's presence, and his immediate outpouring of compliments about her "work," that Felice could not get any part of the nun's attention, and once more retreated to the corner.

The Bishop settled himself in the chair by Sister Agatha's bed, and, taking both her hands in his, praised her paintings until the nun was quite enlivened. By the time he had left, with one final appraising glance at the Eden above her bed, and inquired, "Are you acquainted with the work of Masaccio, Sister?" Sister Agatha was (as Mother Superior gleefully reported later to everyone she saw) sitting straight up, unsupported, smiling, and talking quite reasonably again.

Felice came in for special attention during this visit, too. Sister Agatha nodded toward her, just as the Bishop was leaving, and said, "Now, this is a superior young lady—the most outstanding in the academy, in my view." To which Mother Superior could only add agreement, and the Bishop crossed the room to give her his blessing and "personal congratulations."

The Bishop departed soon after this interview, going with the Abbé to strip the altars and bless the oils, and then on to the priest's house in the village, where he was to be lodged for the visit. He left behind him a noticeably energized community.

Sister Agatha felt so much better that she dressed in a fresh habit and appeared in the dining hall for a second supper. Undaunted by Sister Theodota's pointed remarks about Lenten restraint, Sister Agatha dispatched pollock and riced potatoes with gusto. As she chewed, the nun bobbed her head about the table, her face aglow, and at one point could be heard humming. After the meal, she took Felice's arm and giggled into her ear, "We're winning out, aren't we?"

Good Friday was clear and warm. There had been a light rain during the night that had melted most of the remaining traces of snow, and the trees and windows and bay sparkled in the sunlight, as if the world had been rinsed and hung out to dry. When Soukie went out for cream, she also brought back Mayflowers she had found in the woods near the barn.

Felice pinned one of the flowers in her brushed-out hair for her catechism examination. With the Abbé and Mother Superior standing proudly by, Felice responded to each of His Eminence's sonorous questions with perfect, and melodic, answers. His Eminence was moved, she could not help feeling, both by the sight and sound of her.

After prayers in the chapel, Felice and other members of the League slipped away to the beach to celebrate. They walked sedately, single file, across the grounds and down the cliff, but once on the shore they began to hop and leap about. "Hooray for Felice!" they shouted. "Hooray for Sister Agatha!"

As a special reward for herself, Felice decided to go to her cubicle and open Philippe's Easter present. Even though it was two days early, she didn't think he would mind.

She sat on her bed and shook the gaily wrapped package. As it was light and didn't rattle, she thought it might be a hat, or a white silk shawl she could wear with her confirmation dress.

But when she opened the box she found another, smaller box; it must not be a hat, then, she thought. Within that box was still another, of dark green velvet. A ring, she hoped, thinking of the cameos in Uncle Adolphe's shop. She eased open the lid: it was a ring, but of amethyst set in gold, and beautiful beyond anything she could have imagined. She held her breath, looking at its deep violet prisms; Mama had had a ring like this. She slipped it on her finger—it fit exactly. Then she unfolded and read Philippe's note, sniffing back tears as Seine scampered about the floor in pursuit of the balled-up wrapping-paper.

He was sorry not to be there for Felice's confirmation, Philippe wrote, but he hoped this gift would convey his feelings. He had found the stone at Cape Blomidon and had faceted and set it himself. He thought it would suit her, pretty young lady that she had become, and he hoped it would fit.

"Perfect," she whispered, admiring the oval ring against the graceful background of her hand, and then moved slowly to the mirror, where she looked at the hand and ring against her face. "You are so lovely," she imagined the Bishop, and then Remi, whispering to her.

That afternoon, residents of the convent and village gathered at the village church for the solemn veneration of the cross. Brilliant light streamed through the windows and struck one gilt shoulder of the altar cross as the Bishop undressed it, making it shine like pure gold. Felice felt mounting peaks of elation as the ritual progressed; both she and Sister Agatha had been redeemed, more than redeemed. They were chosen, adored, each having received God's special blessing through the Bishop, who so much resembled Felice's idea of the Heavenly Father.

When she went forward to kiss the feet of the bared crucifix, Felice felt the Bishop's eyes upon her, bathing her in esteem; she nearly swooned from a joy so urgent she thought it must be mystical.

Leaving the church, Felice found herself pushed against Remi in the general crush. Though she was quite keenly conscious of their touching, shoulder to elbow, she did not move away. When they parted at the church door, Felice's arm continued to tingle.

Felice had difficulty falling asleep that night, at first from excitement and then, as excitement curdled, from guilt. She turned and turned, imagining the tongueless man coming back to reveal her for what she really was. When she finally slept, she dreamt he had sneaked into the convent, stowed away in what was thought to be a sack of potatoes. He burst out of his confinement during Easter mass, disrupting the service with an insinuating song, cutting his eyes toward Felice. Even though it was in a foreign language, the meaning of the lyric was unmistakable.

The next day Felice resolved to confess her secret cardinal sin to His Eminence. He would understand—for she was lovely to look upon, and could not help attracting men. Moreover, she had a complex, difficult soul, like Sister Agatha's. He would absolve her; she would be washed clean, even of hypocrisy, and be truly prepared for Easter.

But when she went to the outer chapel she was disappointed to hear the Abbé's familiar drone in the box. His Eminence, she learned from Antoinette, had begun the private interviews with the sisters and did not have time to hear confessions.

When it came her turn, Felice nervously took her place in the confessional. "I am most impure, Mon Père," she said, after the preliminaries.

"Unclean thoughts?" the Abbé said with a sigh, as though this were today's usual, and rather tiresome, complaint.

"Yes, Mon Père."

Felice collected a medium-sized penance, which she took upon herself to double, and she left the chapel feeling several shades lighter of soul.

In the afternoon, the girls and nuns returned to the village church for the rituals of Holy Saturday. After communion, the entire congregation went out of doors for the Blessing of the New Fire. With the Bishop and the Abbé in the lead (and Remi, who had replaced the tongueless man as chief convert, close on the Abbé's heels), they started out and around the church in an orderly procession. Felice and Celeste, little fingers interlocked, walked together behind Sister Agatha. Anne, Françoise, and Marie followed, walking three abreast. In the churchyard, thrown off course by sunken graves and the wooden markers that slanted at all angles like irregular teeth, the lines parted and remingled. By the time they reached the shore where the fire ritual was to take place, the worshipers were regrouped by allegiances.

On one side of the bonfire—which had leapt its bounds—Sisters Theodota, Mary Owen, and Mary Faith stood clotted together; they smirked (with a kind of grim satisfaction, Felice thought) as the village men beat at the smoldering fire with fir branches.

As she stood with other members of the League behind Sister Agatha and the Bishop, Felice carefully raised her eyes above those of admiring males; she let their glances brush her cheeks like rose petals. But she looked—by accident, it seemed—at Remi; his smile held her a moment, and then she pulled away, cheeks flaming, to rearrange the curls of Celeste's forelock.

After the fire had been blessed and then hurriedly doused, sending telegraphic puffs of smoke heavenward, the crowd milled back through the graveyard. Remi tried to press against Felice again. *"Kesalt Sasus?"* she said sternly, moving ahead, hoping that the Bishop —just a few paces behind—understood Micmac.

Everyone reentered the church. Godparents and the catechumens —Remi and several babies, including the Gentil infant—were escorted into the baptistery by the Bishop and Abbé. The worshipers sat back in their pews to think upon, as instructed, the renewal of their baptismal vows.

Felice gazed at the altar rail, stage of her confirmation on the morrow, where she would take the name—rechristened, as it were— Marie Thérèse. She imagined herself rising from the rail, so charged with the Holy Spirit that her face would glow and her dress seem to drift about her like a cloud. The Bishop would be so moved that after the mass he himself would bring up the subject of her vocation.

Felice was distracted from her thoughts as the sprinkled babies began to wail in the baptistery. Godparents emerged jiggling their charges, making the notes of the infants' cries waver and rise toward the ceiling. The Abbé came next, and proceeded listlessly to the altar. It was said that the priest had resolved not to give up entirely on Monsieur until the moment of infusion; that moment had come and gone, leaving the Abbé stooped and defeated. When Remi appeared, wrapped in the white sheet that had served as his baptismal gown, it seemed that he had caught the Abbé's mood, or felt responsible for it. Head and shoulders bent, newly wetted hair plastered to his forehead, he skulked toward his pew. He looked so furtive that Felice felt stung by shame for him and, when he glanced her way, lowered her eyes.

28

EASTER DAWNED AUSPICIOUSLY ENOUGH. THE SUN ROSE IN A cloudless sky, sending its first faint rays across a tranquil bay. The hills and shore and trees and buildings gradually took shape, emerging distinct once again from the formless night, as if in testimony to the miracle of resurrection. Even before the rim of the sun showed itself above the eastern forest, bells began to ring in the village and at the convent. Mute since Maundy Thursday and muffled during Lent, the bells now pealed unrestrainedly, the joyous harmony urging that sinners wake to salvation.

As the chimes resounded, sisters who had been kneeling in the white chapel since midnight rose with some creaking of joints, and silently congratulated one another with gentle smiles. Sister Agatha, who had been standing at her window sill wrapping and rewrapping a present for Felice in a rather crumpled piece of tissue, cocked her head to listen. Soukie, who had taken out stale bread crusts for the birds, clattered the pan noisily against her fist, the noise mingling with the sound of bells; Mother Superior, who was walking down the hall with Sister Claire, covered her ears and confided, "Sometimes my sentiments about Soukie's departure are not the least bit mixed."

Stretching like Seine (who had spent the night at the foot of her bed, in violation of academy rules), Felice looked up at the rectangle of pale sky framed by her window. The cat walked purring up the length of her body and butted his forehead against her face for attention. "It's Easter, kitty!" Felice held him up into the air; he went limp, letting her swing him back and forth, and narrowed his yellow eyes. "I get confirmed, and then—the big concert!"

In the adjoining cubicle Antoinette indicated, with a protesting cough, that she was trying to pray.

"Some people are so *serious,*" Felice said into Seine's ear. But as she jumped out of bed and put on the white organdy dress, with its luxurious smell of newness, Felice's stomach tightened with an emotion that was more complex than mere excitement. She was to perform today without benefit of sheet music; how humiliating it would be if, in the midst of one of the pieces, she made an obvious mistake or, worse yet, forgot where she was and had to start over.

Using her dresser top as keyboard, Felice ran her fingers through the opening bars of the variation. The sight of the amethyst ring reminded her of Mama; her hands grew more confident, and struck noble chords. Felice then leaned toward the mirror, where she looked again at her hand and ring against her face. The sunlight in the room seemed to grow richer, holding her suspended in a precious golden liquid. Her ring shone, her face shone, and the eyes gazing back at her were a deep, strong blue, like Mama's eyes. If only Mama could be here today. She picked up the picture of Mama and Papa and kissed it, then went running out to find Celeste.

When Felice and Celeste went downstairs they found the front hall in turmoil. The Doucettes' Ford, which was to have borne the Bishop and Abbé up to the convent, there to pick up Mother Superior and Sister Agatha, and then to lead the Easter procession to the village, had become mired on the hill. The clerics, who had been forced to

walk up the hill through the mud, stood in the vestibule, their soutanes demurely lifted, while Soukie sponged their shoes and dabbed
at the stains on their hems. The nuns, originally lined up in pairs, were
wandering about—watching Soukie groom the Bishop and Abbé,
conferring with Mother Superior, and adjusting one another's wimples and veils. The girls were chattering excitedly and getting underfoot everywhere; Mother Superior made one half-hearted attempt to
shoo them into the chapel, there to wait quietly until time to start, but
those who had followed instructions were now back out again, drawn
by the rumor that the Doucette twins—just arrived in the hall—were
both wearing rouge.

After looking about in vain for Sister Agatha, Felice learned that
the nun was resting with Evangeline in Mother Superior's office.
Someone who had seen Evangeline, Adele told Felice, had described
the novice as pale and suspiciously red-eyed.

Mother Superior, a hostess' taut smile stretched over her features,
announced that the convent buggy would be used in place of the Ford,
and that His Eminence—she bowed to him, and he, also smiling
stiffly, inclined his head in return—was kind enough to say that this
was totally agreeable. There would be a short delay, however, while
Jacques adjusted a wheel.

"Ma Mère!" Soukie cried. "Antoine's wagon—why didn't I think?
—it's already decorated!" And she flung herself out the door.

"That will take too long!" Mother Superior called after her, but
Soukie did not stop; Felice could see her speeding toward the road.

The superioress started down the hall, muttering, "We're late,
late," and pushing nuns and girls back into line. "Can anything *else*
go wrong?" Felice heard her ask Sister Claire.

But Antoine Gentil's cart, pulled by a team of bell- and flower-
bedecked oxen, arrived so quickly that Mother Superior was greatly
cheered; she proclaimed it a miracle. After the dignitaries had
boarded the wagon, the promenade set off as planned, albeit three
quarters of an hour late.

The cart, with Antoine and Soukie on the driver's seat, and the
Bishop, Abbé, Mother Superior, and Sister Agatha crowded in the
rear, started down the hill. The other nuns walked at a safe distance

behind the wheels of the cart, which spat back red mud. At their center was nested the novice Evangeline, dressed in the white of espousal. After the nuns came the students, led by Antoinette, soon to take Evangeline's place, followed by Felice and the other girls to be confirmed, and then the rest arranged oldest to youngest.

The mud sucked at Felice's boots. She stepped cautiously, looking up only when they passed the bereft Ford, sunk mid-tire in muck. It made Felice think of a cockroachlike sea monster stranded by the tide; when she turned to see if Celeste had noticed, she slipped and fell.

"My dress!" she cried up at the cluster of faces. "My beautiful dress!"

Sister Claire pulled her up, clucking and scolding, and wiped at the mud on Felice's dress with a spittle-moistened handkerchief. "That's the best I can do," Sister Claire sighed, brushing futilely at the back of the girl's skirt.

"I can't go like this," Felice wailed.

"Of course you can. Do you think everybody will be looking at *you?* I wish you had been more careful, though—I put a good deal of work into that dress, and now it's ruined."

The procession resumed. Felice tried to rearrange the folds of her dress as they walked. "That won't do any good," Celeste said in a stage whisper. "It looks like you've got It, Felice."

All the nuns within earshot turned shocked faces toward Celeste, abruptly cutting off a swell of giggles.

As they walked down the village street, Felice consoled herself by looking down at her ring. None of the spectators lining the street could see the back of her dress anyway, and her face must look lovely to them: like a secular bride's, radiant as she stepped forward to meet her Gabriel; or like a postulant's, with achingly beautiful, but ascetic, features.

Some townspeople were already seated in the church; others waited on the steps. Felice saw Remi standing near the door like a bashful young groom. She smiled neutrally and held her head higher; no one could have perceived that her pulse quickened when she brushed by him and entered the church. Though Felice felt other faces turn up to her as she passed down the aisle, she did not look; she and the other girls marched with such dignity to their pews that Mother Superior, already seated, smiled proudly as they slid into place.

Felice breathed in the odors of lilies and Mayflowers. She looked at the sunlight slanting through the high cuneiform windows, washing them all in honey-colored warmth. Pushing back the thought of her stained dress, she watched dreamily as the Bishop and Abbé, vested in silks and laces, circled the Paschal candle. *"Surrexit Christus!"* the Bishop cried, bringing the congregation to its feet in one smooth motion. The Alleluia, unsung for forty days, now rang and crescendoed, proclaiming the joy of resurrection and the triumph over sin and death.

Felice's skin prickled and her eyes brimmed with tears. She felt in love with this music, this Mystery. She *would* be a sister, she thought; just a few such moments would be enough to feed her forever.

When the time for the confirmation ritual arrived, Felice led the three other initiates and the sponsors up the aisle. She walked slowly, trying not to think of her dress; she concentrated on each turned face, the golden light, the incense, the polished wood of the altar rail. She sank to her knees and Sister Claire, her sponsor, took her place behind her. Perhaps Sister Claire would be the mother superior one day, Felice mused; together, they might establish an academy for sacred music. Felice would have a papal dispensation to travel part of the year, giving concerts. The Bishop—he approached her now, magnificent in his crown and rings—the Bishop would recommend this, remembering the astonishing recital that had so enriched his Easter of 1922. And also remembering their intimate discussion, she told herself, during which he had gently unraveled the baroque contortions of her conscience—for Felice intended to speak with him alone, perhaps this afternoon.

His Eminence murmured lovingly above her; she murmured back, gazing into his eyes. Then he held out a hand.

"Your name card," Sister Claire bent forward to whisper in her ear.

Felice felt her empty pocket. "Oh, no," she moaned. She could see it in her mind's eye, propped on her dresser against the porcelain cat where she would not forget it: a creamy white card with her confirmation name written in Mother Superior's flowing script.

His Eminence shifted feet.

"Pretend," Sister Claire said in her ear.

Felice held up cupped hands, as though offering the card. "Cecilia," she whispered.

The Bishop stared for a moment at the empty palms, but he recovered his magisterial presence almost at once. Reaching forward as though to pluck a card from Felice's hands, he called out, in resounding tones, "Cecilia."

"Cecilia?" Felice heard Sister Claire say.

"Marie Thérèse," Felice said, "I meant Marie Thérèse." But it was too late; the Bishop's oiled thumb was crossing her forehead.

Felice could hear a slight commotion in the nuns' pews. Mother Superior must be furious, she thought; first the dress mishap, and now this. It was Mother Superior who had chosen Felice's confirmation name and so carefully inscribed it on the left-behind card. Nevertheless, as the Bishop slapped Felice's left cheek and said, *"Pax tecum,"* her dominant emotion was a fond wonder about herself, that she should be so unpredictable.

But as Felice rose and walked back to her seat, she immediately began devising explanations for her error. She had accidentally taken Mama's name instead of Mother Superior's because of a dream, or vision. She had *said* Thérèse, but the Bishop had misunderstood. No —it was because of the ring, like Mama's ring; she had naturally had poor Mama on her mind. And why hadn't she brought the card? Because Seine had stepped on it with inky paws. But that would precipitate the cat's banishment. Yet if she found no really good excuse, Mother Superior would be so angry that Felice herself might be banished, unless she had the Bishop's support; perhaps Sister Agatha would be willing to speak with him in her behalf, in preparation for their private interview.

So involved was Felice in meditating upon her own predicament that she did not see the novice Evangeline go forward, nor see her waver and fall. Only when Felice heard the congregation gasp did she look up. His Eminence was shaking lustral water toward the floor as though the ceremony had not really been interrupted, but he was frowning and glancing at the Abbé, whose hands were clasped against his chest in what looked more like a gesture of anxiety than piety. Only by rising slightly from her pew—as many others were doing—and craning her neck could Felice see the white heap on the floor, and it was several seconds before she realized it was Evangeline.

Two village men were called forward, and the novice was carried, still in a dead faint, to the vestibule where she was to have walked herself, in modest, joyful tempo, her heart astir, to divest herself of bridal white for the black habit of eternal marriage to Our Lord.

Mother Superior and Sister Theodota fluttered after her, and, after a brief struggle that was heard all over the church, returned alone to their pews. There was some whispering between the Abbé—who went to consult with the novice, now revived—and the Bishop; then the mass was set back in motion, without the ritual profession of Sister Syncletica ever being consummated.

Afterward Felice followed Sister Agatha into the churchyard; conversation there was hushed, as though in the antechamber of a room where a great sickness or tragedy was unfolding.

"Sister," Felice whispered, "did you hear . . ."

" 'Tis the work of the holiest spirit, Felicia."

"But His Eminence, do you think . . ."

"As I told His Eminence just yesterday, I have myself experienced a variety of transcendental swoon—he understood precisely."

"But my name, Sister . . ."

" 'Twas on the eve of bringing forth my first painting. Such colors I saw! Dappled glory!" A small crowd of townspeople had drawn close to Sister Agatha; the nun reached out to touch one village woman, who took her hand and kissed it. "My good woman, you are invited —you are all invited," the nun cried, sweeping her free arm into the air, "this very afternoon. Come ye all to see my works, and I shall myself unfold their symbols—Immanence, as His Eminence says, immanence. Heavenly *immanence,*" she shouted.

Mother Superior suddenly materialized; she grasped Sister Agatha's upraised arm. "Come along, Sister," the superioress whispered. "Time to go."

"I am not Time's Eunuch," Sister Agatha cried back over her shoulder as she was steered toward the cart.

Felice followed close behind. "Ma Mère . . . May I sit with her on the . . ."

"No," the nun said, pushing her back. "Don't be a pest."

In spite of the sky—bright blue as ever—the march up the hill was somber. In the cart, the Bishop, seated beside Antoine, stared silently ahead; on the rear seat Sister Agatha sat slumped against Soukie's shoulder. Mother Superior walked behind the wagon with Sister Theodota, the two of them marching quick-step, with occasional glares at each other, as though bound in some silent race or despised, immutable bond. The Abbé was absent, having stayed behind with Evangeline, who was said to be, Adele whispered to Felice, quite ill.

Felice drooped along feeling utterly disgraced. As not even Sister Claire would meet her eye, she concluded that her accident about the name had contributed, in large measure, to the spoiling of the day.

A splendid luncheon had been prepared. In observing the orderly serving of courses and the guests' appreciation of the fine cuisine, Mother Superior's countenance brightened considerably, a change that was reflected in a gradual warming trend throughout the dining room.

Felice took large helpings of everything; lamb, ham, pâté, duchess potatoes, green beans with almonds, several kinds of relish, and raisin cream tarts. No one mentioned Felice's transgression to her, but she imagined that it must be constantly on every mind, as no one addressed her directly. Other people at her table—all, that is, but Sister Agatha, who fell into periods of silence, often with her fork poised midway between plate and mouth—seemed to be engaged in conversations that Felice could only get to the edge of; finally she gave up all attempts at being sociable and, taking a second helping of everything, ate until her stomach ached. The Bishop, seated beside Mother Superior at the head table, had his listeners spellbound, or at least silenced, by accounts of his travels; for him, at least, the unsettling events of the mass had apparently been put aside.

The celebration party, at which Evangeline was to have been chief honorée, and which was still to include Felice's recital, Sister Claire assured her, was set back two hours. Mother Superior made this announcement after luncheon, following a hasty kitchen conference with the Abbé, who had arrived during dessert.

The nun gave no instructions on how the intervening time was to be spent. Girls whose relatives had come—Anne and Françoise were among this fortunate group—went to sit with them in the parlor, or to show them about the grounds. The other three League members, at Celeste's suggestion, went to the beach.

Celeste wanted to race, or to tell fortunes, but Felice said she didn't feel like doing either. She stood watching the glittering waves roll into the shadowed cove. Even on moonless nights when the waves were unseen by hers or any other eyes, she thought, the motion was the same: gather, rise, strike, hiss. The water had so behaved all the morning, even as she blurted out the wrong name, and when she sat down at the piano bench later, the same steady rhythm would continue, on and on. Felice found some comfort in this, but not enough to quell her vague, queasy fear.

Marie broke the silence. "It's a strange Easter, isn't it?"

Felice looked down at her ruffled dress. "I feel awful about what I did," she said.

Celeste giggled. "You do look like you've got a terrible case of It."

"I mean my name, stupid—the mistake about my name. That's much more serious."

"Well, at least you didn't *faint,*" Celeste said.

"Poor Evangeline," Marie whispered. "I wonder what's wrong."

"She's probably got It too," Celeste said. "That makes people faint, doesn't it, Felice? Or maybe she suddenly fell in love with the Bishop."

"Celeste!" Felice protested.

"Can't catch me!" Celeste suddenly shouted, whacking Felice on the shoulder.

Felice raced after her, with Marie tagging behind. It felt good to run, Felice discovered; she took long, bounding leaps.

"That big rock is home free," Celeste shouted back over her shoulder as she neared the end of the cove. "Ha!" she called, reaching it, and scampered around to its other side, out of sight.

Felice stood panting. "No fair, Celeste." She picked up a handful of small pebbles and sent them pinging one by one against the boulder. Then, indicating with a pointing finger that Marie should guard the bay side of the rock, Felice started around the right edge.

Celeste met her halfway, her face fixed in such a contorted expression that Felice thought at first she was strangling. Celeste's mouth was open wide; she jabbed one finger toward it.

"Celeste?"

"I'm the 'ongueless man," Celeste cried, raising both arms. "And I'm going to *get* you. Aaaaaaaah!" She pounced, lionlike, at Felice.

Felice skittered backward, knocking against Marie, and then turned and ran. She wheeled toward the path and, starting uphill, saw coming down toward her, its hand outstretched, a grinning mirage. She stood screaming, arms over her head.

Celeste pulled at one elbow, pried her arm loose. "Felice. Felice, I'm sorry I scared you. Look, it was just Remi."

Felice lowered her other arm partway and peeked up over it at Remi's astounded face.

"Just your boyfriend," Celeste giggled.

"Shut up," Felice sobbed, and bolted up the cliff, leaving Remi, Celeste, and Marie staring after her.

When Felice scrambled to the top she didn't look back, but ran straight through the balsam grove, vaulted the wall, and sped through the orchard, ducking trees. Even as she gained on the convent, and then was safely inside its halls, hurrying upstairs, a dark shadow pursued her.

In her cubicle, Felice brushed her tangled hair. Then she plaited it into very tight braids and wrapped them about her head in the severe style she hated. She went down the hall to the washbasin and scoured her hands and face until they felt raw. She took off her dress and scrubbed at the stain; it only grew worse. She rushed back to her cubicle and put on her blue silk party dress. Then she went downstairs to the parlor and, choosing the uncomfortable straight-backed chair Evangeline used for readings, sat down to wait.

Soukie, carrying the punch bowl, was the first to appear. "Goodness, Mademoiselle," she said, bending over her. "I didn't know who you were at first. Are you sick too?" She went out, and soon returned with Sister Claire.

"She's just a little worried about her recital," the nun said. "But you'll be fine, won't you, dear?" She lowered her anxious face so that they were eye to eye. "Would you like to warm up a bit while we set things out?"

Felice shook her head no. Soukie tucked a Mayflower into her anchored-down braid. After Soukie and Sister Claire assured each other that the girl would be fine they went off to complete the table arrangements. Others trickled in gradually—Madame Girrard, Mother Superior, Sister Theodota, and the Abbé, and then, in one large rush, all the other nuns, girls, and guests arrived. The Bishop was ushered to the best chair. When Felice felt several heads turning curiously her way, she got up and went to the refreshment table, where she stood less conspicuously in the crowd, pretending to sip at punch.

Though social equilibrium was preserved through the acts of serving, eating, and drinking, there was a decided strain about the affair. Mother Superior, ladling out punch, looked hollow-eyed, and did not even bother to scold Celeste and Marie when those latecomers sneaked into the room. Sister Claire was determinedly festive, handing out gifts to the new novice, Antoinette, and the girls just confirmed, though some whispered that this was a mistake, pointing up all the more acutely as it did the absence of Evangeline. Sister Agatha was not present either; taking a nap, Sister Claire explained to Felice as she gave her that nun's gift. Felice unwrapped it—a sky-blue velvet hair ribbon—and, smiling self-consciously, laid it on the table beside her other presents: a pitchpipe from Sister Claire, a scapular from Mother Superior, a breviary and religious cards from the Abbé, and a totally unanticipated leather bookmark from Sister Theodota.

Sister Claire hung about at Felice's side, murmuring, "You'll do very well, dear, I know you will," and alternately, "Are you going to be sick?" until Mother Superior beckoned to the nun. The two sisters withdrew to a corner of the room for a rather lengthy conversation which Felice knew must concern her, as each turned occasionally to glance her way. Sister Claire walked briskly back to Felice and, smiling in an unsuccessful attempt to mask her consternation, said, "Mother Superior wants you to play just one piece, in view of the, um, situation."

"My confirmation name?"

"What? No, dear. Evangeline. Just the prelude, then."

"The prelude? But what about the invention? I practiced it much more."

"The prelude is shorter. It's for the best, don't you think, since you're not feeling that well yourself? Now, are you ready?"

"No," Felice whispered.

"Ladies and gentlemen," Sister Claire called out. "My excellent student of piano, Felice Belliveau, will now perform for us."

There was silence. Felice felt quite ill as she walked forward. She saw, from the corner of her eye, the Bishop smiling up at her as he readjusted his embroidered gold skullcap; clearly, he expected to be thoroughly pleased.

"The Little Prelude in D, by Johann Sebastian Bach," Felice announced in a quavering voice, and then sat down. Her hands shook as she lifted them from her lap to the keyboard, but with the first chord they steadied and began to move almost of their own will, with Felice following behind, amazed. Soon she forgot her nervousness, and her audience. She concentrated so on her fingers, and the notes, and the wink of her amethyst ring, and the vibration of sonorous keys in her wrists, that when she came to the end, and there was rather noisy applause, she was startled. "Bravo!" the Bishop called out, clapping heartily. "Another artist!" After several demure curtsies, Felice was prevailed upon for an encore. She played "Ave Maris Stella," and then, introducing it only as "Song Without Words," played her willow-tree composition. Its melancholy, quixotic melody stilled the room. Scant applause followed, and congratulations so perfunctory that Felice wished for Sister Agatha: *she* would have appreciated her song.

"Fine, fine," the Bishop said, blinking down at her.

"Nice, dear," Sister Claire said, patting her shoulder. "But what *was* that music?"

Before Felice could explain, a clamor broke out in the hall.

Sister Constance went out to investigate and returned looking agitated. "Some villagers, Ma Mère," she said in an unnaturally loud voice.

The Abbé and Mother Superior jostled each other getting out the door, and the Bishop soon followed. With no one in command, and overcome by curiosity, the nuns and girls gradually eased out too. Felice saw the Abbé trying to round up three villagers, who were drifting about the hall like stray bees, and heard a woman shout into the Bishop's left ear, "The symbols, Your Eminence!"

"Back into the parlor!" Sister Theodota trumpeted.

Felice lingered near the door long enough to hear a villager explain to the clerics that they had come at Sister Agatha's invitation for a lecture tour of the frescoes, and to hear the Bishop respond, in his mellifluent voice, that they had excellent taste, but could they kindly return later, by appointment?

Felice slipped back into the parlor just ahead of Mother Superior, who announced that His Eminence would now continue the individual conventical interviews with the sisters. Felice thought of asking if she might be included in the schedule, but the superioress' smile was so frosty, as she thanked the guests for attending and enjoined the girls to be on time for vespers, that she dutifully filed out with the others.

From that point on, it became clear that all convent activities were being acted out in a superficial realm beneath which lay a vast uneasiness. By suppertime, Evangeline still had not appeared. The meal was quiet, with only bits of stilted conversation launched onto the silence.

When the subdued League members met that night, they whispered their speculations. Françoise thought perhaps Evangeline had changed her mind about being a nun; Celeste clung to her theory that the postulant had It; and Felice wondered if she had died.

The next day, after the Bishop's departure, the silence deepened, permeating every room, corridor, and religious niche, seeming to saturate every crack and crevice. No meetings were called; no announcements were made. Evangeline's name was not publicly uttered.

For two days there was nothing but silent gloom, punctuated only by conferences between the Abbé, Mother Superior, and the other senior nuns in Mother Superior's study. The sisters went about with long faces, and their fingers on their beads, setting a tone more appropriate to Ash Wednesday than the Easter season. The general atmosphere of the convent was distinctly funereal, lacking only a discrete body to be mourned and buried.

29

THE TRUTH ABOUT EVANGELINE'S CONDITION, THAT WHICH IS called "Ruina Maxima" by the Holy Fathers of the Church, seeped into the collective conscience of the convent well before any announcements were made. It was three days before Mother Superior even called the sisters together to describe the circumstances to them, though certainly most of them drew their own accurate conclusions, if not on Easter, at least soon thereafter. The reason she had delayed the meeting so long, the nun said when it was finally convened, was not only that she hoped—though in vain—that Evangeline's confession to His Eminence had sprung from an excess of hysterical, wholly unfounded guilt (indeed, the Bishop had intimated this might possibly be the case), but that she had also needed time to assess her own position in the convent in light of this tragic event. As Sister Claire described the scene much later to Felice, the nun placed a hand on her breast and announced, "Sisters, as her superior, I too am culpable." Mother Superior then went into a self-imposed retreat until Low Sunday, during which time the only rare glimpses of her came when she was slipping in or out of the convent chapel, where she spent the nights praying.

Felice had perhaps been the first student to intuit what was amiss.

On Easter Monday, at breakfast, her eyes strayed again and again to the space where Evangeline's now-removed dishes had been: with the better part of her mind focused—like everyone else's—upon the missing novice, Felice thought of the terrible stories she had told about Evangeline and Monsieur. Then, suddenly, she knew. And, simultaneously with her insight, felt a weight of responsibility, as though, in her stories, she had created, if not the sin itself, the possibility of it. And she herself, after all, had behaved quite similarly. So it was with a sense of terrific personal urgency that she hurried upstairs to visit Sister Agatha, who had also been absent from breakfast.

The nun was arranging and rearranging a shawl, a toothbrush, and a missal in a valise. She did not look up when Felice entered, and the girl stood staring at her for some moments before she spoke. Sister Agatha was squinting, as against an intolerable glare of light.

"Sister," Felice blurted out, "what's wrong with Evangeline?"

"Pregnant as a duck," Sister Agatha said, in a curiously flat voice. Her face still drawn up, the nun turned toward Felice and she laughed, a "hee hee hee" Felice had only imagined in connection with fairy-tale witches. Her laughter stopped as abruptly as it had begun, and Felice fled to the chapel, where she spent the morning murmuring the Penitential Psalms.

The next afternoon when the sisters were singing their office, Emma and Laura Doucette sent word around that any girl wanting to hear the hideous truth about Evangeline should follow them to the barn.

"I think I'll stay here," Felice said to Celeste, lying back on her bed and shutting her eyes. "I don't want to hear poor Evangeline gossiped about."

"Felice Belliveau, you *have* to come." Celeste hauled her up. "I heard Emma say something mean about Sister Agatha—we're going together, as a League."

So the five set out in a group, with Felice walking reluctantly at the rear.

The barn was crowded with students. Felice stood back from the circle, kicking at the straw, trying not to look at, or think about, the loft where she had sinned.

"Evangeline is . . ." Laura and Emma Doucette shouted in unison, and then both collapsed in mirthless giggles.

"What?" the crowd—all but Felice—cried.

"You know, you know," Laura choked; Emma, indicating with her hands a rounded belly, waddled about in a circle.

"Expecting?" Françoise called in a thin voice.

The Doucettes nodded their heads—Yes, yes—and began again to giggle.

"How do you know?" Celeste demanded.

"Our mama told us," Laura said, suddenly prim.

"Our mama," Celeste mimicked in a high, sour voice.

"Mama's sending us to another school, probably in America," Emma said.

"To get us away from this *immoral* atmosphere, and *bad* influence," Laura added, glaring at Celeste.

"Monsieur's gone," Celeste said. "And Evangeline too, I guess. So what do you mean, immoral?" Hands on her hips, Celeste swaggered forward and planted herself before the twins.

"It's more . . ." they cried, backing up.

"Blanche Melanson!" Emma said.

"And Sister Agatha!" Laura said. "She's another example. Mama says it's awful that Sister Agatha is allowed to stay and expose young innocent girls to her warped ideas. Isn't that right, Emma?"

Emma nodded and linked elbows with her sister; the two of them looked smugly at Celeste and other members of the League.

"Sister Agatha is a saint!" Françoise shouted. "My Aunt Febianne says that anybody who doesn't like her paintings is ignorant about art *and* religion."

"The Bishop liked her," Anne said.

"That's right," Celeste joined in. "Your Mama must be sacrilegious, to disagree with the Bishop."

There was some grumbling, and the Doucettes' few supporters went to stand beside them, thus creating two distinct groups.

"It wasn't Mother Superior's fault," Celeste went on. "And it wasn't Evangeline's fault. Monsieur was a wicked, wicked man. He *forced* her. And I'm glad you're leaving, you two Priss-Pots. I hope you go to Timbuktu and never come back."

Some pushing and shoving followed this insult and then a volley, back and forth, about who had sinned most.

"Evangeline!"

"Monsieur!"

"Evangeline!"

"Monsieur!"

Celeste ended this squabble by suddenly shouting, "He *was* evil—he chased Evangeline—Felice saw it!"

They all turned to look at Felice, who had remained aloof. "That's right!" Françoise said. "You *did* see it, didn't you? It wasn't just a story after all."

The girls pressed around, asking for a retelling of the event. Felice backed off, shaking her head.

"Come on, Felice," Celeste prompted. "He *made* her kiss him . . ."

Felice thought of Monsieur's hand snaking out to her, and she standing paralyzed; her heart began to race. "None of you are acting very nice," she said. "What about poor Evangeline, is what I keep thinking. What's going to happen to her, and will we ever see her again, is what *I* wonder."

Felice so successfully diverted interest from the former novice's past act to her present situation that the girls' imaginations remained fixed there for the next week or so; their subsequent discussions contributed to the rich stew of rumor and legend about Evangeline that was already simmering in the village.

Françoise's Aunt Febianne had heard from Beatrice Pinet that Evangeline had been seen walking south on the Chemin du Roi Easter afternoon, on the first leg of a long, futile quest for her illicit bridegroom. Anne, Marie, and Celeste claimed to know people who had witnessed the very same spectacle.

Emma and Laura Doucette said that their mother had it on very good authority that a village woman of excellent reputation had herself escorted Evangeline to the House for Fallen Women in Halifax. In a truly magnanimous gesture, Monsieur had stepped forward and offered to foot all the bills.

One girl said her sister had been told by Madame Tareno, retired midwife, that Evangeline had already given birth. Some people said that she had died; others, that she was scandalously healthy. According to the version that Soukie heard, and reported—as an example of a truly malicious fable—the offspring, a monster whose lower body formed a serpentlike tail, had been killed by a farmer with a scythe, and was now buried in the woods near Maxwellton.

Soukie also told the League that some villagers were whispering that Evangeline's partner in sin was not the tongueless man, but the very devil himself, and a few of Mother Superior's more radical supporters in the populace were insisting, as information about her weakening position at the convent was spread abroad, that the culprit was none other than the Abbé.

What with the tension in the convent and the village, Soukie's wedding, which took place on Low Sunday, was not a gay affair. The sparse crowd was subdued, with the exception of Soukie's red-headed brothers and sisters, who chattered in the front pews and rushed in and out of the church on various urgent missions before the appearance of the bride and groom. Felice watched them scrambling over the knees of their mother, who was seated on the aisle; she was a slight woman whose gray exhaustion was thrown into painful contrast by the vibrance of her progeny. Felice noticed that some of the villagers pointedly ignored the nuns as they entered, and particularly Mother Superior. But when Sister Agatha came in, late, just before the ceremony began, hinged on the elbows of Antoine Gentil and Soukie's father and bowing this way and that, bestowing smiles on her admirers, there were little clucks of appreciation. Sister Agatha's reputation, established in the days of the Great Walk and cemented by the Bishop's approval, had not been tainted by the besmirching of her protégée, Felice was happy to observe.

In the charged seconds before the appearance of the bride, Felice looked around and caught Remi staring at her; she turned quickly back to the altar and recomposed his face to resemble Robert's, a gentle, wholly respectful gentleman who would adore and woo her from afar.

When the congregation stirred, Felice turned with the others to watch the entrance of Soukie, beaming on the arm of her father, a man with nervous eyes and hair the color of dried blood. As the bride neared the front pew, where the Gentil boys were arranged oldest to youngest, their dark heads like the notes of a descending scale, they turned as one to regard their new mother. The eldest, by the aisle, held up the baby, as for a blessing, waking it; its cry mingled with the versicles and responses of the ceremony, for no one thought to carry it out.

Soukie stood firmly on the same spot where, one week ago, Felice had blurted out the wrong name and Evangeline had fainted, but, Felice noticed with awe, the bride seemed totally unconscious of any irony. She repeated the Abbé's mumbled phrases in clarion tones, nodding her fiery head vigorously as she agreed to the conditions of marriage. As she extended her plump, freckled hand to receive the ring, Soukie smiled back over her shoulder, including a quadrant of the congregation in the blissful moment.

Perhaps encouraged by this—but those watching her said she had been in an agitated state throughout—Sister Agatha, just after the nuptial kiss, rose and shouted, "She has found her Gabriel!" She could not be persuaded to sit down, and was ushered out right behind the bride and groom by Soukie's father, the nun declaiming all the way down the aisle the opening lines from Longfellow's "Evangeline."

Though neither Soukie nor Antoine, nor very many of the villagers, found anything to criticize in Sister Agatha's behavior, Mother Superior's opponents at the convent did, and they went up the hill together, in a tight, dark fist. They occasionally turned to stare at Sister Agatha, who was being helped along by Celeste and Marie, as the nun talked, apparently to no one in particular, about Evangeline and Gabriel. Though some points of this soliloquy were hard to follow, it was clear to everyone that the real subjects were not the star-crossed lovers of Longfellow's poem, but the recently departed novice and the tongue-less man.

From that day on, Sister Agatha was garrulous. She could sometimes be heard predicting as she went about the halls and grounds that Gabriel was coming to wake his Acadian sweetheart from an enchanted sleep; at other times, Gabriel was apparently the archangel, descending to tell Eve of an immaculate conception and an assumption bodily into heaven. Once Felice heard Sister Agatha explain to the dining-room door that Gabriel spoke not with his tongue, but with his finger, as he touched and set ablaze the forehead of the woman chosen above all others.

For a time, Felice did her best to avoid Sister Agatha, and her own friends, who were also preoccupied with Evangeline. Celeste organized a midnight expedition to look upon the bed of sin; Felice did not go, giving cramps as her excuse, though in fact her Monthlies had not begun.

As the days passed, Felice began to worry about It's being late. Her fear was exacerbated by Celeste's gleeful reminder that Antoinette had once claimed to no longer get It (or Alice, as Antoinette preferred to say), and that this showed how pure she was; in fact, Celeste whispered, this probably meant the new novice was actually like Evangeline in every way. Maybe Priss-Face had sneaked down to the infirmary at night, or maybe she had even met him in a hotel after his departure, on those weekends when she claimed to be going home.

Felice made numerous trips to the privy to check her underwear, but she remained stubbornly, distressingly dry; she poked at herself, praying for moisture.

Could it happen with all your clothes on? she wondered, tossing in her bed at night. And just what exactly had happened? That sinful scene was too disgusting to think upon closely.

Then, one morning when she awoke, there it was, soaking her gown, staining her sheet: blood. After the initial prick of fear this sight always aroused in her, Felice was joyful. She called out to Antoinette that she wouldn't be at breakfast because of terrible cramps, and would she please tell Mother Superior? Felice stayed in bed all day, happily miserable, her elation not the least spoiled by Celeste's contention that she was fibbing, either today *or* last week. ("Some women get It *twice* a month," Felice informed her. "My mother did, sometimes.") She groaned so when Mother Superior came to check on her condition that luncheon was brought up to her; in the afternoon she read Françoise's fashion magazines, luxuriating in her holiday from classes and in the chaste discomfort of Eve's curse.

30

APRIL GAVE WAY TO MAY, AND THE EARLY WARMTH, AT FIRST distrusted, was now expected to hold. There were no robin snows, only occasional thorough rains that made buds and shoots leap forward. All up and down the Acadian coast there was talk of its being an unusually fine growing season.

By mid-May the hill on which the convent stood had become a thick mat of green, and the first purple and yellow wildflowers had sprung up in the grass. Felice stared out from the dreary classrooms, where the main form of study these days was the memorization of long set passages, at the meadowlike lawn, and at the orchard, where the apple trees were just beginning to whiten into a low cloud; the scene induced a strange lethargy in her. She drifted through the long dull days of classes and prayers, both wishing and fearing for something to happen.

It was a time of waiting. Mother Superior had written to the Bishop to ask his opinion about a change in the conventical leadership, and so, it seemed, had the Abbé and Sister Theodota. At every mail delivery there was a rush to the door; no reply, however, had yet been received, and the nuns continued to go about in small, anxious groups, foreheads bent toward rosary-bound hands.

The Abbé had removed himself from the scene on the first Saturday in May; as he told Sister Theodota, the tension was making his head buzz, and furthermore, the Indian missions were sorely due a visit. On this journey he took Remi, as an example of a recently converted Indian Catholic. After they left, Felice went alone to sit by the cove, both secure and wistful in the knowledge that Remi would not suddenly appear.

With the Abbé gone, the sisters began to hold public confession. Though ostensibly established from practical necessity, to fill the void of absent confessor, the frequency and intensity of the daily ritual manifested its true origin—a prolific species of guilt engendered by Evangeline's sin. The girls were initially not allowed to attend these sessions, though eventually—when news of an unsupervised and possibly harmful similar group confession reached the ears of the nuns —the students were invited to bare their souls at these sanctioned meetings, though not to hear divulgences by the sisters.

Most of the girls, even those most genuinely uneasy on their own accounts, could not help speculating about what their teachers might be saying. Celeste repeated some shocking confessions she claimed to have overheard; Felice did not believe a word of these stories, for they described all sorts of rowdy behavior that was certainly inconsistent with the sisters' present demeanor. Most of the nuns had grown quite pale and thin. Almost all kept indoors, shrinking from the event of spring as though in embarrassment. There were but two exceptions to this: Sister Claire, who took over the back flower garden, attacking friable clods and weeds with great energy, and Sister Agatha.

Sister Agatha could be seen almost anywhere at any time of day: her movements had become totally unpredictable. Felice came upon her one afternoon by the back wall, where the long green whips of the budding willows stirred in the breeze. When the girl approached, the nun raised one hand as though to fend her off and began to declaim, in English:

> Comforter, where, where is your comforting?
> Mary, mother of us, where is your relief? . . .
> O the mind, mind has mountains; cliffs of fall
> Frightful, sheer, no-man-fathomed. Hold them cheap
> May who . . .

Sister Agatha's body wavered; she looked as if she were about to topple. But when Felice leapt forward, the nun began to walk quickly through the orchard, arms outstretched before her to avoid collision with the trees. Felice tailed along listening to the nun recite and watching her unsteady progress. And a good thing she had, she told Celeste and Françoise, for at the final, shouted line, " 'Life death does end and each day dies with sleep,' " Sister Agatha collapsed onto the ground. Felice thought she must be dead, for her eyes were shut and she did not respond when Felice pleaded, and worked one limp arm up and down. She ran, screaming, for help; when she returned with Sister Claire and Jacques the nun's eyes were open and blinking. As Sister Claire touched her, she grunted, but made not another sound as she was half-carried, half-shuffled up to her cell between Sister Claire and Felice (Jacques not being allowed inside the building at all, under the new rules).

"She doesn't eat enough," Felice said, kneeling by the nun's bed and looking anxiously into her exhausted face.

"I'm afraid you are right," Sister Claire said. "Sister!" she shouted —as though Sister Agatha's handicap were one of hearing and not of vision—"did you have lunch? How about some nice custard right now? Would you like Madame Girrard to fix you something special? Anything?"

"Dapple me," Sister Agatha whispered, again in English.

"Apples?"

Felice stood, shaking her head. "She's talking about Gerard Manley Hopkins," she explained to Sister Claire, "her spiritual brother, she always called him."

The nun sent Felice after some warmed milk which, between them, they managed to force down Sister Agatha's throat. Felice then rounded up the other League members and the five of them stood at the foot of her bed and sang hymns. Though this seemed to cheer Sister Agatha somewhat, she still did not speak.

But the next morning, when Felice carried breakfast to her cell, the nun not only ate but talked. She confided to Felice that her wedding had been postponed for her to endure but one more test of her worthiness; a savage was in pursuit of her, but she was keeping him at bay with her absolute purity. "I take no nourishment but His holy body," she whispered.

"That's right, Sister," Felice said, not wanting to remind her that she had just consumed a large dish of gruel. "I'll be coming back a little later." When Felice took in the luncheon tray she persuaded the nun to eat by promising to record her blossoming visions about Evangeline and Gabriel and a dark stranger. Felice went in search of paper and pen, but returned to find the nun asleep.

The League set up a feeding schedule for Sister Agatha, whose cooperation was erratic. The nun had grown so haggard that Felice thought a doctor should be sent for, but could arouse no interest in this. Sister Claire agreed that Sister Agatha was unwell, but said she was beyond medical help. The other nuns, even those who cared for her, had seen Sister Agatha survive so many crises that they were now skeptical of—or inured to—the possibility of real danger.

As in earlier times of difficulty, Felice found herself to be the only really devoted League member. Sister Agatha's condition was almost always at the center of her mind, and she was not able to divert herself by concocting or listening to gossip, as the others were. The chatter sessions made her impatient. She could not bear any of it: parodies of the Doucettes' bragging about their new school; updates on Françoise's romance (a boy from Plympton had spied her during the Easter mass and had begun to write amorous letters); deliberations over whether or not Marie should become a nun ("She might as well," Celeste said, out of that girl's hearing, "since she's not exactly gorgeous"); and the serialized drama, composed by the whole group, about Antoinette and the tongueless man.

Felice's chief occupation, these days, was thinking up persuasions for Sister Agatha. "Saint Catherine appeared to me last night," she said, taking in breakfast. "She told me you were to have fresh eggs today."

Sometimes this sort of approach worked. When it did not, and Sister Agatha jerked her mouth away from the spoon, disregarding the food that slid down her chin, Felice would sit patiently by her for a long while, talking and cajoling. She refused to give up hope of the nun's taking nourishment, for Sister Agatha's liveness seemed as fragile and precious to Felice as her own soul.

Felice prayed to the Virgin Mary for Sister Agatha's recovery. She knelt before her blue and silver figurine of the Madonna morning and evening, and in the white chapel at noon, sometimes forgoing luncheon, saying litanies and novenas devoted to the sister. She also discovered, in her sessions at the piano, that music was a form of devotion. No matter what she played—Bach, Mozart, a piece of her own composing—her fingers felt more authoritative, and the sounds seemed richer, inspired as it all was by compassion for the nun. Even when Felice pretended her audience to be the admissions committee of the Boston conservatory (on which occasions she played the two-part invention and the variation deleted from her recital), she felt empowered by her allegiance to Sister Agatha.

Felice one day tried to persuade Sister Agatha to go with her to the parlor and listen to a melody she had written in her honor. Sister Agatha was either oblivious or unwilling; she made no response. "Then I'll sing it for you, Sister. This is how it goes." Though Sister Agatha did not open her eyes as Felice hummed the song, the girl was rewarded by the nun's reaching out, at the conclusion, to touch her hand.

That night Felice stayed late in the parlor, softly playing the piano until well past bedtime. No one had told her to retire, so she was surprised, when she finally looked at the wall clock, by the lateness of the hour.

Felice lit a candle, extinguished the kerosene lamp, and stepped out into the hall. The building was dark, and so quiet as to seem uninhabited by anyone but herself. As Felice walked nervously toward the stairs, she began to hear, or imagine, distant, ominous footsteps. She quickened her pace, nearly running, and on the first flight of steps collided with Sister Agatha, who was laboring upward in total darkness.

"Sister!" Felice exclaimed, holding up the candle. The nun was without her spectacles, and her face shone with tears. Felice put an arm about the bony shoulders. "Did you come to hear me, and couldn't open the door? I am so sorry."

"All is well," the nun mumbled, reaching for Felice, patting air. "He is feeding me by His own hand. I am divinely nourished." Felice led the way to the nun's cell while Sister Agatha cried and talked, in a mixture of Latin and English and some other language Felice did not know. Whenever the girl tried to offer consolation, Sister Agatha said, switching back to French, "Divine nourishment. Divine nourishment."

The next day, the Saturday before Pentecost, Felice was unable to entice Sister Agatha to eat or to speak. Finally convinced, in midafternoon, that the nun was not going to yield, Felice went to pray for her in her cubicle. As she was reciting the Litany of the Saints Celeste rushed in upon her with astounding news.

"Your boyfriend's here, at the cove. He wants to see you!"

"My . . ."

"Robert, Robert from the train. Hurry up, goosey."

After a hurried examination of herself before the mirror—and the pleasant conclusion that her eyes seemed suddenly larger and dewier —Felice hurried down the steps after Celeste. Only in the orchard when Celeste looked back, giggling, did Felice begin to suspect her.

Felice glanced in at Our Lady of the Willow, crossed herself, and jumped the wall. "If you're lying, Celeste," she shouted, "I'll kill you. What's he doing on the beach, anyway? Why isn't he in the parlor? Celeste!" she called through the balsam grove—for the other girl had run on ahead—"Come back here."

Crossing her fingers, Felice walked on between the fragrant evergreens, praying that he was there, and that he was not.

From the top of the cliff, she saw a cluster of girls on the beach. "Liar. I'm leaving. Stink-pot."

Celeste pulled her back. "I'm not teasing you, Felice. Your boyfriend is *here.*"

Narrowing her eyes at the scene below, Felice did pick out a male head in the group. "But Robert's blond," she protested.

"That's Francie's boyfriend—he came on the train today, and he acts like he's going to propose. But yours is here, too. Come on, you'll see."

"I'm not coming," Felice said, as Celeste started downward. But she did go, muttering "Idiot" and "Stink-pot" to Celeste's back all the way down the hill.

There was cheering when Felice approached. Flushing deeply, Felice crossed her arms over her chest and looked around. Aside from

Françoise's suitor—who had removed his eyes from that girl only for the briefest glance at her—there was no boy in sight.

Angry tears filled her eyes, and she started to stamp away.

"Wait," Celeste said. "You can come out now," she shouted.

From behind the boulder at the end of the cove, Remi appeared, grinning broadly.

"Really, you disgust me, Celeste." Felice stalked toward the path. Behind her was the terrible sort of silence that would soon erupt into laughter. She glanced over her shoulder at them—Celeste was already doubled up, clutching at her stomach—and at Remi. His crestfallen appearance, and the girls' smugness, prompted her action. She turned. Then, smiling as graciously as though approaching a courtier rising from the parlor sofa, she walked toward Remi.

His face brightened as she approached. To her left there was a different variety of silence. "Let's go sit on the other side of that rock," Felice said. "I don't want to be stared at, do you?"

But once she was alone with him her courage failed. She sat clutching her knees, shivering, and when he asked what was wrong, she began to cry. "There's someone I'm really worried about—one of the sisters." And, sorting through cobbles and arranging them in a cairn-like pile, she described Sister Agatha's uncertain health and the continuing trials she had had to endure throughout her life.

"She will be happy, then, in the Land of Souls."

Felice turned to look at him. He was close and vivid; she leaned away. "Did you enjoy your trip with the Abbé?"

"Yes, thank you," he said politely, but his eyes were on her lips. "I think you're very nice," he whispered. "Don't go," he pleaded as she started to rise.

"All right, then. But let's tell stories." Rather frantically, Felice plunged into a narrative of the mystery ship *Marie Celeste*. Though Remi had surely heard this tale before, he attended as breathlessly as though he had not. "Your turn," she said at the conclusion.

Remi told the legend of the great Glooscap's departure for the Land of Souls. "It was when the white man came, and he knew he could not live here any longer. He called all the animals together and talked to them one last time. They all came but the whale. 'Let the small fish rise,' Glooscap called. 'Let the small fish rise.' And the whale rose up from the sea. 'What is it, my grandson?' the whale asked. 'I must go, Grandfather. I must go to a far land in the west, and you are to carry me.' So Glooscap climbed upon the whale's back and sailed away. All the creatures left behind were very sad. They cried and gnashed their teeth, and then they cried all the more when they tried to console one another, and discovered they no longer spoke the same language. The Great Owl flew away into the deep woods. And he has stayed there, crying because Glooscap has gone and because he cannot talk with his brothers. Have you ever heard him? Coo-coo-coos! Coo-coo-coos!"

Felice, entranced by the sound of Remi's voice, had let him inch closer. His face was descending; he seemed about to kiss her. Thinking she heard a sound behind her, Felice quickly rose and brushed at her skirt.

Though there was no one peering over the boulder, as she had feared, Felice sensed many eyes on her. She walked toward the cliff on unsteady legs, feeling oddly, conspicuously tall.

That night Felice dreamt of kissing Remi. They were standing on the deck of a swaying boat, which was also a Latin classroom. *"Amo, amas, amat,"* he whispered, and his lips touched hers. Then, down the lanyards, up through the hatches, came nuns, and girls disguised as nuns, pointing and jeering.

When she awoke, Felice lay remembering the dream, and then revising it; with the intruders erased, the kiss went on and on, and the ship grew still beneath them.

She tossed; the bed felt rumpled; she began to be exhausted. She should get up now and say her prayers. But still she turned from side to side, her mind empty now of everything but a formless, gummy indecision.

When Felice finally rose and dressed it was late. She would have been tardy for the mass of Pentecost, had it not been indefinitely postponed.

When she went downstairs, Felice found the convent in an uproar, with sisters dashing up and down the halls, searching classrooms, bumping into one another. The Abbé was pacing in a circle near the chapel door and chewing his knuckles. The girls were huddled in the dining room. Though there was some confusion about what was going on, Felice soon pieced together the story from Celeste, Madame Girrard, and Sister Claire, who was sitting at the kitchen table with her head in her hands.

It seemed that when the Abbé went to ready the altar in the white chapel for mass that morning, he had found the tabernacle door open. The ciborium, in which was kept the bread of Holy Communion, the body of Christ, was empty, even of crumbs. As the Abbé told the hastily assembled sisters, he stood pressing his fingers against the metal of the ravished bowl for fully a minute, so stunned was he, before he realized that the most dreadful of all profanations had taken place. Then he saw that the tabernacle key, which he usually kept on a shelf just below it, in its holy place, was gone. There were no words to describe his feelings, he told the sisterhood, when the fact and implications of this most execrable crime, this theft from God Himself, became clear to him. Did they have any idea who would have perpetrated such a deed?

According to Sister Claire, it was Sister Theodota who, after a long silence, stood up and said, "Sister Agatha is the only one of us not present. Perhaps she could explain. This act might well put some of her recent bizarre—and unfortunately, neglected—comments into their true perspective."

After the convent building had been searched from bottom to top, and Sister Agatha still had not been found, Sister Theodota and the Abbé went outside to look. Mother Superior followed, but not before ordering the girls to their cubicles.

Felice obeyed, reluctantly, and watched from her window as the search party went into and out of the outer chapel, and toward the garden house. Then Felice caught sight of Sister Agatha as she rounded the opposite side of the building and made her way into the orchard. When she disappeared into the light green leaves, Felice ran downstairs. She dashed down the hall and out the back door, brushing past Madame Girrard, and ran to the orchard, ducking this way and that between trees, calling, "Sister Agatha! Sister Agatha! It's me, Felice."

Though she had no clear plan in mind, she felt it urgent that she reach the nun first, to caution her. She did not find her anywhere in the orchard, or among the willows. With a sense of premonition, she thought of the cliff, and was looking in that direction, into the balsams, when she heard the Abbé shout, "There she is! Stop! Thief!"

The sound came from near the building, and Felice realized at once that Sister Agatha had gone along the south wall up toward the road, and had been spied by her pursuers as they circled the building from the other directions.

"Stop, thief!" Felice heard again, and, "Give me that key!"

"No, Abbé, don't chase her." Felice recognized Mother Superior's voice. "Don't chase her—she'll fall."

As Felice hurried back through the orchard, she saw Sister Agatha running across the grass toward her. White legs flashing beneath the habit held bunched at her knees, she was moving faster than Felice would have believed possible.

The Abbé, close behind, was slowed momentarily by Mother Superior, who managed to get a firm grip on the sleeve of his cassock. "Stop," she screamed, "you don't know what you're doing."

The Abbé slashed his arm free and took up the chase again, Mother Superior close behind him. A group of sisters who had been watching from the back stoop joined in pursuit as Sister Agatha neared the orchard.

Felice stepped out from behind the trees, one hand extended. "Sister? It's Felice." But Sister Agatha rushed past her, and plunged into the orchard.

Felice ran parallel, a line of apple trees between them, calling out, "Sister, it's Felice. *Sister!*"

Branches slapped about Sister Agatha's face and shoulders. When a limb caught her veil, the nun flailed like a drowning swimmer. Felice heard the cloth rip just as she reached out to her.

"No!" Felice heard her shout as she dove onward. "Dirty man, filthy. Never touch me. Never."

Felice stood still, paralyzed, as the Abbé ran past, Mother Superior and several other nuns close on his heels, all of them panting as they darted around trees.

"Give me that key!" the Abbé shouted again and again.

"Wait! Wait! Don't be such a fool!" Mother Superior called after him, reaching toward his shoulder.

Not until their voices grew fainter did Felice realize they had cleared the wall, which meant Sister Agatha must have gotten over too.

Felice dashed through the orchard, jumped the wall, and ran through the balsam grove, emerging just in time to see Sister Agatha heading toward the cliff, the Abbé still in pursuit, and Mother Superior still vainly trying to hold him back.

"The key, woman, the key!" the Abbé yelled, even when it was evident to Felice what was going to happen.

"Noooo," Mother Superior bellowed, "Sister Agatha—no—don't."

Sister Agatha's arms opened. She rose to tiptoe, seemed to dance forward. "Come!" Her voice resounded over the bay. "My bridegroom," she called, as her foot struck air, "come!"

Felice saw her leap and, for one second, soar. Then she plummeted, hands folded above her head. "Come," she called, as she fell; the long vowel rose in the air like spume.

Felice sped to the cliff and down the path, running and praying so hard that she gave no thought to slipping. She was on the shore in seconds, and had begun to run toward the still, black figure before the Abbé and sisters had so much as moved.

Though she was sprinting, it seemed to Felice that it took a very long time to reduce the expanse of beach between herself and Sister Agatha. "Please, God," she said over and over, "please," but there was no stirring in that form at the base of the cliff.

Felice was suddenly there, on the wind-sculpted rock with Sister Agatha. She knelt beside her. The nun lay face down. One thin leg was exposed, and twisted at an impossible angle.

Felice lifted Sister Agatha and pulled back her veil. There was a deep gash in one cheek; the lower half of her face was already bathed in blood. Her unspectacled eyes were open wide, and ecstatic. As Felice lifted her the nun stared up at the sky, as though mesmerized by the splendor of a final glorious vision emblazoned there.

Felice sat cradling her, looking up into the blue sky at the high bank of white clouds with elaborately whorled edges, like the clouds in one of Sister Agatha's paintings. She breathed in and out, in and out, listening to the subtle harmony of her breath and the waves against the shore, feeling strangely calm, and out of time, until the Abbé came stumbling across the beach toward them.

THE POWERFUL FUNDY TIDE HAD SWUNG OUT AND IN BUT ONCE before the first pilgrims found their way to the cove where Sister Agatha had died. By the close of the day following that Pentecost Sunday which was later called, in French Acadian villages up and down the coast, the birthday of Saint Agatha, a sizable group of people were searching the cobbled beach and fissures in the cliff for amber beads from her rosary, said to have miraculous powers of healing.

From the hour when Sister Agatha's body was carried up the cliff, the popular impression was that she had died a martyr; it was some time, however, before all details of the standard version of the event could be filled in.

The Abbé's contention that Sister Agatha had committed suicide met with such outrage from most of the nuns that he went ahead with plans for a Christian burial. No tabernacle key was found, giving credence to the view advanced by Soukie, and soon by many others, that the Abbé's accusation of larceny had been, to put it most kindly, the work of an inflamed imagination.

A few of the sisters charged that the priest had, by his insensitivity, caused the nun's demise; Soukie embroidered liberally upon these remarks in the village, where there was already some gossip—among those who had professed greatest shock about recent evidence of licentious behavior in the convent—that the priest had pursued Sister

Agatha for wholly dishonorable purposes; the tenacity with which this belief actually took hold, however, was greatest at distances where the Abbé was little known.

As a lascivious Abbé was unthinkable to most villagers, the tongueless man was, from the first, the leading suspect. The myth—and this was the one that endured, passed down from mother to daughter—that the tongueless man's attempt to ravish Sister Agatha had precipitated her martyrdom might have arisen spontaneously; after all, the mysterious stranger, who had profoundly affected the local imagination ever since his emergence from the sea, was known to have ruined another, frailer, member of the sisterhood.

But, as it happened, Antoinette Mouton played a large role in the formulation of this legend. In the days following Sister Agatha's death, Antoinette reminded the girls, sisters, and Soukie of the aged nun's predictions that a villain would try her virtue. And the girl confided that she had had an eerie premonition (even before the revelation of Evangeline's sin; since Monsieur's disappearance, in fact) that Monsieur would one day return and take action against other virgins in the convent. In recent weeks Antoinette had dreamt urgently of danger; though she had originally thought these dreams concerned herself, she now realized, she said, shaking her head in sad relief, that all omens had pointed toward Sister Agatha's trial by Monsieur. Yes, Monsieur; for she had seen him, she whispered, on the night before Pentecost, lurking about the corner of the convent building when she returned from a private round of the stations in the outer chapel. At the time she had thought the shadowy figure might be a warning set before her by the Virgin; but now she realized that the shape had been all too corporeal, and most definitely Monsieur's.

Felice's part in the interpretation of the glorious tragedy was more subtle. The fact of Sister Agatha's death so affected her that for a long while she could not speak of it, and she never felt an inclination to spin stories about the final moment in the nun's life. Aware that some deep cleverness of the nun's had contributed to the manner of, and conclusions about, her death, Felice neither advanced nor disputed the tongueless man theory, but let the speculation take its natural course.

Felice most directly influenced the Sister Agatha legend by narrating the events of her life, many of which might otherwise have passed into oblivion. She first told the story on Monday night, to a crowd gathered in the Doucettes' parlor.

Felice described Catherine Comeau Starr's early home: conflict between a French Catholic mother (whose great-grandmother, one of the earliest female settlers of Nova Scotia, had been martyred by Indians) and an English, Baptist father. Conversion of her father was the young Catherine's first religious act, and the earliest indication of her future direction. Attracted by the beauties of nature and art, and possessing a rare talent for drawing the figure, she first pursued a career in painting. But it was when studying with the great masters in Florence, Italy (one of whom was madly in love with her), that she had received her call to return to her homeland to teach Indian children and young Catholic girls. When she had first come to L'Académie du Sacré Sang many, many years ago, she had begun to paint the series of frescoes that had, over the course of time, kindled so many souls. The depiction of her namesake Saint Agatha's passion—the sacrifice of her breasts—was symbolic of the tribulations in store for the young postulant. The first trial had been the loss of her eyesight to cataracts; those veils across the eyes, however, she later came to understand as necessary to the development of an inner vision which emerged as the central focus of her life. And she had endured many other adversities: a general misunderstanding of her nature, for example, which had on one occasion even caused her to be incarcerated; and, also at the close of her life, retirement from the teaching which she had so loved. But during this last, especially difficult year Sister Agatha had been blessed by a lush flowering of visions, Felice said, and visits from her heavenly bridegroom and several other residents of heaven, Duns Scotus, Gerard Hopkins, and Catherine of Beaubassin among them. Felice also told her listeners that the nun's painting of Our Lady of the Willow had blazed with light on Saint Agatha's Day, a revelation in which the entire audience—but particularly Antoinette—displayed much interest.

But, Felice went on, cutting off questions, though Sister Agatha had certainly been an inspired teacher and a great mystic, her most wonderful, and unappreciated, quality was the warmth and love she had felt for others; and especially those beings who were lonely and misunderstood. At this point Felice, overcome by tears, abruptly ended her narrative; as Madame Doucette guided her upstairs, the girls, women —and even a few men—applied handkerchiefs to their eyes.

On Tuesday afternoon, Felice went to the infirmary with the other girls and the nuns to view Sister Agatha's laid-out body. She dropped to the end of the line, so that she might have a moment alone with the nun. While waiting outside the door, she tried to console herself with thoughts of how happy Sister Agatha must now be; she took out her beads and fingered them, but could not pray.

Finally she entered the room. A heavy drape had been pulled over the window, so that the only illumination was from candles flickering at the head of the bier. The sickbed had been removed for the wake, and in its place, beneath the frescoes of the Holy Virgin's Dormition and Assumption, stood the raised coffin. As Felice shuffled forward in the lily-perfumed darkness, she imagined how Sister Agatha's face would look: peaceful, asleep. Sleeping here but awake in heaven, Felice told herself.

But when her turn came to kneel beside Sister Agatha, Felice was so stunned that she cried "No!" and fell against the coffin, making it wobble slightly on its supports. The nun's face looked peevish, and peculiarly small, like that of a wizened infant. Felice gripped the coffin's sharp edge and bent closer. She could see cotton wadded beneath the starched headdress; either Sister Agatha had really shrunk, or this was a new wimple of an inappropriate size. Then Felice saw that the black cloth of the habit was also new, as were the coarse chain and silver cross arranged on Sister Agatha's chest. The cross was of recent vintage and not well-modeled; its points were blunt, and the figure stretched between them utterly without artistic grace. Sister Agatha would have hated it, Felice thought.

Felice reached to touch one hand: cold, and horribly still. It seemed to have nothing to do with Felice, nor with Sister Agatha herself. Her body had deserted them both.

Felice rose to find Sister Claire beside her. The nun led her into the hall, where Felice clung to her waist and sobbed.

Sister Claire patted her face with a large, soft handkerchief. "Would you like to sit in the parlor with me?" she whispered, "or go to the dormitory and lie down?"

"No—I want to walk."

Felice went down the hall, looking into classrooms and offices; everything had a distant, grating familiarity. From the front door, she stared at the road, unable to imagine setting out in either direction. She would visit her willow tree, she thought, and perhaps then go to the shore.

She circled the convent building and entered the orchard, where she was surprised to hear voices. She hesitated, but then, drawn by curiosity, and an instinct to protect her tree and its relics, went on.

She found semicircular rows of girls facing her willow. Those in the back were standing and talking, and those nearest the tree, she discovered upon pushing into the crowd, were kneeling. At the base of the tree was a prostrate figure whom Celeste—one of those in the back row—identified as Antoinette. "She's having visions," Celeste whispered to Felice. "The Holy Virgin and Sister Agatha, she *says*. Emma Doucette and Marie said they saw them too, but I don't believe it." Celeste squinted upward. "Antoinette says there's a big light all around the tree."

Felice stepped closer to the willow; the only light that she could see was that of the sun quivering in the long, narrow leaves. The recess where Sister Agatha's painting hung was shadowed, and no luminescence poured forth from Our Lady's face.

Felice watched as Antoinette rose and genuflected, her hands clasped ecstatically to her chest; and then, looking down once more, Felice's eye was caught by a glimmer in the tall grass by the tree. She narrowed her eyes, thinking at first this might be some evidence of a miracle—for the gleam was but inches from the place where Antoinette's outflung hand had lain.

But something told her otherwise, and she quickly looked upward to avoid drawing attention to the spot; she waited, seeming to gaze into the branches, while Antoinette and her train walked with measured steps back through the orchard to the convent.

Celeste and Françoise lingered. "What is it?" Françoise whispered. "Do you see something too?"

"She's pretending," Celeste said. "Like Priss-Face."

"Go on," Felice said crossly, turning around, "I just feel like being by myself for a while."

When Françoise and Celeste were out of sight, Felice ran to the tree and knelt beside it. She combed the grass with her fingers until she touched metal; then, trembling, she held it up to the light of day: the tabernacle key.

The small gold key was elaborately wrought, and worn to an elegant thinness; there could be no doubt of what it was. The circle was made of tiny interlocking baroque curves; the opening mechanism was delicate and fine. Felice felt wonder, but no surprise. It was as if she had sensed, even before it lay gleaming in her hand, that the key would be hers to find—a legacy, a responsibility. For it was clear— Felice never questioned this for a moment—that Sister Agatha had tried to put the key in the hollow for her to guard and keep secret.

After carefully checking for holes, Felice put the key in her pocket. Then she reached into the hollow and took out her other treasures for inspection: brocade-wrapped painting, cobbles, glass, iron—all were in order. She considered, but only for a moment, putting the key in the bottom of the hollow; no, she thought, replacing the objects one by one, a permanent, and completely safe, resting place was required.

Hand in her pocket and key tight against her palm, Felice walked slowly back to the convent. To avoid any possibility of accident or inspection she went around to the front door, slipped in through the vestibule, hurried down the hall, and ran lightly up the steps. She hid the key in her bottom bureau drawer, between the pages of a missal, which she inserted into the folded-back arms of a sweater. But all through supper she worried about the safety of the key—for if it was discovered, an entirely new light would be shed upon Sister Agatha's life and death, and her glory might be dimmed.

That night, when other girls gathered in Marie's cubicle to discuss the afternoon's miracle, Felice stayed alone, keeping watch by her treasure. She stayed awake late that night, considering alternatives. She would like to wear the key on the chain about her neck with her Saint Cecilia medallion, as a memento of Sister Agatha, but knew that would be too risky. Her jewelry box wouldn't do, nor a plush-lined watch case she had once taken from Uncle Adolphe's study, nor the lining of her suitcase. Burying it in the ground seemed wrong—and it might be inadvertently dug up some day, by an animal, or a farmer tilling new ground. She could throw it into the water. At first this seemed a good idea, but then the thought of her sea treasures reminded her of the tide's long net. The key might be flung up on the shore, sparkling there on the rock for anyone to pick up. She could return the key to the chapel, but that might prompt an investigation, and, besides, Sister Agatha would not approve.

After a mostly sleepless night, however, Felice had a solution. She went to Mother Superior and requested, as a close associate of Sister Agatha's, some time alone with her before the coffin was closed and carried to the village for the funeral. Mother Superior agreed, kissing the girl on the forehead. "Poor Felice. I know you loved her. But she has now met her reward."

In the infirmary, Felice pushed a chair against the door to prevent anyone from suddenly entering. She took the tabernacle key from her pocket, slid it beneath the nun's loose collar, and, stroking her hand along the material, worked it down to a safe distance on her chest. She rearranged the cross, which had shifted slightly to the left during this maneuver, and, after one final inspection of the nun's face, left the room.

Anxiety that the key might be found kept Felice hovering outside the infirmary door until it was time for the procession to Nevette to begin. And she followed the bier closely down the hill, front and center among the nuns and girls. The suspenseful possibility of discovery distracted Felice throughout the service in the church—which was packed with emotional mourners and spectators—and sustained her until the moment when the coffin lid was shut for the final time, and the box was lowered into the earth. Then she buckled beneath her sorrow. Life without Sister Agatha was hard to contemplate.

FELICE STAYED AT THE CONVENT INTO THE SUMMER, WHICH WAS uncharacteristically hot and dry. Dust filmed the surfaces of leaves by the road, and even the willows along the back wall looked thirsty. Felice dragged through the days in a state of torpor and spiritual aridity that she attributed—when she thought of it—to the weather. Sometimes she stood on the rim of the cliff, looking out at the wisps of cloud above the bay, praying for them to gather, darken, and fan out into a low, cool blanket over sea and land. Long, thorough drenchings were needed, days of rain that would restore trees and grass to vividness and make her feel cozily purposeful indoors, kneeling in the white chapel or helping Madame Girrard in the kitchen.

Remaining at school during the holidays had been surprisingly easy for Felice to arrange. Mother Superior had granted permission almost casually, and without the close questioning Felice had anticipated.

Felice had written to Philippe, asking him to inform Uncle Adolphe that she did not intend to come to Wolfville this summer, or ever; she also inquired about the status of money left to her by Papa, for if and when she entered the order of Sacré Sang, she would need to present a dowry. In a postscript, she begged Philippe to visit, perhaps even move to Nevette—Monsieur Doucette would be glad to employ him, she felt sure.

Philippe's reply was terse. Her trust fund was being held at the Wolfville bank; when Felice needed the dowry money she should write and tell Philippe the exact amount and he would have Uncle Adolphe sign it over to the convent. If she was determined to shut herself away, there was no preventing her, he supposed. As to a summer visit, he would try but couldn't promise, as he was very busy; to the proposed move to Nevette he made no response.

Felice took this depressing letter to Sister Agatha's cell and threw herself on the narrow bed. When her attempt to weep resulted only in dry, coughlike sobs, she jumped up and paced the rectangular room. Now that she had cut herself off from it, Wolfville seemed almost attractive. She thought of the populated streets, the pretty white house, her large bedroom, long talks with Philippe. But as she began to compose a letter of retraction, she remembered Uncle Adolphe's dour face and Philippe's aloofness. She didn't belong there. She walked to the window and looked out at the rusty grass and, beyond it, the shield of silent firs. Those were the tree shapes Sister Agatha had known best, and that the canvas of sky—today a merciless blue—upon which she had most often gazed until her eyesight failed. If Felice joined the sisterhood, perhaps she could occupy this very cell, revere this same beloved scene. Perhaps she should speak to Mother Superior right now, and declare her intention clearly.

Yet Felice did not go to Mother Superior that day, nor the next; she lapsed into a state of monotonous suspension.

It was not that she feared rejection; indeed, the superioress seemed to be waiting for her to announce her candidacy for the novitiate. And since Marie's and Emma Doucette's petitions had been accepted, surely hers would be. Yet the thought of being grouped with those two made her angry; her spiritual struggle had been much deeper, more complex. They were, as Sister Agatha would have said, innocents.

Felice preferred to feel scorn for the series of apparitions that had prompted Marie's and Emma's decisions to join Antoinette in the novitiate. She did grudgingly admire Emma's brave defiance—her parents were said to be appalled, and Laura, still planning to enter an exclusive American school in the fall, now barely spoke to her sister. But as for the visions, Felice thought—and sometimes prayed—that they must have been delusions.

Because the trio continued to hold daily vigils before the willow, Felice removed her treasures from the hollow, for fear they might be molested. She put the cobbles on top of her bureau, and the more sacred objects—glass, iron, brocade, and painting—in the bottom drawer. After moving the relics, she rarely visited the grove.

When she did go, it was alone, and in a fit of penitence. For Felice was occasionally tormented by fears—confession day invariably provoked them—that her wickedness had prevented her from seeing Mary. Perhaps even—but she thought this only on her blackest days —Sister Agatha. Her dreadful sin, acted out beneath this very tree, in the spot where she now knelt, had filmed the eyes of her soul and blinded her to the apparitions. The Virgin had offered her the first opportunity, she thought, staring at the ridged trunk, and what had she done? Scorned it, dashed it to the ground, reduced her miracle to smithereens.

Throughout June Felice kept to the convent, there wandering the halls and grounds, shifting on her knees in the white chapel, sitting on her bed with Seine, and staring out at the bay. With all the other students gone but Antoinette, Emma, and Marie, the building was quiet, and the absence of Sister Agatha—which created such a void for Felice—seemed to have brought peace to the convent's other inhabitants. Without Sister Agatha to remind them of the soul's darker side, most of the nuns settled into what seemed to Felice a bland serenity. Though the group confessions were continued, these meetings now had a pleasant, almost social air. The question of a change in conventical leadership had apparently been dropped; Mother Superior and the Abbé were coexisting harmoniously, and even Sister Theodota's scowl lines had relaxed. Sister Theodota had taken up a new, time-consuming hobby—the reproduction of illuminated manuscripts—about which she insisted on talking at mealtime.

The sameness of the long, slow days suffocated Felice. She wanted to slam doors, break things, run shouting down the halls. She poured her violence into the piano, making the chords thunder and resound. Mother Superior accused her of banging and, finger to her lips, drew shut the parlor door. When even Sister Claire commented that Felice was playing without her usual grace, she stopped practicing and began to make excursions away from the convent.

She went twice to Sister Agatha's grave in the village churchyard, but the sight of the mounded earth—now littered with religious cards, scapulars, icons, and decaying wildflowers left by pilgrims come to seek heavenly intercession—made Felice unbearably sad. She visited Françoise and her Aunt Febianne in Nevette, and she spent some weekends with Anne in Pointe l'Eglise. But Felice felt most comfortable at the Gentil house, over which Soukie ruled from the kitchen.

Felice liked the good-natured rowdiness of Soukie's stepchildren, and the smells of cooking, and Soukie's chatter. Perched on a table by the stove, Felice listened to Soukie talk about the new Saint Agatha, tales of whose numinous appearances had been reported from the farthest reaches of French Acadia.

Felice felt no envy about these visitations, partly because they all occurred at great distances, and also because of Soukie's exuberant storytelling style, which made the miracles seem believable, though not necessarily true.

Soukie told of the aged, nearly-destitute farmer in Hants County who had seen the figure of Sister Agatha walking in his drought-stricken potato field; it had rained all the next day, and only upon that one acre of land. Sister Agatha had also appeared on the deck of a storm-tossed fishing vessel near Prince Edward Island; French Acadian sailors had lived to tell of being guided around treacherous shoals and into port. And the nun had recently visited a woman at Truro who was routinely beaten and otherwise abused by her husband when in his cups; on Sister Agatha's advice, Soukie said, this woman retreated from her marriage bed to a small chamber in the attic, the door to which she locked when necessary.

Thanks be to the Madonna that she herself need take no such measures, Soukie said, for Antoine was every inch a gentleman. And did Mademoiselle know, by the way—this announcement accompanied by the only shy smile Felice had ever seen upon Soukie's face —that they were expecting a little one?

In the latter part of July, Felice went every afternoon to Soukie's house. She sat by, listening, as Soukie canned tomatoes and beans and squash, and sometimes helped stir the slow-bubbling vats of blackberry preserve. And she stored away, for repetition to Celeste (who would be wonderfully jealous that Felice had this all first-hand), every detail of Soukie's confidences about the physical and emotional symptoms of her interesting condition.

An increasingly attractive feature of these visits was the walk to and from the convent. Felice was aware that her progress through the village drew much attention; when she walked past the shipyard there was a long silence (which she both loved and hated) that was finally broken by a medley of whistles. And Remi had learned her schedule; he always managed to emerge from the cod-drying house, where he now worked for Antoine, just as she appeared.

All this admiration, and her response to it, gave Felice material for fresh spiritual tension. Her hours at the convent were enlivened by memories of grown men's glances, and the ardor in Remi's eyes as he spoke of the weather or yesterday's catch. Felice's prayer sessions were now passionate, wrestling as she was with a legion of devils. Though the image of herself as a nun had dimmed, that of Felice Belliveau, Virgin Martyr, had not. She imagined herself stripped and lashed; burnt at the stake; crucified; boiled in oil. And always gloriously rewarded, ascending with seraphim, for her death-defying rejection of lust.

One afternoon, as Felice was returning from the Gentil house, Remi persuaded her to walk to the beach with him. He wanted to show her something, he said.

"What is it?" she asked, following him across the dunes, looking nervously about to see if anyone was watching. "What?" But she knew: Remi's nervous smile, and the wild beating of her own heart told her. "What?" Felice demanded, glancing up and down the empty border of sand, and then out at the retreating water.

"You have to come here," Remi said, sitting in the shelter of a beached dory. "Then you'll see."

"Oh, no. I couldn't. And it's getting awfully late." But she sat, and had closed her eyes even before Remi bent forward and kissed her.

His lips brushed hers, tickling. She giggled and opened her eyes. Remi stared back, startled, then pulled her close and kissed her again. She relaxed against his chest and let it happen: his mouth pressing hers, then gently sucking her upper lip, as though for nectar; his hand caressing her head, her cheek, her neck, and—gingerly at first—her breasts. Felice's eyes flew open, and shut: she could not seem to awaken. She did not pull away until a finger began to work between the buttons of her blouse. Then she jumped up, pushing Remi back, and bolted across the dunes.

Felice pelted down the street between large-eyed houses, and up the hill. Even if people didn't follow her and tell, Mother Superior would know everything; her wrinkled dress, her red lips, her eyes, all would testify against her. Once at the convent Felice sped up to her cubicle and wedged herself in the tight corner beside the bureau to pray. But the Virgin wanted nothing to do with her: she stank of sin. Felice scraped her knuckles against the wall until they bled, and she vowed to reform.

For several days Felice did not leave the convent. She prayed long hours in the chapel and begged chores from Madame Girrard. She scrubbed the kitchen and pantry floors, cleaned the woodstoves of ash and soot, and polished the nuns' black shoes, all the while planning her atonement.

Then one afternoon Felice, her tightly plaited hair concealed beneath a kerchief, walked to the village. Remi ran out to meet her by the road. He stood panting, his hands hanging awkwardly at his sides.

"I will not sin again, ever," Felice announced.

Remi did not speak, but in his eyes Felice saw anguish and desire.

"This evening at sunset I will be alone on the cliff by the convent," Felice whispered. "You must not come."

Then Felice slowly turned and walked back to the convent, certain that he would come. And she would be prepared, this time. She went to the white chapel, knelt before the statue of the Virgin, and fortified herself with prayer.

Then at sunset she went to kneel at the top of the cliff where the downward path began. She took out her rosary and bowed her head, imagining the tender nape of her neck as he would see it, exposed and white in the gathering dusk. He would come close, reach to touch her neck. She would entreat him to keep his distance, but if he did not, if he forced himself upon her, she would leap, and repay all her debts of sin. This cliff would be sacred to Agatha and Felice, Virgin Martyrs of Nevette.

Her rosary would break in the fall, and its blue beads would be sought after, more precious than sapphires. And the amethyst ring—Felice loosened it on her finger—she hoped Philippe would find that, and treasure it sadly forever, along with his belated understanding of his sister's noble character. Uncle Adolphe would finally become aware of Felice's purity, and of his own dark savagery. "O forgive me, my little niece," would be his unavailing cry. "My dear little niece, most holy virgin Felice."

The sun, now lower in the western sky, threw a shimmering path across the water. The salt air was warm upon Felice's cheeks and folded hands. Tears filled her eyes as she thought of how everyone would cry when her broken body was found upon the rock below. Sister Claire would be inconsolable—a thought so distressing that Felice pushed it from her mind. But after the mass for a virgin martyr had been said, Sister Claire might play Felice's compositions (which the girl had recorded on sheet music and left prominently displayed on her bureau); that might make her feel better.

Felice shifted on her knees—the rock was growing uncomfortable —and smiled out at the setting sun. Mary was most pleased with her now, and was protecting her. She could almost sense her hands descending, caressing her contrite head, and her lips whispering consolation, promises of paradise.

Felice remained at the top of the cliff as the bay consumed, inch by inch, the fiery sun. The sky blazed; the air seemed to tremble with event. Yet, though Felice thought she heard, once or twice, a sound in the balsam grove behind her, no one came.

Then the sun was gone. The sky faded to orange, to violet. The air cooled. Felice began to say the Litany of the Virgin aloud. The supper-bell rang. Her stomach growled. Perhaps he was waiting for darkness, so that he could do his very worst. Her knees were aching, perhaps bleeding. She sat, rubbing her knees, watching the stars begin to wink into place. Her purity had kept him back. With that consoling thought, she jumped up and ran to the dining room, for she was very hungry.

It was two days later, during public confession, that Felice told her story.

Antoinette, Emma, Marie, and Felice were admitted to the room after the nuns had finished their confessions. Antoinette led off, with the dreariest list of peccadilloes Felice had ever heard. Either that girl didn't do much examination of her soul, or it was a highly under-developed soul indeed. Emma and Marie weren't much better, except for Marie's admission that she would like to see a certain sister un-clothed. This awakened the listeners, who had seemed hitherto lulled, and the nuns looked with interest at Felice as she stepped upon the platform.

Felice had not been a regular participant in these gatherings, mostly from inertia, but partly because of Sister Claire's expressed opinion that there was something unhealthy about them. Sister Claire was not present today, Felice noted with a mixture of disappointment and relief.

She had been lustful, Felice began. Her soul was being eaten alive by concupiscent desire. Torturous longings kept her awake all night, and only the hand of the Virgin restrained her from private sin.

This was impressive. Her audience was captured.

But there was worse. Men desired her, dozens of men—here Felice modestly lowered her eyes, and then raised them—and she, sinful creature that she was, must confess that she had occasionally encour-aged them. She had smiled, answered softly, allowed approaches. And she had even been—kissed.

But the Virgin had appeared to her, and had shown her a picture of her soul ten years hence, were she to continue on this path: black-ened, pitted, pocked, oozing with slime. Though outwardly lovely, she would be inwardly a charnel house; altogether, a whited sepulchre.

But she had reformed, taken action. She prayed for the Virgin to help her, and went forward to meet her tempter—but not to acquiesce. To do battle.

"It was evening," Felice said. "The sun was setting. I was on the cliff. I thought"—here she crossed herself—"of Sister Agatha. I could feel her presence, and those of the other virgin saints, and of the most holy Virgin Mary. And then—a man came."

The nuns and girls stared up at Felice, every eye fixed upon her.

"I could feel him at my back. I held to my blue rosary—the one you gave me, Ma Mère. I truly thought I was going to die, but I had no real fear. Though I would have missed you all.

"He came closer. He touched my shoulder. I protested, but he moved his hand toward my breast. Then, sisters, I ran, and I started to jump—and then—most holy miracle!—the Virgin appeared!"

The audience gasped and leaned forward. Even Sister Theodota stared, waiting, her disbelief suspended. Emma and Marie, with their mouths frozen open, looked like little frogs awaiting flies.

It was that sight, or so Felice later told herself, that made her laugh. She had looked away from the girls, but still the image of those gaping mouths was with her as she said, "And the Virgin caught me—she would not let me fall!"—and then she began to giggle. "Mary spoke to this man—this boy . . . he fell to his knees . . ." More giggles from Felice, and rustlings, coughing in the audience—"It was a mir—"

Spasms of held-in air shook Felice. She doubled over. At first some thought that she was ill. But when Sisters Constance and Mary Owen ran forward to support her they found her eyes streaming with tears of merriment. And then she could restrain it no longer: there, in the sight of them all, Felice laughed and laughed. She could not stop herself—though she tried, the results were hiccups which provoked her into further hilarity—and was finally ushered out by Mother Superior, who returned to tell the shocked assembly that Mademoiselle Belliveau "is hysterical, and perhaps quite unwell."

From that day forward it was obvious to Felice that she would have to leave. No one needed to tell her that it would hardly be appropriate for her to apply for the novitiate after making such a scene—not only shameful to herself, but insulting to the sisterhood. Even remaining as a student of the academy seemed unthinkable. Though neither Mother Superior nor any other nun actually said so, Felice could sense, in the way that most deliberately avoided looking at or speaking to her, that departure was the only solution. Some nights she spent away from the academy, at the Gentil house, or with Françoise, or at the Doucettes'. On these occasions she merely left notes letting Mother Superior know she would be absent—for she feared actually confronting her—and never encountered any resistance about this.

She had all sorts of advice, both solicited and not, about what she could do. Françoise recommended marriage; Laura Doucette, the finishing school; Sister Claire, the music conservatory. Soukie said she could stay with them to help her mind the baby in exchange for board. That had an appeal for Felice, for she was reluctant to leave her friends, the cove, Sister Claire, Remi. (If he would promise to reform.) Seine. And most keenly, she felt compelled to remain near the scenes of Sister Agatha's life and death; to be with her spirit.

One Saturday in early August, Felice went alone to the cove to gather periwinkles for Madame Girrard's stew. She took off her shoes and stockings and waded among the large boulders, feeling along the rocks for the snaillike shells. The tide was coming in, and as she reached deep for a cluster of winkles, a wave surprised her, throwing her against a boulder, soaking her dress, wetting her face. The cold water stung her cheek, but not unpleasantly, and she had the impression that the wave had acted in a deliberate way. For as she stood and looked at the scene around her, at the bay, the sky, the clouds, the birds scooping air, she felt its loveliness so acutely that it seemed to her it had all just been freshly etched. And the smells—salt, balsam, seaweed—and the sounds—birds, the clatter of pebbles in the advancing surf, the slap of water against the shore—pierced her, and commanded her attention. And there was the sensation of sun on her head, which felt to the touch like a warm, friendly animal, and the cold water foaming at her knees. The world was beautiful and sacred, and she was a part of that world.

Felice went to sit on the shore, on the shelf of rock where Sister Agatha had died, and looked out at the water. Sister Agatha must have come here, too, as a young woman, and studied the movements of waves, and clouds, and the colors of rocks. Whether the visions of her blindness had indeed been her life's climactic experience Felice did not know, but certainly they had been nourished by memories of what her eyes had seen.

Felice closed her eyes, thinking of Sister Agatha in her coffin; of Sister Agatha in her last months, feeling her way along the corridors, her fingers nibbling at the painted figures forever lost to her sight. The girl sighed away sadness in a long, deep breath and listened for a moment to the music of waves: quiet, complex, unceasing. Its rhythm was as dependable as the beat of her own heart, as her own breathing. More dependable, for it would survive her, contain her, continue her.

The melody of one of her own songs, perhaps suggested by the sound of water, entered her head. Felice lay back, listening to it, humming it, and then—sitting bolt upright—recognized it. This was meant to be a song for Sister Agatha; already some words were coming to her, lines beginning to take form. She stood. Yes. A song, songs for Sister Agatha. Felice would celebrate her, and the wild, dappled world she had loved. And if she had a daughter—daughter Agatha—she would teach the songs to her.

Felice ran toward the cliff, and then up the path, hurrying to paper and pencil before the lyric dissolved, and hearing, as she went, the line of the melody, the rhythm of words not quite shaped, and, beneath, a dark bass tone that permeated the whole.

It was because of the experience on the beach—which Felice later described to Sister Claire as mystical—that she made up her mind to attend the music conservatory. Sister Claire pronounced herself relieved, delighted, and not surprised—she had thought for a long time that this was Felice's true inclination.

Arrangements fell quickly into place. Sister Claire confessed that although she had not wanted to press the girl, she had taken it upon herself to write to the school's directress—just in case—and her admittance had been secured. Mother Superior, who was immediately consulted—and seemed pleased, both for Felice and for the painlessness of this solution—said she would send a telegram to Uncle Adolphe and help with arrangements for funds. Felice would travel in the company of Laura Doucette and her parents, who were leaving for Boston from Yarmouth on a steamer in just one week. Soukie would keep Seine, and would of course give him back when Felice returned; or perhaps, Soukie consoled her, he could even be sent for. That place might be rat-infested; so many schools were. And, at the last hour, Sister Claire decided that she would go too. She wanted to see Felice settled, and, who knew, she just might want to teach there herself some day. Mother Superior gladly gave her permission; Sister Claire needed a holiday, she said—she had been thinking too much, and her cheeks were consequently altogether too pale.

The night before her departure, Felice gave a concert in the Doucettes' parlor. Present were the nuns, the girls staying at the convent and those who lived nearby, the Abbé, Philippe, who had come to see her off, and Remi. Following the Bach two-part invention and the variation, Felice played some French Acadian songs which they all joined in singing. There was some crying and an exchange of small gifts. Felice's parting with Remi was constrained by the presence of Philippe, who, when the pair walked outdoors and to one side of the Doucettes' house, took up a post at the corner. Remi gave Felice a mussel-shell necklace he had made for her, and squeezed her hand until she thought it would break. She gave him the blue rosary from her pocket, and promised to write.

Felice cried unobtrusively all the way back to the convent. But once there, caught up in the bustle of departure preparations, she found that her sadness mellowed into a pleasantly melancholy state of reverie. Mother Superior sewed buttons on the girl's clothes, and she and Sister Claire helped her to pack. Downstairs, Madame Girrard was ironing the dress Felice was to wear tomorrow, and readying a hot tub of bathwater just for her.

When it was time for her bath, Felice went downstairs to the kitchen. She put her dry underwear, gown, and towel on a chair behind the screen that had been set up, and undressed, taking off everything but her chemise and petticoat.

The metal tub groaned as she stepped in. She eased into the bath and lay back, listening to Madame Girrard stack dishes in the pantry. She paddled her fingers in the water, looking at the moonlight that streamed through the high window above her and made a star of her submerged amethyst ring. She rested her head against the back of the tub and let her body float. Soon Madame departed, calling out, "Just leave things as they are, Mademoiselle, I'll clear up in the morning. Don't dawdle about forever, though—you'll catch cold."

Taking up the soap, Felice began to wash her feet and ankles. She looked at her toes planted against the sloping end of the tub and thought, wonderingly, how graceful they seemed, wet and gleaming in the moonlight. She raised her petticoat to look at the curve of her lower leg and then, drawing it up further, saw the length of her legs, like pale stems beneath the water. Her heart beating faster, Felice lay back and pulled the chemise up to her chin. She looked for the first time in her life at the entirety of her newly blossomed body, her breasts and stomach and the dark place between her legs where the delicate tendrils had grown thick. Closing her eyes, and sinking neck-deep in the water, she lightly touched her breasts and stomach, and the slight curve of her hip. When her fingers reached the silky hairs, she pressed her legs tight together. She lay there, swaying slightly in the water, humming, until she heard a noise in the outer kitchen. She froze, her hand cupped against her body. It was the tongueless man, stalking through the darkness, and here she was all alone.

She pulled her underwear down and leapt from the tub, sloshing water onto the floor. Her teeth chattering, she pulled the nightdress over her head. As she kicked away the shucked wet underthings, she felt a silken touch against her ankle.

"Seine, you silly cat." Giggling with relief, she reached beneath her gown to dry off, then picked up the cat and carried him in her arms as she went barefoot up the stairs.

About the Author

A native of North Carolina, ANGELA DAVIS–GARDNER was born in Charlotte, graduated from Duke University, and received a Master of Fine Arts degree in creative writing from the University of North Carolina–Greensboro.

Ms. Davis-Gardner, an avid outdoorsperson, lives in Raleigh, North Carolina, with her husband, Charles, who is a geologist.